About the Authors

Award-win... ...nter writes con... ...exy, and sparkl... ...joys reading, c... ...nba classes, ro... ...and anything spa... ...ith her adorable ... ...poodle mix, Harry. Kerri... ...chatting with readers. Visit her at kerricarpenter.com or on Facebook, Twitter or Instagram to connect today.

There was never a time when **Elle Wright** wasn't about to start a book, wasn't already deep in a book—or had just finished one. She grew up believing in the importance of reading, and became a lover of all things romance when her mother gave her her first romance novel. She lives in Michigan.

Essence bestselling author **Donna Hill** began her career in 1987 with short stories and her first novel was published in 1990. She now has more than seventy published titles to her credit, and three of her novels have been adapted for television. Donna has been featured in *Essence*, the *New York Daily News*, *USA TODAY*, *Black Enterprise* and other publications. Donna lives in Brooklyn, NY with her family.

Wedding Belles

Wedding Belles: Falling for Mr Right

KERRI CARPENTER

ELLE WRIGHT

DONNA HILL

MILLS & BOON

First Published in Great Britain 2021
By Mills & Boon, an imprint of HarperCollins*Publishers,* Ltd
1 London Bridge Street, London, SE1 9GF

www.harpercollins.co.uk

HarperCollins*Publishers*
1st Floor, Watermarque Building,
Ringsend Road, Dublin 4, Ireland

WEDDING BELLES: FALLING FOR MR RIGHT
© 2021 Harlequin Books S.A.

Bayside's Most Unexpected Bride © 2017 Kerri Carpenter
Because of You © 2019 Leslie Wright
When I'm with You © 2018 Donna Hill

ISBN: 978-0-263-30270-7

MIX
Paper from
responsible sources
FSC™ C007454

This book is produced from independently certified FSC™ paper
to ensure responsible forest management.

For more information visit: www.harpercollins.co.uk/green

Printed and bound in Spain
by CPI, Barcelona

BAYSIDE'S MOST UNEXPECTED BRIDE

KERRI CARPENTER

For my very own small town, the place that made me who I am today. To my hometown of Monessen and all of those fellow Greyhounds who have been supporting me since day one.

Chapter One

It's beginning to look a lot like Christmas... Well, kind of. Thanksgiving is right around the corner and before we know it, the Yuletide season will be here. Looks like everyone's favorite editor in chief is starting the festivities early by spending time with local hottie Holly Carron. The duo were spotted at The Brewside yesterday looking quite cozy. And right when everyone thought Bayside's forever bachelor would never settle down! Stay tuned for more developing details...

Riley studied the screen in front of her and pursed her lips. Yep, Sawyer was going to be pissed. *The Bayside Blogger strikes again.* He hated when she wrote about him.

Who didn't?

Riley fluffed her red hair, held back with an oversize blue headband to complement her green-and-blue-plaid dress with the adorable white collar. She'd seen this dress in the store and knew instantly that she could rock the retro vibe. What would the ubiquitous Bayside Blogger say about her outfit? Riley grinned. She knew exactly what she'd say.

Everyone's favorite ex-Manhattanite Riley Hudson is sporting her wannabe New York fashion in small-town Virginia. Hard to be fashion forward when she's just copying Kim Kardashian's recent ensemble. Always the bridesmaid, Riley.

"Hey, Ri, did you file that article on the upcoming holiday movies?"

Riley glanced up to see her coworker Claudia Thomas hovering above her cubicle. Claudia was the most striking woman Riley had ever seen, with her long, jet-black hair, delicate features and statuesque six-foot height. Definitely didn't fit into their quaint coastal town on the Chesapeake Bay. She was also the senior editor in the Style & Entertainment section, which Riley wrote for.

"Yep, just sent it your way. I think I covered the majority of the new ones, plus I added my top-ten holiday classics. Got a couple good quotes from the guys over at the Palace Movie Theater, too."

"Excellent," Claudia said with a big smile. She spotted Riley's computer screen and gestured toward it. "I see you're reading the Bayside Blogger's column today. Sawyer is gonna be *pissed*."

"Uh, yeah, just finished it. But I don't know why he would be. A ton of people saw him at The Brewside with Holly yesterday."

Claudia leaned onto the wall of Riley's cubicle. "But you know how he hates to be featured in that column. The Bayside Blogger should really tread lightly, especially since Sawyer is the only person who knows her identity."

Riley fidgeted in her chair. "It's not like he would out her. Or him. Not after all this time."

"Maybe not." Claudia lowered her voice conspiratorially. "You think it's serious with him and Holly?"

Riley suddenly felt uncomfortable. She shrugged. "Who knows?"

Sawyer Wallace was more than the editor in chief and owner of the *Bayside Bugle*. More than her boss.

She'd known him her entire life. Two years older than her, their families were very close and had always shared holidays, vacations, barbecues and practically every important milestone.

Sawyer was like an annoying older brother, only... not brotherly at all.

"My friend Vivica asked him out a couple weeks ago."

Riley perked up at that tidbit. She straightened in her chair. "Really? I didn't know that."

"Probably because Sawyer turned her down. Crazy, because Vivica is the most gorgeous woman I've ever seen. But, personally, I think something's going on with him."

They both turned toward the glass office in the corner of the newsroom where Sawyer was intently studying his computer screen.

"Something bad?" Riley asked.

"You tell me. Your families are tight."

Riley eyed Sawyer in his office again. Apparently not that tight. Although, he had been extra surly lately. Sawyer did that whole stereotypical moody-writer thing well. But it never bothered her. In fact, she always knew how to make him lighten up and laugh.

"I say we get him drunk at this year's holiday party and force him to reveal the identity of the Bayside Blogger," Claudia said.

Riley smiled. "I don't think there's enough spiked eggnog on the planet to get that closely guarded secret out of him. Besides, I've tried."

Everyone in town had tried at one point or another. The Bayside Blogger not only had a daily column in *The Bayside Bugle*, but she—or he—also had a blog and utilized every social media channel imaginable. No one was off-limits—the blogger always seemed to know everything about everyone, anytime, anywhere.

"I can't believe he won't tell anyone who she is. Even us. We work here, for goodness sake. And that damn Blogger is published in my section."

"We should go on strike," Riley stated dramatically, making Claudia laugh.

"You may be onto something. In the meantime, I'm going to read over your article. Oh, by the way, my husband and I are going to take a weekend trip to New York in December. You know, see the holiday windows and the big tree and Rockefeller Center."

Riley tensed. "Cool."

"I know you lived there for a while. Maybe you can give us some restaurant recommendations."

She twisted her fingers together. "Well, you know New York. Everything's constantly changing. I haven't been back in a couple years. I'm totally out of touch."

But she wasn't. After graduating from Syracuse, Riley had moved to the city that never sleeps. She'd worked at a start-up marketing firm writing copy and social media posts. She'd lived in a massively overpriced studio apartment where she'd had to store her shoes in her oven and hang her laundry from her curtain rods.

It had been fabulous. Everything she'd always wanted. Living in the greatest city in the world. She'd stayed out late and seen Broadway shows and walked down Fifth Avenue at night. As often as her entry-level salary allowed, she'd tried new restaurants and bakeries. She'd been dazzled by the lights, the sounds, the people.

At least, that's what she let people think of her experience in the Big Apple. It was easier to pretend her life was closer to *Friends* than *Two Broke Girls*.

When she'd returned to Bayside for holidays, she'd

never been able to let the truth slip, which was that pretending to be a sophisticated young twentysomething in Manhattan was exhausting. And frustrating. And expensive. And...disappointing.

She'd wanted to live in Manhattan forever. She'd had a whole picture of what her life would be like, but the reality never matched up to it.

She was supposed to have an amazing job, a large apartment with tall windows that overlooked Central Park, a group of friends to rival Monica, Rachel and Phoebe. And, of course, her cool boyfriend would be the icing on the cupcake.

But that's not how Connor McKenzie turned out to be.

She frowned. She'd seen no harm in dating her co-worker. After all, their company hadn't had a policy against it. At least, that's what he'd told her. Why wouldn't little old naive twenty-two-year-old Riley believe the dazzling, successful thirty-year-old Connor?

So, all had been well...until it wasn't. She'd moved back home.

Well, more like run back with her tail between her legs. Now she never talked about her time in Manhattan if she could help it. Or she'd tell people the version she knew they expected to hear. At twenty-nine, Riley had definitely learned her lesson.

Claudia's face fell and Riley relented. She hated letting anyone down. "I mean, I guess I could put a list together. Remind me."

This seemed to appease Claudia. "Great. And don't forget, editorial meeting this afternoon."

"Wouldn't miss it."

Riley watched her editor walk to her office before returning to her screen and studying Sawyer's name embedded in the Bayside Blogger's column. Maybe Claudia was wrong. Maybe he wouldn't get too mad about it.

"Hudson." Sawyer's voice boomed out from his office. "Get in here."

As she got up and adjusted her dress, more than one head turned in her direction with sympathetic eyes. Never a good thing when Sawyer used his outdoor voice. Or called her by her last name.

"What's with him?" Dennis, her next-door cubicle mate, asked quietly.

"Dunno. Probably pissed about that restaurant review I did. They were an advertiser."

"Hold strong." He touched his stomach. "I ate there, too. It wasn't good."

Riley grabbed her notebook and pen. "Will do." Then she headed toward Sawyer with the sinking feeling she already knew what this was about.

When she reached his office, she stayed where she was in the doorway. She crossed her legs, accentuating the fabulous brown suede knee-high boots she'd bought in DC last weekend when she and her best friend, Elle, had driven to the city for a girls' weekend.

"Hey, boss. What's up?"

He steepled his hands on his desk and peered at her with his dreamy hazel eyes.

Damn. *Dreamy?* She meant *irritating. Beady* even.

The weather was unseasonably cold already and he was sporting a pair of corduroy pants and a somewhat ugly argyle sweater that she knew had been a Christmas gift from his mother last year. Not the most stylish of outfits and yet somehow he looked like he'd walked out of the pages of an L.L.Bean catalog. Just because he was tall with broad shoulders and had really cute sandy-brown hair that flopped on his head because he needed a haircut. And today he was wearing his glasses. What was it about a large lumberjack-looking man who wore glasses? Why did that make her stomach twist up into knots? And then there was his lopsided smile…

What in the heck was she doing? This was Sawyer Wallace, lifelong friend and, more importantly, boss. She couldn't size him up like a piece of meat. Especially because they worked together. Especially because of what had happened to her in New York.

"Riley," he began.

"Sawyer," she countered, and bit her lip in anticipation.

He reached into his top desk drawer and pulled out a colorful silk scarf. "Before I forget, Tony found this at The Brewside. Said you left it there a couple of weeks ago and he kept forgetting to give it to you."

She reached for the bright yellow scarf with lime-green polka dots. One of her favorites.

"Thanks," she mumbled. "Tony must have given this to you while you were on your date." She used air quotes for the word *date* and wiggled her eyebrows.

Sawyer exhaled a long breath.

"What?" she asked, feigning innocence.

"'Bayside's forever bachelor'?" he quoted. "Really?" She shrugged.

"I thought I told you to keep me out of the Bayside Blogger's column."

Riley stepped into his office and closed the door. She didn't sit in either of the chairs in front of the ancient oak desk in his office. The desk that had belonged to his great-great-grandfather. Instead, she remained standing in front of him, wearing a sexy little dress that looked like something he'd once seen on a rerun of *The Mary*

Tyler Moore Show. Not to mention those boots that showcased her shapely legs.

She was wringing her hands, he noticed. That meant she'd already realized he wasn't going to like being an item in her gossip column.

"You wrote about me? Seriously?"

Riley scrunched up her nose in a way he found distracting. And...cute. "I've written about you before. Besides, it wouldn't be fair to exclude you just because you work at the *Bugle.*"

He arched a brow. "Because I own the *Bugle*, you mean?"

"Well, no one's off-limits. That was the deal we made when I started doing this."

"I know. Believe me, I know." Did he ever. When Riley had originally pitched him the idea of a gossip column he'd had no idea what the Bayside Blogger would become. He'd only said yes because she'd been so excited about it.

After she'd returned from New York City, the usually bubbly girl he'd known forever had been different. Somber, quiet, less bubbly. Not for the first time, Sawyer wondered what exactly had happened to her in Manhattan. But she never talked about it and changed the subject if New York was even brought up.

His phone chirped and he saw a text message from his mother. He gestured to his phone. "Do you see this? You have my mom reading your column."

"I love your mom. Tell her I said hi."

Sawyer gritted his teeth. "My mom follows the Bayside Blogger. My mom mentioned the article and I told her it wasn't true. She just asked me via text if I was planning to propose to Holly and when I said no, she asked if I was gay."

"Fair question," she said with a wry smile.

He nailed her with a hard stare. Riley remained completely unaffected. They'd known each other too long for intimidation. Hell, they'd known each other their entire lives. Of course, that's what happened when you grew up in a small coastal town like Bayside, Virginia.

"You know I'm not gay."

Her gaze ran over him. "Of course you're not gay. Look at that outfit."

"Cute."

"Thanks." She plopped down in a chair. "Honestly, I don't know what you're upset about. I didn't write anything that bad."

He leaned toward her. "You said I was on a date."

"I had multiple sources email and direct message me on Twitter about your little daytime rendezvous."

Sawyer knew Riley got tips all day long from her many sources. For, as much as they complained, the residents of Bayside couldn't keep themselves from joining the gossip train. They apparently loved helping the Bayside Blogger report on one another. They emailed her directly or through the *Bugle*'s website and left Facebook and Twitter messages. Last summer Riley had been able to take a weeklong vacation without the gossip stopping.

He'd claim the whole thing was preposterous, but the numbers didn't lie. The gossip column was the most viewed area of the online edition of the paper. He couldn't help but wonder what his ancestors who'd started the newspaper would think of that.

Still, he wasn't letting her off the hook that easily. "You know I wasn't on a date with Holly."

She raised her nose in a regal gesture. "I know nothing of the kind."

"She's one of our best freelance photographers. We

were meeting about an assignment." Even he could hear the defensiveness in his voice. And why did he feel the need to explain himself to Riley?

"You could've met here at the office."

"I needed caffeine." And he'd needed to get away for a little bit.

Running a daily newspaper wasn't the easiest of jobs these days. Not that it ever had been. Balancing editorial with the business side, advertisers and marketing. Not to mention the dwindling circulation numbers.

He really wished he didn't have to mention that.

"Is the *Bugle* in trouble?"

Damn, she was the most perceptive person he'd ever met. Probably why she was so good at being the Bayside Blogger.

He noticed the concern on her face. It probably mirrored his own. Still, he didn't want to worry her or anyone on staff. So far he'd been able to keep all of the financial concerns to himself. "No more than every other paper in the country."

"Maybe you could raise the price. I'm sure people would pay…"

He shook his head as she trailed off. "You know that circulation doesn't keep newspapers afloat. Advertisers do."

A small line formed on her forehead as she considered that. "But you said that advertisers have been fighting to get in."

"Just in your section." Which was true. Everyone wanted to appear in the Bayside Blogger's section since they knew that everyone in town was reading the gossip. Bayside had its fair share of restaurants and local businesses, but a small town offered only so many resources.

And without more advertising, they'd be closing up shop by the end of the next summer season.

The truth was, Riley's question was on target. The *Bugle* was in trouble. Sawyer had tried to stay on top of it by utilizing their website and digital edition and making sure the design was up-to-date. He'd even downsized the print edition to cut costs at every corner.

But now he had some tough decisions to make, the biggest being layoffs. He was already running with a skeleton crew in the advertising department. He hated to think about shrinking the editorial team. He swiped a hand over his face. Employee layoffs at Christmastime. Could there be anything worse?

"Sawyer, are you okay? What's going on?"

Riley's voice pulled him out of his funk even though he knew he was going to have to deal with it soon. In the meantime, he'd explore all options and do everything in his power to not have to fire anyone. At Christmas or any other time. And he'd definitely work hard to keep this from his team. Even if it meant not drawing his own salary.

"Nothing is going on and I'm fine. Stop worrying. On to other business. The upcoming Christmas Kickoff Festival."

Riley eyed him skeptically for another moment before flipping open her reporter's notebook. "Day after Thanksgiving, just like always."

"With a twist," Sawyer interjected. "Usually, this is a townie thing. But I was at the council meeting the other night. They want to go big, attract people from other towns and areas of Virginia."

"Impressive."

"They want it to be a smaller version of New York's lighting of the Rockefeller Center tree."

He noticed her pen skip at the mention of New York. "I want you to cover the event. This is right up your alley. Plus, you lived there, so you'd have the experience of knowing what their ceremony is like."

"I never went to the tree lighting when I lived there," she said in a soft voice.

Sawyer knew that wasn't true. Riley had lived in New York for four years. During that time, she'd always been active on social media, and he remembered seeing her Facebook pictures of tree lightings over the years. But, once again, she didn't want to talk about New York. So, once again, he would let it go. For now.

"Still, I'd like you to head up the festival for the *Bugle*. Let's start getting some pre-event coverage in both the print and online editions."

Now she was scribbling in her notebook. Concentrating. Looking sexy as hell.

Get a grip, Wallace.

"Oh, I wanted to ask you about that recent social media promotion you and Claudia ran. Why were the numbers so low?"

Her gaze flicked up quickly to his. Her eyes narrowed. "The numbers were fine. Normal."

"Not from the report you sent me. The reach was lower than the last contest."

She gifted him with an overdramatic sigh. "How many times do I have to explain social media to you?"

The side of his mouth twitched but he held in the smile. One of his favorite things about Riley was how bright she was. Most people didn't realize that under her coordinated outfits and talk of the latest docudrama airing on Bravo, Riley had a shrewd eye for social media, pop culture and how to use those things in business.

"Humor me," he told her.

"You were looking at the total reach of the posts on all the platforms. Did you check the organic reach? The numbers were fabulous, especially considering how you cut our social media advertising budget to shreds."

"I don't see how that—"

She continued on her rant and Sawyer couldn't follow it, although, he was impressed as hell. He might not understand a lick of what she was saying, but he really loved watching how passionate she became as she explained it.

"Are you listening to me?"

Her question jerked him away from his thoughts. He decided that talking to Riley about social media wasn't going to help anything. Especially because he didn't want to reveal that she was going to have even less money in the budget next year.

"What are you up to this weekend?" he asked.

If his change in topic came as a surprise to her, she didn't show it. "Same as you," she said with a bemused smile. He racked his brain and couldn't think of any shared family gatherings until Thanksgiving. Riley rolled her eyes. "Tomorrow is Elle and Cam's engagement party at the Dumont estate. There's no way you could have forgotten that."

His turn to roll his eyes. "Blocked, perhaps."

"Sawyer, it's not that bad. Most people love when the Dumonts throw parties."

"Which is practically every week."

The Dumont family had also been in Bayside for generations. They owned Dumont Incorporated, headed up by Jasper Dumont now. Jasper was Cam's brother and Sawyer was close with both of them. He was happy his friend had popped the question to Elle. Thrilled to celebrate with them. What he didn't particularly look forward to was dressing in a monkey suit and mingling with most of the town at yet another black-tie party.

He saw the excitement on Riley's face, though. This kind of event was much more her thing. She was so good at socializing and enjoying large crowds. Not to mention, she looked damn fine in a gown.

"Come on," she cooed. "There has to be something about tomorrow's party you can look forward to."

An image of her in a tight black dress from the last Dumont soiree flitted into his mind. All of that amazing red hair had been piled in curls atop her head. Her shoulders had been bare and she'd worn the sexiest pair of stilettos… His mouth went dry thinking about it.

He almost jerked backward. What in the heck was he doing? He couldn't think about Riley like that. He could still remember the doll she used to carry around when they were kids.

"Earth to Sawyer," she said impatiently.

"There's always the free alcohol," he covered.

Oblivious to his thoughts, she nodded. "There you go. Now, you just have to get your date Holly on board."

He gritted his teeth. "I am not dating Holly."

"I wouldn't care if you were." Her eyes narrowed as she considered. "Are you bringing anyone else tomorrow? Like, as a date?"

He shook his head. "Nope. You?" He held his breath.

"No. It's hard to be Riley Hudson, the Bayside Blogger, and enjoy being on a date. You know that."

He did. She committed her life to the *Bugle*, sacrificing much of her social life to write the column that was keeping the paper in the black—barely. He opened his mouth to thank her, but the words caught in his throat. The sun was slanting through the blinds, highlighting her coppery hair, the freckles on her ivory nose, that amazing body.

Had she always been this beautiful? Why was he only noticing her now, when he couldn't possibly make a move?

Ah, heck. He was feeling something for his lifelong friend that he had no business feeling.

She stood to leave but hesitated next to her chair. "Sawyer, are you sure you're okay?"

"Uh, yeah, I'm fine."

She reached for the door but turned back again. "And the *Bugle* is fine, too? It's not in any trouble?"

Her hand was on her hip, accentuating the fact that even for a petite woman she had curves. He swallowed hard. "Don't worry, Riley. Everything will be fine."

Sawyer wasn't entirely sure if she believed him. She lingered a moment more before departing.

He felt bad about lying to his oldest friend, saying the *Bugle* wasn't in trouble. But it sure was—and so was he.

Chapter Two

Who's excited for tonight's party at the Dumonts'? I can't think of a better way to ring in the holiday season than champagne and dancing with a view of the bay! And you just never know who might show up at a Dumont affair, so this blogger is keeping her eyes open, Baysiders!

Riley crossed the terrace and took in the sight of the Dumont estate in full party mode. A cold breeze caused goose bumps to rise on her skin, hardly surprising since it was almost Thanksgiving. Not to mention that Riley was wearing nothing more than a gown and a thin wrap. Still, she couldn't help but take a moment to soak in her surroundings.

With its cascading terraces and gorgeous grounds, this was so much more than a house. It was like something out of an old black-and-white movie. With tennis courts and swimming pools, even an atrium, the Dumont mansion sat right on the bay, surrounded by strategically placed fences and bushes for privacy.

Riley made her way into the large heated tent set up on the lower grounds. Several bars occupied the corners of the space, while waiters flitted throughout the crowd of black tie–bedecked guests listening to a large band seated on a raised platform. Crystal chandeliers hung from the ceiling and tasteful twinkly lights were strung from one corner to another. And then there were the candles. Riley had never seen so many in one place. Mrs. Dumont had gone above and beyond tonight.

All Dumont parties were special, but this one was extra special. Cameron, the oldest Dumont brother, had recently popped the question to Elle Owens, one of Riley's two best friends. Everyone in town was thrilled to see the two of them together, but Riley in particular. She liked to think the Bayside Blogger had had a hand in their relationship. Sometimes people just needed a push.

And speaking of pushes…

Riley did a quick glance around the tent, taking in all the players. She had a keen memory, which came in handy for recalling details when she wrote her column.

She snagged a glass of champagne from a passing waiter as she continued surveying the party. A handful of people were already dancing, but mostly there was a lot of chatting over appetizers. And…she grinned. Over in the corner she saw Simone Graves getting her flirt on with Sam Roberts, who'd just taken a job at the high school. Interesting. She whipped her cell phone out and quickly made a note.

"What's that sly smile for?"

Riley looked up to see her other best friend, Carissa Blackwell, smirking back at her. "Look at you, gorgeous," Riley said, instead of answering the question.

"You like?"

Carissa was wearing a navy blue floor-length dress. Her blond hair was piled on top of her head and her makeup was flawless. She was tall and curvy with the most beautiful gray eyes. If they weren't friends, Riley would hate her on principle.

"Stunning," Riley replied. "I can see the drool on Jasper's chin from here." She waved at Jasper, who was all the way on the other side of the tent. He'd been beaming with adoration at his girlfriend the whole time. Carissa turned and winked at him.

It was official. Both Dumont brothers were off the market. Too bad for Bayside's singletons, but hooray for her friends. She couldn't be happier they'd found their soul mates.

She sighed. Well…mostly happy. Totally happy, she amended quickly. She was thrilled for Carissa and Elle. It was just that it would be kind of nice to find someone for herself.

Of course, last time she'd had a serious boyfriend it hadn't turned out so great. Maybe she should watch what she wished for.

"Riley!"

She shook her head and tuned back into Carissa, who was standing with her hands on her hips, an expectant look on her face.

"Sorry, what?" Riley asked.

Carissa narrowed her eyes. "I said, you look great, too."

Riley was wearing a new curve-hugging, low-backed dress in her favorite color, emerald green. She'd put her hair up in a messy yet chic ponytail, leaving wild strands loose around her face.

"Oh well, thank you. And speaking of looking good…" She wiggled her eyebrows as Elle, the bride-to-be, sidled up to them.

"You look very bridal," Riley said, gesturing to Elle's off-white gown. Of course, she'd helped her pick out the dress a month ago. "Practicing for the big day already?"

"Don't mention the big day. I'm stressed." She grabbed a champagne flute from a passing waiter.

"Oh no," Riley said. "What can we do?"

"Are you kidding? You've both been bridesmaids of the year so far. Between you two, my soon-to-be mother-in-law, every bridal magazine ever written, and even my dad, I think I may be approaching too much help."

"Too many opinions?" Carissa guessed.

Elle grimaced. "Too many *very* strong opinions."

As they chatted about the upcoming spring wedding a little longer, Riley couldn't help noticing that something was off with Carissa.

"What?" Riley asked.

"What do you mean what?" Carissa countered.

Riley wiggled her pointer finger in front of Carissa. "Something's up. I can tell."

Carissa turned to Elle. "I swear, she's a psychic or something."

"It is eerie sometimes," Elle agreed. "But is something wrong, Car? You look a little pale."

"No, not wrong. The opposite of wrong, actually. Just scary."

"Can you be a little more cryptic?" Riley laughed.

"Sorry." Carissa glanced across the tent. Riley followed her gaze and saw that Jasper was deep in conversation with his brother. "Jasper asked me to move in with him this morning."

"Whoa, that's huge."

Riley wondered if the Bayside Blogger should mention this. She chewed on her lip as she considered. It was pretty major news. Carissa and Jasper had been hot and heavy back in high school. Then they'd broken up right after graduation and hadn't seen each other for years. After Carissa's divorce, she'd moved back to Bayside to start her catering business, Save the Day Catering, which had really taken off. She'd not only gotten back together with Jasper, but they would be opening a bookstore and café soon. And now they were taking the next step. Cohabitation.

All of this was right up the Bayside Blogger's alley, but Riley knew that her friends—just like Sawyer—hated being written about. Still, she couldn't leave them out of the column. She'd become tight with Elle and Car. Everyone in town knew that. If she didn't mention them from time to time, then her identity would be obvious.

Maybe she should wait a couple days and see how this played out.

"There's more," Carissa said, drawing Riley and Elle's attention. "A lot more."

Riley immediately let her gaze drop to Carissa's ring finger. The all-important finger was empty of a ring.

"What's going on?" Riley asked.

"Well, um, I went to the doctor yesterday."

Elle's face washed of color. Her father had dealt with bladder cancer recently and Elle was particularly sensitive to talk of doctors. "You weren't feeling well a couple days ago. I remember. You had to run out of our brunch when you got sick."

"Right," Carissa said.

Elle grabbed one of Carissa's hands. Riley took the other.

"Are you okay?" Riley asked, her pulse skyrocketing.

"Well, turns out I'm…pregnant."

A long moment of astonished silence passed between them. Riley didn't know who started it, but then all three of them were screaming and hugging.

"Ohmigod, ohmigod, ohmigod. How did this happen?" Riley asked. "I mean, I know how it happens."

Carissa laughed. "We've always been so careful. Except, well, this one time."

Elle hugged Carissa again. "And one time is all it takes. Congratulations."

"Thank you. I wasn't going to tell anyone yet, but I just couldn't keep it from you two. So mum's the word until I say. Especially from the men."

They agreed and hugged some more.

"Speaking of men," Carissa began as she pinned Riley with a knowing glare.

Uh-oh. She had a feeling what was coming even though they weren't talking about men. "Don't start, Car," Riley begged.

"I'm just saying. When was the last time you went on a date?"

Riley shook her head. "I'm focusing on my career right now." Which was a total lie. Elle saw through it immediately.

"You were just saying the other day how you could do your job with your eyes closed." Elle wagged a finger at her. "I know for a fact that Jason Wellington asked you out last week and you blew him off. What gives?"

Riley opened her mouth to answer, but the words caught in her throat as she noticed Sawyer walk into the tent. Her mouth went dry at the sight of him in his tux, which was stupid really because she'd seen him in a tuxedo before. Many times. She supposed it had to do with the fact that he usually wore jeans and... Wow, he'd shaved today instead of leaving his face all scruffy. Although, normally, his scruff was appealing too.

What was she doing? What was she thinking? This was Sawyer. She'd known him her whole life. She couldn't get all swoony over him. Only he'd just noticed her, too. He grinned and she felt like someone had punched her in the stomach.

He started to walk toward her and once again her

friends faded away. Her knees actually went weak like she was one of the characters in those Hallmark Channel movies she loved so much.

Only this wasn't a movie. The way her heart started racing was very, very real.

Riley always looked amazing. But tonight? For an editor, a man who dealt with every aspect of a newspaper every single day, he had no words.

At first, he'd thought the green dress was a bit demure for her. Then she'd turned around—the back of it was close to nonexistent. It dipped low, almost to her shapely behind.

Again he chastised himself. He wasn't supposed to be thinking about her behind. Or her front. He shook his head. Or any side of her. Except the friend side. They'd practically grown up as siblings. No, that wasn't quite right.

He should stop walking toward her, yet he couldn't. He noticed she wore dangly earrings that sparkled so brightly they practically lit up the whole tent on their own. Very Riley-esque. Because when he thought about her, he thought about a bright light.

When he reached her, she smiled, but otherwise stayed silent. He turned to Elle and Carissa, who were both wearing the oddest expressions. They exchanged mysterious looks with one another.

"Congrats again, Elle," he offered. "I'm thrilled for you and Cam."

"Thanks, Sawyer. Have you said hi to Cam yet?"

"Uh, no, I just got here."

"And came right over to us," Carissa said. Then she exchanged a second look with Elle, who bit down on her lip like she was trying to keep from laughing.

Women were enigmatic to him sometimes.

"Well, I really must find my fiancé," Elle said.

Carissa jumped slightly. "Yes, and I need to find Jasper and check with my assistant. Save the Day catered tonight's soiree, so I expect you all to make copious yummy noises throughout the party."

Sawyer laughed as Elle and Carissa said their goodbyes and disappeared into the crowd. He turned to Riley.

"Hey," he said lamely.

"Hey you," she replied. "You look…" She trailed off and tilted her head. Then she reached forward and fiddled with his tie. "There. It was crooked."

"Thanks." The word lingered on his lips the same way her hand lingered on his chest. He could smell her perfume. He didn't know what it was, but it smelled amazing, like flowers dipped in more flowers.

"Quite the dress, Ri," he said when she finally took a step back. "You should consider yourself lucky that your dad is out of town or he would have thrown his coat over you and hauled you out of here."

She waved him away. "Oh, please. It's not that bad."

To prove her point, she did a little spin. His mouth went dry at seeing all that silky skin up close. Not to mention he couldn't help but realize she couldn't wear a bra. Suddenly his tie felt incredibly restrictive.

He tried to make light of the situation. "If I remember correctly, you always did give your parents a run for their money with your various fashion choices."

Again she waved her hand. "Experimenting with outfits and accessories is part of finding yourself."

"And I imagine all those times you came home late from dates was also some sort of experimenting? Now that I think about it, you were a bit of a wild child, Riley Hudson."

"Hardly. I think I was a fairly normal teenager. And anyway, easy for you to say. You've always been Mr. Dependable, son of the year."

He didn't have to see himself in a mirror to know his face fell. "Not always, Ri."

Sawyer really didn't know why he was goading her. He'd been called into the principal's office more than he should ever admit. Wasn't his fault he'd had a penchant for pranks.

Of course, that was all child's play compared to his antics after he'd graduated from college. He'd been in love and like many young people in love, he'd made Rachel his whole life.

Unfortunately, it had taken him a couple years to realize that Rachel wasn't the right fit. In fact, some might call them polar opposites.

But he'd been besotted with her so he'd moved away from home. Shunned Bayside, if he was being honest, which he hated being because then he had to admit that he'd been selfish.

He'd turned his back on his family, on his town and on the *Bugle*.

"How long are you going to beat yourself up for that?" Riley asked gently, kindly.

Sawyer shrugged. He'd put his parents through hell. Just another reason why the *Bugle* couldn't fail now. He would make sure of it.

Riley stepped closer. "You know, everyone has at least one bad relationship under their belt."

Something crossed her face. He wanted to jump on it and ask her what caused those shadows to appear, but she beat him to it.

"Heck, most people have multiple crappy relationships. You and Rachel lived in DC for a hot minute. And you came to your senses and moved back."

"I don't want to talk about Rachel."

"That's fine. What do you want to talk about?"

"How about you?"

She rolled her eyes.

"You look beautiful tonight."

He didn't know why he'd said that. It just slipped out. Her eyes widened in surprise. Had he never told her how gorgeous she was before? Riley was an insanely appealing woman who lit up any room she entered. Somehow she had the ability to be both the girl next door and the fantasy.

He didn't know when she'd reached that status. She'd been a cute kid. Freckles and pigtails and skinned knees. She'd been kind of an annoying preteen, always following him around at family functions. Maybe the change had occurred during high school, or college, when he was away too often to take note? Who the hell knew.

Right now, he couldn't take his eyes off her.

"Oh," she said to his comment. She scrunched up her nose, something he often saw her do at work.

Sawyer never danced at these events. Ever. So he was more shocked than anyone when he blurted out, "Dance with me."

Riley couldn't contain her surprise at the statement, either. Her green eyes widened. "Are you serious? You can't dance."

"I can." He reached for her hand. Her skin was so soft, so smooth. Like silk. "I just choose not to most of the time." He led her to the dance floor.

"What makes tonight the exception?" she asked, her voice husky.

You. But he couldn't say that. Shouldn't say that. This

was Riley, after all. Riley Hudson. Lifelong friend. Close family acquaintance. Employee. Gorgeous redhead who managed to sneak into his thoughts more than he'd like to admit.

"Tonight is a celebration," he said instead. He could tell she had another question, so he drew her to him, pressing one hand to her back and the other wrapped around her tiny, delicate hand.

And then all questions stopped. In fact, all talking ceased. While he was sure there was music playing, he didn't seem to hear it. Because being this close to Riley, inhaling her sweet perfume, taking in her tempting red lips, took over all his senses. It was like he didn't have room to notice anything else.

It should have been weird. Or awkward, at least. But for the first time, he wasn't thinking of her as his oldest friend or the kid he'd grown up with. She was an adult now and his body was taking notice.

He drew her closer. Her body felt good up against his. His hand traveled over the exposed skin of her back. He could feel her breath tickling his neck as she moved closer to him.

He had no idea how long they danced, Riley in his arms as they swayed to a song. Two songs? More than two songs?

Sawyer would have remained just like that forever but Jasper Dumont appeared at his side.

"Sorry to interrupt, guys."

Riley jumped back, a deer-in-headlights expression on her face. She gave Sawyer a long once-over before mumbling something and quickly making her way off the dance floor.

"Riley, wait," he called. Shoot. What had just happened? Seriously, what the hell had just freaking happened between them?

"Sorry, dude," Jasper said, a sheepish expression on his face. "I didn't mean to…" He gestured between Sawyer and Riley's retreating back.

"No, don't worry about it. We were just dancing."

Jasper's eyebrow quirked as the two of them made their way toward one of the bars. "Just dancing, huh? Trust me, I know all about *just* dancing. Well, I am sorry, but I interrupted for good reason. There's someone here who really wants to meet you." He turned to the man next to him. "This is—"

"Dan Melwood."

Sawyer accepted the handshake from the tall man with dark hair, just beginning to gray at the temples.

"Dan was born in New York but he lived in Bayside during his high school years," Jasper said. "He left years ago and is an entrepreneur who is considering adding to our local economy. Dan, this is—"

"Sawyer Wallace," Dan once again jumped in. "Publisher of the *Bayside Bugle*."

Sawyer raised a brow. "Publisher, editor in chief, reporter, head of ad sales, you name it. Life at a small-town newspaper."

Jasper left them to talk. Sawyer and Dan grabbed drinks at the bar and moved to a quiet corner. Dan was in his fifties, only a little younger than Sawyer's parents. As Jasper had informed him, Dan graduated from Bayside High, went off to college and business school, and then spent the next couple of decades building his businesses. He dabbled in real estate and construction. He explained to Sawyer that occasionally he invested in struggling companies, helping them improve their processes so they could turn a profit. Sounded like he'd helped out quite a few restaurants and commercial businesses in the state.

Now he was interested in Bayside. Particularly in the *Bugle*. He seemed to know a lot about newspapers, as if he'd done his research. Sawyer was impressed.

"I have to admit that I'm intrigued by this Bayside Blogger you have in the Style and Entertainment section."

Sawyer fought an urge that was somewhere between pride for Riley and protectiveness over her. "The Bayside Blogger is certainly our most popular column." He offered a small chuckle.

"And your most enigmatic."

Dan's smile faltered. Just slightly and only for a fraction of a second. But it was long enough for Sawyer to note.

"The blogger is definitely mysterious."

"And not always accurate."

Sawyer took a step back. "Actually, the one rule I've made with the blogger is that every article, every tidbit of gossip has to be true."

"That's interesting," Dan said, rubbing a hand along his jaw. "She happened to write about me last summer."

Sawyer racked his brain and then remembered. "Oh, yes," he said, choking slightly on bourbon. "I vaguely recall the piece. Maybe that's why your name is so familiar."

"I was back here visiting for a month or so. I can assure you what she wrote was not true."

He couldn't remember exactly what Riley had written, but he made a mental note to go back through the archives when he left tonight. Sawyer prided himself on journalistic integrity. It was the number-one thing he required of all his reporters. "I apologize if that's true.

I will certainly speak with the blogger and we'll print a correction if it turns out we were wrong."

Dan's face paled slightly. "Don't worry about that. Anyway, I won't leave you in suspense any longer. There's a reason I wanted to meet you tonight and talk about the paper."

Sawyer perked up and put his empty drink on a nearby table.

"I know it's hard times for print publications," Dan said.

Not what Sawyer had been expecting to hear. It was also a subject that he went out of his way to avoid. He had so much to figure out in the next couple of months. No matter what, he had to save his family's legacy.

Dan leaned closer. "Quite frankly, I can't believe you've lasted this long."

"A lot of new businesses have been flooding the area. That's helped," Sawyer explained. "Our online edition is going strong and we're utilizing our new app, and social media, of course."

"All good things. And I'd like to discuss this more in depth because I want to make a proposal."

Sawyer was all ears.

"I suggest that I come on board as a partner for the *Bugle*. I can offer you financial support, and maybe together we can figure out a way to save the newspaper."

Sawyer wanted to jump for joy, but he spotted his father across the dance floor. His head was tilted toward his mother's ear and, whatever he was saying, his mom was laughing hysterically.

Every single person in the Wallace family who had touched the *Bugle* had left an indelible mark on it. His father, in particular, had really done his best to keep the

paper afloat. He'd been the one to go digital, long before most small-town newspapers looked to the internet.

Legacy firmly in mind, he refocused on Dan. "That's
quite an offer. But, as I'm sure you know, the *Bugle* is
a family-run business. It's been in the Wallace family
since its launch issue."

"I realize that. In fact, I heard you're celebrating the
one hundred and fiftieth anniversary this year. Quite a
milestone. But, as I told you, I have made my fortune on
turning around failing businesses."

"Do you have any experience in media?"

Dan's head bounced from side to side as he considered. "Some, but print media is a bit of a passion proj-
ect for me." He swirled the amber liquid that was in his
glass. "I already have some numbers put together for you.
Why don't I revise them a bit? We can discuss investor
options or even silent partnership."

Sawyer didn't know what to say. This was more than
he could have asked for. "I'm overwhelmed," Sawyer
admitted easily.

"There's only one thing I'd like in return."

At that moment, he heard Riley's laugh from the bar
where she was talking to Jasper and Carissa. She threw
her head back, exposing her long neck. She had the most
beautiful laugh.

"What do you think?"

Embarrassed that he'd tuned out this possible *Bayside Bugle* savior, Sawyer struggled to refocus and get
his mind off of Riley's...everything. "I'm sorry. I didn't
quite catch that." He indicated the speakers, hoping Dan
would think he hadn't heard over the noise.

Dan clapped a hand on his arm. "If I'm going to become involved in the *Bugle*, I want to be involved in
every area."

Made sense to Sawyer. Who wouldn't want to know where their money was going?

"Meaning," Dan continued, "that I would want to know about every nook and cranny. Every secret. In particular, I will need to know the identity of the Bay-side Blogger."

Sawyer froze just as Riley caught his gaze. She smiled at him.

Well, *damn*.

Chapter Three

Happy Tgiving! Hope all my gossip birdies are enjoying their family time. I know at least one person who will be eating her pumpkin pie alone. Poor little Riley Hudson has no one to watch the Macy's parade with since her parents swapped turkey day for a tropical cruise this year!

Sawyer scrolled through the Bayside Blogger's latest article. His finger hovered over the screen when he read the last part of the column.

He sighed. Riley didn't usually post things like that, especially about herself. After all, it wasn't as though she was alone. The Wallaces were hosting Thanksgiving this year and had invited her, along with half the town. Mr. and Mrs. Dumont would be there, as well as Cam, Elle, Jasper, Carissa, Elle's dad, Carissa's aunt and more. Riley was as much a part of his family as he was.

He reread the tweet one more time and considered shooting her a quick text of encouragement. But she'd been acting weird all week, avoiding eye contact with him and even working from home one day.

He could pretend to be oblivious, but he knew exactly why she was acting odd. That dance at Elle and Cam's engagement party. Something had shifted in their relationship and he would be outright lying if he didn't fess up to being shaken by it, as well.

He'd had no business dancing with her in that way. They'd been friends for far too long for one dance to feel like that.

Sawyer pulled his car up to his parents' house, put it in Park, but made no move to get out just yet.

Despite the three-day workweek, he'd been busy. He'd met with Dan Melwood and he was no closer to giving him a decision on his proposal than he had been at the party last Saturday. He'd asked for time to consider all options.

Dan was offering full financial assistance as the main investor. If Sawyer agreed, he wouldn't have to lay any-one off and he'd save his family's business. It also pro-vided him with some wiggle room so he could play around with a couple ideas of branching out. Even with financial help now, at some point, he would be right back in the same position.

If he looked at the situation from that side, he'd be a fool not to accept what Dan was offering. But there was another side.

Riley.

Or the Bayside Blogger, he amended quickly. Dan wanted to know the identity of the Bayside Blogger. He claimed that as an investor, he was owed that right.

After Sawyer researched Riley's old columns, he'd fig-ured out why the man was upset. Apparently, last sum-mer, Dan had returned to Bayside for a month or so. Riley had insinuated that Dan had carried on an affair with a local woman. She hadn't named the woman. She hadn't even said the word "affair." But it was clearly implied what Dan had been up to.

Sawyer also learned that Dan and his wife separated after the summer. Coincidence? Probably not.

But what Dan was proposing was wrong, both morally and ethically. Sawyer wanted to save the paper, but was he ready to stoop to this level to get it done?

Sawyer pushed a hand through his hair. The only restriction Sawyer ever put on Riley in her position as the *Bugle*'s gossip columnist was that she be absolutely positive about the accuracy of anything she committed to print, and she'd never failed him. Not once. If she said Dan was carrying on an affair, he was.

He couldn't out her, though. She would be beyond humiliated. Sure, Dan was only one person. But he could easily share Riley's alter ego with another person. And that person could tell someone else. And so on. That was exactly why neither he nor Riley ever talked about the blogger. He hadn't even told his parents.

Speaking of his parents, maybe he should vet this whole situation with them. Since the newspaper didn't have a board, it would be nice to have someone to talk to about this. Although, that would mean revealing the financial trouble the paper was in. His dad would launch into a lecture about how he shouldn't be publishing every day of the week. A fact that Sawyer was proud of. He wanted to make his mark on the *Bugle*, too.

A rap on the car window scared the crap out of him. He turned to see his father standing next to the car with a questioning look on his face. Sawyer grabbed the bottle of wine and flowers he'd picked up for his mother and got out of the car.

"Everything okay, son?" his dad asked.

Henry Wallace had the same mischievous smile Sawyer was constantly told that he possessed. They were the same height and same build, with wide shoulders and long legs. They also shared a love of mystery books, seafood and fishing.

"I'm fine." He embraced his dad. "Happy Thanksgiving, Dad."

"Happy Thanksgiving. Come in." They walked down the path that, in the warmer months, was lined with flowers. Twin pots of mums flanked the door of the colonial two-story house that sat right off the bay.

"How's the *Bugle*?"

"Everything's great." It was a standard answer he gave his dad, but he felt guilty, nonetheless. At some point, he needed to tell his father the true picture of what was happening. But once he did that, everything would be more real.

Henry made to open the door, then suddenly covered the handle with his hand and gave his son a long once-over. "You know, you can always talk to me. About anything."

Sawyer felt like he was back in high school being questioned about making out with his girlfriend or drinking after the big game. "I know."

"Because I do have some experience in the newspaper biz."

He certainly did. Sawyer had always looked up to his father. Idolized him, really. And not only because of his role at the *Bugle*. People in the community respected him, valued his opinion. He was a family man. Loyal to the very end.

Everything Sawyer wished he could be.

"I've heard that somewhere," Sawyer said as they finally entered the house. Immediately, they were assaulted with the aromas of Thanksgiving. The smell of sage and roasting turkey wafted out to greet him, as did all of the spices of pumpkin pie, yams and his mother's famous green bean casserole.

"But what I want to talk about is your retirement. Heard your golf game is actually regressing."

Henry stopped walking and wagged a finger in his face. "You've been talking to your mother. Never listen to her."

"I heard that," Patty Wallace called from the kitchen.

Sawyer and his dad exchanged a look before entering the room. As soon as they did, a flurry of activity greeted them in the way of hugs, handshakes and holiday greetings. Someone thrust a mug of spiked cider into his hand and his mother was fussing over him and thanking him for the flowers.

But Sawyer was busy surveying the room. A lot of their guests had already arrived, but not everyone.

"Where's Riley?" he asked his mom.

His mother patted his cheek. "She should be here soon. She was making that whipped Jell-O you like this morning."

"But she's coming, right?"

His mother cocked her head curiously. "Of course. Why would you ask that? She's spent practically every Thanksgiving here since she was in diapers."

"I know, it's just…" He trailed off because he didn't really want to get into her tweet with his mom.

"If I know Riley, she'll be flouncing through the door at any minute in a fabulous outfit."

"Did someone say my name?"

Sawyer twisted his head so fast he almost got whiplash. Just as his mother had suggested, there she stood in a forest-green sweater and polka-dot pants. She'd left her hair down in loose curls and it was bouncing around her as she entered the room carrying a covered dish and a bottle of wine.

Riley was greeted even more enthusiastically than he'd been. He moved to welcome her but was blocked by the entrance of Elle and Cam.

Elle, Carissa and Riley were in the midst of planning Elle's bridal shower, so it didn't surprise Sawyer to see the three of them joined at the hip all afternoon. They helped his mother in the kitchen, enjoyed wine in the family room while football blared from the television.

Every time Sawyer made a move to get closer to her, someone would intervene. Or a timer would go off in the kitchen and Riley would race away. Or one of her friends would want to show her something on their phone. Or she'd refill her drink.

The universe was clearly against him.

He thought dinner would help. He and Riley usually sat at the far end of the long dining room table. But this year, there had been a seating adjustment. Instead of sitting next to his oldest friend, he strained to hear her hearty laugh from way at the other end of the room. He couldn't even enjoy his mother's turkey, which was always amazing.

The real question was whether Riley was actually avoiding him or if all of the distractions were coincidental. He got that their dance the other night had been a little much. Hell, he was still thinking about it. All the time. But that was no reason to avoid someone you've known your whole life.

In any case, he resolved during dessert and more football that he would get to the bottom of her cold shoulder. Just then, opportunity presented itself when Riley went out on the deck. Alone. Sawyer jumped up, grabbed a fresh beer and joined her.

It was cold and the breeze coming off the bay didn't help matters. His parents had started a fire in the family room and the smell of wood smoke was a comforting and autumnal aroma.

Riley had wrapped one of his mother's throw blankets around herself. She was standing at the far end of the deck, away from the windows of the family room. Her glass of wine sat on the banister, untouched. She was lost in her thoughts, staring out at the water.

He quietly approached, suddenly unsure what to say. The moonlight played over her face and he longed to reach out and touch her.

"Hey, Ri," he finally said.

Riley jumped a mile and then spun around. Her wine glass wobbled but luckily didn't take the plunge over the railing.

She placed a hand over her chest. "Good grief, Sawyer. Where'd you come from?"

"That's a very esoteric question. How deep do you want to get tonight?"

She smiled at him and he felt it all the way in his gut.

"I never get deep unless I've had at least three pieces of pumpkin pie. Right now, I'm only up to two."

He joined her at the railing and put down his beer bottle. "Are you warm enough?"

She nodded. "I'm fine. I needed some air."

The two of them had never had any problem keeping a conversation going, yet tonight it felt strained. Awkward.

"Listen, Ri," he said.

"Hey, Sawyer," Riley said at the same time.

They laughed. "Go ahead," she said.

He wanted to ask about their dance. Wanted to know if it had made her feel the same way he'd felt that night. Wanted to know if her feelings about him were starting to change too. Instead, he said, "I saw your column this morning. I didn't realize you were upset about your parents' cruise. Why didn't you tell me?"

She shrugged and continued to look out over the water. "You know how it is. Sometimes we don't realize how we feel about something until we write it down."

True. Which was exactly why he needed to stay clear of any kind of writing assignment at the moment. His emotions and feelings were too jumbled. Making sense of them might just scare him.

Riley took a sip of her wine. "I don't know why I'm even bothered about my parents. They deserve this vacation and they'll be back next week. I guess... I mean... it's only that I miss them and..."

He reached for her arm and turned her to face him. "What, Riley?"

"I'm lonely."

It was such an un-Riley-like statement and the combination of her words and the frightened expression on her face was like a punch to his gut.

"Oh, hon, why? They're only on vacation for ten days. You just said so yourself."

Her eyes were looking everywhere but at his. "It's not just that. It's stupid, really."

"We've been friends for a million years. You can tell me anything."

She finally met his gaze. "Friends. Right." She tightened the blanket around her. "Elle is engaged and Carissa is going to be moving in with Jasper. Plus, she's also..."

He cocked his head. "She's what?"

Riley shook her head. "Never mind. It's nothing. The point is that Elle and Carissa are both making huge changes."

So that's what this mood was about. Her two closest

friends were taking big steps in their lives and relationships.

"And you wish you were in a relationship, too?" he asked. He held his breath, uncertain of what he wanted to hear her say.

"Yes. No." She shook her head. "I don't know. It's not that."

He leaned toward her. "What is it?"

"It's confusing and...and..."

"Ri," he said, his voice sounding husky even to his ears.

"Sawyer, I don't know..." She gestured helplessly between them.

He reached for her hand. It was so small wrapped up in his. When he met her gaze again, he saw something he'd never seen there before. At least, not whenever she'd looked at him. But there it was, pure lust. And he knew exactly how she felt.

Without analyzing it, he did what felt natural to him. He pulled her to him and covered her lips with his.

For the second time that night, Sawyer shocked her. But this time, he wasn't sneaking up on her. He was kissing her.

And quite well.

His lips moved over hers, softly at first. Her surprise lasted for only a second and, before she knew it, her hands were winding up around his neck, the blanket she'd wrapped herself in falling to the floor of the deck.

He pulled her even closer as his lips became more and more greedy. His hands were in her hair and then moved down her body until they reached her hips.

He smelled so good. His cologne was tickling her nose as she ripped her lips away to place a soft kiss against the column of his neck, apparently a sensitive spot. He made a sound, something like a growl, and feasted on her lips once more.

Riley felt like stars were exploding around her. She hadn't experienced pure, unadulterated passion like this since...

Suddenly she pushed away from him. They were both struggling for breath, their chests mirroring each other in a rapid up-and-down rhythm.

"I can't," she said in a very unsteady voice.

"I'm sorry," he said, his eyes wide and dark with desire.

She wasn't sorry. Not in the least. That was part of the problem. She couldn't kiss Sawyer. He was her friend, not to mention that he currently handed out her paycheck.

But it had felt so good, so natural.

No. She shook her head, trying desperately to clear it. At the same time, she shivered.

"Ri," Sawyer said, bending to retrieve the blanket. "You're going to get sick. Here." He placed the blanket around her shoulders, adjusting it so that it covered all of her. He lingered, and his fingers brushed over her collarbone, inciting another shiver that had nothing to do with the weather.

Sawyer must have noticed and his eyes focused on her lips. Before she could protest, he was tugging the blanket toward him, which had the added effect of bringing her right to him. She raised her head. Big mistake—it put his sumptuous mouth in front of her.

How could she resist?

They stood like that for a moment. A long, heated moment. She didn't know who moved first. Maybe it was both of them. She let out a gasp, and then once again their lips met.

Who knew Sawyer Wallace could kiss like this? If he wasn't holding her up by the blanket, her knees would give out.

After what felt like hours, they parted. Gently he kissed the tip of her nose and then her forehead before pulling her in for a long hug.

"Riley, that was—"

"Something that absolutely cannot happen again," she finished sadly.

He released her and pinned her with questioning eyes. "Ri," he began. Instead of finishing, he scratched his head. "Are you seeing someone?"

"No, of course not. You'd know if I were."

"Then what?"

"It's not you, Sawyer. It's me. I can't do *that* with you."

After their dance at Elle and Cam's engagement party last week, this kiss wasn't really a surprise. When they'd danced, it had felt like they were the only two people in Bayside. And that had scared the crap out of her.

She'd spent the week avoiding him, which frankly hadn't been that hard. He'd met with Dan Melwood. Riley wondered what that was about. Dan had been in Bayside last summer, but as far as she knew he didn't have any reason to be back so soon.

"Talk to me," he said firmly.

She put space between them. Bided her time by taking a sip of her wine. She owed him some kind of explanation.

"Okay." She nodded. "When I lived in New York, there was a guy there. A guy that I dated."

"I always wondered," he said more to himself.

"We worked together."

"Ah." He ran a hand through his hair. "Let me guess. There was a policy against dating in your office?"

"Actually, no." She drank a much bigger sip of wine. "I wish there would have been. But I was young and stupid so I probably would have ignored it anyway." She tightened the blanket around her. "Connor and I hit it off right away. Before I knew it, we were dating."

Sawyer's face was serious. "What happened with him?"

"He got promoted." She swallowed hard. "To my supervisor."

"Damn."

"Exactly," Riley agreed. "I don't need to go into all the details."

More like, she didn't want to go into the details, because if she did, Sawyer would know that she was a major idiot. She'd have to tell him how wonderful she'd thought Connor was. How she'd stupidly thought they would get engaged and married one day. How she made him the center of her universe only to have that universe come crashing down around her when she learned that Connor was already engaged to another woman.

There had been signs, but she'd ignored them. Connor had made a fool out of her and out of her belief in love.

"Riley," Sawyer urged.

She opened her eyes. She hadn't even realized she'd closed them. "He became my boss and the situation became so complicated."

"He didn't fire you, did he?"

Was it her imagination or was a vein ticking in his neck? It was too dark to tell.

"No, he didn't fire me. It was an incredibly uncomfortable couple of months. I tried to find work elsewhere, but nothing panned out."

"So you came back home to Bayside," Sawyer said.

"Not at first. I wanted to give it some time, see if

things got better. But after four years in New York I was ready to return."

"I see."

"Do you?" she asked. "When I came home, I promised myself that I would never, ever put myself in a situation like that again."

"A situation where you date your boss."

"A situation where I could possibly humiliate myself. That's why I can't kiss you. Or date you. Not now, not ever. Even if I want to."

He stepped closer. "Do you? Do you want to kiss me?"

She held up a hand. "It doesn't matter what I want, Sawyer. The fact is, nothing can happen between us. You're my boss."

"I'm your friend, too, and I always will be."

Yes, he was. Another stark reminder. Kissing him had the potential to damage both their working relationship and friendship. Not to mention the drama that would ensue if anyone found out about them. And Riley just couldn't—*wouldn't*—go through that again.

Chapter Four

Ho-ho-ho, Baysiders! Who else is excited for today's Christmas Kickoff Festival? You know I'll be mingling in the crowd. Hopefully, Santa won't put me on the naughty list. But I'll tell you someone who should be...;)

Sawyer's plan for the town's annual Christmas Kickoff Festival was to do a quick lap to check out the scene, stop at The Brewside for coffee and then get back to the action.

He'd attended this festival every year of his life except for two. He shook his head, willing the guilt over that lapse in judgment to fade.

Instead, he took in the center of the town square where a huge Christmas tree had been erected, decorated and awaited the ceremony tonight, when its hundreds of strands of lights would illuminate the square. A cute picket fence surrounded the tree, and an old-fashioned electric train made its way around the base. Sawyer had loved trains when he was a boy and just seeing the one today brought back all kinds of warm childhood memories.

Beyond the train were oversize presents wrapped in red, green, gold and silver paper. He was happy to see the large bins on the other side of the tree that had been set up to collect toys and coats for local charities, too. He needed to remember to bring the things he'd bought for that. Maybe they could even take up a collection at the *Bugle*.

More guilt washed over him. How could he ask his employees for donations to charity when he might have to lay some of them off soon?

Sawyer wished he could go one day without thinking about all of the troubles in his life. Especially at this time of year. He cared about each and every person on his staff, almost as if they were family. Until he knew they were taken care of, he'd never stop worrying.

Once again, he pushed his thoughts to the back of his mind and continued his lap of the square. Every business boasted wreaths, garlands and decorations in their windows. From experience, he knew they would all be outlined in twinkly lights, as well. Lampposts, benches and pretty much all free space in the town square had been devoted to the holiday cause.

He had to admit the festival was always fun, but this year the town council had gone all-out. A band was on a stage playing lively carols. Some of the businesses displayed tables and stands outside of their doors with special festival prices. Stands were set up throughout the square selling holiday cookies and other baked goods. Sawyer knew Carissa had provided some of them. She'd left Thanksgiving early last night to bake. They also had coffee, tea, cider and hot chocolate.

Sawyer hoped that with all the beverages outside there wouldn't be a line in The Brewside, but as he pushed through the door, he saw he was out of luck. As the town's favorite source of caffeine and a great gossip hotspot, the place was always busy.

Situated between a shoe store and a high-end clothing shop, the coffeehouse had the same look of the other shops around the square. They were all painted white with blue shutters. He noticed quite a few pots of poinsettias beside the entrances.

In Sawyer's opinion, each store on the square was unique, but The Brewside was the only one that felt like home. It was cozy with its quaint decor, raised ceiling made up of exposed beams and dark wood floors. Tony had decorated it with antiques like old vinyl records, framed black-and-white photos and old-fashioned kitchen items. His favorite piece was the refurbished brass cash register that sat on the long bar.

The staff had already put up their Christmas tree in one corner. Sawyer knew that Tony encouraged the local elementary school kids to donate homemade ornaments. Stockings with the employees' names hung behind the counter, and poinsettias dominated every free space.

He offered a wave and a nod to Tony, owner of the joint, and got in line. As he waited his turn, he tuned into a conversation between two women about the Bayside Blogger.

"I mean, she didn't really write anything scandalous today," one of them said.

"Well, yesterday *was* Thanksgiving. Maybe she's in a food coma like the rest of us. Or maybe she went to the amazing Black Friday sales at the outlets at four in the morning like we did," the other woman contributed.

"Or maybe she doesn't have any gossip today."

The two women looked at each other for a beat. Simultaneously they shook their heads and laughed. "Nah," they said together.

Sawyer pushed a hand through his hair. The women were right. Riley not having gossip was like The Brewside not having any customers. Unlikely.

Besides, he knew firsthand that she happened to have one hell of a scoop. He could just see her column now.

Everyone's favorite editor was spotted making out in the dark shadows of his parents' deck last night. Guess someone's lips tasted better than the pumpkin pie!

Riley *had* tasted better than pumpkin pie. Better than every other dessert combined.

When he let himself think about their kiss—*really* think about it—the air left his body. He'd kissed his fair share of women over the years, and none had felt like that.

He kept mulling over their conversation just before the kiss, when she'd admitted she was lonely. Confessed that it was a little difficult to watch her two best friends find such happy relationships. Did Riley *want* to date someone? Did she want to be in a relationship?

Did he want to date her?

The thought surprised him so much that he actually took a step backward. Whoa. Where had that come from?

He certainly wanted to kiss her more.

She was his friend, who could kiss like a dream and who, if he was being truly honest, had started becoming more to him over the last couple of years.

She was also his employee. He was her boss, as she'd pointed out last night. He'd been glad she'd opened up about her time in New York City, although he did suspect there was more to that story. Still, she'd told him she would never date her boss again. Never put herself in that position again.

So, he needed to stop thinking about her in that way. Even if he would give up The Brewside's coffee for the rest of his life for one more chance at feeling her lips against his. One more time to...

"Yo! Sawyer, dude."

His head snapped up at the sound of Tony's amused voice. Heat rushed into his face. "Sorry."

Tony gestured to him. "Sawyer Wallace, everyone. Our esteemed editor in chief."

Sawyer received a nice little round of applause. He bowed and then stepped up to Tony to place his order.

"Sorry, man," he repeated.

"No worries." Tony accepted Sawyer's frequent-customer card and cash. "I mean, I saw you standing there. I know you were physically in the room. But mentally?" He whistled. "You were on a planet in a galaxy far, far away." He punched the card and gave it back. "Working on a big story?"

"Nah. Just this holiday festival. Lots to cover."

"Yeah, Riley was in here earlier complaining..." He trailed off, catching himself. "Did I say complaining? I meant, she was excitedly chatting about how much she loves her job."

Sawyer accepted his extra-large black coffee and chuckled. "I just bet."

"Oh, I almost forgot. Some guy named Dan Melwood was in here asking about you. Actually, about you and the Bayside Blogger."

That got Sawyer's full attention. "Really?"

Tony nodded. "Who is he? Gotta admit, I didn't get a great feeling from him."

Despite being everyone's favorite resident now, Tony wasn't a Bayside native. He'd met his wife, a local woman named Georgia Cooper, in college, and they'd started The Brewside when they'd moved back to town after getting married. Sawyer didn't know all the details but, unfortunately, he did know that the marriage hadn't lasted. Georgia had hightailed it out of Bayside and Tony had stayed. The town had come to love him as their own.

Sawyer explained who Dan Melwood was. "What did he ask about the blogger?"

"The usual questions. Do I know who it is, that kind of thing." Tony paused, considering. "But he seemed *really* intent on finding out her identity. I mean, who isn't?" Tony's face fell.

"What is it?" Sawyer asked.

"He wouldn't let it go. Made me feel a little protective of her. Or him, although most people do think it's a her. But whoever the blogger is, I found myself defending her." Tony held up a finger. "Even though she did write last week that I hadn't been on a date in three years and wouldn't know what to do if I were to go out with someone."

Sawyer cringed. *Dammit, Ri.* "Sorry about that."

Tony offered a good-natured smile. "Not the worst thing she's ever written. Besides, she brings people into this place. She writes about The Brewside so often that people think she's going to be here. So in they come."

"Everyone in town is always here."

Tony nodded emphatically. "Exactly."

Sawyer raised his cup of coffee in salute. "Happy to help. And let me know if Dan asks you any more questions."

"Will do," Tony agreed as Sawyer exited The Brewside.

He didn't like the idea of Dan badgering Tony or anyone else in town. He knew that what Riley had written about him had been intense—tougher than she usually went on people. Still, everything had been true.

To hear that Dan was asking questions at The Brewside made him seem obsessed at this point.

Journalism ran in Sawyer's blood. Part of that was a distinct nudging, a reporter's hunch. In any case, he was feeling it now. What exactly did Dan plan to do with the knowledge of the blogger's identity if and when he got it?

If Dan only wanted to know for himself, that was one thing. Maybe Sawyer could live with that. But if he wanted to take it further and reveal Riley's secret to the entire town... There was no way Sawyer could let that happen.

The only thing that was keeping him from telling Dan Melwood to take a hike was the chance that his investment in the paper could save jobs for the rest of the staff.

The other big question regarding Riley was what Sawyer was going to do about that kiss.

Sawyer continued walking toward the festival, stopping frequently to chat as he ran into family and friends. He checked in with his reporters as he saw them interviewing people, taking photos and jotting notes for their stories.

The ceremony portion of the festival started. The mayor gave a speech as the town council and Santa Claus joined him onstage. Sawyer made to move closer to the stage until he spotted Dan Melwood in the crowd. He really didn't feel like dealing with the man at the moment, so Sawyer averted his eyes and quickly made his way into the shadows. He saw an isolated spot between two of the buildings that actually had a great view of the stage and Christmas tree. He took another step and ran right into— "Riley?"

"Ow! Hey—oh, Sawyer?"

"What are you doing hiding here?"

She poked him in the chest with her index finger. "I could ask you the same thing. Are you following me?"

He took her in. She was wearing tight dark jeans, tall gray boots and a matching gray wool peacoat, which was pretty subdued for her. But she'd accentuated it with a large sparkly pin, purple leather gloves and one of those fleece headbands that covered her ears and had a large purple flower right on the front. Her cheeks were pink from the cold weather and her lips... Her pink lips were adorably pouted as she questioned him.

"I'm not following you. But I think we had the same idea."

She shook her head, curls bouncing around that headband. "Nope. I don't think so. I picked out this spot days ago to watch the tree lighting because it's a great vantage point. You, my friend," she said with another poke to his chest, "are hiding. The question remains, who are you hiding from?"

"I don't know. Are you asking me or is this an inquisition by the Bayside Blogger?"

She gave him a "duh" look. "Uh, the blogger. I'm here on your dime today."

He leaned against the wall to give himself some space. Standing that close to her had her rose-smelling perfume infiltrating his senses and shutting down his brain. "Sorry about that. How's the coverage going?"

She took a moment, considering with a cute little head tilt. "Okay. We definitely got more than in years past."

"But?" he guessed.

"But if the town council had given us more time, more of a heads-up that they were trying to turn our little small-town Christmas festival into something grandiose, I could have done even more. Maybe a cool online piece."

She was always so hard on herself. The Bayside Blogger aside, Riley was one of his best reporters. She was a fast writer who needed little editing, and she had an intuitive knack for interviewing people and getting them to reveal the real story. Not to mention she was an ace when it came to social media. "I'm sure what you got will be amazing. I liked the pre-event coverage."

She rapped him on the chest for the third time. "Again,

it would have been better if I'd been given more time. We could have done a contest for the kids. Or we could have created some Facebook and Instagram ads. With a little more money toward—"

"We don't have the money for..." Realizing his mistake, he let the sentence trail off and prayed that Riley wouldn't pick up on it. Naturally, she did.

"Sawyer?"

"Don't start," he said, throwing his hand up for emphasis.

"I'm not. It's just that—"

"It's nothing," he said. But the statement didn't seem to appease her any more than it calmed him.

The *Bugle was* in trouble, a fact that he wanted to keep to himself for as long as possible. At least, until he had a viable solution.

His earlier thought of Riley's great journalistic skills was backfiring on him. She had that look in her eyes, that glimmer of a story.

"But you said we don't have money. I've asked you this before and I'm going to ask you again. Is the *Bugle* in trouble?"

Those keen green eyes narrowed as she searched his face for any kind of tell. It wasn't that he didn't trust Riley, but admitting the failings of the newspaper out loud would make it real. And Sawyer desperately wished that none of this were real.

"How about this? When I need to talk to you about the newspaper, I will." She didn't seem placated. "You will be the *first* person I talk to."

"Do I have a choice in the matter?"

"Not really." He shifted his weight and changed the subject. "Heard some people talking about you in The Brewside."

One of her eyebrows rose in a delicate arch. "Me or my alter ego?"

"Your alter ego, of course. They were surprised you didn't have any good gossip today."

She rolled her eyes. "Oh, please. Ye of little faith. I've been tweeting up a storm since I got here. Sharon Wright and Elliot Walker were totally getting it on behind the Boathouse."

"No kidding?"

She grinned. "This is an interesting development because Elliot only got out of a serious relationship like a month ago. He'd been dating Amanda Wright for four years and Amanda told everyone with ears that she dumped him because he had no sense of spontaneity or passion." She snorted. "He certainly looked, ah, passionate to me."

She was on a roll now and Sawyer enjoyed watching her eyes light up with enjoyment. "I also happened to notice Mrs. Glamore, the librarian at the public library, winking at Ted Owens."

Sawyer practically choked. "Elle's dad?"

"Hey, he's available."

"He's in his sixties," Sawyer countered.

"So what? Love has no age limits," Riley said passionately.

"Speaking of love, the women I overheard talking about you were also wondering if the Bayside Blogger had a boyfriend."

"Shut up."

She made to jab him and he easily caught her fist. His eyes searched hers before skimming down to take in that appealing heart-shaped mouth again.

"What are you doing?"

Her words snapped him out of it. "Uh, nothing."

"Well, stop it."

"Stop what?"

"Stop looking at me like you want to…like we've already…like you want to again…"

He couldn't stop himself. He cupped her cheek. "Maybe I do want to again."

"Well, you can't. We can't," she said even as she leaned into his palm.

Sawyer moved closer, his eyes intent on her lips. Riley shivered. Her eyes began to drift closed, and his followed as he imagined the softness of her mouth beneath his. Then a dazzling light had them flying open again. The Christmas tree had just been lit, and all of the shops and buildings lining the square—even some of the boats bobbing in the bay—were decorated in beautiful lights.

"Wow, beautiful," Riley whispered.

"Yes, you are."

He waited for her to hit him again or to at least roll her eyes. She didn't. Instead, she stood there, with those big green eyes, her face aglow from all of the twinkly lights.

He'd never wanted anyone more.

And she was the only woman he couldn't have. Ever.

Chapter Five

Well, well, well, looks like everyone's favorite high school sweethearts, Jasper Dumont and Carissa Blackwell, are moving in together. I heard that...
DELETE, DELETE, DELETE

Riley blew out a long, frustrated breath. She was having a major case of writer's block. No, not writer's block. Blogger's block.

She stared at her computer screen, willing it to come up with words on its own. When that didn't happen, she tried again.

The usual suspects were all at the Wallace family house for Thanksgiving last week. Including Bayside Bugle heir and playboy Sawyer, who was looking fine. Especially when he kissed his lifelong friend, Riley Hudson!

DELETE, DELETE, DELETE

She kept hitting the delete button long after all the words were erased. And then she hit it one more time for good measure.

Never in her entire career as the Bayside Blogger had she struggled this much with her column. Maybe that was because she'd never been part of the story before.

"You are a hypocrite, Riley Alexandra Hudson," she said to her empty apartment. Anyone else and she would have blogged about their first kiss so fast that it would have been posted before they came up for air.

However, most couples were probably happy about kissing, while she remained completely undecided.

It wasn't that she hadn't enjoyed it. She had. A lot. A whole heck of a lot. That was the problem. Besides being a beyond-stellar kisser, Sawyer happened to hold two other titles in her life: friend and boss.

Riley let out a long, deep groan and began circling her apartment. She loved this space. When Dumont Incorporated had erected this apartment building right in the center of town she'd jumped on it. Now she was the proud renter of an adorable one-bedroom with hardwood floors, tons of natural light, and killer views of the bay and the town square. Her kitchen was full of upgrades, her bathroom had an amazing soaking tub, and there were plenty of built-in shelves for all of her books and knick-knacks. And the closet had lots of room for her shoes. Many, many pairs of shoes.

Plus, it was decorated flawlessly, if she did say so herself. She'd opted for crisp white furniture and accented every room with pillows, artwork and accessories in every color of the rainbow.

She flopped onto her oversize couch—highlighted with turquoise, red and yellow throw pillows—and tapped a finger to her lips. Taking a deep breath, she inhaled the scent of the coffee she'd made earlier that morning, still lingering in the air.

She'd been down this road before. The "I kissed my boss" route to hell, and it had ended badly. She wrapped her arms around her stomach. Even after all these years, the pain was still fresh and she still felt raw. Connor had betrayed her trust. Not only had he been engaged to someone else while they dated, but once everything was out in the open, he'd let her take the blame for everything. Not once had he stepped in to clear her name.

If she closed her eyes, she could still see the judgy eyes of everyone she'd worked with. Every time she'd entered a room, the hair on the back of her neck had stood straight up, a sure sign everyone had been talking about her.

A loud banging on the door thankfully pulled her out of her head. She bounced to the door and greeted her two best friends.

"Who's ready for some serious downward dog?" Carissa asked, moving past Riley into the room.

"I would never miss our Saturday yoga dates," Riley said loyally.

The three of them headed to the yoga studio, only a block from Riley's apartment building. On the way, they chatted about the Christmas Kickoff Festival. While Elle and Carissa discussed the decorations, Riley couldn't help remembering the look in Sawyer's eyes as he'd cupped her face as he'd brought her closer to him.

"Hello," Elle's voice rang out. "Earth to Riley."

Riley shook her head. "Sorry, what?"

"I said, you'd better be on your best behavior."

Riley waved a nonchalant hand in the air as they strolled into the studio and stashed their stuff. "I don't know why the instructor is so hard on me."

Carissa unrolled her mat as the class assembled around them. "Kyra is hard on you because you never stop talking."

"Hey, that's not true."

Elle waited a beat before snorting. "Yoga is supposed to be calming and peaceful."

"Totally," Riley agreed, getting her own mat ready. "I'm always at peace in this class."

"You're the only one," Carissa said.

Undeterred, Riley stuck her tongue out at her.

Kyra, their instructor, entered the room then and glanced around the studio. "Good morning, everyone." She put on her favorite playlist and moved to her spot at the front of the room.

"Namaste," Riley offered heartily.

Carissa and Elle started laughing. Kyra gave a pained smile, then turned back to the class. "Time to forget the outside world, everyone. Center yourselves in the room. Focus on your breaths. In...and out." She moved into child's pose, and for the next hour, Riley did her best to concentrate on her breathing and how her body was feeling.

How what she'd like to be feeling was Sawyer's lips on hers again.

No, no, no. What is wrong with me! She let out a frustrated sound while everyone else exhaled the troubles from the week.

"What's wrong?" Elle whispered.

"Nothing," Riley said. "Do you want to grab coffee and some of those yummy glazed doughnuts after this?"

"Let us move our minds from the material world and take them to a place of reflection," Kyra's lyrical voice instructed. "A place where there are no glazed doughnuts."

"I'd like to go to a place where the glazed doughnuts didn't have any calories," Carissa said quietly. "I'm in for coffee and carbs."

"Me, too," Elle agreed. "I could use some non-wedding-planning girl time. I think Cam is hanging out with Sawyer today."

Riley stumbled. Her warrior pose was less warrior,

more cowardly lion. "Why are you asking me about Saw-yer?" Riley asked defensively.

"I'm not," Elle said with a head tilt. "I just mentioned him in passing. Why are you getting so defensive?"

"And channel your inner child. Your inner *quiet* child. Your child that stops talking," Kyra said from the front of the room.

"Just because I've known him forever doesn't mean anything," Riley said. "And even though… Okay, okay, we may have kinda, sorta kissed."

Carissa and Elle both froze in the middle of their sun salutations.

"What!" Carissa blurted out loudly.

A resounding *shh* came from about six different people. Kyra tapped her foot in a very impatient way.

"Sorry," Carissa mumbled, and Elle snickered. "What?" she repeated in a much softer tone.

"I know. It's…shocking."

Her friends exchanged an amused look. "Um, yeah. You and Sawyer kissing is about as shocking as the sun rising in the east," Carissa said.

"What do you mean?"

Elle moved into child's pose but turned her head toward Riley. "After seeing the two of you dance at my engagement party, it was clear to the entire town just how much you guys are into each other."

"What are you talking about? We danced for one song."

Carissa snorted. "Try three songs in a row."

"Ladies," the yoga instructor said. "I'm going to have to ask you to lower your voices. Or, better yet, stop talking altogether. The quiet will help your mind and body connect."

"You're right. I'm sorry, Kyra," Riley said to the instructor.

Had she and Sawyer really danced for that long? Holy cow.

Somehow, and she truly had no idea how, Riley managed to finish class. At the same time, she was somewhat horrified she'd told Elle and Carissa about that kiss. Even though they were her very best friends, she just hadn't planned on opening up about something she couldn't quite understand herself yet.

Luckily, neither of them mentioned it again during class. And not on the walk to The Brewside, either. They ordered three coffees and a bunch of glazed doughnuts and found a somewhat private table in the back corner.

Maybe luck would be on her side and no one would mention Sawyer and kissing again.

"So? Are you ever going to tell us the details about this kiss or what?" Carissa asked, licking the glaze off her doughnut.

Riley sighed. Luck had never been her thing anyway. "I mean, there's not really much to tell."

"Um, there's a whole bunch to tell, so hop to it. Where? When? How long?" Elle was practically bouncing in her seat.

"Tongue?" Carissa added.

Riley rolled her eyes dramatically. "Were we at a seventh-grade dance? Of course there was tongue."

Elle pointed her doughnut at Riley. "See, I knew she would spill for carbs."

Carissa edged closer to Elle so they were shoulder to shoulder, a united front, staring her down. "You might as well tell us everything. We're not going to leave you alone until you do."

Riley held her ground. For all of point-three seconds.

Then she relented, took a huge bite of her doughnut with sprinkles and launched into the story.

"It was Thanksgiving night," she began.

"Hold up." Carissa pushed a finger into the air for emphasis. "We were there?"

"Yep."

Elle looked thoughtful. "Oh right. The two of you were out on the deck for a while after dinner."

"Right. We were just talking and I let it slip that I had been feeling kind of lonely."

Both sets of eyes watching her grew in size and filled with worry.

"Lonely?" Elle asked.

"Ri, what's wrong?" Carissa asked.

Riley waved her hand nonchalantly. "It's nothing. Just a passing feeling. I was missing my parents." As much as she loved her friends, she didn't want to tell them the full truth, which was that she'd been feeling left out since they'd both gotten into extremely serious relationships. She would never want them to feel bad. Besides, she was beyond happy for them.

Elle tilted her head, studying Riley. "Are you sure that's all it was?"

"Positive." Riley crossed her fingers under the table. "Anyway, Sawyer and I were talking about that and then one thing led to another... Next thing I know, we're kissing."

Neither Elle nor Carissa said anything for a moment. Finally Carissa beamed. "About freaking time."

"Totally," Elle agreed.

"What are you talking about?" Riley asked. Clearly her friends had lost their minds.

"You and Sawyer have this insane chemistry," Elle

said. "I noticed it as soon as I returned from Italy last year. It's palpable."

"What?" Riley felt completely gobsmacked. "We don't… I mean, we can't. It's too complicated."

"Because he's your boss?" Elle guessed, sympathy in her light green eyes.

"Yes. No." She shook her head. "Not exactly. I mean, he's my boss, but he's also my friend. My longtime family friend. And he knows…" She trailed off.

"He knows what?" Carissa asked. "Like some deep dark secret that you've been keeping from us?"

Riley gulped down her coffee. Hard. The liquid burned her throat. She coughed and turned her head, her gaze landing on a discarded copy of the *Bugle*, her latest Bayside Blogger post staring back at her. It felt like a huge neon light was pointing straight at her.

"Oh, please. Riley never hides stuff from us," Elle said loyally.

Maybe not, but right now she wanted to hide under the table.

"But going back to the amazing chemistry between you and Sawyer," Elle continued. "I even asked Car if you two had dated in the past, or were currently dating. Or, at the very least, hooking up."

"I knew you hadn't," Carissa piped in. "But I'm not sure why. The way he looks at you when he thinks you're not paying attention…" She whistled, long and low, and then fanned her face.

This was all news to Riley. She wanted to hear more about how Sawyer looked at her, but, instead, she focused on something else she'd noted. "Wait a minute. You guys have been talking about me and Sawyer?"

Elle nodded. "For months."

"You're lucky that we're the only ones talking about it," Carissa said.

"What do you mean?"

Carissa deliberated between two doughnuts before choosing a chocolate glazed. "I mean, you're lucky the Bayside Blogger hasn't mentioned you and Sawyer getting all smoochie-smoochie."

Oh, crap. "Uh, yeah, that is lucky." She swallowed. Hard. "But you know, how would she even know? Sawyer and I were out on his parents' deck. In the dark."

"How does she know anything? Come on. Think about all the embarrassing things she posted about me and Cam. And you and Jasper," Elle said to Carissa.

"She's such a beyotch," Carissa said.

"That's kind of strong," Riley said, trying to keep the defensiveness out of her voice.

"Oh, come on, Ri. She put me through hell."

"Yeah, but maybe she was just trying to help."

Carissa rolled her eyes. "Oh, please. Jasper and I almost didn't get together because of her meddling."

The comment was completely unexpected to Riley. And the complete opposite of what she'd thought. She liked to think that her blogs and tweets helped couples find each other. Like she was the final push they needed to realize they were meant to be together.

"Same with me and Cam," Elle said. "I was so freaked out by all the attention that I kept pushing him away."

Riley was flabbergasted. Sure, she realized she'd blogged about Elle a ton. But that was hardly a surprise. Elle hadn't been back to Bayside in ten years. Of course, her homecoming had been a big deal.

To hear that Elle had almost pushed Cam away because of her blogs was insane. She'd assumed they'd become a couple *because* of her gossip.

"But, in the end, you wound up together. That has to count for something." Riley could hear the desperation in her own voice.

"Why are you defending the Bayside Blogger?" Carissa asked.

Riley didn't know what made her do it or why. All she knew was that her brain turned off and her heart kicked in. These were her two best friends and they deserved to know the truth.

And maybe she really needed to tell the truth. Maybe spilling her guts would help her feel less lonely. Finally. As much as she'd been telling herself that Elle and Carissa's relationships had come between them, it wasn't the only thing. There was a big, fat elephant who was constantly present with the three of them. That elephant's name was the Bayside Blogger.

"I'm actually—"

"What?" Carissa asked.

"I'm the Bayside Blogger," she whispered so low that even she had to strain to hear herself.

"Huh?" Elle asked.

"I said…" She took a deep breath. "*I* am the Bayside Blogger."

"Get real, Ri." Carissa took a long gulp of coffee.

Elle snorted. "Seriously. She's written about you plenty."

Riley looked down at her hands. Somehow they had become tightly twisted together. She could feel the sweat on her palms. "I had to write about myself." She glanced around the coffee shop and dropped her voice even lower. "To make it more believable."

"Whatever," Carissa said with a head shake.

But Elle caught on more quickly. "You're serious."

"No, she's not." But Carissa looked from Elle to Riley and then back to Elle.

"I am. It's me. I'm her. I'm the Bayside Blogger." She went on to tell them how she returned from New York and came up with the idea. Neither she nor Sawyer had had any idea that the simple gossip column she'd pitched would turn into what it became.

When she was finished explaining, she sat back feeling like a weight had been lifted from her shoulders. For the most part, she'd been able to keep the secret with little fuss. Besides, she'd had Sawyer to talk to when she needed him. Still, there were times she'd wanted to let Elle and Carissa in.

Her feeling of calm came to a screeching halt when she saw the expressions on her friends' faces.

"Oh, Riley," Elle said, a combination of hurt and disappointment laced in those two simple words.

Carissa was worse. She was mad, extending a finger in Riley's direction. "You wrote all that stuff about me?"

"Uh, yeah," she answered quietly. "I never lied, though. All of the things I wrote were true."

"And hurtful. You told the entire town that my ex-husband cheated on me. Dammit, Riley. Do you have any idea how embarrassing that was?" Tears welled up in Carissa's eyes.

"But it brought you and Jasper together." Riley felt desperation creeping into her voice. She realized that what she'd believed all along to be a matchmaking plot might not have gone the way she'd intended—and she was about to pay a price.

"It's a lucky coincidence that Jasper and I rekindled our relationship and, trust me, it had nothing to do with you. How could you do that to me?" Carissa stood quickly, her chair toppling over. Every pair of eyes in

The Brewside turned in their direction. Riley could feel the heat on her cheeks.

"Car, please just sit back down and we can—"

"We can what? Talk? What can I say to you now that won't end up in your column?" She quickly righted the fallen chair.

"I've *never* written about anything we agreed to keep secret between the three of us. I wouldn't do that. And I never would. I keep my promises, Carissa."

One tear spilled over, falling down Carissa's face, a rare occurrence for her typically stoic friend. "I feel like I don't know anything about you anymore. I need some space." With that, she grabbed her tote bag and quickly fled the café.

Riley's heart sank. "Aren't you going to storm out on me, too?" she asked Elle softly.

Elle shook her head. "Don't get me wrong, Riley. I'm furious, too. But with me, the Bayside Blogger was more of a pesky fly. With Carissa, she was a fly carrying some disease. You really hurt her. How could you do that?"

"I don't know," she said, her voice hitching.

The truth was, keeping something of this magnitude from her two besties was brutal. Especially since she told them every other minute detail of her life.

"The whole Bayside Blogger thing just became so much bigger than everything else."

That was certainly true, but if Riley was being completely honest, being the Bayside Blogger offered her a respite from her real life. It was like a shield that she got to wear. An invisible shield that only she and Sawyer could see. By enabling her to concentrate on everyone else in town, she didn't have to think about her own life.

And how empty it really was.

She didn't have to remember how she'd spectacularly

messed up in New York. Or feel the poignant sting of her heartbreak and betrayal.

"I'm going to go check on Carissa," Elle said.

"Okay, let me know how she is."

Elle shook her head. "You betrayed my trust, Riley."

Riley swallowed past the lump growing in the throat. "Please don't be mad, Elle. Please don't hate me."

"I need some time, too. This is a lot to take in, to be honest." Elle gathered her belongings and walked out of the coffee shop, leaving Riley alone with a pit in her stomach.

What had she done? How could she fix this? Make it right?

Her own tears threatened, but she was very aware that people were still watching her. She felt naked suddenly. Was this how her friends had felt when she'd been writing about them?

"Everything okay over here?"

Riley startled at the sound of Tony's voice. His eyes were kind as he looked at her.

"Uh, yeah, of course. Carissa wasn't feeling well," Riley covered smoothly. "It came on pretty fast. Elle just went to check on her."

"Hope it wasn't anything she had here."

"Nah. She wasn't feeling great before our yoga class, either."

"Sorry to hear it. And even sorrier to say that you guys will probably be in the next Bayside Blogger column," he said.

Riley didn't have to see her reflection to know that the color had drained from her face.

"You think?" she asked.

Tony nodded. "Definitely. I don't know if she has this

place bugged or what, but seems like she always captures gossip from inside these walls."

Riley wanted to protest. She wanted to call Tony out on his statement. She got tips and leads nonstop, every single day. And the absolute biggest contributor to her site was from the man standing right in front of her. If only the rest of the town knew how many tips Tony passed on to her, his business would be cut in half.

Her phone sat deep within the shadows of her oversize purse. She didn't need to look at it to know that Tony had just sent her a message. His preferred method of communication was via direct message on Twitter.

As Tony returned to the front counter, she gathered up the remnants of their carb-fest. She was pretty sure that she'd never regain her appetite after what had just transpired with her two best friends.

Idiot. Stupid. Dumb. If she didn't write about their fight, that would be as good as outing herself as the blogger to Tony—who might out her to Bayside.

Yet how could she break a promise to her best friends?

She knew chastising herself couldn't reverse time. But, for the first time in the two-and-a-half years she'd been acting as the almighty gossiper of Bayside, she regretted ever saying anything at all.

Chapter Six

My, my, dear readers, you've been active this morning. Plenty of you witnessed something going down between Elle Owens, Carissa Blackwell and Riley Hudson at The Brewside. Unfortunately, no one seems to know just what set off the fireworks between these Bayside besties! But I do...

Sawyer was restless. He had six articles for the Sunday edition of the newspaper sitting in front of him, waiting for their turn under his final review, and for the life of him he couldn't concentrate on any of them.

He had a lot on his mind. Well, that was the understatement of the year. From saving the newspaper to his mixed-up emotions for Riley to his family's legacy and back to Riley again, his mind was overflowing with thoughts.

Leaning back, he took in his home office, his favorite spot in the house he'd purchased two years ago. It overlooked the bay and offered plenty of natural light. A large desk was set up between two picture windows. There was a cozy fireplace against one wall, and at Riley's suggestion he'd added a comfortable recliner and table in front of it.

He crossed to the fireplace now, leaned on the mantel.

The answers he sought didn't spring up from the ashes left in the hearth.

Damn.

He returned to his desk and that's when he noticed the date. Sawyer cringed. His wedding anniversary. Or it would have been if they'd gone through with it. But Rachel had called it off at the last minute.

He stretched back as far as his leather desk chair would allow. He'd been so bitter with her back then. And embarrassed, if he was being honest. Now he realized he owed her a debt of gratitude from saving them both from what would have been a huge mistake.

He'd met Rachel in college. They'd started dating junior year and it didn't take long for her to take over every aspect of his life. He'd been in love in the stupid way only a young man could be. Totally, wholeheartedly, without regard to anything besides his ever-present libido.

In essence, he would have done anything she asked.

He *did* do anything she asked.

How could he not when Rachel was so much fun? The first couple of years they knew each other, she'd been vivacious and exciting, with a love of exploring. She could turn a simple weekend into a huge adventure.

Coming from a small town where people took life slowly, Sawyer had gravitated toward her zest for life. He'd never met anyone like her. She introduced him to new cuisines and different bands and musicians. In the middle of the night, he'd wake up to her phone call and the next thing he knew, they'd find themselves in a different state. Just for fun.

After college graduation, he'd returned home and worked for his father at the *Bugle*. It hadn't taken long for Rachel to suggest they go on an adventure. She thought a move to Washington, DC, would be fun.

"Come on, Sawyer. When else are you going to have the opportunity to spread your wings and live a little? You're only young once."

It had sounded like a sound argument to him. So he'd quit the *Bugle*, abandoned his family, left his friends and moved to DC. He would never forget his parents' faces when he'd announced that he was leaving home. Quitting the newspaper.

He'd taken a job at the *Washington Post* that he hadn't particularly liked. After being the second in charge at the *Bugle* it was tough to become the small fish.

They'd lived in a tiny apartment they could barely afford. Rachel had loved it. Sawyer had been massively discontented. He was used to yard work and a big bay to swim in and actually knowing and talking to your neighbors.

But as long as Rachel was happy...

Of course, it hadn't taken long for the glimmer and shine of DC to fade away. Soon Rachel became bored with her own work as a graphic designer for a small ad firm and her wanderlust returned.

She began hinting about moving again. To New York City or Los Angeles. Yet another adventure. Only, Sawyer wasn't enjoying their current one.

He'd decided to take action. Getting engaged would fix the fissures in their relationship, or so he'd stupidly thought.

A week before the big day was set to happen, Rachel came home. She gave him one long look and admitted she wasn't happy. She was ready for a new experience. The last he heard she'd gone to live in Prague, Budapest, and at some point, she ended up in Iceland.

He guessed her explorations weren't quite over.

And Sawyer had had the pleasure of returning to Bayside, his family, his friends, and the *Bugle* with his tail between his legs and a mountain of apologies to dish out.

His parents had been saints. They'd never thrown it back in his face.

Well, Sawyer certainly had Rachel out of his system. And he had swore that he would never, ever be that selfish again.

So he'd made the *Bugle* his life. He devoted everything to it. That's why it couldn't fail now. *He* couldn't fail. The *Bugle* was his family's legacy and he'd be damned if he saw it wither away and die.

That's why he had to consider all options, including Dan Melwood's offer, no matter how extreme his demands seemed.

He reread an email exchange he'd had with the man earlier and then turned to scan the notes he'd taken during their meeting. Maybe there was a way he could convince him to move forward with his offer without bringing the Bayside Blogger into it.

Or maybe revealing the identity of the Blogger wouldn't be that horrible. Maybe Riley was sick of living a double life. Maybe no one in Bayside would even care.

His doorbell rang. Sawyer wasn't expecting anyone. In fact, he'd bailed on plans to meet Cam for some beers in order to brood alone.

He yanked open the door and sucked in a breath. Riley stood there, her red hair framing her pretty face. She wasn't wearing a coat, and the athletic clothes she sported outlined to every curve of her body. But it was her eyes that really caught his attention. The green color wasn't as bright as usual and they were puffy and red tinged. She'd been crying.

She let out a sob and he pulled her inside.

"Ri, what's wrong? Did something happen?"

He didn't even think. With one hand he shut the door while the other reached out and drew her to him, enveloping her in a hug. She came willingly, curling into him, pressing her face against his chest. She let out a long sigh and tightened her grip.

They stayed like that for a long time. Finally she pushed back. "Sorry."

"Don't apologize. Come on. I'll make you some tea."

She had no idea that he kept it stocked only for her. Sawyer despised tea.

They entered the kitchen and while he set to make the tea, she hopped up on the counter, a habit of hers that amused him. He had a table and a peninsula with three bar stools, but she always went for the counter.

"What's with the outfit?" he asked. "Pretty subdued for you."

"What?" She seemed dazed. "Oh, this. I was at a yoga class with Elle and Car—" She broke off on Carissa's name, let out a delicate hiccup.

Ah, now he was getting to it. "Did you guys have a fight?"

"You could say that." She looked down, studied her gray UGG boots.

She stayed quiet for another couple of minutes while he finished getting the tea ready. He handed her a mug and then leaned against the opposite counter. He could wait this out. Sawyer was patient. Luckily, Riley was not.

"It was a fight. A horrible fight."

"That's unusual. The three of you have been joined at the hip for the last couple of months."

She frowned. "They're my best friends. At least, they were."

"Come on. What could you have possibly done that would sever that relationship?"

Riley sighed. "I really love them. They both mean so much to me, and I would never hurt either of them. But apparently I did."

Sawyer held up his hands. "Whoa. What are you talking about?"

"We were having carbs and they were talking about much they hated the Bayside Blogger. I was shocked because I always thought I was helping them. Or, you know, the Bayside Blogger was helping them. And then…" She met his stare. "I told them I was the Bayside Blogger," she said in a fast whisper.

Sawyer gripped the edge of the counter hard so he didn't fall off in shock. "You did what? I thought we had an agreement. No telling anyone your identity." As soon as the words left his mouth he felt like a hypocrite. Dan Melwood's emails were still up on his computer in the office.

Not to mention that given the fact he was pretty sure Carissa and Elle had not reacted kindly to this news, it was doubtful that others would be fine knowing the Bayside Blogger's true identity.

"Oh, Riley," he said, suddenly feeling tired.

"I know, I know, I'm horrible." She covered her face with both hands. "You hate me now, too, don't you?" she asked between shaking fingers.

He relented. Sawyer jumped off the counter and crossed to her. Gently he removed her hands from her face and held on to them. "Ri, look at me." It took her a long moment, but finally her gaze slid up to his. He could see the moisture pooling in her eyes.

"I could never hate you. And I certainly don't hate you over this…incident."

"But you wish I hadn't told them, right?" She tried to remove her hands from his, but Sawyer held on tight.

"No. Yes. I mean, I'm not really sure at the moment. I know that I would have liked for you to give me a heads-up before you told them or anyone else."

She tilted her head, causing a piece of hair to fall and cover her eye. "So you could talk me out of it?"

He pushed the strand of hair off her face, lingering for a moment. Her hair was so shiny and silky. And despite coming from a yoga class, she smelled fresh, like a new bouquet of flowers. "I'm not sure if I would have tried to talk you out of it. But you and I have been keeping this secret for a long time now. Maybe it's been getting too hard to keep the truth from the people we care about."

It was this thing that brought the two of them together. But what if it was beginning to separate them from everyone else, too?

Sawyer met her gaze for a second before taking in her perfectly shaped nose and full lips. She was the most beautiful woman he'd ever seen. She was studying him just as intensely. Her chest was rising and falling and her mouth opened slightly into an appealing little O.

Perhaps the Bayside Blogger secret wasn't the only thing bringing them together.

He wanted to kiss her again. That's all he'd wanted to do since the last time it happened. But there was hurt and sadness in her eyes, and that needed to be dealt with first.

"How mad were they when you told them?"

She whistled. "Pretty pissed. Carissa especially. Elle was a little more reasonable. But that's Elle's personality."

"Do you think either of them will tell anyone else?"

"No," she said quickly, the loyalty to her friends evident. "Like I said, they're pissed for sure. But I think they get the repercussions. At least, I hope they do."

"Give them some time. A couple days to cool off." A thought occurred to him. "Elle and Cam are engaged. I hear Jasper and Carissa are moving in together. What if there's pillow talk and the guys end up blabbing?"

Riley's face deflated. "Oh, God, I don't know. What have I done? I'm such an idiot."

Sawyer disagreed. An idiot? No. Impulsive and often times overzealous? Absolutely. He stepped closer to her and framed her face in his hands. "Riley Hudson, you are not an idiot. You're one of the most caring, loving, smart, funny, loyal people I know. I hate when you're down on yourself."

She scrunched up her nose. "Yeah, well, I hate when I go and do something really stupid that I can't take back."

"Everyone has regrets."

"Not as many as me, apparently." She laughed lightly but there was still a hurt expression on her face.

Sawyer realized, and not for the first time, that there were things Riley was still keeping to herself. Secrets that might bring them closer if she would only open herself up to him.

He stepped even closer to her. "I wish you would talk to me, Ri."

"I do talk to you. Like, every day."

He placed a finger against her lips. "Really talk to me. Let me in."

The indecision was clear as day. It was a struggle for her. Maybe it was that, or maybe it was the fact that her eyes still held so much emotion after her rough morning. Sawyer wasn't sure. All he knew was that they were close, so close, and he gave in to his wants.

He touched his lips to hers. She inhaled a quick breath, and followed it up by lacing her arms around his neck and pulling him closer to her. The longing to feel her lips on his again subsided, only to be replaced by something much more potent. Lust, pure lust, washed over him.

His mouth moved greedily over hers, reveling in the taste of her, the smell, the touch. She made a little sound of longing in her throat and it almost undid him.

She was still sitting on the counter, and next thing he knew, he was scooping her up. She gasped when he lifted her.

"Sawyer."

He nipped at her lips. "Is this okay?"

"Yes. Oh, yes."

He didn't need to hear more than that. Somewhere in the back of his mind, he was wondering how they'd gone from her bad morning to him carrying her into the living room and gently placing her on the couch. But it was very far in the back of his mind. Right now, all he wanted was more of her.

He covered her body with his and she welcomed it with open arms that twined around him, moving up and down his back. When her fingers snuck under the bottom of his shirt, he jumped at the touch.

She giggled. He looked down at her face. She was smiling and her eyes had finally lost some of the hurt. "Is someone ticklish?" she asked with humor in her voice.

"If I remember correctly, I'm not the only one who is." With that, he ran his hand up her side. She bucked and would have jumped right off the couch if he hadn't been lying on top of her.

"Touché," she said, trying to move his hand from her sensitive spot.

But Sawyer simply ran his other hand up her other side, lightly grazing the skin under her shirt. She shuddered and he covered her mouth with his again. Soon, it wasn't about one ticklish spot or another, and their hands were all over each other, caressing every spot they could reach. Over clothes, under clothes, it didn't matter.

He trailed his mouth down the column of her throat, eliciting something that sounded very similar to a purr. Riley took the opportunity to try to remove his shirt. He shifted helpfully but, somehow, they got twisted, and the next thing he knew he was falling.

Sawyer hit the floor next to the couch with a *thunk* and before he could recover from that, Riley landed on top of him. They were both stunned, and there was silence for a long moment before they started laughing.

"Are you okay?" they asked at the same time. Obviously they were if the laughter said anything.

"Holy crap. Did we just fall off the couch?" she asked, propping herself up on her elbows and looking down at him.

"Seems like it. That's definitely a first for me. Now that was quite a kiss." He'd meant it lightly but a shadow passed over her face. "Ri, what's wrong? Are you sure you're not hurt?"

"I landed on you, remember?"

"You weigh like two pounds."

"There's a comment I'd like to hear over and over for the rest of my life."

She made to move, but he yanked her back to him. He kissed her lightly and tightened his arms around her. "Where did you go just now?"

She averted her eyes. "Nowhere."

"Don't avoid me. You gave me the same look you did back in the kitchen when I asked you to talk to me."

She bit her lip, deciding. "There are things from my past that I just don't like talking about. And when you pointed out that we'd been kissing—and of course we had—I kind of, well…"

"Freaked out a little?" he guessed.

She nodded. "You're my boss."

"But I'm also your friend."

She cupped his cheek. "That makes it worse. We shouldn't keep doing this."

He didn't second-guess himself. Instead, Sawyer went for it. "I want to keep doing this."

"You do?" Her voice was filled with shock. "Why? I mean, really? What would our parents think?"

"Ah, I really don't want to think about my parents at this particular moment."

What he did want to do was probe into that secret she was keeping from him, find out just what it was holding her back. But before he could do any of that, the doorbell rang and Riley jumped off him. She was already straightening her clothes and the couch cushions by the time he righted himself.

He took one last long look at her and decided that anything he was going to ask would have to wait. Instead, he walked to the door and pulled it open to see Cam standing there with two six-packs of beers and a grin.

"Since you refused to come meet me for a drink, I'm bringing the drinks to you." He handed one of the six-packs to Sawyer. "You're still lame for pretending to work on a Saturday."

Having hung out for years, Cam was comfortable in Sawyer's house, and he headed toward the living room. When he saw Riley, who, for her part was looking extremely guilty, he stopped in his tracks.

"Wait, were you actually working?"

At least Cam seemed oblivious to what they'd actually been doing. "We were just going over some edits on late deadlines," Sawyer lied smoothly.

"Nice work outfit," Cam said to Riley.

"I was at yoga earlier," she said, blushing.

"I'm just teasing you, Ri. But speaking of yoga, did

something happen? Elle was in a weird mood when she came home."

Riley jumped. "Um, I don't know. It was fine. I mean, um, I have to go." She pointed toward the door and then quickly made her retreat.

"Riley, wait." Sawyer gave Cam an apologetic look, handed the six-pack over, and ran after Riley, who was faster than he realized. He caught up with her in the driveway, her hand clutching her key fob.

"Sorry, Sawyer," she said. "I need to go."

"Was it Cam's question or the couch? Or the floor?"

She blew out a long breath. "All of the above?" she asked. Her face grew serious. "It's been a weird morning. I have a lot to think about."

"We both have a lot to think about. But I meant what I said in there. I don't know when or why or how this all started. All I do know is that there's something between us that I want to explore."

"But...but," she stammered. "We've known each other forever. And we've never done any of that before. I mean, except for Thanksgiving." She wiggled her finger toward the house as if that was a clear indicator of their earlier make-out session.

"Things change and I'm okay with that. The question is, are you?"

"Sawyer, I just hurt my two best friends. I need to fix that first."

"And you will. Like I said earlier, just give them some time."

She nodded firmly, although her face belied the action. She was uncertain and nervous. He got that. It had been a big morning for her.

Sawyer waited until she got in the car and watched as she pulled out of his driveway, drove down the street and turned the corner. Before heading back inside to Cam, he took a moment in the brisk November air.

The one thing that had come out of the entire day was that Sawyer had finally realized all the feelings and urges he'd been suppressing about Riley were out in the open now.

He wanted her. It was as simple as that.

Chapter Seven

Spotted: Sawyer Wallace "working" over the weekend. Only...he wasn't alone. What member of the *Bugle's* staff kept him company? Or, should I say, what FEMALE staffer... New couple alert? Keep me updated, faithful gossip birdies.

"Where you off to, boss?"

Sawyer halted in his tracks. He'd been trying to sneak out quietly without drawing attention to himself. His sports reporter's question had squashed that hope. Every head in the bull pen turned in his direction, including Riley's, the one person he was really trying to avoid.

"I'm just running out for an hour or so to do some errands. Carry on, everyone."

He hated acting suspicious and shady. He knew his intentions were noble, but he didn't want to share the details of his outing until he returned. Since it involved Riley and her new predicament, he'd been laying low all morning.

He could feel those gorgeous emerald eyes burning into him now. *Don't look at her. Don't look.*

Of course, he looked.

As usual, she was beautiful. She was wearing a pink sweater and had her hair pulled back in a ponytail. But those who really knew her would notice the shadows under her eyes. Because he understood what was happening in her life, he realized she'd probably spent the whole weekend fretting about the fight with her friends.

That's why he was sneaking out now.

She tossed him a questioning stare. He responded with a nod and continued out the door, zipping his coat as he went.

It didn't take long to walk from the *Bugle*'s office to The Brewside, which was great since it was a particularly cold day. The wind was biting and there was a feeling of snow in the air.

He pushed open the main door to the coffee shop, soaking in the aroma of freshly brewed coffee beans. A blast of air from the heater washed over him, warming his chilled skin.

He sidled up to the counter where Carissa was talking with Tony. "What's that amazing smell?" he asked. Besides the coffee, there was something sweet in the air.

Carissa beamed. "Just some of my world-famous cinnamon raisin scones."

"Carissa's catering company is going to start offering one specialty item every day," Tony said around a large bite of the scone.

"Want one?" she asked Sawyer, gesturing to the tray of fresh-from-the-oven scones.

"Do you really even need to ask me that?"

Tony wiped his mouth with a napkin. "So, Sawyer, what brings you in this time of day?" He looked at his watch. "You want the usual?"

"Sounds good," he said. "I'm actually here to meet with your new baker and..." They all shifted their attention to the front of the room as the door let out a little jingle. "Here's my other date," he said as Elle smiled at them and crossed to the counter.

"Dates with two of Bayside's most beautiful women,"

Tony said with a wink. "Lucky guy." He leaned across the counter. "I should warn you, though. They're both taken."

Sawyer faked shock. "Ladies, you deceived me."

"I'm making up for it with scones," Carissa said, and led them to a table near the window.

"Fair enough."

After Tony brought over their drink orders and they'd dispensed with the pleasantries, Sawyer jumped right into business.

"You're probably wondering why I asked the two of you here today," he began.

Carissa sat back in her seat. "I think we figured out the crux of it."

"You want to talk about Riley," Elle added.

He nodded and sipped his coffee.

Carissa huffed. "Riley or the Bayside Blogger? Seems they're the same person."

Suddenly Sawyer wasn't sure how to proceed. Riley had been right when she'd said Carissa was upset. Even now, there was an angry tint to her cheeks and her eyes had narrowed. But he'd decided yesterday to try and right this situation. Riley was an employee of the newspaper, and therefore he had a responsibility to try to fix this.

Hell, even he didn't buy that.

He was going to try to fix this because it was Riley.

"I can't image how you felt learning that Riley is…" He glanced around the nearly empty coffee shop. Still, he lowered his voice. "Learning about Riley's alternate identity."

"Alternate identity? It's not like she's Batman," Carissa said with a snort. "She's a gossip columnist."

"How could we have not figured this out?" Elle asked. "How does she know all the information and details that she does? We took a trip to DC together a while back and I remember that the Bayside Blogger still put out a column."

"Technology," Sawyer answered. "She can write from anywhere. As to all the details, well, let's just say that as much as the fine citizens of Bayside complain about the gossip, they sure do love to contribute to it."

"You mean, people help her write her columns?" Elle asked.

Sawyer nodded. "She gets tips and items all day long, every day. She could probably stay in her house for a month straight and still put out a column every single day."

"I still can't believe that she hid this from us. We're so close." Elle worried her lip.

"Couldn't have been easy. She came to my house after she told you on Saturday. She was a mess."

Elle seemed sympathetic to the statement, but Carissa held firm. "Oh, so sorry that Riley was distraught over something she caused. Poor little blogger." She sighed. "You don't understand, Sawyer. You're not the one she keeps writing about."

"Um, I beg to differ. Thanks to one of her items, my mom started grilling me on these imaginary girlfriends Riley threw in her column."

Elle and Carissa worked hard to stifle smiles. In the end, they both lost the battle and it didn't take long for Sawyer to join in on the laughter.

"See, it's not that bad," he said.

"But, Sawyer, you weren't dating anyone else and you're not getting engaged." She paused. "Right?"

"Of course he's not," Elle chimed in. "He wouldn't have kissed Riley on Thanksgiving if he was into someone else."

Gah. "She told you about that?"

Elle and Carissa exchanged a look that clearly read, *Duh*.

"Of course, she did, although, it's really not that surprising," Elle said.

"It's not?" he asked. "What else—"

Carissa interrupted him. "Can we stay on topic here? I went through a lot of tough times that I would have preferred to keep to myself. The Bayside Blogger didn't give me that option. She told the whole town my very personal business."

"I know she did and that sucks. But let me ask you this. Was any of the info she reported on false?"

"Huh?" Carissa asked.

"Was it gossip or fact?"

"Well, fact, I guess."

"See, Riley and I had two rules when it came to the blogger. The first was that every single item she posted, tweeted, wrote about, had to be fact. No presumptions. No lies. No embellishments. If she reported that someone cheated on their significant other, they did. When she says someone is raising havoc in The Brewside, they are."

Elle leaned forward, interest shining in her eyes. "So Mrs. Winters really did take a burlesque dance class over in Riverdale?"

"My eyes are still burning over that one, but yes," Sawyer admitted.

"What's the second rule?" Carissa asked. "Between you and Riley?"

Sawyer waited a beat, making sure he had their full attention. "That she wouldn't tell anyone her identity."

They all paused, realization settling in.

"Then why would she tell us?" Carissa asked softly.

"Because she loves you and respects you."

"And she trusts us," Elle added.

"I think she was probably feeling a little bad, too. It's a big secret she's been keeping completely to herself all this time. Couldn't have been easy. In fact, it must have been pretty lonely."

"She betrayed my trust," Carissa said, and crossed her arms.

Sawyer stifled a sigh. "You could argue that she betrayed the whole town. And that most of the citizens of Bayside betrayed one another. There's a lot of betrayal going on here."

He finished his coffee and put the empty cup back on the table. "I understand you're mad at her. I'm just asking you to forgive. Riley really loves both of you and she's devastated to realize how much she's hurt you. And I know you both love her."

Elle leaned her arms onto the table. "What about you, Sawyer? How do you feel about Riley?"

Heat washed over his face and suddenly Sawyer felt uncomfortable in his chair. "Riley and I have known each other our entire lives. She's a talented writer and a good employee. And she's my friend. She always will be."

Elle's eyes softened. "Sometimes relationships change."

If he thought he was uncomfortable before, it was nothing compared to how he felt now. "Well, I don't know that we need to…"

"Oh, give him a break, Elle." Carissa rolled her eyes. "They have to come to it in their own time."

"I suppose you're right," Elle agreed.

"I appreciate you meeting with us, Sawyer," Carissa said. "But I just need a little more time to work out how I feel about all this."

He supposed that was the best outcome he could hope for at this point. Besides, when it came to things concerning Riley he had quite a bit of thinking to do himself.

Interesting meet-up at The Brewside today between Sawyer Wallace, Elle Owens and Carissa Blackwell. The three had their heads together for a long time. Couldn't catch any snippets of the conversation, but maybe it had something to do with Carissa and Elle running out on Riley the other day.

Riley stared at the message that Tony had sent her over direct message on Twitter. Why in the world had Sawyer, Elle and Carissa gotten together? Of course, Elle and Car were on friendly terms with Sawyer, but that was still an unlikely trio.

Maybe this had something to do with how weird Sawyer had been all morning. She knew something was up with him when he left earlier.

Riley turned her attention back to her computer screen, but she couldn't stop thinking about Tony's message. Not to mention the fact that, as usual, Tony had been sending her tips all weekend and she'd yet to post any of them.

The blank Word document staring back at her was like a big neon sign shining the word *loser* over and over again. She had a major case of the blogger's block. Ever since she'd spilled the beans to Car and Elle she'd been unable to post anything other than a couple of lame tweets. Pretty soon people would start to notice.

Since she'd spent the entire weekend moping in her apartment with Chinese takeout and bad reality television, she took some time to go through all of the tips she'd received. She'd have to cobble an article out of them.

She was halfway through a column about a possible new romance between two of the teachers at the high school when Sawyer's voice bellowed out from his office.

"Hudson. Get in here."

When had he gotten back? Must have used the back door.

Riley got up. She shook her head at the *oohs* emanating throughout the bull pen as she walked to his office, entered, and shut the door behind her.

"So?" he asked.

"So what?" She took a seat in front of him, smoothing down her black wide-leg pants, pink wool sweater and leather belt with polka dots. Her matching pink pumps peeked out from the bottom of her pants as she crossed her legs.

"It's almost noon. Where's the blogger's column?"

"Ah, I see, I knew you loved reading it."

"Riley." His voice may have taken on a hard tone but sympathy shone in his eyes. "What's going on? Is this because of what happened with Elle and Carissa the other day?"

She shrugged. "A little. I mean, it was a pretty tame weekend around here, too. Nothing exciting to report."

He leaned forward on his desk. "No tips came in from your usual sources?"

"Actually...let's talk about that." She leaned forward, mirroring his pose. "I did happen to get the most interesting tip just now."

She paused and he waited.

"Well? Are you going to tell me what it was about?"

Riley tapped her foot in a quick staccato. "Why don't you tell me, since the tip was all about you."

Confusion crossed his face, followed by awareness and a cute reddening of his cheeks. "Someone told you that I met your friends at The Brewside this morning, didn't they?"

She nodded. "Was it just a coincidence? Maybe you

went in for some of Tony's Monday-morning sticky buns and ran into Elle and Carissa?"

"Or maybe I asked them to coffee."

She frowned. "Why would you do that?"

He removed his glasses and the confused expression she thought was adorable crossed his face. "I guess I was just trying to help you."

Her heart melted. When was the last time someone had helped her? When was the last time someone had spoken up on her behalf?

Certainly not when she was in New York.

"Well? Do they still hate me?" She held her breath, fearing the answer.

"Your friends don't hate you, Riley," he responded quickly. "But they are angry."

"I deserve that." She stood and crossed to the window. Peering out at the street below, she said, "I shouldn't have told them. I can't believe I did."

"Neither can I. Riley?"

She turned back to face him.

"Why did you tell them? What made you pick that moment?"

She shrugged as if the answer was inconsequential or elusive when, really, she knew exactly why she'd spilled the beans.

She was lonely. Revealing her secret to her two best friends gave her a moment of inclusion. Of course, that only lasted a second before reality came crashing down. Now she felt even more isolated.

"I wanted to unload my biggest secret," she told Sawyer.

He saw through her words immediately. Sometimes it was like he had an insight right into her mind, as though he could edit through her thoughts to get to the crux of the matter.

"I don't think the Bayside Blogger is your biggest secret."

She crossed her arms around her stomach protectively. "Oh really? Think I have some other identity that's bigger than the blogger?"

He'd been watching her from behind his desk. Now he joined her by standing. "Yes." He skirted the desk and stopped in front of her. "I think you have a whole story from your time in Manhattan. One of these days, you'll trust me enough to share it."

Her mouth fell open. How did he know?

They stood like that, in front of his desk, only inches apart, for a long time. Vaguely, she wondered if any of their coworkers noticed them. Surely someone was watching the two of them staring into each other's eyes.

He had the most alluring hazel eyes. She'd always been able to get lost in their depths.

Eventually Sawyer broke the spell by sitting down on the edge of his desk. "In the meantime, I have a favor to ask of you."

Not what she was expecting him to say. "Okay?" she said, uncertainly.

"You know I go to the annual Technology in Print Publication Conference every year." She nodded. "It's two days from now and Bob had to back out. He has a family commitment he can't get out of."

She had noticed Bob was out of the office this week. "And you want me to go with you?"

"In Bob's place. Yes. You know how you always think of me as Superman?"

"I literally have never thought of you in that way."

He ignored her. "Turns out I can't be in more than one

place at once. There are some workshops on social media and communications I think would be beneficial to the newspaper. You're the perfect person to cover them."

Something felt fishy about this invite. She *was* the perfect person to cover anything related to social media. Heck, she'd taught most of her coworkers how to use Instagram and Snapchat. But why hadn't he asked her to go to this conference in the first place?

Unless…it was due to money.

"Sawyer, why didn't you ask me about this earlier?"

He coughed. "We never send more than two people and Bob has seniority over you." He didn't meet her eyes. "Is that a yes then?"

She ignored his question. "So we'll be going away together. Just the two of us."

He made a low, guttural sound. It was pure male and pure sex.

She knew the feeling. A couple days away with Sawyer. Alone. Despite her hesitation to get involved, she knew her resistance was wearing thin. Besides, this was for work. Her job. "Uh, I guess I can do that."

"It's a couple hours away at a ski lodge. Not sure if they have snow yet or not. But there's all kinds of things there—sledding, exercise facilities, spa, that kind of stuff. Bring warm clothes. The conference is pretty casual."

"Do I need to register or anything?"

"Um, no. Don't worry. The paper will take care of everything. Just be ready to head out early in two days."

She left his office, but stopped right outside the door. Leaning against the wall, Riley took a moment to compose herself. She would be ready for the conference. The real question was, would she be ready for Sawyer?

Chapter Eight

Ho. Ho. Ho. Anyone guess the *Bugle's* potential new couple yet? The lovebirds didn't get the memo about going south for the winter. I heard they're traveling to a swanky ski resort in the Blue Ridge Mountains. Is *conference* the new term for *tryst*?

Having Riley by his side was torture.

Especially when she smelled so damn good and looked even better in an outfit that she had deemed was "ski-chic casual" when he picked her up. Whatever that meant. One hour into their car ride and he was already having a heck of a time keeping his eyes on the road and off her. Not to mention the itching in his fingers to reach out and touch her.

For her part, Riley seemed oblivious to the frustrated attraction on the driver's side of the car. She was singing along to some Christmas song on the radio.

The truth was, he'd lied about Bob. In fact, he'd just used this whole conference as an excuse to get her out of town for a few days to clear her mind.

Clear her mind, but cloud his.

He stifled a grumble. While he might have lied about Bob, who was never supposed to attend this conference, he hadn't been completely dishonest. There would be workshops and lectures on social media. When it came to anything remotely related to the internet, Riley was the best.

After what felt like a million years, they arrived at the hotel. The Pine Ridge Ski Resort was nestled in the Blue Ridge Mountains, a couple of hours from Bayside. The backdrop was stunning. Snow fell onto the forested peaks from the cloudy sky.

The resort looked just how he'd imagine a ski resort to be. It was constructed of a dark brown wood and had a plethora of tall windows. He could see smoke rising from several chimneys and a chairlift traveling to the top of a mountain behind it.

There was actually snow on the ground already and a flurry of activity as other cars pulled in, no doubt also attending the conference. A large sign greeted the attendees as hotel employees helped collect baggage and usher the guests into the lobby.

Sawyer and Riley made their way inside the rustic lodge and to the front desk, where they waited in line for about ten minutes. Sawyer felt nerves in his stomach as he stepped up to the counter. He glanced at Riley, who was busy checking her phone. No doubt, dealing with the Bayside Blogger.

"Checking in?" The man behind the counter smiled at them. His name tag read James.

"Yes. Room under *Wallace*." He eyed Riley, who was still ensconced with her phone. Perfect. He leaned closer to the counter and lowered his voice. "And I had called about getting a possible second room."

James typed quickly on the keyboard as his eyes stayed trained on the computer screen in front of him. "Yes, I see the note here. One moment."

Sawyer held his breath. He really hoped they could accommodate his request for a second room. He'd had no problem getting Riley into the conference, although he did have to pay the highest rate for registering her so late. Still, if his libido was so out of control during one car ride, there was no telling how he'd handle sharing a hotel room. Not to mention how irritated Riley was likely to be.

He was determined to stay positive.

"Unfortunately, we don't have any spare rooms."

There went that.

"We've been booked with this conference for several months. Plus, the weather forecast is calling for snow so every other available room has been reserved by skiers and snowboarders. I do apologize."

Sawyer stifled a groan. "I understand. Do you think we can get a room with two beds at least?"

More fast typing. "Hmm. I'm not sure we can do that, either." He studied the screen. "Tell you what. Check-in is not for another couple of hours. I know the conference starts before that. Why don't you leave your bags here and see to your conference sessions? No promises, but I will do the best I can to accommodate you."

"The best he can for what?" Riley asked, suddenly appearing right next to Sawyer.

Before Sawyer could answer, James said, "A room with two beds."

Riley tilted her head in question. "We're sharing a room?" She bit her lip and appeared nervous.

"Yes, we're sold out this week," James answered helpfully.

"That's odd. What about Bob's room?"

"We don't have a reserve—"

Sawyer sprang into action. "Uh, I think that Bob canceled his reservation when he realized he couldn't attend." He sneaked a glance at James, who was watching him with an amused expression on his face. "They must have given it to another guest."

James grinned. "Exactly."

"Oh. Well, um, okay."

Was it his imagination or did Riley seem as nervous about bunking together as he was?

"James is going to do his best to get us a room with two beds." Sawyer gave the attendant the eye. "Right, James?"

James spoke up quickly as he took Sawyer's ID and credit card. "Absolutely, sir."

Riley twisted her fingers together. "It's not like we haven't shared a hotel room before."

That was true. Their families had gone on countless vacations together over the years. Of course, they were no longer kids and their parents were nowhere to be seen. This time, it would be the two of them. Alone. In a hotel room. For three days.

Suddenly, Sawyer's face felt flushed. He accepted his driver's license and credit card from James and shoved his wallet back into his pocket.

They secured their bags with the bellman and did a quick tour of the hotel. If Sawyer hadn't been feeling so anxious he would have been charmed by the high ceilings, exposed beams and countless fireplaces with comfy sitting areas. Not to mention the views of the snow-covered mountains.

They registered for the conference, received a packet and name badges, and reviewed the schedule. "I guess we should go to this first session. It's for all attendees. After that, I'm going to meet with some different vendors for our app."

"Thinking about switching?"

"I just want to see what else is out there. Can we save any money." He noticed her raised eyebrow. "Don't start."

"Fine," Riley said. "I'd like to attend the workshop on Facebook Live and videos for Twitter."

As they walked toward the meeting rooms, he could feel the tension rolling off Riley in waves. Couldn't blame her. They'd kissed twice now. Besides all of the issues Riley was having with her friends and the Bayside Blogger, she had made it clear that they really shouldn't kiss again. Well, mostly clear.

Sawyer ran a hand over his face as they found two seats and settled in to listen to the first lecture. Three days with the woman he wanted to kiss—and perhaps more—but who he absolutely should not kiss—or do more with. Great.

This was going to be the longest three days of his life.

It had been one heck of a long day.

As they rode the elevator up to the third floor, Riley rolled her head back and forth trying to dislodge the tension that had formed as she'd sat through lecture after lecture.

While most of the sessions she'd attended had actually been interesting, it had still been a lot to take in at one time.

Technology in Print Publications. Riley knew it was an important subject. Keeping up with the latest trends was important for all publications but especially for a small outlet like the *Bugle*. Hadn't she been pushing social media for years now? How many reports had she compiled for Sawyer so he could see the benefits of increasing their use?

God bless Bob for attending this with Sawyer in the past, although she didn't know how he'd managed it. Bob was an amazing writer and an even better editor. But he was very much the stereotype of the old-school news reporter. As far as she knew, he never went online. She wasn't even sure if he had a Facebook page.

At least she'd had a good time at the mandatory cocktail hour and dinner. She'd loved meeting reporters and editors from different publications. And if she did say so herself, she'd dazzled quite a few stuffy librarian-types with stories from her various experiences.

She'd told a table of freelance reporters all about the Bayside Blogger. Well, not everything, obviously. In third person, she was able to convey how popular their blogger was. And how the residents of a small town that was rather dead during non-tourist times had come alive with the opportunity to gossip about one another.

She glanced at Sawyer. He'd seemed to be in his element, as well. He knew a lot of the attendees and speakers. More, they all knew him. Even though he tried to downplay it, they'd been impressed with him.

Was it crazy that she found him even sexier than before? The way he'd taken the time to really listen to each person he spoke with. How he'd fiddled with his glasses when he was intrigued with a new idea. How he was dressed in another argyle sweater and corduroy pants that should have made him look like one of her college professors...but made him look completely sexy.

She was out of her mind.

She'd overheard more than a couple conversations praising him for sticking it out. Their fellow attendees appeared to believe that small newspapers were soon to be a thing of the past and they couldn't believe the *Bugle* was surviving.

What exactly did that mean?

She'd had a feeling for a while that Sawyer was keeping something from her regarding the newspaper. She'd even asked him a couple times, but every time she did, he'd brushed her question off.

Riley opened her mouth to ask him again, but he beat her to it.

"Did you enjoy the sessions today?"

She could tell he had. Besides the constant compliments, he'd been busy scribbling notes, eyeing different exhibits and excitedly talking to vendors.

"They were interesting."

The elevator stopped on the third floor and they stepped out into the hallway. Sawyer grinned at her. "So, tell me, could you have taught any of them?"

She held her own smile in. "Maybe. Just a few."

"Before you came along, we didn't have much of a social media presence. You really upped the bar for all the departments." His grin faded. "I hope you weren't bored today."

"Are you kidding? Social media is constantly evolving. There's always something new to learn."

He mock-wiped his forehead. "Phew."

They started walking down the hallway toward their room. "I'm here for you."

He stopped outside their room and looked at her. A crease formed on his brow, a sure sign he was deep in thought. "Yes, you are and I appreciate it, Riley. I really do."

Sawyer let them into their room with the key card and stopped in the entryway. Riley ran right into his back.

"Hey, what gives?" she asked, even as her hands lingered a little too long on the strong muscles of his back.

"I don't think you're going to be too happy but…"

He trailed off and she peered around him. "What? I

don't see any…" And it was her turn to trail off because what she did spot was a bed. A large king-size bed that certainly appeared to be extra comfy with plush white bedding and an ample amount of pillows. The operative word was *one*. One bed. As in, oh my God, she was sharing a bed with Sawyer.

Sawyer, her boss. Who she was now lusting after day and night. Night and day. Around the clock.

"Riley!"

Sawyer's loud voice pulled her out of the merry-go-round of thoughts. "Sorry, what?"

"I said, I can call down to the desk. They told us we would have two beds."

She pushed past him and walked into the room. "Actually, they said they would *try* to get us a room with two beds." He picked up the phone on the bedside table and she held out a hand to stop him. "I think we've put them through enough downstairs. They're obviously fully booked, so let's try and figure this out ourselves. Maybe they can work out another arrangement tomorrow."

Sawyer slowly lowered the phone. "You're right."

She threw her big tote bag onto the bed. "Of course, I am. Besides, we're both adults."

She didn't mean to linger on the word *adults*. But she did and Sawyer took notice. His gaze landed on her lips. He shoved his hands into his pockets, and quickly averted his eyes and looked at the bed.

Yep. They were two adults who were clearly lusting after each other staring at a big comfy bed.

Not awkward at all.

"I can always just sleep on the couch," Sawyer offered.

"No," she said. "I'm smaller. I'll fit better on a…" Riley did a quick lap of the room, which had been decorated in soothing white, beige and warm brown tones.

There was the infamous bed with two end tables. A sliding door led out to a balcony with a beautiful view of the mountains. The snow was falling faster and heavier now, reflected by the nighttime ski lights. To the left of the door was a closet and to the right was a dressing area and bathroom. She saw a little sitting area with two oversize chairs, a table and a television.

And absolutely no couch.

Well, damn.

Sawyer shook his head. "Why don't I ask the front desk if they have a cot?"

She shimmied out of her cardigan. "No."

"No?" His eyebrow arched.

"Sawyer, we have to get over this. So we made out a couple times."

He sat on the edge of the bed and studied her for a moment. "Is that all it was?"

She gulped, her throat suddenly feeling dry. Very dry. "Of course. Anyway, it's a huge bed and it's only a couple nights."

Again he remained quiet for a moment as he considered her words. "If you're sure."

"Yes, I'm sure. It's fine. Totally okay."

Since she'd known him her entire life, neither of them had ever had any problem talking to the other. They had a lifetime of conversations and inside jokes to fall back on. However, the tension in this room was thicker than the snow covering the ground.

Sawyer cleared his throat. "I think I'll just go grab a coffee."

"Sawyer, it's ten o'clock at night."

"Oh, right. I meant I'll get a decaf. Want anything?"

Yes, you. Ugh. "Um, no, I'm fine," she said as he

started walking out of the room. "I'm going to jump in the shower. I can't wait to get out of these clothes."

Sawyer stumbled and fell into the closet door.

"Ohmigod, are you okay?" She rushed to him.

She'd never seen his face—or anyone's really—quite that shade of red.

"I'm fine. I don't know how that just happened," he said, trying to right himself awkwardly.

"Here, let me help you." She grabbed onto his shirt and gave one big yank. Next thing she knew, she felt Sawyer's body launch toward hers, and they both fell against the opposite wall.

"Oomph."

Their bodies were flush together. In an attempt to break their fall, his hand had landed on her breast and her mouth was snug up against his throat. Even at the end of the day, he still smelled amazing. She tried to move her mouth to say something and her lips brushed against his skin. Sawyer shivered.

He must have realized where his hand was, and he swiftly removed it as they tried to untangle themselves. Still, they were close. So close. His warm breath fanned across her face and her lips parted.

Next thing she knew Sawyer muttered, "To hell with it," and his lips were on hers.

There was nothing sweet or subtle about this kiss. It was fast and furious and completely intoxicating. Riley heard herself groan as her fingers clenched his shirt, pulling him even closer. His mouth devoured hers.

When they finally came up for air—a minute later? Five minutes later? Who knew. They stood, staring at each other. Her chest was rising and falling as she attempted to calm down her pulse and get her breath back in check.

He searched her face, looking for something as his mouth opened and closed. Finally he pointed to the door. "Coffee."

She nodded. "Right. Shower." She inched back toward the bathroom as he slipped out of the room.

Yeah, she was definitely getting into the shower now. A nice *cold* shower.

Chapter Nine

Sawyer slept a total of fifteen minutes that night. How could he sleep longer than that when Riley's warm, soft body was lying right next to his?

When he'd returned from getting his coffee, she'd emerged from the bathroom, smelling even better than before. If that was possible.

As he'd lain in bed, his senses had been assaulted by the smell of her freshly washed hair. The lotion she'd used had a hint of lavender, which he'd always heard was supposed to be calming. Then why was his heart beating triple time?

He'd never stayed so still in all his life. It was as if moving, even to turn onto his side, would break some kind of spell. Instead, he stared at the ceiling, replaying their earlier kiss over and over in his mind.

What had he been thinking?

Easy answer. He *hadn't* been thinking.

Hence, now he was lying in this bed, not sleeping.

At some point, Riley began dreaming. She was murmuring in her sleep. Sawyer watched as she turned onto her side and curled up into a ball. His fingers were itching to reach out and stroke her hair, but he knew if he touched her, even once, he'd never be able to stop.

He had to wonder what his teenage self would think of this development. They'd always been in each other's lives, but when they were growing up, he'd never experienced feelings like this. In fact, he used to offer her advice about boys.

He remembered her first crush, a guy named Josh. She'd written him a note and they'd had a typical two-week-long junior-high relationship. When Josh dumped her for another girl in their class, Sawyer took her out for ice cream.

As he thought about the happy memory, he finally drifted off.

Morning came way too soon. Despite barely getting any shut-eye, Sawyer had never been happier for a new day to come. He sprang from the bed and hit the shower, then dressed quickly.

He peeked at the bed, where Riley remained asleep. She was on her back with one arm thrown over her face, her red hair a stark contrast to the white sheets.

He didn't want to wake her, so he scribbled a quick note and left it on the table next to her. Before he left, he took another moment to study her beautiful features. Again, the urge to touch her washed over him. It seemed to grow stronger and stronger each day.

As that thought entered his mind, he realized he had to get out of the room immediately. He made his way quickly down to the lobby.

"Good morning, Sawyer."

"Hey, Jack." Sawyer shook hands with his friend, Jack Rodger. The two had met when they worked together at the *Washington Post* in DC. Jack had stayed in the city and was now running a successful magazine. "Didn't see you yesterday."

"I got in late," Jack explained. "I couldn't make it here until the end of the day. Coffee?"

"Absolutely."

They hit the free breakfast buffet and caught up. Sawyer filled him in on the first day of the conference, the *Bugle* and Riley. Well, most of the Riley situation.

"Riley Hudson." Jack sat back in his seat, the remnants of his pancakes dotting the plate. "I haven't seen her in years. Didn't she visit you in DC when she was still in college?"

Sawyer smiled. "Yeah, took the train down from New York. That was a long time ago. She's definitely not in college anymore."

Jack studied him before a grin broke out on his face. "Oh, really?"

"What does that mean?"

"You tell me."

Sawyer groaned. "It's complicated."

Jack waited patiently. It was unnerving.

"What? We're not together," Sawyer said.

Jack leaned back, studied him. "Do you want to be together?"

He knew he should deny it, but he found himself too exhausted to resist. "Yes."

"Well, then, that's new."

Sawyer shook his head. "Not really. What's new is me acting on things I've been feeling for some time."

"What does she think of this?"

Sawyer accepted a refill of coffee from a passing waiter. "She's...cautious."

"Interesting that she's here at all, then. Last time we emailed, you said you were coming alone." He arched an eyebrow.

"It's not like that. I didn't bring her to... I mean..."

Jack's face broke out into a grin. "I wasn't implying anything."

"She's going through a rough time back home. I

thought it would be good for her to get away. Plus, most of this digital information is right up her alley. I don't know why I didn't think of bringing her before."

"Back to all those feelings you have for her," Jack said.

At that moment, his phone went off. Saved by the bell. But when he saw who was calling, he stilled. Dan Melwood was surely calling to pressure Sawyer into this deal. He shoved the phone back in his pocket without answering. "More complications."

Jack watched him with curiosity. "How about a subject change?"

"Yes, please."

"How in the hell are you making the *Bugle* work?"

Sawyer groaned. "That's part of that whole complicated subject. Fact of the matter is that…I'm struggling." He sat back in his chair and let out a long exhale. It was the first time he'd admitted out loud to anyone that the newspaper was in trouble. Surprisingly, it actually made him feel a little better.

"I'm not surprised. Small papers are folding across the country. And you're still publishing every day. Crazy. How in the hell are you doing it? More importantly, why are you doing it? Why not go down to a couple days a week?"

It wasn't like he hadn't thought of this. The *Bugle* was probably the last paper of its size to publish daily.

Not to mention, he had a tradition to uphold. The *Bugle* was his family's legacy. Each generation made it work. He refused to be the weak branch in his family tree.

When his dad had been at the helm, everyone had insisted that newspapers were dying. His dad ignored the naysayers and started the digital edition.

He'd made his mark and Sawyer was determined to

make his, too. If there was anyone in the world he wished he could emulate, it was his father.

"I'm proud that we publish every day."

Jack considered that for a long moment. "Are you sure you're not mixing pride with stubbornness?"

Jack's words shocked him into silence. That's not what he was doing. Sawyer didn't consider himself a stubborn man. And yet…

"Listen, Sawyer, you have a lot going on in your life. You want my advice?"

More like, he *needed* his advice. He nodded.

"Make some decisions. Go for it. Whether with the *Bugle* or with Riley. It's time to act."

Sawyer couldn't get his friend's words out of his head all morning. *It's time to act.*

Jack was right. Decisions needed to be made. When he returned from the conference, he had to tackle the newspaper. Right now, he still didn't know what to do about Dan Melwood. And maybe Jack was right and had a point about his unwillingness to cut the paper down to a couple days a week.

Thoughts and ideas swirled around his head. This conference was no place to make big decisions regarding work.

Riley however… He may not be able to act on his whims with work, but he could address his feelings for Riley.

It's time to act.

Again he felt bolstered by Jack. He wanted Riley. Yes, he was her boss. Yes, they'd been in each other's lives forever. But the feelings he had for her weren't going away. If anything, they were growing stronger by the day.

He didn't want to belittle her concerns, but he did want

to show her that he could be a good guy. He was someone she could trust with her heart.

So far, they'd kissed in the cold on his parents' deck
and in an alleyway. Where was the romance? She deserved more.

A plan began to form during his morning meetings.
Between sessions, he worked with the hotel staff on lo-
gistics for his plan, including keeping Riley occupied.
He knew from her text messages that she was attending
an all-morning workshop. He had the front desk find
her and present her with a gift certificate for a pedicure,
something he knew she loved to get.

While she was busy getting toenails painted, he
stopped at the gift shop and bought her two dozen roses
in a variety of colors. Sawyer didn't have any kind of
eye for design, but when the food he'd ordered appeared,
the waitress delivering it helped him set everything up.

Pleased with how it turned out, he barely had time
to take it all in before he heard the key card at the door.
Riley entered the room.

"You'll never guess what I got?" she said excitedly,
rushing toward him and showing off her bright red toenails, still clad in fuzzy spa slippers. When she noticed
the flowers and the table set with candles, she froze. "Am
I in the right room?"

"I believe so," he said.

She touched one of the roses. "Do you have a date I
don't know about?"

"Kind of."

It was as if all the air left her body, deflating her. "Oh."

"Riley," he began, but she was already inching backward toward the door.

"I'm sorry. I didn't realize… You probably know
women here."

"Riley," he tried again.

"We should have had a system. Like a hanger on the door handle or something."

"Riley!" At that she stopped. "My date is with you."

She dropped her bag on the floor and cocked her head. "Huh?"

He ran a hand through his hair. "I mean, if you want to have a date with me."

"I…well…" She peeked around him at the set table. "You did this for me?" He nodded. "Why?"

"I wanted to thank you for coming up here with me." He blew out a frustrated breath. "No, that's not the truth."

"You're not trying to thank me?"

"No. Yes. I mean, of course I appreciate you attending the conference." He gestured at the table with his arm. "But all of this is for you."

She bit her lip as she walked to the table and ran her hand across the white tablecloth. She leaned over and smelled the flowers. "First, a free pedicure and then…"

She trailed off, her green eyes growing in size. "Did *you* pay for my pedicure?"

"You deserve to be pampered every now and then."

She laughed. "Are you trying to romance me, Sawyer Wallace?"

"Yes." He didn't offer more. He wanted her to know he was serious. Needed her to know.

Her smile faded.

He stepped toward the table and began removing lids. "I wanted you to have a good dinner. Since the local options are limited and there was no dinner at the conference tonight, I ordered in for us."

She studied the dishes and her mouth formed an O. "Is that…?"

"Mac and cheese with lobster."

"Diet be damned. Holy hell, that smells amazing."

"I couldn't decide what to get with it, but I figured filet mignon goes with everything."

"Oh, yum."

Her mouth was practically watering. His eyes fastened onto her lips. They were so close, so enticing.

"What's that?" she asked, breaking his lustful thoughts.

"I ordered a special dessert just for you."

He removed the lid of a fancy silver dish with a flourish, secretly hoping the hotel had gotten his special request right. And not only because he'd paid through the nose for all of this.

Riley stepped closer. "Chocolate cake," she said with awe.

Sawyer finally sneaked a glance at the dessert. He smiled at the sight of two huge pieces of Riley's favorite treat. "Not just any chocolate cake. It's made with dark chocolate."

"You really did this for me?" she asked, wonder in her voice.

"Of course." Now he felt nervous.

As if Riley sensed it, she inched closer, a sly smile spreading across her face.

"Tell me something. If Bob had come with you instead of me, would you have ordered him chocolate cake?"

Relaxing, he grinned. "Nah. Bob's a potato-chip man."

She took another step closer and placed her hand on his chest. "Sawyer, why am I here?"

"I told you—"

"Why am I *really* here?"

Since he'd known Riley her entire life, he knew the set expression on her face. She was the most stubborn person when she wanted to be. So he relented.

"It's just that you've been going through a lot lately.

Missing your parents, being the blogger, admitting you are the blogger, your friends. I thought a couple of days away would help."

Sawyer didn't know what he expected her to do or say, and, as usual, Riley surprised him.

Tears pooled in her eyes and her lip trembled. Then she took a deep breath.

The tears never fell. Instead, she burst into laughter.

Riley could not believe she'd started laughing. She certainly hadn't meant to. She just couldn't believe what was happening, or she was completely insane. Maybe a combination of the two.

Once again, the idea of someone taking care of her and thinking about her needs was overwhelming.

And not just anyone. Sawyer. The man she could no longer deny she had romantic feelings for.

All morning, as she'd been attending workshops and lectures, she'd thought long and hard about her fight with Elle and Carissa. And she couldn't help but be reminded of all those nights in Manhattan. When she'd been surrounded by millions of people and yet had never felt more alone in her life.

It was bad enough when she found out that the man she loved was engaged to someone else. But when her coworkers discovered that she'd been dating him, they'd all turned on her.

Not one person had supported her. She'd had no one to turn to.

Her laughter abruptly stopped.

It's not like it had been her fault. How in the world was she to know her boyfriend had a whole second life? Maybe she'd just been stupid and naive.

Wasn't a person entitled to make a mistake now and then without being crucified for it?

An image of Elle and Carissa's faces when she'd told them she was the blogger flashed into her mind.

Not quite the same scenario as New York, yet she still felt that mind-numbing loneliness.

She'd almost forgotten he was there for a second. But when Sawyer scooped her up into his arms and hugged her it was, without a doubt, exactly what she needed at that moment. The special dinner and amazing dessert were an awesome mood-boost, but this hug was even better than a pedicure.

"Thank you," she mumbled against his shirt. Then she rapped a knuckle against his chest. "You're overly kind to me, Sawyer." She swept her hand out to indicate the meal he'd had delivered. "This is the nicest thing anyone has done for me in a long time."

"You almost started crying and then you started laughing hysterically, instead. If the chocolate cake didn't bring on the emotions, what did?"

"Uh…" she stuttered. "It's just that…" She couldn't bring herself to tell him.

"You know, Ri, maybe if you tell me what it is that seems to be frustrating you it might make you feel better. I might be able to help you. Because I know it has to be more than the fight with Elle and Carissa."

"I don't want you to think differently of me."

He sighed loudly. "Do you really think so little of me?"

"No, of course not."

His face was so earnest and his eyes held such patience. It undid her.

They sat on the bed and she told him everything.

"I'm a fraud, Sawyer."

"What are you talking about?"

"You know how glamorous I used to make my life seem when I lived in New York? How I would post all those pictures on Facebook and talk about how fabulous everything was when I came home for holidays?"

"Sure."

She took a deep breath. "None of it was true."

"What do you mean?"

"It was…awful." Her voice hitched. She placed her hand on her chest to calm herself. "There was nothing glamorous about my life. I think my cubicle at the *Bugle* is bigger than my apartment was."

"Most people's first apartments are pretty crappy," he said diplomatically.

"Most people don't leave their windows unlocked and return home to find their laptop, television, iPod and cell phone stolen."

He winced and then swore under his breath. "I never heard about that."

"I never told anyone." He cursed again. "I mean, I obviously called the cops. They never found my stuff. In fact, they told me I was in the wrong for leaving my window open when I lived on the first floor in broad view of the street."

"Ri…" He covered her hand, but she abruptly pushed him away.

"No," she said, taking a deep, shuddering breath. "I need to tell you everything."

He took her hand. "Okay."

"I was always so popular in high school. I got along with everyone. College was a lot of the same. Then I moved to Manhattan, and all of a sudden I didn't know a soul." She twisted her hands together. "I thought I would meet people quickly. It had never been a problem for me before. I found my job so fast that I figured I would hang with my new coworkers."

"You didn't?"

She shook her head slowly. "I was a fish out of water at that place. It was a social media company that began as a start-up and most of my coworkers had been around since the beginning. I was the youngest by at least five or six years. It was also a very male-dominated staff. And the few women were, well, kind of intense. I mean, completely brilliant and talented, don't get me wrong. But you should have seen them. They were so sophisticated and put-together. They looked like they'd just walked off the runway and found their way to the office."

"What are you talking about? You always look amazing."

"Not compared to them. These women were sitting front row at fashion week while I was cowering outside the tent wishing and hoping I could get one glimpse inside. They carried Gucci purses and I bought knockoffs down on Canal Street.

"Every day I went into that office and was reminded that I didn't fit in. Not completely." She took a deep breath. She had to in order to say this. "I felt so incredibly lonely."

"Why didn't you ever talk to me about this? Or your parents? Or anyone from Bayside?"

She'd been embarrassed. Even now, her shoulders were tensing up simply from speaking aloud her memories of that time.

"I'd wanted to live in New York my entire life. How could I ever tell anyone that it was miserable?"

She ran a hand through her hair. "Then I met Connor."

Sawyer sat up straighter, but he remained silent.

"He was thirty, which seemed so old and mature and worldly back when I was twenty-two."

His lips twitched. "Not so much anymore?"

"Nah." She slid the slippers from her pedicure off and folded her legs under her. "Instead of making friends to go to happy hours with, I ate lunch by myself every day. I was always broke so it was usually ramen noodles."

Sawyer rose, poured two glasses of wine and handed one to her. "Go on."

"Connor must have noticed I was constantly alone. I thought he was sensitive. Now I see his behavior differently."

"I'm not going to like this, am I?" Sawyer asked, his fingers tightening around his wineglass.

She didn't answer him. She had to keep going. "Connor and I started dating. At least, I thought we were dating. Turns out, I wasn't the only person he'd been dating. In fact, he was engaged to someone else."

Sawyer rolled his neck. She could hear it crack. "You never suspected this Connor guy was cheating on you?" His words came out terse.

"Never." She shook her head adamantly. "Then he was promoted in a reorganization. That new position made him my boss."

"None of your coworkers knew you were seeing each other?"

"Nope. He made a point of telling me we had to be even more covert about our relationship because he didn't want anyone to think I'd be getting special treatment because I was dating my manager. There was no policy against it—he was just worried about appearances. Again, I didn't see it for what it was."

"What was it?"

"He took advantage of the fact that I was all alone."

Sawyer rose and poured more wine in his glass before returning to the bed. "There wasn't anyone else in the office you could talk to? What about HR?"

"It was a small marketing and communications company. The president had started it out of his living room. We had an HR consultant but he didn't work in the office."

She took a deep breath. "I didn't feel comfortable talking to any of the guys. As for the women on staff, I kind of got the impression they were disgusted. Like they thought I was the new, young girl sleeping with the boss."

He hadn't said much during her story. She'd noticed a tick in his jaw a couple times, and it seemed his eyes had darkened once or twice. But she could be making up both of those things.

This was it. The only person she'd ever told the complete truth to. Not even Elle or Carissa knew about Connor.

"Who else knows about this?" he asked, as if reading her mind.

"No one."

He whistled long and low. "That's why you came back to Bayside. This is what you've been hiding all this time."

She couldn't meet his gaze.

"Riley," he urged, scooting closer.

He was judging her. She knew it. She should have kept her big mouth shut, with him and with her friends. When would she learn that some secrets had to stay hidden forever?

"I shouldn't have told you," she whispered.

"What are you talking about? I'm glad you did."

"I told you that you would think differently of me."

He sat back, studied her. "You were right. I now realize how brave you are."

Her head snapped up. "Wh-what?"

"I think you're one of the bravest people I know. Look at what you went through all on your own. I don't know how you dealt with all of that. You were so young."

"I stayed in New York until I was twenty-six. I felt like I'd aged about twenty years in those four short years."

She let out another long sigh. "Well, now you know everything. I don't have any more secrets."

His face fell, and it was as if an invisible wall went up between them.

"Sawyer?" she asked tentatively, already afraid she understood the hesitation. "What is it?"

He shifted, putting his wineglass on the end table. "It's just that…"

She knew she should give him time. Sawyer was a methodical man. He was measuring the situation.

After a moment, he spoke. "I get it now. After everything you just told me about Connor, I understand."

She had a sinking feeling. "Understand what exactly?"

"Why you don't… Why you can't be with me."

His voice held so much sadness she wanted to weep.

"That's just it," she said quietly. "I shouldn't want to be with you because I would be repeating the same mistake I made in the past." And that hadn't turned out so great. "But…" Now it was her turn to trail off.

Sawyer straightened. "But what?"

"But I want you anyway."

She sealed her words by pressing her lips to his.

Chapter Ten

Sawyer felt blindsided by Riley's kiss—but not so much that he couldn't enjoy the feel of her lips against his. The heat of her body against his.

She'd revealed a big piece of her past tonight. His heart broke for that young girl who'd been so lonely and scared. Not to mention, how she'd been mistreated by her coworkers and by the man she loved.

The idea of Riley being in love with another man made him burn. Then again, the thought of any man mistreating her had his fingers curling into a fist.

"Relax," she whispered against his lips.

"Sorry," he murmured before moving his lips to travel along her jaw, down to her neck and back up. When he nipped her earlobe, she shuddered and pulled him closer.

"More," she said, and he was only happy to oblige.

He paid special attention to one ear and then the other. Then he returned to her lips, kissing her softly, almost reverently. Her taste was so heady. It got to him in a way that nothing else ever had.

As the kiss deepened, her lips opened and he took that as invitation to push his tongue inside, gently touching hers.

As always, she smelled so good. Like fresh fruit in the middle of summer. Or maybe flowers. Hell, he didn't know. He couldn't think.

When she pulled back, he groaned. She smiled, her eyes sparkling. She had to know she was driving him crazy.

Riley reached down and curled her fingers around the bottom of his shirt, lifting it over his head and dropping it to the floor. Before he could respond in kind, she was running her hands over his chest. Her fingers circled his nipples and gently pulled at his chest hair. When she began the descent toward his pants, he knew he needed to slow things down a little or this would be a very short interlude between them.

So he went to work on her top. In true Riley fashion, she was wearing some kind of complicated, one-shoulder stretchy sexy blouse. Sighing, he tried to figure out how to remove it, but his efforts were useless. How the hell did this thing work? How had she even gotten it on?

Riley giggled. "It's easy. See?" With one fast move, she pulled off her top and stood before him in a sexy strapless lace bra that displayed her breasts perfectly.

He unsnapped the front closure of her bra, her breasts spilling out. She reached for his hand, her own shaking. He knew the feeling. Sawyer couldn't believe he was about to touch her so intimately.

She placed his hand on her breast and he was amazed at how perfect she felt. Like silk. As he ran his thumbs over her tight nipples, she sighed deeply and her head fell backward.

Sawyer leaned in and nipped at her bottom lip, then kissed her again, harder this time. He was so involved in kissing her he didn't realize she'd unbuttoned his jeans.

"Aren't we in a hurry?" he joked.

But the tender smile she gave him erased any joking. "I think we've waited long enough for this," she said.

He couldn't agree more, and he shucked his jeans by kicking them off.

Riley wrapped her arms around his shoulders and kissed him deeply, sighing as she did. His hands roamed over every inch of her.

Their kiss intensified by the second and so did his desire for her.

Then, she playfully snapped the waistband of his boxers. "Off," she said.

"Yes, ma'am." Sawyer stood quickly. But before he could shed the underwear he paused. It was a moment of realization. They'd seen each other in fancy clothes, bathing suits and even pajamas. But never before had they gone this far.

The metaphorical line between them was about to be erased. From friends to lovers.

He opened his mouth to say…he didn't know what. But Riley stood up in the middle of the bed. Even towering over him, she was still so petite.

"I'll go first." With that, she hooked her thumbs under the thin straps of her panties and slowly pulled the flimsy silk down her legs.

With the panties dangling from one finger, she stood before him completely exposed, completely vulnerable. Yet, she seemed so confident, so sure.

As if honing in on his thoughts, she threw her panties at him. He caught them, running his fingers over the soft material while taking her in. She was so beautiful.

"Your turn," she said.

His nerves were still there, but they were rapidly being drowned out by his libido. He yanked his boxers down to the floor and stepped out of them.

Then he met her gaze. There was heat in them so intense that the usual emerald color was a dark forest green.

She eyed him, taking her time running her gaze over every part of his body. It was erotic and made him even harder, a feat he would have thought impossible.

"Sawyer." Her voice was raspy. "Come to me."

He didn't need more than that.

He joined her on the bed. Skin to skin.

"Touch me," she whispered.

Complying, he trailed his fingers up her arms. She shivered. He continued by roaming over her shoulders and down her back until they rounded her bottom. He cupped it, bringing her even closer.

Her lips met his in a deep, wet kiss that knocked all sense from him. After a few minutes of exploring hands and the intense kiss, they were both breathless. He ripped his lips from hers and moved them down her throat again. Her fingers were entwined in his hair, keeping his head close to her.

Gently he laid her down right in the middle of the large bed. Then he did something he'd wanted to do for a long time. He took one of her taut nipples into his mouth, sucking, tasting. She moaned and arched her back, bringing her breast even closer. After he lavished attention on that one, he moved on to the other. Then he ran his lips over her collarbone and up to her neck.

He ripped his lips from her throat. "Ri?"

"Yes?" Her voice was raspy and her lips were swollen. It was the sexiest vision he'd ever seen.

"Are you sure?"

Was he kidding?

They were in bed, naked, limbs intertwined. She was pretty damn sure.

At the same time, she knew that Sawyer was only

asking for her. He wanted to make sure she was okay with this.

She lifted her hips, pressing them into his pelvis. "Yes, I'm sure."

"You're not nervous?" he asked.

That's when she realized that he was nervous. "I feel like I should be."

"But you're not?"

She shook her head. "Nope." To prove it, she pushed with all her might. Sawyer appeased her by rolling onto his back and taking her with him. She straddled him.

"I don't know when this started," she admitted.

"What?" he asked.

"This wanting you. I think I've been fighting it for a long time. Now that we're here, together, like this, it just feels right."

She placed her palms firmly on his strong chest and grinned.

"What's that smile about?"

She ran her hands up and down his body. "For someone who spends most of his time behind a desk, nose buried in a newspaper, you are deceptively built, Sawyer Wallace."

He offered her a look that was purely comical. Like he had no idea what she was talking about. It made her giggle.

"Now she's laughing at me," he said with a smile.

"Not for long."

She kissed him again, feeling as though she could do this forever. She loved the feeling of his mouth against hers. Loved the way he took his time. Loved how he cupped her head, making her feel so secure. Loved... him?

She reared back. Sawyer's eyes flew open.

No way. She couldn't love him. Obviously, she loved him as a friend. But…more than that?

"Ri?" he asked, confusion on his face. "You okay?"

"Sorry." She took a deep breath and did everything in her power to push that errant thought to the back of her mind. She would need to deal with it, but not now, not tonight. "Your hand hit a ticklish spot," she lied.

He relaxed. Then he sprang from the bed. Before she could wonder why, she heard the crinkling of a condom wrapper. He was back in bed in a second, towering over her. His hands were on either side of her head as he gazed down at her. The expression in his hazel eyes was so intense, so serious. She ran a fingertip along his jaw.

He kissed her again, deeply, and gently spread her legs with his knee, positioning himself between them.

"Sawyer?" He met her gaze. "Now."

Oh my. Her breath caught as he filled her.

Then he paused, peering down at her. "Are you okay?"

She nodded and sighed. "Oh yes."

He pulled out, his eyes never leaving her face. Then he pushed back in, slowly. She breathed a sigh of contentment. Still, he continued to watch her, their gazes locked onto each other. It was the most erotic moment of her life. Never before had sex been like this.

He reached for her hands, clasping them in his much larger ones. Then he pulled them above her head, securing them into the mattress. They were in the middle of the bed. Her legs were wrapped around his hips tightly as they moved together.

They continued, their bodies moving faster until they were both gasping for breath. A feeling started deep and low in her belly, trickling to the surface in the most exquisite way. She felt as though she were seeing stars, growing brighter and brighter until they appeared to be exploding all around her. The only thing she could think to do in the moment was yell out his name as her body bucked against his.

He fused his mouth to hers as she succumbed to her release. It didn't take long for his body to tense, and then he joined her on the other side.

Exhausted, she barely had the strength to wrap her arms around him as he collapsed on top of her. She was aware somewhere in the far recesses of her mind that his weight should be overbearing, but at the moment, she didn't really care. She was warm and sated, and Riley knew she never wanted this moment to end.

They stayed that way, melded together in the center of the bed, for a long time. Limbs locked around each other, breathing finally slowing down. Most of the lights were still on in the room, which ordinarily would have made her feel self-conscious. But, tonight, there was nothing awkward about this scenario.

She turned her head toward the window. The snow was falling thickly outside the window.

Finally she let out a sound. It was something between a yawn and a purr. Amused, he went up on his elbows and grinned down at her.

"What was that?"

"Shh, I'm basking."

"Sorry," he whispered. "Bask away. But in the meantime, are you cold?"

She grabbed his arms and tugged, forcing him to fall onto her once again. "Not as long as you're on top of me keeping me warm."

He nuzzled her earlobe. As he did, she felt one of his hands move down to cup her breast.

"Hey, haven't you had enough?" she said playfully.

He squeezed her breast and bit her ear. "Not even close, Hudson."

Satisfaction rolled through her body. Not to mention, pleasure. Deep, impenetrable pleasure.

Like a queen being adored, she lay on the bed and allowed Sawyer to do as he pleased. He kissed and licked and fondled. All of it felt amazing. All of it had her sighing, gasping, moaning and writhing on the bed until her hands fisted in the sheets.

Riley knew what she wanted, but they'd only just finished the first time.

"Riley, look at me."

She opened her eyes and took in the strain on Sawyer's face.

"I need you. Again."

"Already?" she asked on a strangled breath.

He nodded. "No one has ever turned me on the way you do."

"I bet you say that to all the girls."

She meant the comment to be light and funny, but Sawyer kept his solemn expression. His eyes were narrowed and lines had formed on his forehead. She knew that look. He got it when he was deadly serious about something.

"No other girls. You and only you."

Her smiled faded. She wanted to weep at his sweet and tender words, but she didn't have time. Sawyer had her in his arms and was entering her again, slowly, gently first, then faster, harder, and before she knew it, she was calling his name, her body shaking from pleasure.

Riley's eyes felt heavy and she fought to open them. When she did, she was met by Sawyer's lopsided smile. She must have dozed off. She was now wrapped in the blankets with her head cradled on his chest and his arms around her.

"Hi," he whispered.

"Did I fall asleep?"

"Mmm," he murmured against her head as he kissed her hair. "I think you were tired."

She glanced around the room. Their dinner sat untouched across the room. He'd turned the lights down, which illuminated the falling snow outside the windows.

"That's beautiful," she said.

"So are you." He leaned down and placed a kiss against her lips.

Suddenly she felt shy. "Well, that's something we haven't done together before."

"After that, I'm not really sure why we haven't." He shifted, taking her in as he did. "Ri, you okay?"

"Um…"

"Uh-oh, that's not good."

She sat up in bed, and as she did, the blankets fell away and she realized she didn't have any clothes on. Quickly she tried to cover up.

She was glad the lights were turned low because, no doubt, her pale skin was bright red.

He clasped her hands in his. "Riley, be honest with me. You don't…" He coughed. "You don't regret this, do you?"

Her answer was fast and immediate. And the truth. "No. Absolutely not." She leaned over and kissed him again.

"I can tell you how I feel," he said with a wink.

"Oh, I bet I can guess. Men, only one thing on their minds." She laughed.

"Our relationship is changing now. You know?"

Her earlier thought of love flitted around her mind,

and once again she had to push it away. It was too soon for that. Wasn't it? Besides, sex didn't equal love. And anyway, who knew where this thing between them was going to go?

She didn't want to do it, but her mind had other ideas. Thoughts of Connor and her time with him in New York had her stomach clenching and her palms sweating. She'd learned a valuable lesson from that experience. She had to protect herself and her heart.

Being with Sawyer had felt beyond amazing. But as much as she wanted to pursue the possibility of a real relationship with him, she needed to take it slow. She needed to protect herself.

His eyes held so much hope as he waited for her to answer his question. While she wanted nothing more than to throw her arms around him, she reminded herself what it had felt like to have her heart crushed by Connor.

"I think that right now... I'd really like to eat."

Despite the disappointment that crossed his face, he recovered quickly and offered her a grin.

"I happen to know where you can get some food. It's nearby and already paid for."

"How convenient," she quipped.

He rose from the bed and threw on a shirt and his boxers. He went into the bathroom, returned with one of the plush white robes and held it open for her. She allowed him to wrap her up in it. Then his arms snaked around her middle and he drew her to him. He whispered in her ear.

"Tonight was amazing. But after everything you told me earlier about your ex, well, I understand that you may need time. I'll give you whatever you need."

She turned to face him. "Thank you," she said.

Their mouths met and they stayed together for a long time as the snow continued to fall outside and she continued to fall harder for her best friend.

Chapter Eleven

Cocooned in Sawyer's strong arms, Riley slept like a rock. She woke feeling more content than she had in years.

Before she opened her eyes and let the morning in, she took a moment to consider the man beside her.

She had to admit that she'd thought of being with him before. He was gorgeous, sweet, silly, funny. Over the years, when she thought about her ideal man, it was always someone who she could laugh with. Someone who was sensitive and romantic. Someone who valued family and appreciated community.

Holy cow. She'd pictured Sawyer.

The reality of being with him so far exceeded her expectations that she could barely keep her stomach from fluttering. The way he kissed her and lavished so much attention on her… It was overwhelming.

The very real and scary thought that had filtered into her head last night came roaring back in the light of day. Love. Something Riley didn't even know how to deal with—or want to deal with, really. She pushed that scary four-letter word from her mind and decided she would contemplate what it meant later. Much later.

After an early morning spent in bed with Sawyer and a mound of blueberry pancakes, they enjoyed a dessert of something that was even sweeter than the blueberries.

Then Riley took a long, decadent shower in the spa-like bathroom. She could get used to being pampered like this.

Sawyer kissed her goodbye and headed off to his meetings. She browsed through the on-site program and picked a couple of sessions for herself.

The information was really interesting and probably useful to her career. She noticed, though, that when one of the speakers began talking about longevity in publishing Riley started to feel uncomfortable.

Wasn't that strange?

She'd always assumed she would stay at the *Bugle* until retirement—unless she moved to another city. But after her time in New York, she knew that Bayside was where she wanted to live.

For the first time since she'd started at the newspaper, Riley actually took a moment to consider the possibility of a different job. Maybe it was the first time she'd allowed herself to admit it.

Strangely, it had nothing to do with Sawyer, either. Obviously, taking their relationship to a new level changed things. But maybe a new job, a new career, would help her claw her way out of this life slump. Elle was getting married and Carissa was having a baby. Perhaps it was time for Riley to make a leap into something new and unknown, as well.

"Someone looks deep in thought."

Sawyer's deep voice pulled her out of her musings. She shook her head and offered a bright smile.

"Hey, you." She tapped him on the chest and tilted her head. "All done for the day?"

"Yep." He laid a finger to her forehead. "What caused this line to form just now?"

"I was just thinking."

"About what?"

"About…work, I guess."

At the urge to break eye contact with him, she glanced around the lobby of the hotel, which was bustling with energy. A line formed near the elevators as badge-wearing conference attendees were exiting the meeting space to return to their rooms. On the other end of the large space, she could see the hostess of the on-site restaurant rushing to seat the influx of lunchtime patrons.

"New story idea?" he asked.

Not even close. But how to say that to Sawyer?

"Something like that," she lied. "Anyway, are you hungry?"

"Nah. I had a snack during my last session. I was going to see if I could tempt you into doing something with me."

She felt her cheeks warm as an excited sensation began low in her belly. She wiggled her eyebrows. "Oh, I think you can tempt me to do something with you."

He offered her a wicked grin. "Mind out of the gutter, Hudson. That's not what I was thinking."

Damn. "Yeah, me neither," she said smoothly. "In fact, I was hoping we could go to one of these super-fascinating lectures together."

"What a great idea," he said in response to her sarcasm. "Sadly, there are no more lectures today."

She snapped her fingers. "Darn."

"Since we don't have to be at dinner until seven, I thought we could try skiing."

Riley used to love skiing, but she hadn't been in three years. It had been even longer for Sawyer.

After they were geared up and had their lift tickets, they made their way to the ski lift and rode up to the top of the mountain.

Over the next couple of hours, one thing became obvious. They were both pretty horrible skiers.

After falling more times than was humanly possible, they returned to their room and changed for dinner. Unfortunately, there would be no repeats of last night's feast of chocolate cake and cold salmon since they were dining in the hotel's ballroom with the other conference attendees.

Riley washed down her overcooked chicken with a sip of bad wine. At least the people seated at their table were interesting and conversation flowed.

Still, it was kind of hard to concentrate when Sawyer kept sliding heated glances her way.

A few hours later, they were lazing in bed with a bottle of wine that they'd ordered from room service.

"I don't want to go back home." Even she could hear the wistfulness in her voice.

The last few days had offered her a much-needed respite from life. Returning to Bayside would mean dealing with her best friends' anger and fixing that situation. It would mean returning to work, to a job that she was no longer sure she completely wanted. A job that used to be fun and interesting. And a great hiding place.

Not to mention, when she'd left a couple days ago, she hadn't been sleeping with her boss.

"No?"

She shook her head. "Not so much. Reality lives in Bayside."

"Speaking of Bayside, what happens at home? How do you want to handle this?"

She didn't need him to define *this*. He was asking about their very new relationship, so she took a moment. "I don't think we should tell anyone." At his disappointed expression—and how cute was that—she added, "Yet."

He didn't seem completely appeased by her answer.

"There's the Bayside Blogger to consider."

"If you're worried about appearing in her column, I have an in with her," he said.

"That's just it. If we were anyone else, we *would* be in her column. If someone sees us together, like this," she said, and gestured between them.

He raised an eyebrow at their state of undress.

"Well, not exactly like this. I hope no one sees the two of us naked. But, if they see us doing anything couple-y, they might tip the blogger off. Then what am I supposed to do?"

He shrugged. "Write about us."

His answer surprised her. "And you would be okay with that?"

"Yes," he answered with zero hesitation. "I want to be with you."

Her palms began to sweat. "What about work? You're my boss, Sawyer."

"You could get a new job."

He was joking, but she couldn't let it go. "A new job? Where exactly? To the other newspaper in town? There's not a lot of options in Bayside."

Sawyer collapsed back against the pillows, too. "I know it."

"If I didn't work at the *Bugle*, where would I work?" Was she asking Sawyer or herself?

Something crossed his face, but Riley couldn't explain it. It was as if a dark shadow fell over them. Even though Sawyer shrugged it off and turned the conversation to discussing a book they were both reading, Riley couldn't shake the feeling that something was very wrong.

The next morning she still sensed something was off, but then they got busy packing up their things. They attended the closing seminar of the conference and checked out of their room.

Before they could exit the hotel, they took some time to say goodbye to fellow attendees. Sawyer was talking to a man who looked awfully familiar to her. Riley ventured over to them.

"Riley Hudson," the man said. "I heard you were here."

"Ri, do you remember Jack Rodger? We used to work together."

Realization hit her. "At the *Post*. Right. It's been a long time. How are you?"

"No complaints. Unlike this guy." Jack jabbed Sawyer in the stomach.

That was strange. Sawyer had complaints? About what, she wondered. She glanced at Sawyer, but he avoided her stare.

"What did you think of the conference?" Jack asked, causing her to rip her eyes from Sawyer.

"I enjoyed it a lot more than I had anticipated. I went to this really fascinating lecture on how to boost circulation with different social media events, like contests."

"Uh-oh," Sawyer said. "Does this mean you're going to force me to do that 'take a selfie with the editor' contest again?" Pain etched across his face.

"Oh, shut up. You loved that."

Jack laughed. "Yep, same Riley I remember."

They played catch-up for a few more minutes before checking their weather apps and deciding it was time to head out.

Jack reached out and shook her hand. "Great to see you again, Riley."

"You, too." Riley began putting her coat and gloves on.

Jack turned to Sawyer and offered him a hearty slap

on the back. "Don't worry about the *Bugle*. Everything's gonna be fine."

Riley's ears perked up as she was buttoning her coat. She knew it. She'd been guessing for months that something bad was going on at the paper. How many times had she asked Sawyer about that very subject, and every time he dodged her questions.

Obviously, he'd confided in Jack. She got that the two of them went back a long time. Maybe he wanted financial advice from his old connection?

Still, why hadn't he talked to her about this? She was one of his closest friends; someone he'd known forever and a day.

"Ah, thanks," Sawyer said awkwardly, darting a worried expression in her direction.

"Remember what I said. There's more than one way to go at this juncture, even for a small-town newspaper. Give me a call if you need anything."

Riley tilted her head as Jack walked across the lobby toward the doors. When Sawyer didn't budge, she planted herself smack in front of him with her hands on her hips.

He sighed. "Just some ideas I'm considering."

She frowned. "I've asked you this before and you always manage to change the subject or avoid it completely. Is the *Bugle* in trouble?"

"All newspapers are in trouble right now."

She pointed at him. "See, that's not a real answer, either."

"It's the truth."

"Maybe. But it's not the full story." She worried her lip as she tried to find the right words. "You can talk to me, you know."

"Of course I know that. But, right now, we really need

to get on the road. I still have to stop in at the office to-night."

"I thought you said we didn't have to go back to work today." He'd already begun walking toward the door and she increased her pace to keep up with his long legs.

"*You* don't. I do." He handed the valet his ticket. "I'm the editor, Ri. I'm in charge of everything that has to do with the *Bugle*. The good, the bad, the ugly."

What in the world? His voice held a wariness she rarely heard from him. Like the weight of the world was resting on his shoulders.

She placed a hand on his arm. "Sawyer?" she tried with a soft voice.

He faced her, finally meeting her eyes.

"I told you the most personal things about me the other night. Because I trust you." She suppressed the urge to fidget. "I only hope that sentiment is reciprocal. You can trust me, too."

"I know it."

"Then what's going on?"

He opened his mouth and Riley could tell he was about to reveal what this was all about. Then his face changed, as if a shield had dropped and he'd changed his mind.

Her heart sank.

Before she could do or say anything else, the car showed up. Sawyer loaded their bags into the trunk and Riley slipped into the front seat. He adjusted the seat and the radio. Then he set the heat. Didn't matter, she thought sadly. No amount of warm air was going to heat up the cold spot in her heart.

If she was giving herself to someone else, all she wanted, the only thing she wanted, was to get that back in return. She'd bared her soul the other night, told Sawyer her deepest secret. Then they'd shared an amazing time together.

Would their relationship start and end in the bedroom? While that aspect had been nice—okay, more like phenomenal—it wasn't the only thing she wanted. What she needed was a partner who could be there fully for her, and part of being there for someone was opening up. This was something she'd never had with a romantic partner before.

When she looked at the way Elle and Cam shared everything and how Carissa and Jasper were so in tune with each other, she couldn't help feeling pangs of jealousy. She knew now that's what she wanted, too. A man to connect with in every way imaginable.

Sawyer shifted. "Ready?"

She nodded. She was definitely ready. Ready for love and passion and understanding and sharing.

Her stomach clenched at the idea that Sawyer might not be on the same page. There might always be a wall between them. Could she live with that?

They drove back to Bayside in relative quiet. Riley had a lot on her mind, the main thing being if she'd made another mistake with a man.

She glanced at Sawyer as he switched lanes on the highway, eyes focused straight ahead on the road.

Riley knew she couldn't make a mistake with him. Not Sawyer. He was far too important to her.

Chapter Twelve

Who else has been caught in the dark cloud that hangs over the *Bugle's* fearless leader, Sawyer Wallace? Didn't he get the memo that it's the holidays? Rumor has it Sawyer hasn't found a date for the *Bugle's* upcoming anniversary gala. Perhaps that's what has him so surly...

Sawyer was in a bad mood, and not only because Riley had once again written about him in her column. Although he couldn't deny her accusations about his crappy attitude.

As usual, he returned to the *Bugle* after the conference with a pile of work. Articles needed editing, bills needed paying, advertisers needed to be appeased and staff needed guidance. Everything fell on his shoulders. He couldn't imagine being out of town for more than three days.

But what a three days it had been.

Despite his less-than-cheery mood, when he thought about the feel of Riley's silky skin or the way she looked as he moved over her, it was hard to stay sour. Their time together had been beyond ideal, which was why the way it had ended really sucked.

The car ride home had been awkward, something the two of them had never experienced before. They'd known each other too long for uncomfortable silences and tension. All he'd wanted to do was reach over and stroke her cheek, ask her what was on her mind.

He hadn't done either of those things. Now, here he was wondering what she was thinking and how he could fix this situation without telling her the truth about his dilemma with Dan Melwood.

Sawyer rolled his shoulders. He'd been hunched over his computer for the better part of two hours. No, he glanced through the door of his office, out into the bull pen. No one was left. The lights were turned low and the cleaning crew would be coming through shortly.

He saved the document he was working on and shut down his computer for the night. It was Saturday and he knew damn well that he would be working over the rest of the weekend.

He walked past Riley's cubicle on his way out, stopping briefly to take in her colorful decorations. Photos lined the walls, tacked up with multicolored pushpins. Her wall calendar displayed a beautiful cherry blossom tree, the pink-and-white hues popping out. There were Mardi Gras beads hanging from a lamp shaped as a peacock, which stood next to her computer, complete with a body made of glitter and tall turquoise-and-green feathers that stuck as high as the cubicle wall. She'd left a purple cardigan on the back of her chair and an oversize travel mug on her desk.

He knew she would soon decorate for the holidays, as she did every year. Last December, she'd strung twinkly lights around her desk and put up a small desktop tree. He wondered what she'd do this time.

Riley Hudson, he thought with a long exhale. His lifelong friend and employee. She was always able to get him to have fun. Get him out of a funk.

Except, this time, the funk had to do with her.

Sawyer finished walking through the floor and exited the building. Instead of turning right to head to the parking lot and his waiting car, he automatically turned left toward the center of town. He knew where he was headed. Riley's apartment.

It wasn't only the secret that he was keeping from her that bothered him. That, he could admit to himself out here on the cold, dark street. He wasn't happy that she didn't want to return to Bayside as a couple, something he realized more each second he did want.

New or otherwise, he didn't want to keep their relationship under cover. He would have been perfectly content to announce they were dating.

Sure, he understood her point about the blogger. How could he not? Especially when he was feeling so bad about keeping the *Bugle*'s financial troubles from her. Their time away together had been a brief respite from thinking about that. But decisions would have to be made. And soon. Too many people were relying on him.

His mind was a roller coaster tonight. When he entered her apartment building, a calm suddenly took over.

He rode the elevator to the sixth floor and made his way down the hall to her apartment. When she opened the door, surprise crossed her face. Her bright eyes widened and she automatically raised a hand to check her hair.

She'd mostly avoided him since they'd returned. Or maybe he was imagining that. They'd both been busy. But it was Saturday night and he wasn't busy at the moment. Neither was she judging by the yoga pants and oversize teal sweater she wore. Her hair was pulled back in a ponytail.

"Hi," he said lamely.

"Hey," she replied. "Is everything okay?"

"No," he said automatically. Her mouth dropped open

into an O shape and he instantly regretted his answer. Even if it was the truth.

She gestured him inside. Her Christmas tree was set up in the corner of the room near the windows. It was decorated with white lights and strands of crystals and beads. The topper was a bright star with long ribbons that cascaded down most of the tree. And every single branch held a different ornament. He chuckled silently to himself because, once again, it was so typical Riley. Fun and sparkly.

"I just opened a bottle of wine. You look like you could use a glass."

He followed her into the kitchen, which was separated from the rest of the living room by a counter. Not waiting for his answer, she was already pouring him a tall glass of red.

The kitchen smelled great. Like tomatoes and onions and garlic. Something was simmering away on the stove.

She followed his gaze to the pan. "I'm making spaghetti and meatballs. Nothing special really. The meatballs are premade. So is the sauce, but I'm doctoring it up a bit."

"Looks good," he said.

"You're, um, welcome to stay. I have plenty."

Sawyer found it interesting that she was rambling. Clearly, she was nervous having him in her apartment. Another first—she'd never been nervous before.

He crossed to her and enveloped her in his arms. She was stiff for a fraction of a second. Then she sighed, molding her body to his and winding her arms around his neck. He indulged himself by running his hands up her back. He removed the elastic holding her hair and his fingers dove into all that gorgeous red hair. It smelled like flowers in the middle of the spring.

When he placed a chaste kiss on the top of her head, she shifted, tilting her head to his. Her lips were right there, tempting and alluring.

Nothing could have kept him from kissing her.

Their lips met and it was as they hadn't seen each other in a month instead of a few days.

Her fingers dug into his neck and she hung on for dear life. He pulled her in as close as humanly possible. She tasted so damn good, like the wine she'd been sampling.

A timer went off and he reluctantly loosened his grip.

She grinned, her lips swollen and her cheeks red. "Sorry about that. It's the pasta."

He nipped her bottom lip one more time and offered his own smile.

She turned, flipped the knob on the stove, grabbed two pot holders and emptied the pot into a waiting colander in the sink.

"Can I help with anything?" he asked.

"You can check on the bread in the oven. I made garlic bread to go with this."

"This is a nice little spread you got here."

She shrugged. "I needed some comfort food. There is nothing more soothing than spaghetti and meatballs. Homemade or otherwise."

He frowned. Couldn't help it. After he removed the bread from the oven and she arranged the spaghetti, meatballs and sauce on a large platter, he touched her arm.

"You're upset with me," he said.

She didn't say anything for a moment. She didn't look at him, either. He knew her well enough to tell she was working out what she wanted to say. Then her eyes flicked up to lock onto his gaze.

"I'm not upset with you."

"Then why the comfort food? What has you upset?"

"I guess I'm disappointed." She nodded for him to grab the bread and wine as she lifted the platter of pasta. After she placed it on her small dining table, she returned to the kitchen for plates, silverware and napkins.

"I had planned on eating this on the couch. But this is kind of nice. I don't use this table often."

"You're avoiding the subject."

She sipped her wine. "I know it."

"Come on, Riley. It's me. Talk."

It didn't seem that she was going to say anything, but then it was as if someone uncorked her mouth, and the words flowed out.

"We slept together and it was amazing. But that doesn't change the fact that we've been friends our entire lives. No matter what, you'll always be my friend first, Sawyer. You can tell me anything. I know you've been holding back. I know something is going on with the paper."

She took a break to scoop spaghetti onto his plate.

"Jack confirmed my suspicions and you still didn't talk about it with me. It hurt my feelings."

A huge knot formed in his stomach over that statement. "I'm sorry, Ri. I really am. It's just, you're not only one of my oldest friends, not only someone I just slept with. You're also my employee."

She blinked, waiting.

"It's my job to protect my employees."

She studied him for a long moment. Then a smile spread slowly across her face.

"Oh, Sawyer. I don't know what I'm going to do with you."

Just like that, the atmosphere of the room changed. Everything seemed lighter.

"Are you making fun of me?" he asked, half-amused.

"A little bit."

They ate their meal and chatted about a million different things. Like always. But Sawyer knew he wanted to tell her the whole story of what was happening with the *Bugle*. Needed to.

When they were finished, they cleaned the dishes together. She cleared the table, he rinsed and loaded the dishwasher. It was such an easy domestic task, and yet it felt so very right doing it together.

As he wondered if she felt the same way, she crept up behind him and placed a kiss behind his ear.

He could envision this scene playing out every single night of his life and he would be a very happy, content man.

They moved to her couch with their refilled glasses of wine. She'd turned the lights low, and the illumination from the Christmas tree cast a soft glow over the room.

They were sitting close, holding hands. The time felt right. He began telling her his dilemma.

"The *Bugle* is in trouble."

She placed her wineglass on the coffee table and leaned forward. "Tell me."

So he did.

"I understand the situation. But how bad is it?" she asked, her brows furrowing. "Like, no hopes of bonuses ever again or a cut travel budget?"

He rubbed the back of his neck. "More like we shouldn't even order supplies." This was the part he really didn't want to say out loud. "I'm going to have to lay people off."

She squeezed his hand tightly. That simple gesture meant so much to him. Her support wound through his body and warmed all the places that were cold because of what was happening in his professional life.

"The publishing industry is tough right now," he said. "Really tough."

"I know. It's a different world. The internet has changed everything."

He hesitated before speaking, feeling completely weighed down. "People are now used to getting their news and information instantaneously and often for free."

"Our online edition is doing pretty well, right?" she asked.

"Really well, actually."

"Why not switch to online only?"

He got up abruptly from the couch and crossed to the window. He looked down at the town square below them. People were moving in and out of The Brewside. Kids were gathered in front of the large Christmas tree in the town square. He used to do the same thing in high school. Congregate in the middle of town, hang out, laugh. So many things were the same, yet everything felt different now, too.

"I wonder what my ancestors would think about going to a digital-only publication?"

"I think they wouldn't have any idea what a computer or the internet is."

He barely cracked a smile.

"Come on, Sawyer. I think they would be willing to change with the times. They did leave everything they knew in Europe to venture across the ocean to come here and start a new life. Trust me, they were ready to change. You have to be willing to adapt, too."

"All I feel right now is overwhelmingly guilty."

She crossed to him, but he continued to gaze out the window. She wrapped her arms around him from behind and pressed her cheek to his back. It was such a comforting gesture.

"What in the world are you feeling guilty for?"

"For having left the newspaper after college. For moving to DC with Rachel. My parents must have been so disappointed." He shook his head.

"Sawyer, there is no way your parents could ever be disappointed in you. In fact, I remember how excited your dad was that you were working at the *Washington Post*. You're being really hard on yourself."

He shrugged. "Still, that's how I feel. Now I have to feel guilty for what I'm going to have to do to all those employees who count on me. Riley, it's the holidays. I don't know how much longer I can drag this out. I will be solely responsible for putting people out of work."

He felt her shift. Her hands grabbed his and she spun him to face her. "Sawyer, you're a good man. A really good man. And this isn't your fault. You've been holding everything together for a long time. You need to cut yourself a little slack."

"I can't. I feel responsible for every single person who walks into that building every day." He hesitated before continuing. "The thing is, I have an out. Someone has presented me with a proposal. Only I don't think I can accept it."

"Want to tell me about it?"

More than anything. She was being so patient and so kind. It was killing him not to spill his guts to her now.

"I would." He should. "The details aren't ironed out yet."

"What's stopping you from accepting?"

He looked deep into her eyes, knowing he could get lost there. Knowing that he could hurt her if he ever accepted Dan's offer. Then again, he could hurt a lot more people if he didn't. "It may not be the right thing to do."

"Maybe you should talk to your dad. I mean, he ran

the paper before you. Plus, he's crazy smart. I'm sure he would be able to help you sort things out."

"No way." He scrubbed a hand over his face. "I can't tell either of my parents about this."

She stepped back and studied him with surprise on her face. "Why not? Who better?"

"They retired and they deserve this time to relax."

"I think they would both smack you for that comment."

"Maybe, maybe not. But I can't burden them with this, especially my dad."

The newspaper had been passed down through generations on his dad's side of the family. Because of Sawyer, his dad had been able to retire early. Even though the idea of taking over an entire newspaper had scared the bejesus out of him, Sawyer had stepped up to the plate. He'd had to because he'd owed his dad. He should have never left Bayside and run off to DC with Rachel.

"What's going on in there?" she asked, running a soft finger along his temple.

"The *Bugle* is more than a newspaper. It's my family. We may not have saved lives or found the solution to world peace. But this was the Wallace contribution to society."

"Your legacy," she said with a knowing nod.

"Exactly. A legacy that is now my sole responsibility."

Again she gave a curt nod. "Then I think you should do whatever you need to do to save the newspaper and our coworkers' jobs. Really, Sawyer. No matter what."

The option before him was to either save the newspaper or save Riley. His family's legacy or Riley. All those jobs or Riley.

Now she was essentially telling him to pick the newspaper. But doing that would make him lose her forever.

* * *

When Riley had donned one of her comfiest outfits earlier and made plans with a box of spaghetti, she'd had no idea her evening would evolve into this.

She'd been surprised to open the door and find Sawyer standing there. But getting him to finally open up about his troubles meant the world to her. It showed that he trusted her. Really and truly trusted her.

She was worried about him, though. The stress he felt was palpable.

Sawyer was such a good man. He was honest and kind. He loved his family and friends. Not to mention how much the *Bugle* meant to him and how he so wanted to protect it.

Riley wished she could help. She wanted to soothe the stress line that had formed in the middle of his forehead.

Maybe there was a way she could.

She took his hand, which she was still holding, and brought it to her lips. Kissed his knuckles. Then she went up on tiptoe and pressed her lips to his.

"You are the best man I know, Sawyer Wallace. Trust me that this whole thing will work out."

"Riley—" he began, but she cut him off with another kiss.

"Shh," she whispered. "Come with me."

He didn't move. "Where?"

She smiled. "Don't you trust me?"

"You know I do."

She tugged his hand. "Come." When he finally budged, she led him through the living room, down the short hallway, and into her bedroom.

Rather than turn the overhead light on, she moved around the room, lighting the many candles she liked to keep around her room. Then she opened her laptop and set it to play soft music.

When she was finished, she turned. Sawyer hadn't moved from the doorway.

"Are you trying to seduce me, Riley Hudson?"

She shook her head. "No. I'm trying to make you feel better. Any seduction is simply a happy perk for both of us."

"I feel better just being here with you."

When he said things like that, she was filled with a tingly sensation that made her breathless and light-headed.

She held out a hand and he moved to her.

She pulled him onto the bed beside her. Their mouths sought each other, immediately fusing in an intense kiss. Following suit, their hands were moving over each other, touching, enticing, igniting fires of desire.

They rolled over and over as clothes were shed. Her breath was coming faster as her heartbeat skyrocketed.

Finally all clothes were shed and they lay on their sides facing each other. "Sawyer," she said as her fingers traveled up his side, delighting in all of his angles and curves.

"Yes?" he answered. His own hands were having one heck of a time tracing the outline of her breast.

"I have to tell you something." She bit her lip. *I love you.* It was on the tip of her tongue, but she couldn't squeeze the words out. Not yet, even though her heart was full of such love for him.

"You mean more to me than any other man ever has."

He didn't say anything, but his eyes seemed to darken. She wasn't sure if that was a good or bad thing. Suddenly feeling anxious, she blurted out, "I shouldn't have said that."

"Why not?" he asked on a half laugh.

"Because I know it's fast."

His hand moved up to cup her cheek. "Ri, it's been twenty-nine years."

When he put it that way...

"Here's something to hopefully make you feel better. You mean more to me than any other woman has. I never thought I would feel like this."

"Again?" she asked. Surely he wasn't discounting Rachel. They'd been engaged after all. "You never thought you would feel like this again, you mean."

He shook his head. "I've never felt this strongly about any woman, ever."

She leaned into his hand and he kissed her then. She gave a little push and moved him to his back. Then she straddled him. Looking down into his eyes, she smiled.

"Really?" she asked.

"Really. You have no idea what you mean to me."

And he had no idea that she'd fallen head over heels in love with him. Maybe she'd always loved him. Maybe they were destined to be together. Riley had no idea, and, instead of telling him, she decided to show him what he meant to her.

She leaned over and pulled a condom from her bedside table. Quickly she protected him. Then, raising her hips, she lowered herself onto him, slowly, so slowly. Her breath came out as one big, desirous moan. He reared up and covered her mouth with his. They were joined together in every way possible.

Then she gave him a little shove and he fell back to the pillows. She began to move, never taking her eyes off his. His hands clamped onto her hips, urging her on. She covered his fingers with her hers as she rose and fell above him.

Their bodies rocked together in total sync, their rhythm increasing with each passing second. Soon the world around her began to blur. When she fell over the edge, he was right there with her.

She collapsed onto him as his arms came around her heated body—exhausted, sated and more in love than she had ever dreamed possible.

Chapter Thirteen

Bayside Blogger @BSBlogger
Seems like the big @BSBugle gala is bringing all the old alums out of the woodwork. Any guesses which big business honcho is in town? #Bugle150

Sawyer read Riley's latest blog post and stifled the urge to pop an antacid. He knew exactly who she was referring to. Of all times for her to report on Dan Melwood, this was definitely the worst.

Not that she realized that, of course.

Now he was going to have to deal with Dan, who would no doubt be displeased. Sawyer felt the beginnings of a headache.

To think he'd been having a great week. How could he not when he'd been spending every night in Riley's arms. The way her body moved, the sounds she made when her body was being devoured by his, went a far way to making his life seem better than what it currently was.

Something had changed between them last weekend. He couldn't pinpoint it. For a journalist, he was having a tough time coming up with the right words.

It was no longer the two of them hanging out as friends. And it definitely was a hell of a lot more than sex. She'd always been important to him. But now? It was as if everything revolved around her.

To celebrate getting through another work week, they'd made plans to see a movie tonight. She was still feeling apprehensive about revealing the shift in their relationship. He was still pretending to be okay with that. At least at the movies they could hold hands in the dark.

He picked up his ringing phone without glancing at the caller ID. Maybe if he had, he wouldn't have choked at the sound of Dan Melwood's voice on the other end.

"Sawyer, the time has come for your final decision. It's been weeks now and I need to know if I should move on and invest my money elsewhere."

Sawyer stifled a groan. He leaned back in his chair as he considered how to approach this. "I appreciate you giving me time, Dan. This is obviously a big decision."

"I understand that, but I'm still wondering why you aren't jumping on the opportunity for financial help when I know very well that the *Bugle* is floundering."

Leaning back in his chair, Sawyer decided to go for it. "I welcome the financial freedom your company would bring. What I'm struggling with is your very unusual caveat of revealing one of my reporters' identities."

Dan laughed. It was a bitter, almost metallic sound. "I would hardly call a gossip columnist a reporter."

"Nevertheless, I can't tell you the name of the Bayside Blogger, Dan. Journalistic integrity."

"I can appreciate that."

"You do? Great."

"Not so great for you. Without that name, I won't back the paper. Ethical or not."

A weary groan escaped Sawyer's otherwise pinched lips. "I don't understand why this is so important to you,

Dan. I know the blogger wrote about you last summer and I apologize for that."

"Damn blogger was the cause of my divorce."

Actually, his infidelity was the real cause, but Sawyer wisely chose to keep that opinion to himself.

"Again, I'm sorry to hear that. But if I give you his or her name, what exactly do you plan on doing with that information?"

"I'm not sure yet. But I'll tell you what. We're going to keep talking in circles here. You have my proposal and all the numbers and projections. I will be at the Dumont party tomorrow night for the one-hundred-and-fiftieth anniversary of the *Bugle*. I expect an answer there."

With that, Dan disconnected. Sawyer rubbed a hand over his face. Initially, he'd been thrilled when Lilah Dumont offered to throw the *Bugle* an anniversary party. Of course, he knew Mrs. Dumont was on board with any party, any time, but it wasn't like he had room in his current budget to celebrate, and one hundred and fifty years was a long time. The entire town apparently thought so, too. He'd seen a recent guest list and it looked like everyone would be there. Despite the current financial climate—or maybe because of it—his reporters and staff had earned the right to a night of celebration.

One hundred and fifty years. Something to be proud of. Again Sawyer thought about his ancestors. What would they think knowing the Wallace family had continued their legacy?

More importantly, what would they think knowing he was screwing it up?

Sick of feeling powerless, Sawyer turned to his computer. Whenever he needed help sorting through an issue, he always wrote out each and every detail. Then he would sit back and study the list. Make a pros-and-cons list if necessary. He would do the same now. He started typing Dan's initial proposal, but then was interrupted by a question from one of his editors.

He would get back to it, though, because he was determined to figure out the best course of action. He wouldn't let his family down.

Even though the day was overcast, with thick gray clouds biding their time before they unleashed what was sure to be a huge amount of rain, to Riley it felt like the sunniest of mornings.

Something was different between her and Sawyer since he'd stopped by last weekend, and she could no longer pretend that their relationship was some kind of fluke. They were together as more than friends, more than coworkers. He was her boyfriend, and she was—she gulped—in love with him. Definitely, irrevocably in love.

She sat at her desk, unable to contain the grin at that thought.

"Do I even want to know what that look is for?" Claudia asked as she sidled up to Riley's cubicle, leaning over the edge and peering down at her with an amused expression on her face.

"Hmm? Oh, it's nothing. I'm just in a good mood today."

Claudia eyed her for a long moment. "Oh, really? I know that expression. If I had to guess, I would say you're dating someone."

"I might be," Riley replied coyly.

"It's not like you to withhold info. Who is he?"

Riley opened her mouth and quickly shut it. She couldn't exactly tell her supervisor that she was sleeping with the big boss.

"You know, I think I want to keep it to myself a little bit longer."

Claudia's face softened. "Oh, Riley."

"What?"

"You really like this guy, don't you?"

More than like. She loved him and she was having a heck of a time keeping that to herself. She wanted to shout it from the roof of the *Bugle*. Maybe take out an ad.

Her stomach took a huge dive and Riley knew she was lucky to be sitting down, or else she'd be on the floor.

Big, fat raindrops began to fall against the window and Riley suddenly understood why she'd been thinking it was sunny earlier. Because she was in love with Sawyer and she hadn't felt this good in a long, long time. Since she had dated Connor...

That thought made her sit up straighter.

Claudia leaned closer. "Okay, I feel like sixteen different emotions just crossed your face."

"Um..."

"I'm not going to push you on this guy because I'm happy for you. But you know what's interesting? The Bayside Blogger hasn't picked up on this yet. You and your new man must be really stealthy for her not to write about you."

"Uh, yeah, we've been pretty discreet." She quickly looked away.

"Hey, boss," Claudia called out as Sawyer made his way out of his office.

Riley glanced up. Sawyer tripped over a garbage can. He looked really out of it. He removed his glasses, which was a good thing since they were on crooked anyway. His mind was definitely somewhere else.

She knew how worried he was about the state of the *Bugle*. They'd spent every night together, eating dinner, watching television, making out. It had been one of the best weeks of her life. Just the two of them, enjoying each other, laughing, kissing. Maybe he was feeling relaxed because he hadn't mentioned the financial trouble again since he'd finally told her about it last Saturday.

In fact, he'd looked relaxed all week long at work, too. He'd joked around with their coworkers and brought doughnuts in almost every morning.

Now those shadows had returned under his eyes. There was definitely something up today.

"Ready for the big anniversary gala at the Dumonts' tomorrow?" Claudia asked.

The expression on his face was enough to make Riley laugh. It was as if Claudia had asked him to cut off his own hand.

"Come on, Sawyer," she said. "It's going to be fun. It's not like we have to do anything, either. Mrs. Dumont took care of everything."

"I still have to put on a tux—again—and go be social."

"Maybe Riley will bring her new boyfriend."

Sawyer's head shot up at that. Riley could feel the heat on her cheeks as she studied her desk, suddenly finding her mouse pad extremely interesting.

"Riley has a new boyfriend?" Sawyer asked, amusement in his voice.

"Yep," Claudia said. "It's serious, too."

Sawyer propped his elbows on the top of Riley's cubicle wall. "Oh, really? How do you know?"

"Because she won't tell me who he is," Claudia said, oblivious to the fact that she was talking to Riley's new "boyfriend."

Sawyer rubbed a hand over his chin. "That *is* serious."

Riley rolled her eyes and stuck her tongue out at Sawyer. "Claudia also pointed out how incredible it is that the Bayside Blogger hasn't written anything about my new relationship."

He met her gaze for a long, intense moment. She knew he was remembering her words about the blogger. Anyone else would have been busted by now. Another reason to keep their dating under wraps.

"You're lucky," Claudia said, oblivious to what was passing between them. "And I'm happy for you. About time you found a nice guy. He'd better be treating you right."

"He's…not bad," she said slyly.

Sawyer snorted.

"Has he, you know, stayed over yet?" Claudia asked, her eyes gleaming with curiosity.

"You know, he has. Although, I have to admit, he snores."

Sawyer straightened. "He does not."

Riley stifled a giggle as Claudia swiveled toward Sawyer. "And how would you know if he snores or not?"

Sawyer shoved his glasses back on his face. "I'm just saying that it's unlikely Riley would know if this guy snores because…well, um…"

"Yes?" Riley asked helpfully, enjoying Sawyer's discomfort.

"Because you always fall asleep so early," he finished lamely.

"Nice save," she whispered.

Luckily, Claudia seemed oblivious. "By the way, thank you so much for all of your New York suggestions, Riley."

Riley smiled. "Did you and the hubby have a good time?"

"It was wonderful. I've always wanted to visit at Christmastime." She glanced down at her watch. "Oh, shoot. I didn't realize the time. We have that budget meeting in a couple minutes."

Sawyer groaned.

Claudia laughed. "Did you get the latest numbers I emailed?"

"Darn," Sawyer said. "I left them on my desk. But I want to run to the restroom before the meeting."

"I'll grab them," Riley offered, popping up. "I need to get that story you edited for me anyway."

"Thanks, Ri."

As she moved from behind the cubicle, Sawyer lingered, allowing his hand to brush against her arm. It was the lightest of touches that shot a surge of awareness through her system. Her breath caught in her throat.

"You're welcome," she whispered. She desperately hoped no one detected the breathy quality to her voice.

But Sawyer did. He grinned and winked at her. Riley made her way quickly across the room and stepped into Sawyer's office.

She crossed to his desk and found her article. Her nose crinkled as she took in all of the red-pen markings. Another editing job by He Who Loved the Red Pen.

Scanning the rest of the large desk, she located the budget numbers from Claudia. As she reached for them, she bumped the mouse and Sawyer's computer sprang to life. She couldn't help but read the words that filled the screen. It was an email from Dan Melwood to Sawyer.

Riley's mouth dropped open. Holy smokes. Dan was offering to become an investor of the paper.

She wanted to throw her fist in the air in triumph. This would solve all of the *Bugle*'s financial problems. She felt so happy for Sawyer. He must be ecstatic.

But as she continued to scan the email, the hair on the back of her neck stood up.

In exchange for financial backing, the terms of which are laid out in attachment 3, the investor shall retain the right to full disclosure and transparency, including employee salaries, bonuses and legal names.

She reread that paragraph three times. What did he mean by legal names? It wasn't like anyone used a pen name. After all, they weren't writing fiction or some salacious novel or...

A secret gossip blog. *Oh no.*

Riley froze, her breath whooshing out of her as if someone had punched her in the gut. She didn't know how long she stood there, staring at the computer screen, willing it to morph into something else. At some point, the papers in her hands fell to the ground.

Try as hard as she might, every time she reread Dan's words, they were the same.

Sawyer was planning on outing her as the Bayside Blogger to get help with the *Bugle*. He was going to sacrifice her anonymity to protect the newspaper.

And why did Dan even need to know she wrote the blog? Why did he care? But, most importantly, how could Sawyer do this to her?

Once again, she wasn't important enough.

Not to mention that she knew Sawyer had been talking to Dan Melwood for a couple weeks now. This whole thing must have been planned even before they went to the conference. Before they became lovers.

A wave of nausea passed through her. She had to put a hand on the back of Sawyer's desk chair to steady herself. He'd been talking about this before he slept with her.

A sound slipped out from between her clenched lips. It was a pathetic whimper as she realized that he had no regard for her. How could he?

"Ri, what's taking so long?"

She snapped to attention when Sawyer spoke from the doorway. Seeing him brought about two very different emotions. Anger and sadness. She didn't know which one of them to focus on.

Anger won out. Big-time.

"How dare you?"

"What?" His gaze swept over her face in question.

She pointed at the computer screen. "This."

In two strides he was across the room. She put a hand up to halt him before he moved around the desk. Instead, she started reading.

"'The investor shall retain the right to full disclosure and transparency, including employee salaries, bonuses and legal names.' Sound familiar?"

He crossed the room and pulled the blinds so they wouldn't have an audience.

Sawyer pointed at his computer. "That's not what you think."

"Really? Because I *think* Dan Melwood offered you financial help and part of the agreement is revealing that I write the Bayside Blogger column."

He ran a hand through his hair. "Okay, that's pretty close. Dan does want to become an investor—"

"But what?" she interrupted. "How could you even consider this? You made me a promise when I first started doing this that it would stay between me and you."

"You told Elle and Carissa."

Her mouth fell open. "You can't compare me telling my two best friends with this." She pointed at the screen, once again reading the hurtful words typed there.

Sawyer started skirting the desk, but she moved to the other side of the room. "Riley, please?"

"Please what? Please get on board with the whole town

finding out I've been gossiping about them for years? Why does he even care?"

"Apparently you wrote something about him that pissed him off."

Her chin jutted out. "I never write anything that's not true. You know that."

"Of course."

She glared at him. "You were going to humiliate me, Sawyer. And after everything we—you and I—we've been together." A pained expression marred his handsome face, but she didn't care. With a sweeping of her arm, she tried to encompass all of the people on the other side of the door. "What would they have thought? They're my coworkers and they respect me. You know I've already been through a bad situation with coworkers. And with a guy." Her voice caught on that.

"This isn't the same situation as what you dealt with in New York."

"No? Because it's feeling pretty damn similar. Man I lo—" She stopped herself just in time. Sawyer didn't deserve to know her true feelings. Not now. "The man I like sells me out."

He stepped toward her. "Riley, it wasn't like that. I mean, it wasn't going to be. I hadn't made any decisions yet. Not really."

She threw her hands into the air. "Oh, well. You hadn't definitely decided to rat me out." She crossed the room and got in his face. With her index finger, she poked him in the middle of the chest. "But the fact that you even considered it is more than enough."

"Riley, please," he repeated, the desperation evident in his voice. He grabbed her finger, pulling her hand so her palm was flat against his heart.

"You were going to tell the whole town that I'm the

Bayside Blogger." Tears were welling up in her eyes. She took a long, deep breath, willing them not to fall.

"Dan offered me a proposal that would save the entire paper. It would keep me from having to lay off staff."

She tried to free her hand, but he hung on tight. "Save the paper at the expense of my reputation. I trusted you."

"Ri..." No other words came out. Just one syllable of her name in a weak, defeated voice.

"I thought that after this last week, things had changed between us."

"They had. This week has been amazing."

She couldn't agree more. That's why this hurt so much. "You opened up to me. You told me so much. What I don't understand is why you didn't tell me about this. Were you just going to let me be blindsided?"

The expression on his face was all the answer she needed.

Again. Just like Connor in New York. That thought was enough to have her yanking her hand away from him. Riley needed space and she needed it now.

"Sawyer, I can't."

"You can't what?" As she retreated toward the door, he followed. "Don't leave. Not like this. We need to talk about this."

She stopped when she reached the door, but she didn't face him. She couldn't. So, as she looked at the fake wood paneling of the door, she gathered herself.

"There is no we. There is no us."

"Riley," he muttered.

But she didn't listen. She wrenched the door open and left without looking back.

Chapter Fourteen

Riley quickly weaved her way through the cubicles of
the *Bugle* and flew out the front door.

All she knew was that her heart was breaking and she
wanted to crawl into a deep, dark hole and hide for the
rest of her life.

She ran across the town square, bypassing The Brewside, and made a dash for the door of her apartment building.

Huffing and puffing, she got out of the elevator on her
floor and headed to her apartment. When she reached it,
she pulled up short, a gasp escaping her lips.

Elle and Carissa were standing outside her door.

"Wh-what are you doing here?" she asked through a
strangled breath, which at this point was half sobbing.

"Riley, what in the world happened?" Carissa asked.

All she could do was cry harder at the questions. At
seeing her two friends who she'd missed so much.

"Oh, Ri-Ri, come on." Placing an arm around her
shoulders, Elle urged Riley forward. She gently took

Riley's key from her hand and opened the door. All three of them entered the apartment.

Riley moved to the couch and sank down. Exhausted. Spent. But, to her disgust, the tears wouldn't stop.

She curled up into a ball and let herself cry.

All she could think about was the deep hurt and betrayal she felt. In the distance, she heard Elle say, "That's it. Let it out, honey."

She had no idea how long she stayed like that, scrunched up on the couch with her eyes firmly shut. When she finally did open them again, she had been covered up with a blanket. Elle sat on the other end of the couch and Carissa was in her oversize chair. There was a box of tissues on the coffee table in front of her, as well as a mug of what smelled like her favorite tea, a bottle of wine, a glass of water, a jumbo bag of potato chips and a box of cookies.

She sat up, adjusting the blanket around her. "What's all this?" Her voice was scratchy. Had she cried herself to sleep? "Did I fall asleep?"

Elle nodded. "For about an hour."

Carissa gestured to the coffee table. "We didn't know what you would want so we tried to cover all bases. There's ice cream in the freezer, too."

"I don't have any ice cream. I haven't been to the store."

"I went for you. You're stocked up now," Carissa said, and quickly looked down at her folded hands.

"You did?" She was overwhelmed. "Why?"

Carissa scooched forward. "Because you were upset."

Elle wrapped a hand around Riley's foot and shook it. "Because we love you."

It only took a moment for more tears to surface.

"No, no, no more crying. At least not for a little while," Carissa said.

"But I ruined your lives by being the Bayside Blogger and here you are being so nice to me."

Carissa and Elle exchanged a glance. It seemed like they were silently saying, *You go first. No, you.*

Finally Elle relented. "You didn't ruin our lives, Ri."

Riley sneaked a peek at Carissa.

Carissa sighed. "You didn't ruin my life. But I was pissed at you."

"I know," Riley said.

"We've wanted to talk to you for days, but you disappeared on us. I called the *Bugle* and they said you and Sawyer went off to a conference. After you got back, we just didn't see you anywhere."

She'd been too busy hibernating with Sawyer. Playing house. Only that had turned out to be a big fat lie.

Carissa cleared her throat. "We missed you, Ri."

She wanted to weep but for an entirely different reason. "Really? I missed you guys so much. And I'm so sorry that I didn't tell you about the Bayside Blogger. And I'm sorry I wrote about you. Really, truly, I didn't mean to hurt you in any way. Please forgive me."

"I do," Carissa said.

"Me, too," Elle agreed.

Then the three of them piled onto the couch for a long group hug. Riley felt lighter than she had in weeks. Well, until she remembered Sawyer and what she'd found on his computer earlier.

"Now that that's settled, want to tell us what got you so upset?" Elle asked. "When we saw that tweet about you running through the square crying today, it was clear that something horrible had happened.

She nodded. "But, first, I think I'll take some of that ice cream. What kind did you get?"

Carissa laughed as she rose and walked toward the kitchen. "Mint chocolate chip, cookie dough and basic chocolate. Which one do you want?"

"Yes," Riley said firmly.

"All three it is."

Not bothering with bowls, Carissa brought all three cartons and three spoons to the couch. After they'd each sampled the different flavors, Riley finally began to tell them her story. She started with her time in New York and didn't stop until she'd revealed everything about her short relationship with Sawyer.

When she was finished, she collapsed back against the couch cushion, taking the carton of mint chocolate chip with her.

"Um, wow," Elle said.

"Wow is right," Carissa agreed. "I don't even know where to start."

Riley shoved a huge spoonful of ice cream into her mouth, reveling in the minty chocolaty goodness. "We could start with how I'm an idiot. How I continue to fall for the same kind of guy who is intent on making me into a total fool."

"You're not an idiot," Carissa said loyally. "And I don't get why you think you were the foolish one in New York. You didn't make a mistake there. That lame-wad Connor did. How were you to know that the guy you were seeing was a two-timing bastard?"

"But I…" She paused. "My coworkers wouldn't talk to me and…"

"Your coworkers sound horrible. Why in the world would they blame you for that situation? Couldn't they see you were the victim?"

Elle piped up. "Not when Connor got to them first. Still, pretty shortsighted and judgy of them, in my opinion."

"Totally."

Hmm, she supposed her friends had a point. All these years she'd been blaming herself. She'd felt so disgusting thinking she'd dated an engaged man that she never stopped to admit that she'd been the victim in the situation.

Sawyer had tried to point that out, though.

Just thinking about him made her stomach clench. She still couldn't believe what she'd seen on his computer that morning.

"You're right," she told her friends. "That situation wasn't my fault. But it still happened and it was still a pretty awful time in my life. And that leads us to me coming home with my tail between my legs and working for Sawyer."

"And then doing other things with Sawyer," Carissa said with a wink. "I wish we could spill the dirt on the sexy times. More reason for me to be mad at Sawyer for ruining that, too."

"Sawyer didn't deny it when you spoke to him this morning?" Elle asked. "He really considered outing you to this guy."

Hearing it out loud made Riley want to cry. She fought the urge to grab the ice cream again.

Carissa looked perplexed. "I still don't get it. I know Sawyer. He's one of the kindest men on the planet. Why would he be willing to reveal your identity and cause you that much pain and embarrassment?"

Riley sucked in a breath as she tried to decide how much to tell her friends. In the end, she knew she needed their opinions.

"I get why."

"You do?" Elle asked, astonishment on her face.

Riley nodded. "The *Bugle* is in financial trouble. Sawyer has been faced with the possibility of laying off employees."

Suddenly she remembered her conversation with him. She gasped and her hand flew to her mouth as realization dawned.

"What is it?" Elle asked.

He'd hinted at this offer. Hadn't he told her someone had presented a way out but he didn't want to take it? She racked her brain to remember the details of that particular conversation. Sawyer had said there was something holding him back from accepting help. And she'd encouraged him to take it anyway.

As of today, he still hadn't said yes to Dan. For her.

"He loves me," she whispered.

"Hold on, everybody. The merry-go-round just made a sharp left," Carissa said. "What is this now?"

He was going to protect her over the entire rest of the staff. "I'm such an idiot."

Elle scratched her head. "I have to admit, I'm no longer following, either."

Riley quickly filled them in. "Don't you see? The *Bugle* is his family's legacy. He can't let it fail."

"So what are you going to do now?"

Buoyed by a new determination, Riley rose.

"I'm going to help him."

Simone Graves @SimGrav
Come on @BSBlogger. We're dying. What's up with Riley Hudson?

Bayside Blogger @BSBlogger
Rumor has it everyone's favorite Manhattan wannabe is

having career trouble. Will Riley be jumping the *Bugle's* ship soon? Stay tuned...

Sawyer read Riley's response to the Twitter question and let out an exhale.

What did he expect? Did he honestly think she would answer with the truth? That she would reveal that someone she'd trusted her entire life had just broken that confidence for an easy way out of a bad business situation?

His head started pounding for the hundredth time that day. Every time he thought about Riley he got a lump in his throat. Riley had never returned to work that day. Not that he could blame her.

He had sat through a boring budget meeting, two different editorial sessions and a phone call with the printing facility. If someone offered him a million dollars he couldn't say what had happened in any of those meetings.

It was dinnertime, but he wasn't hungry. Sawyer was fairly certain he wouldn't be able to eat again. The idea of putting food in his stomach made him nauseous.

He's left a message for Riley and tried texting her twice. But she wasn't answering.

So he left his house and drove over to his parents'. Despite the darkness, his dad was outside hanging Christmas lights.

A huge green wreath with a red bow hung from the front door, and candles glowed from every window. It was such an inviting and friendly scene.

Too bad it was the exact opposite of his current mood. A bad mood brought on by his own stupidity.

He threw the car in Park in front of the house, got out and slammed the door hard. His father paused with lights wrapped around his arm to eye his son.

"Hey," Sawyer called out as he walked up the front walk. The word came out terse and unfeeling.

"That's some greeting," his dad, Henry, said. "Did you have a bad day?"

Sawyer kicked at a pebble.

Henry unwound the lights and placed them on the porch. He stepped toward Sawyer.

"Today sucked," Sawyer admitted.

Henry nodded. "I'm putting these up for your mother." He gestured to the lights.

"Kinda dark," Sawyer said.

"As your mother would say if she wasn't at the grocery store. She told me to start earlier. Sometimes she's right. Don't tell her I said that."

Sawyer simply grunted.

"I could use a break. Come on."

Sawyer followed him through the house. His dad snagged two beers from the fridge and, despite the chilly temperature, they made their way onto the deck.

The water was choppy, mirroring Sawyer's mood. The air held a distinct crispness. It smelled like snow, something Sawyer really couldn't describe but knew intimately from growing up here.

They sat in silence for a few minutes, drinking their beers. Sawyer didn't mind the cold. It was cooling off the anger he had toward himself.

"So, son," Henry finally said. "What brings you here?"

Sawyer decided to get right to it. "You always say I can come to you with any problem at the newspaper? Well, I have a problem. A huge problem. And I really need your advice."

If his dad was surprised at his bluntness or the reason for visiting, he didn't show it. Instead, he nodded for them to start walking.

They descended the steps of the deck and strolled slowly around the rim of the bay, and Sawyer told his father everything. How the paper had been losing money and subscribers. About his feelings for Riley. At first, he could barely look at his dad as he revealed how he'd fallen hard for his lifelong friend. He explained Dan Melwood's proposal and what had transpired with Riley that morning.

When he finished, he stopped walking and waited for his dad's remarks, unsure of how he was going to take all this news.

To his shock, his dad threw his head back and laughed.

"Well, gee, thanks for the sympathy and support, Dad." He took a long swig of beer.

"Sorry, sorry." He continued laughing for a few more moments before pulling himself together. "It's just that... well, that was quite a mouthful."

"Tell me about it."

"Our little Riley is the Bayside Blogger." He laughed some more. "Your mother had guessed that a while ago. I told her she was crazy."

"Mom is pretty intuitive."

"Now that I think about it, I guess it makes sense. But what's more interesting...you and Riley."

Sawyer cringed. He was hoping his dad would focus on the business and newspaper portion of the story. He should have known he'd go right for Riley. "It's weird for you, isn't it?"

"Are you kidding me? Your mother and I have been waiting for the two of you to sort out your feelings for years."

Sawyer felt his mouth drop open.

"Aw, I see you're surprised. Well, I'm not. There has always been something there between you."

Fascinated, he simply stared at his dad. "How did you know?"

"Intuition. Experience. The fact that you never take your eyes off her when she's in the room with you." He rapped Sawyer on the chest. "And she doesn't, either."

Henry continued. "I always thought the two of you were perfect complements to each other. Always reminded me a little of me and your mother. Riley is the only person who can make you laugh when you're in one of your serious moods. And, likewise, you have that ability to calm her down when she becomes frenetic."

Really? He couldn't believe it. He wondered how long that had been going on. He wanted to ask his dad but couldn't get the words out. Not after their fight this morning.

"Yeah, well, it doesn't matter anyway. I really messed it up. She'll never trust me again."

"Poor kid. That must have been really hard for her to read on your computer."

"Not making me feel better, Dad."

"Answer me this. Were you really going to out Riley to Dan Melwood?"

"I don't know. I've been trying to talk him out of it."

"Why does he want to know her identity so badly? Who cares?"

"She wrote about him last summer and it didn't sit well with him. Apparently her article contributed to his marital problems."

"I don't think the words of a small-town blogger could really have that much effect on someone's marriage. There were obviously problems to begin with."

Sawyer nodded. "I agree completely."

"Plus, if you did tell him, there's no way to control who he would pass the information to."

"Again, I agree."

Henry threw his beer bottle into a recycling can as they started making their way back toward the house. He scrubbed a hand over his face in the same way Sawyer often did.

"She's written about a lot of people in this town. I can't see any of them punishing her for it and I get the feeling that's what this guy wants to do."

"I would never let that happen," Sawyer said passionately.

"You already have your answer, son."

"I do?"

"This Melwood guy sounds like a real prize. You don't want to get into business with someone like that."

"But, Dad, he could save dozens and dozens of jobs. I love Riley, but I can't put all of those people out of work for her."

"You don't have to."

"The newspaper has been in our family for a century and a half. I already failed it once when I abandoned it for DC and Rachel."

"Stop that." His father rarely raised his voice, so when he did Sawyer took notice. Just like now. "This guilt has been going on for long enough."

"But, Dad, you can't rewrite the past."

"Neither can you."

"You and Mom were so upset when I told you I was leaving Bayside for DC. I'll never forget your faces."

Henry groaned. "We were wrong, Sawyer."

"To be upset?"

"I'm not going to lie to you. It was hard for us to see you leave, to know that you didn't want to stay here and follow my exact footsteps. It wasn't long after you left that I realized how unfair that was. How much I would have hated it if my dad had done that to me."

Sawyer was dumbfounded. He didn't know what to say.

"You were twenty-two, Sawyer. So you went and worked in another city. So you made the wrong choice with a girl. You're hardly the first man to follow your—"

"Stop, Dad!" Sawyer let out an exasperated laugh.

"It's true. Rachel was gorgeous and you were young. You found your way back. What's more important is that you found your passion. Even if that passion had been in a completely different field, your mother and I would still be proud of you. So stop beating yourself up over that time in your life. You're doing an amazing job with that newspaper during a really tough time in publishing."

"Yeah, real boss-of-the-year material."

"Don't make me hit you upside the head."

Sawyer grinned because the likelihood of his dad ever hitting anyone was about as plausible as finding an envelope full of enough cash to save the newspaper.

Still, maybe his father did have a point. He'd been carrying this guilt around with him for so long. He'd always felt he'd messed up all those years ago. As long as the newspaper was doing well, he felt he was making amends for leaving his family.

"Dan Melwood gave you a great idea. An investor. That's all you need to find."

Sawyer groaned. "It's not the first time I've thought about an investor. But, Dad, how many people out there would be willing to back a small-town newspaper? Newspapers are dying."

"A fact that continues to make me sad, but that's the way of the world. You are approaching this problem from the wrong angle."

"What do you mean?"

"If you really want to save the *Bugle*, and, remember, your mother and I are okay if you don't, you need to find an investor. But not for a newspaper. Why not try searching for someone who wants to back the town." He tapped Sawyer on the head. "Think about it. And if you want even more of my advice?"

Sawyer nodded.

"Cut the paper down to a couple days a week. With the online edition, there's no need to print seven days a week. Make those issues you do print special."

"You would be okay with that?"

"It wouldn't matter if I wasn't." He rapped Sawyer on the chest. "You are the boss. And, yes, I've been waiting for you to cut back for some time now."

"Dad, you're a genius."

"Why don't you mention that to your mother next time you see her?"

"Will do."

They started walking back up the stairs to his parents' deck.

"Now, you just have to realize one more thing." Sawyer paused, waiting for his dad to reveal it. "You said you loved Riley back there." He grinned.

He did? Wow. He did.

"I, uh, well, um…"

His dad clapped him on the back. "Keep repeating that over and over. In the meantime, how about you help me finish hanging the Christmas lights and stay for dinner?"

"I can do that."

Henry slapped his son on the back. "And next time you have problems with the newspaper or problems with a female or problems that involve both the newspaper and a female, don't wait so damn long to come talk to me."

* * *

Sawyer had left no less than five messages for Riley the night before. After dinner with his parents, he'd almost gone over to her apartment, fully prepared to grovel, and grovel hard. But Cam and Jasper had shown up unexpectedly at his house with beer, cigars and a homemade chocolate pie from Carissa.

Somehow he had the feeling that Elle and Carissa had put them up to it. They'd insisted that they'd heard he'd had a rough day and wanted to help him take the edge off.

He'd called Riley once more, only to get her voice mail yet again. Then he'd stayed inside with his friends and moaned about his own stupidity.

The next morning, he drove to the *Bugle* offices and parked in his usual spot. His plan was to go over the Sunday edition of the paper, just as he did on most Saturdays. Once he was satisfied that everything was in good shape and ready for the printer, he'd head to Riley's apartment and wouldn't leave until she agreed to talk to him. Even if it took all night and they both had to miss the big anniversary party.

He entered the quiet office and flicked on some of the lights. Pausing at Riley's cubicle, he looked around once again at her funky, personable decor and the realization hit him deep in the gut.

He loved her.

He loved every last inch of her. From her bubbly attitude to her over-the-top outfits. He was head over heels for his best friend.

Sawyer continued to his office and found his proof of the paper in the middle of the desk, where his deputy editor always left it. As usual, he began with page one and barely glanced up until he'd been over the entire thing.

When he flipped to the last page, he was surprised to see another page underneath.

"What's this?" he asked into the silence.

He scanned the page briefly until he saw Riley's name at the bottom. It was a letter addressed to him.

He read through slowly, taking in every word. He could practically hear her voice saying them.

A resignation letter.

"Oh, hell," he muttered.

His heart rate accelerated as he read over the letter again, but the words were still the same.

Riley was leaving him.

She felt it was time for her to make a fresh start. That while she'd loved her experience at the *Bugle* she needed to look for new opportunities.

His palms were sweating as he put the resignation letter back on his desk. He'd really messed up this situation.

He rose and began pacing his office from the windows to the door and back again. The smell of the disinfectant the cleaners used permeated his senses. He desperately wished it was Riley's sweet scent surrounding him instead.

Had he lost her forever? Was their friendship over as well as their romance? He knew he'd blown any chance of working with her, not even in her secret role as the Bayside Blogger.

The hair on the back of Sawyer's neck stood up at red alert. A nagging feeling washed over him and all he could think about was the Bayside Blogger.

He rushed to his computer and logged in to the back end of their website. After a quick search he saw the saved article for the blogger page. It was set to publish soon.

Opening it, his eyes scanned the contents in shock.

She was outing herself.

There, in the black font that distinguished the blogger's column from all the others, was Riley admitting her true identity. As all of her articles were, it was well written and concise. She talked about how much she loved Bayside and her friends and family. She'd only meant to help and, on occasion, offer small pushes—and here she'd included her favorite winky emoticon, and Sawyer had to roll his eyes despite grinning)—to play matchmaker for couples she believed could use a little extra nudge to get to their happy ending. She'd never, ever meant to hurt anyone's feelings.

Sawyer sat back in his chair and removed his glasses. He ran a hand over his tired, weary face.

He grabbed her resignation letter again and located a particular line. *I know the* Bugle *will be fine now.* Yes, it would, if this blog posted. Riley was exposing the blogger so Dan Melwood would offer him the money and backing he needed.

She was being completely selfless. For him. And he hadn't done a thing to deserve it.

A feeling of love so strong and so visceral surged through him.

This was the polar opposite of Rachel. In fact, this was the opposite of him. He'd thought of himself when he'd left Bayside with Rachel. And he'd been thinking of nothing but himself since he'd returned.

Riley was thinking of him.

Moved beyond words, he was helpless to do anything but stare at his computer screen. After a few minutes of deep reflection the answer he needed came to him. It was so simple really.

He wasn't going to let Riley do this. He couldn't. Instead, he was going to step up and be the man she needed. A man who would actually protect her. Unlike that idiot in New York she dated, Sawyer planned to defend her to the last word.

Chapter Fifteen

This is it, Dear Readers. My moment of truth. I know you've all been dying to meet me. Well, tonight your wish is granted. The *Bugle's* anniversary party just got a heck of a lot more interesting. After all, it's not every day you get to unveil a real live gossip darling! Who do you think I am? Big hint: I'll be the one wearing the very sheepish expression...;)

Elle and Cam gave Riley a ride to the *Bugle's* anniversary party. Ordinarily, when she pulled up to the Dumonts' impressive mansion, she took a moment to take in the beauty of the estate. The classic architecture of the house, the immaculate grounds and well-tended gardens always made her sigh. Tonight she was in no mood to enjoy their lush beauty.

Instead, she began running toward the grand foyer. Well, as much as her three-inch heels would allow. It was more like stilted power walking.

She hadn't even put her usual time and attention into her outfit. She'd grabbed a vibrant purple dress that she'd worn to another Dumont party a few months back— gasp. She'd left her hair loose and kept her accessories to a minimum. In her mind, she might as well be at the grocery store.

But, after her article had published earlier in the day,

all hell had broken loose in Bayside. She knew when her revelation article posted. Not only because she'd scheduled it, but when any of her blogs went live, an automatic tweet was sent out letting her readers know.

Today, as usual, she started getting replies to her tweet almost immediately.

No way!

Is this a joke?

OMG! The Bayside Blogger is out. Do you believe it?

No way that's the Blogger? No freaking way.

At first, Riley wanted to hide. Skip the party and bury herself under the blankets on her bed until the holidays were over and it was a new year. Or, maybe forever.

But, in the end, she knew Sawyer would be here and she desperately needed to talk to him. Hiding wasn't the answer. This wasn't New York all over again. She'd run away that time. Returned to Bayside like a scared little ingenue.

Time to face the music. As if on cue, the band began playing a song. She walked into the house and was greeted by a waiter offering champagne. She ignored him and the alcohol and quickly made her way through the atrium and out the French doors to the attached tent. This party was set up just as it had been for Elle and Cam's engagement party, with heated tents, food stations and pop-up bars. Plus, a dance floor in the center of the area.

She scanned the party, her eyes searching for any sign of Sawyer. She spotted Carissa and Jasper. Carissa was waving at her frantically, but she ignored her friend, making a quick round of the tent instead.

When she was positive Sawyer was nowhere to be found, she paused. Riley had to admit that this wasn't what she'd expected. After revealing her secret identity today, she thought she would have people coming up to her left and right. Some would be curious, but some might be angry.

She even had all kinds of excuses ready to go. She was prepared to apologize profusely.

But, as she stood in the middle of the dance floor, not one person approached her. She didn't even receive the questioning glances she'd anticipated.

What is going on?

Before she could follow that train of thought, an out-of-breath Carissa grabbed her arm. "Damn, Ri, you're fast."

"Sorry. I'm just looking for Sawyer."

Carissa nodded, her eyes holding understanding. "Of course. I just can't believe he did that."

"Right. Wait, what?" For the first time, Riley gave Carissa her full attention. Carissa looked lovely. Riley didn't know if it was the simple black dress or the early stages of pregnancy, but Carissa was glowing. "What did Sawyer do?"

Carissa opened her mouth, a questioning expression on her face, but no words came out. "You don't know?"

Riley frowned. "Know what? What are you talking about?" An uneasy feeling crept up her spine.

"Oh, my God, you have no idea. Where have you been all day?"

"I've been… Carissa, come on." She shook her head, her hair landing over her shoulders. "What are you talking about? What did Sawyer do?"

Carissa grabbed Riley by the arm and pulled her off the dance floor and toward a quiet corner of the tent. "He said he was the Bayside Blogger."

Riley could feel her eyes widening even as she became light-headed. "Excuse me?"

"A blog posted to the *Bugle* site this afternoon."

She began blinking in rapid succession. "I know. I told everyone that I'm the Bayside Blogger."

Carissa shook her head. "No, Ri. The blog said that Sawyer is the Bayside Blogger."

Riley whipped her phone out of her gold clutch purse. Quickly she scrolled through the replies she'd received from Twitter. Now it all made sense. She'd thought those responses were a bit...off.

She looked up, met Carissa's expressive gaze. Carissa held out her phone. "Here, read it."

Riley took the phone in her unsteady hands and read the words she hadn't written. The blog was short and sweet. At the end, Sawyer revealed that he was the Bayside Blogger. He was the one who had been reporting on the residents of town. He stressed that he hadn't meant to hurt anyone's feelings, pointing out that every blog, every tweet, every word, had been truthful.

He'd covered for her.

He'd protected her.

He loved her.

The realization hit her harder than having every single person at the party throw their smart phone at her head. Sawyer was in love with her. Unlike her last boyfriend, he'd stepped in to shield her from pain and embarrassment. Instead, he'd sacrificed himself for her.

"Oh, my God, Carissa," she whispered to her friend as she handed her phone back.

"I know," Carissa said. "Pretty unbelievable."

Riley didn't know what to say. Luckily, she was saved by the murmur of the crowd, which was becoming increasingly louder. She and Carissa both glanced around until they saw the source of the whispers. Sawyer had just stepped into the tent.

Her breath caught. The man she loved. Her oldest friend. Her everything.

She felt a light push against her back. "Go," Carissa whispered in her ear.

Riley made her way toward Sawyer. As she did, she couldn't miss the speculation of the other guests.

Sawyer Wallace is here. Or should I say the Bayside Blogger.

I don't know. I just can't see him being the blogger. I mean, our blogger.

Why would he say he's the blogger if he isn't?

I kinda never wanted to know the identity of the blogger. Not really.

As she got closer, Riley increased her speed, even though her heels were not a fan of this decision.

"Hi," she said.

"Hey," he replied.

They stood like that, staring at each other as if they'd just met three seconds ago instead of twenty-nine years. He said, "Listen, Riley."

At the same time, she uttered, "Sawyer."

They both laughed awkwardly. He opened his mouth, but she put a hand on his arm to stop him.

"No, please let me go." He nodded and she continued. "I... I, um..."

"Riley?"

She took the deepest breath of her life. It did nothing to settle her nerves. "I love you, Sawyer," she blurted out. "And you love me, too."

The first expression to cross his face was shock. It was followed quickly by realization and then a large smile. Her favorite smile of his. The one that was slightly lop-sided and made him look mischievous and handsome at the same time.

"That's right," she said. "We love each other."

He pushed a hand through his hair, messing up the tidy style he'd attempted for the party. She loved that, too. "I knew you and I were going to have a talk tonight, but I didn't think this is how it would start. I'd assumed I would begin by groveling and begging your forgiveness."

"Oh, you can still do that."

He chuckled. "Trust me, I plan to. Because I really hurt my friend."

She nodded. "Yeah, you did."

"See, I considered doing something that would have devastated her."

"True." She stepped closer to him. "But the thing is, I get it."

"You do?" His voice was filled with surprise.

"I understand. The *Bugle* is your legacy, your fam-ily, your…thing," she supplied for lack of a better word. "If outing me is all it takes to get the help the newspaper needs, I understand."

"But in the end, I couldn't let you sacrifice yourself."

She wound her arms around his neck and stared into his amazing hazel eyes. "I wanted to help."

"I couldn't let you do that, Ri."

He tilted his head and their lips met in a sexy, soul-ful kiss that made its way through her entire body until Riley felt like she was glowing with love.

When they broke apart, she sighed. "Sawyer, I can't believe you changed my blog."

"I found your resignation letter. I knew that there was

more to it, and when I checked your blog... You are the most selfless person I know and I love you, Riley Hudson."

If she thought she was glowing before, she now felt like she was flying. Hearing the words *I love you* from his lips was too much. It was more than she'd ever hoped for.

"I can't believe you told everyone you are the Bayside Blogger," she said. "I can't believe you did that for me."

He grinned. "Allow me to repeat. I love you, Riley Hudson." Then his expression grew serious. "I don't want you to leave the newspaper," he said.

She'd known this conversation was coming, one way or another. It was never going to be easy, but now that they'd finally admitted their true feelings, it was even harder.

"I have to leave." She put a finger to his lips when he was about to protest. "It's time, Sawyer."

He appeared to take that in, thinking deeply about her words. "Are you not happy?"

She bit her lip. "I am happy at the *Bugle*. But I'm not content. Does that make any sense?"

"How long have you been feeling this way?"

She couldn't keep the sign from escaping. "I'm not sure. I think it's been coming on for a while. It has nothing to do with you or this Dan Melwood situation. I went through something horrible and crappy in New York, and instead of sticking up for myself, I ran away and came home. You gave me a job at the *Bugle* and I hid behind it. Not just as the supersecret blogger in town. But you made me feel safe."

He cocked his head. "Isn't that a good thing?"

"It's a cowardly thing. I'm twenty-nine years old. It's time for me to try something new and exciting, no matter how scary that might be."

He nodded slowly before a smile gradually lit up his face. "I'm proud of you, Ri. But I'm really going to miss seeing you and your outfits every day."

Again she twisted her arms around his shoulders and kissed him soundly on the lips. "I think you're going to be seeing me and my outfits on a daily basis anyway."

"Good. I couldn't imagine not having you in my life every day."

Nor could she.

They leaned in to seal their new arrangement with a kiss, but were interrupted by a loud cough. Together, they turned toward the sound.

Dan Melwood stood there, a cocky smirk on his face.

"Sorry to interrupt," he said, not looking sorry in the slightest. "But the time has come, Sawyer. Tell me, who is the *real* Bayside Blogger?"

Sawyer held in the groan that desperately wanted to slip through his pinched lips.

He'd stepped into the Dumont party with anxiety and fear that he'd lost Riley forever. Now, after she'd admitted that she was in love with him, he considered himself the luckiest man on the planet. It felt like everything in his world was right.

But Dan Melwood's interruption reminded him that one thing was still very not right.

The fate of the *Bugle*.

"I gave you until this party as a deadline. Do we have a deal or not?" Dan asked.

Without thinking, Sawyer faced Dan and angled his body so he could shield Riley from this pariah. To his surprise, she joined him at his side, linking her hand with his and facing Dan head-on. It was a bold statement and one that set his pulse racing. They were partners now.

As if reading his mind, she squeezed his hand and then whispered softly, "We're in this together."

"Come on, Sawyer. It's time to make some decisions," Dan said with little patience. "I told you I needed an answer by tonight. What's it going to be? Feel like saving your family's newspaper?"

He really was conceited. Sawyer couldn't believe he'd even considered this proposal or working with this man.

Over the last couple of days, and particularly the last twenty-four hours, he'd been replaying the events of his life. Of course, he felt guilty for leaving his family and his town to run off to DC with Rachel. But after talking with his dad, he decided to give himself a break. It had been one moment in time. In the end, he had done what was right. He had come back home.

While he may have contemplated Dan's offer for a moment, in the end, it wasn't right, and not only because of Riley. Sawyer loved the *Bugle* and he loved Bayside. Dan Melwood was right for neither.

It was going to be hard and it was going to take sacrifice, but Sawyer was determined to save the paper no matter what. If Riley could be brave and branch out to another job, another career, then he could figure a way out of this mess.

Still, he decided to play with Dan a bit more.

"Why, Dan, you must not have been online today. I do believe the Bayside Blogger revealed himself."

Dan rolled his eyes. "Oh, please. You're no more the Bayside Blogger than I am." He inched toward Sawyer. "Tell me who it is, really."

Sawyer wasn't going to be intimidated by this guy. He stepped forward, as well, ready to defend Riley, his newspaper, his town. Two little letters, *n* and *o*, hovered on his lips. But before he could get them out, the music stopped, and he found himself and everyone else in the tent turning toward the small stage.

Lilah Dumont was standing there in all her regal glory. She thanked everyone for coming, as she always did at these things. Then she went on to talk about the *Bugle* and how it meant so much to the community. Her husband, Collin, joined her and reiterated her thoughts, adding that he was well aware newspapers were a dying breed and how he couldn't be happier that the *Bugle* was surviving. If Sawyer wasn't radiating with such irritation over Dan, he would have been beyond touched.

He would have also noticed that Dan had moved away from him and Riley. In fact, he'd made his way to the stage. Next thing Sawyer knew, Dan took the microphone from Mr. Dumont.

"Hi, everyone," he said to the crowd. "The name's Dan Melwood. I lived here in Bayside for a few years and graduated from Bayside High."

"What's he doing?" Riley hissed.

Sawyer shook his head as the two of them moved closer to the stage. "I have no idea, but my suspicion is that he's up to no good."

They continued to make their way through the crowd as Dan began talking again.

"I am happy to be here supporting the *Bayside Bugle* tonight. Happy one-hundred-and-fiftieth anniversary." He raised a glass and most of the crowd did the same.

"However," Dan went on, "Mr. Dumont is right. Newspapers and most print media are going the way of the VCR, cassettes and floppy disks. In fact, I recently learned that the *Bugle* is in serious financial trouble."

Sawyer froze in his journey toward the stage. Riley ran into his back before coming around his side and reaching for his hand again. The crowd let out shocked sounds at Dan's admission. The whispers started up immediately.

Back at the stage, Dan waved his hands to settle the noise. "I know. Believe me. When I found out that the *Bugle* is barely able to pay its employees, well, I simply couldn't believe it."

"Is that true, Sawyer?"

Sawyer turned to find Jim and Ted, two of his reporters with worried expressions. Bob was right behind them, looking concerned.

"Newspapers are struggling all over the country," Riley said.

"I certainly know that," Claudia said, "but I didn't realize we were one of them."

Bob took a long swig of his beer. "I didn't want to think it. How naive."

Dan coughed into the microphone to get all of the attention back on him. "I know it's scary and unsettling to hear these things about a long-running and respectable institution like the *Bugle*. But don't worry. There is hope. There is a plan. At least, I hope there will be." His gaze shifted, searching the crowd until he found Sawyer. The look Dan offered was equivalent to checkmate.

"Sawyer, why don't you join me up here?"

Sawyer stifled a groan. Riley stood next to him, unmoving.

"Come on, Sawyer. Don't be shy. I know writers tend to be introverts." Dan offered a little laugh. "Let's give Sawyer Wallace, the fearless editor of the *Bugle*, a hand."

That's how he wanted to play it? Fine. Sawyer had taken his share of turns at chess. He made his way to the stage as his fellow citizens applauded. The clapping grew even louder when he stepped onto the stage.

Sawyer crossed to center stage and stood next to Dan.

"Sawyer has been doing his best to keep the struggling newspaper afloat and I commend him. But I told you not to worry. That's because I have a plan. A business plan."

He went on to relay his bio in business and all of the deals he'd made over the years, but Sawyer tuned it out. Instead, he searched and found Riley's supportive gaze. She nodded.

"I offered Sawyer Wallace complete financial support to save the *Bugle*."

The crowd roared its approval. He even heard a *hip hip hooray.*

Sawyer perused the audience. He knew almost every person in attendance. From former teachers and classmates to his employees and friends, it felt like each person contributed to his life in some way, no matter how small.

He loved Bayside. It wasn't just a town. It was a community. They looked out for one another. When someone was down, they all pitched in.

Maybe they did like their gossip a little too much, but didn't all small towns? He smiled.

His dad was right. There was another way out of this mess. And it was staring him in the face right now in the form of every person in the heated tent in the Dumont family's backyard.

He stepped up to the microphone. It was time to put his town to the test. If they responded the way he anticipated, Dan Melwood wouldn't stand a chance. It was Dan's turn for checkmate.

"It's true," Sawyer said, flinching at the sound of his voice echoing throughout the tent. "Dan did offer me a proposal to save the newspaper. It was tempting, let me tell you."

"What do you mean?" someone called from the crowd. "Are you not going to accept it?"

Sawyer paused for a long moment. He saw his parents standing off to the side of the stage. Both of them were smiling at him. His dad nodded. He definitely wasn't letting them down now.

"Here's the thing. This help came with a stipulation. Dan offered to bail out the *Bugle* if, and only if, I revealed the identity of...the Bayside Blogger."

Everyone had been quiet while he spoke; now they became even more hushed. Like they were all holding their breath.

"You said today that you were the Bayside Blogger," someone said.

Sawyer nodded. "That's right, I did."

Dan grabbed the microphone. "Sawyer Wallace is not the blogger. He lied. He is protecting the real blogger."

Sawyer didn't need a microphone. He raised his voice. "Maybe I am. Maybe I'm not. But Dan wanted a name and he got one."

Dan stalked across the stage, baring his teeth. "I'm offering to save the newspaper. All I want to know—all I deserve to know as a silent partner—is the real identity of the Bayside Blogger."

"Not at the expense of journalistic integrity," Sawyer's dad called.

"Please. We're not talking about some international headline in the *New York Times*. This should be a no-brainer. Who is the Bayside Blogger?"

The crowd was reacting exactly as he'd anticipated. They didn't like being cornered any more than he did.

But what he hadn't expected was to see Riley walk onto the stage. His heart dropped.

She took a deep breath and faced the town. "I'm the Bayside Blogger."

Chapter Sixteen

She didn't look at Sawyer. She didn't need to. She could feel him staring at her with his mouth hanging open. As soon as she'd stepped onto the stage, his eyes had darkened.

But she needed to do this.

"Sawyer is not the Bayside Blogger."

Sawyer pivoted toward her. "No, Ri, don't," he whispered.

"I am. It's been me the whole time. I'm the one who's been writing about all of you."

A hush fell over the crowd. Every pair of eyes in the house was trained on her. Riley gulped, suddenly feeling very, very uncomfortable. She bit the inside of her cheek as she rocked back on her heels.

No one offered any words. Nothing. No angry tirades. No supportive gestures. Perhaps she hadn't thought this whole thing through.

Too late to change her mind now. Riley pushed her shoulders back and faced the firing squad, er, her fellow townsfolk.

"You're the Bayside Blogger?" someone asked.

"Yes. I am." She wanted to say more, to offer some kind of explanation, but a muffle in the crowd caught her attention.

Claudia was elbowing her way to the front of the stage.

When she reached it, she turned back. "That's not true, either. I'm the Bayside Blogger. I'm the one who's been writing all those blogs and social media posts."

Whispering began in the audience as Riley started stuttering. "Wait, no…"

"So am I. I'm the Bayside Blogger."

Everyone turned to see another member of the *Bugle* staff who was standing near the closest bar. He raised his glass in salute and took a long chug. "I've been following all of you. I get tips every day."

"No, no, no. You guys don't have to…" Riley tried again, but no one was paying her any attention. No one except Sawyer, who sidled up to her and grabbed her hand.

She whirled to face him. "Why are they doing this? They don't have to help."

"They want to," he said kindly. "So let them, Riley."

"They're all lying," Carissa called from the back of the room. With Jasper's help, she climbed up onto a chair. "I am the Bayside Blogger."

"No, you're not. You weren't even in town when it started," Simone Graves called out, annoyance in her voice. "I am the blogger."

"Wrong again," Elle said, joining Riley and Sawyer onstage. Every head in the place swiveled toward her. "It's me. I've been doing it this whole time. Even when I was in Italy. I just utilized the internet."

"Oh, please. Everyone knows I like to blog and I've been gossiping about all of you for years."

Riley couldn't keep her mouth from falling open at this latest admission from Elle's father, Ted Owens. Mr. Owens rarely even attended a Dumont event, let alone talked when he did.

Still, she couldn't believe what she was witnessing.

Every person was defending her. Or did they even realize she was the one telling the truth?

"Sawyer, are they covering for me?"

He leaned close, his breath a whisper on her neck. "I don't think they even realize that you're the real blogger. I don't think they care."

Elle put an arm around her waist. "They're protecting this town, Ri. And you're an important part of this place."

At that moment, Cam stepped onto the stage and opened his arms wide. "Now, now, I can't have my fiancée and soon-to-be father-in-law lying on my behalf. Time for me to man up."

Riley almost choked. Cam Dumont was one of the most masculine men she'd ever met and probably the least likely to even have a Facebook account, let alone know how to write a gossip column.

"I am the Bayside Blogger," he called out.

People couldn't contain their amusement at this admission. Whistles and catcalls echoed throughout the space. Cam took a bow and snagged Elle for a long, dramatic kiss.

"He must have had a few drinks. I've never seen Cam act so gregariously." Sawyer grinned.

"This night keeps getting more surprising by the second," Riley said.

"Sometimes I'm the Bayside Blogger."

Everyone stopped talking and turned toward Mrs. Dumont. She flung back her head and leveled a bold stare at the crowd. No one dared contradict Lilah Dumont.

"Hey, I've tipped the blogger off more than once," admitted Tony from The Brewside from the middle of the room. "Guess that makes me the blogger, too."

"You've tipped off the Bayside Blogger?" Jasper asked with shock in his voice.

"Hey, I work in the heart of the town. I know all the good gossip."

"Dude," Jasper said with a smirk and a head shake.

Dan tapped his finger against the microphone. Apparently he was done with this charade. "Who is really the Bayside Blogger? I demand to know."

"We all are."

"The Bayside Blogger is part of our town. And our town sticks together. So don't think you can come in here and try to rip us apart."

Riley wasn't even sure who was saying what at this point. Tears threatened her eyes. She was beyond moved at the loyalty of Bayside.

Mrs. Dumont moved to the center of the stage and reached her arm out. Dan immediately handed over the microphone. "I believe you have your answer, Mr. Melwood. Now, we are going to continue celebrating the *Bugle* tonight. You are welcome to join us or you are free to leave. Your choice."

With an expression of defeat, Dan slumped off stage and made his way to the nearest exit, shaking his head. A loud round of applause roared through the crowd.

"Now, Bayside," Mrs. Dumont corrected them. "Let's keep it classy." But she was grinning from ear to ear as she said it.

It definitely took some time, but eventually talk of Dan Melwood, the Bayside Blogger and the very exciting start to this party died down.

"Wow, just wow," Carissa said as she and Jasper found Riley and Sawyer.

"Tell me about it," Riley agreed.

Cam and Elle made their way over with champagne for everyone. Well, everyone but Carissa, who enjoyed a large ginger ale in a champagne flute.

"I just love this town," Elle said.

Riley had to hold in a smirk. She remembered not too long ago when Elle was ready to pull her hair out at the thought of staying in Bayside. Of course, Riley may have been responsible for that attitude since the Bayside Blogger had kinda, sorta made it difficult for her. But in the end, Elle and Cam fell in love, so the end justified the means.

Riley took a moment to glance around at the party. The band was playing. People were dancing. Guests were enjoying the drinks and the food.

And she and Sawyer were in love.

Everything was perfect.

"Tell me about the *Bugle*'s financial troubles," Jasper said to Sawyer.

Well, almost perfect. For a few minutes there, Riley had allowed herself to forget that there was still one very big problem. The fate of the newspaper hung in the air.

Sawyer must have allowed himself a brief reprieve from his worries, too, because at Jasper's question his face fell. The smile he'd been wearing slipped away and his eyes narrowed.

But he explained what was happening with publishing and specifically with the *Bugle* to Jasper. Riley couldn't help noticing that Elle, Carissa and Cam were all listening attentively, too.

It was bad. The newspaper needed help.

She'd never seen Jasper in business mode before. The usually charming and fun-loving Dumont brother had become serious while he took in every word from the editor. His arms were crossed over his chest. He didn't ask any questions, only occasionally nodded.

When Sawyer finished, Jasper responded. "What I'd like to know is, why didn't you come to me sooner?"

Sawyer appeared to blush. "Honestly, I did think of your family. But you're in real estate. I didn't think you'd be interested in signing on to the publishing world." He rocked back on his heels and scrubbed a hand over his face. "Although, you are opening that bookstore on the other side of town."

Jasper raised an eyebrow.

"It's official. I'm an idiot," Sawyer said, as he worked through everything out loud.

Jasper chuckled. "Come with me."

Carissa placed a hand on Riley's arm when she wanted to follow the two of them. Carissa smiled and shook her head. "Let them talk."

"But…" Riley protested.

"But nothing. I filled Jasper in on all of this last night after you told me and Elle what was going on. He was up all night on his computer. I think he has the solution to two problems."

That was great. Then something dawned on her. "Two problems? What's the second?"

Carissa remained tight-lipped. After what felt like an eternity, Sawyer and Jasper returned, wearing matching grins.

Riley jumped in front of Sawyer. "What happened?"

"Meet my new silent partner. Mr. Jasper Dumont has agreed to work with me to keep the *Bugle* going," Sawyer announced.

Riley let out a long, relieved sigh. It felt like the weight of the world had just lessened. She couldn't even imagine how Sawyer felt although, the way his eyes were shining, she had a pretty good idea.

"We have some details to work out, but I think that can wait until Monday." Jasper stuck his hand out and

Sawyer didn't waste time shaking it. "I couldn't be happier to help such a worthy institution."

Carissa crossed to her boyfriend and wound an arm around his waist. "What about the other thing, Jasp?"

"Ah, yes." Jasper placed a kiss on the top of her head. "I probably shouldn't do this in such a public forum, but since we're all friends and tonight is a celebration, why not." He faced Riley. "As you all know, I'm opening a bookstore."

"How's that going?" Elle asked.

"Everything is right on schedule, except for one tiny thing. I don't have a manager. There's a certain type of person I'm looking for and I've yet to find her." He continued staring at Riley.

Did he think she knew someone to manage a bookstore? In all honesty, she couldn't wait for the Bookworm to open and planned to spend a lot of time there. How fun to have a place that would sell new and used books. Bayside really needed someplace small and local that catered to the community and—

"Ri," Sawyer said, amusement in his voice.

"What?" She realized that Jasper wasn't the only person watching her. Everyone in the group had turned their attention in her direction. "What?" she repeated.

Jasper cleared his throat. "I was wondering if you had any interest in applying for the manager position?"

"Me? You're kidding."

Jasper shook his head. "Nope. I need someone who is good with people, who knows the town, who likes reading. I want someone who not only knows books but understands social media and more current forms of communication. I think you might just be that person."

Riley was stunned. She clasped Sawyer's arm in excitement. "Ohmigod. Jasper, this is amazing! Of course I'm interested! I'm thrilled that you'd even consider me."

"I may have told him you recently resigned from the *Bugle*," Sawyer added.

"Let's have lunch this week and talk it over," Jasper said.

In the matter of a few hours, everything seemed to go from dark to light. Dan Melwood's threat was gone, the *Bugle* was saved, and she might have a new career to look forward to.

Then there was Sawyer.

As their friends dispersed to enjoy the party, Sawyer reached for her hand. He led her to the middle of the dance floor and swept her into his arms.

She'd never felt more at home.

"Happy?" he asked.

"Beyond words," she replied. "I'm just so ecstatic the way everything has turned out."

"Me, too," Sawyer said. "Plus, I've made a decision. I'm going to take some advice a good friend offered me."

Riley cocked her head.

"My favorite redhead suggested I learn to evolve. I think she was right."

"She sounds really wise. And beautiful."

"She's both." Sawyer kissed her. "We're going to stop printing the *Bugle* every day of the week. We're going down to three times a week plus a Sunday edition. Some special editions throughout the year."

She knew that decision must have been hard for him. At first, it would have made him feel like a failure. But she knew it was the right way to go and she couldn't be prouder that he'd come around to it.

"You're going to have some extra time on your hands."

Her arms tightened around his neck. "However will you fill it?"

Sawyer met her gaze. "I'm going to be spending it with my new fiancée."

Oh. Oh? *Oh!*

Her hands started shaking as she backed up from him. "What did you just say?"

"Hmm," he said lazily. "I thought you heard me but I guess not. So let me make it crystal clear."

Sawyer got down on one knee right in the middle of the dance floor. People stopped dancing and faced them. She thought she saw phones being held up to capture the moment, but she couldn't tear her eyes from Sawyer. Especially when he pulled something out from his back pocket and she realized it was a ring box.

"Ohmigod," she exclaimed, her hands flying to her mouth. She was so caught off guard that she barely noticed everyone in the tent was sighing and gasping.

"Now you're sounding more like yourself. And you know what? I love who you are, Riley Hudson. I love how obsessed you are with *The Real Housewives*, but that you read *Newsweek* while you watch them. I love that you never miss an episode of *Entertainment Tonight*. I love that you're the Bayside Blogger," he whispered. "I love that behind all those outrageous outfits you parade around in, you have the biggest heart on the planet. I love how well you know me and how you've always been there for me."

Sawyer coughed.

"I love you, Riley."

She leaned over and kissed him. "And I love you, Sawyer Wallace."

"Marry me?" he asked.

She couldn't stop the smile from blossoming if she'd tried. "Of course."

Sawyer twirled her around until she was dizzy. Or maybe that was from being so in love and so happy.

The crowd applauded wildly and Sawyer grinned.

"Wait, wait," she said, fumbling in her tiny purse. "We have to snap a selfie." She turned to him. "You're not going to get away with being camera shy this time, Mr. Editor in Chief."

As she held her phone up, Sawyer leaned in, wrapped his arms around her and smiled—for real. They took a whole round of selfies showing off her new ring, their matching smiles, and the love that had been steadily growing between them since they were kids. Even as a brand-new bride-to-be, Riley couldn't help imagining the headlines her own engagement could make for her column! Not that she'd ever write about herself again…

Then Sawyer yelled out, "Can someone make sure to tip off the Bayside Blogger about this?"

Riley laughed as her phone vibrated, the tips no doubt pouring in. Finally, the blogger would have the scoop she'd been waiting on for a long, long time.

Epilogue

What a great start to a new year.

Smiling, Riley crossed to the window of her apartment and hip-bumped Sawyer. Her fiancé. She still couldn't believe it.

Sawyer's arm shot out and wrapped around her waist, bringing her snugly to him. The room was dark except for the pretty light emanating from her Christmas tree. Riley never took down her tree until after New Year's.

They stared out at the bay, aglow with the twinkly lights the town had put up after Thanksgiving. All of the boats were decorated, the large tree still stood in the town square, all of the stores and businesses were illuminated. Most of the town's residents were down there. She and Sawyer had been in the crowd until ten minutes ago.

They'd eaten dinner at the Boathouse with all of their friends and family. It had been one of the best nights of her life.

Tony closed The Brewside early and joined them for dinner. He joked about not having anyone to kiss at midnight, but Riley suspected there was something deeper under the laughter. Hmm, wouldn't the Bayside Blogger be all over that one, she thought with a smirk.

Jasper and Cam chastised him for giving tips to the blogger but Tony simply grinned. "I work in the eye of the gossip storm. Besides, I didn't want the blogger to get any details wrong."

More reason to love Tony. "Truth in reporting is important," Riley said.

Elle and Cam sneaked glances at each other all night. Mrs. Dumont excitedly talked about their upcoming wedding as Mr. Dumont pretended to be exasperated by his wife.

Elle's dad announced that he'd been at the doctor's that morning for one of his checkups and was still cancer-free. Everyone at the table let out a collective sigh of relief and they all toasted the wonderful news.

Riley's parents kept hugging Sawyer throughout the dinner, something they'd been doing his whole life. But tonight it had been different. It was a kind of blessing and she loved watching Sawyer blush with the attention.

Riley chatted with Sawyer's mom and dad, who couldn't believe she was leaving the *Bugle* in a couple of weeks. But Riley was excited to start her new career. She toasted Jasper and thanked him for the millionth time. She was going to run a bookstore. She could barely believe it. Plus, a new job called for a new wardrobe.

As they finished up dessert, Jasper and Carissa shared a glance. Then Jasper tapped his knife against Carissa's glass of water to get everyone's attention.

To a rapt audience, the two of them announced they were expecting the newest Dumont in seven months' time. Riley had to hold back tears as she watched everyone explode with congratulations and well wishes. If she thought Mrs. Dumont was excited to plan Cam and Elle's wedding, it was nothing compared to the idea of planning for a first grandchild.

They all left the restaurant together, strolling lazily through the town square where there would be an official countdown to the New Year followed by fireworks over the bay. But Sawyer whispered a suggestion to Riley and she couldn't agree more. He wanted to share this moment with her, and only her. Since they could see everything from her apartment, they decided to quietly slip away.

Before they did, she took a moment to hug her two best girlfriends. She and Elle teased the always-gorgeous Carissa about how excited they were she would be getting fat.

"Bitches," Carissa said with a laugh. "But, seriously, who's in for a little prenatal yoga?"

"You know I am. Some of my best conversations happen in yoga," Riley said with her best mischievous smile.

Elle grabbed both of them into a group hug. "I love you both so much. I can't believe the last year."

"It's been wonderful," Carissa agreed.

Riley peeked at Sawyer. "Feels like we're all exactly where we should be." And what a wonderful, empowering feeling that was. To be happy. To be loved. To be content. There was nothing better.

So, she left her friends, joking that she would see them next year. Then she and Sawyer made their way back to her apartment. It would be the last New Year's Eve she would live on the sixth floor of this building. They had big plans in the coming months. A summer wedding. Before that, she was going to move into Sawyer's house where they'd have more room.

She opened one of her windows so the happy sounds from below could filter up to them. The countdown began.

As for the Bayside Blogger? Well, except for one thank-you tweet to the town of Bayside, she'd been quiet this week. She might be quiet for a long time. Then again, when it came to the Bayside Blogger, who knew. She did love a good surprise.

Ten, nine, eight...

The day after the *Bugle*'s party, Riley had received a big tip to her Bayside Blogger email. A video of Sawyer proposing to her. Happily, she posted it on the website and watched it a million times as she snuggled on the couch with her lifelong friend, her soon-to-be former boss and her very amazing fiancé.

Three, two, one!

"Happy New Year, Riley."

"Happy New Year, Sawyer."

She kissed him for the first couple minutes of the New Year, happy knowing that at last she, too, had been saved by the blog.

* * * * *

BECAUSE OF YOU

ELLE WRIGHT

To my mother, Regina—you are missed

Chapter 1

Turning thirty was almost like a sudden death. One day, Bailee Sanders was twenty-nine, working as a nurse anesthetist, dating one of the most eligible bachelors in Columbus and living what she thought was her best life. The next day...well, let's just say she panicked when she felt like her "best life" was choking her. So she did what any person would do in that position—quit her job, ended her relationship and purchased a first-class ticket to the Big Easy for a weekend of fun with her bestie.

It couldn't be that easy, though. Hence, her current predicament. In her defense, it was hot in Louisiana—so hot she was pretty sure the New Orleans air had destroyed her brain cells and rendered her incapable of making good decisions. How else could she explain her behavior?

First, she'd knocked back three too many Hand Grenades on Bourbon Street. Two...*or is it second?* Anyway, after her last drink, she'd cozied up to a stranger at the hotel bar. Not only did she chat with him like she'd known him for years, she'd made matters so much worse when she invited Mr. Hottie McHotStuff back to her room after they'd closed down the bar. And—

"Damn, baby, I can't get enough of you," Mr. Hottie whispered as he thrust into her once again. He circled her nose with his before he nipped her chin with his teeth.

Oh God.

Bailee couldn't think straight. Not when his scent seemed to invade her mind. Not when his lips brushed against her neck, her cheeks, her forehead. Not when his body conquered hers in such a way that made her forget all the reasons why it was a bad idea to get busy with a stranger.

Her gaze dropped to his full lips. She'd been the one to set the conditions for the night—no kissing, no love, just sex. Hell, she'd even given him a fake name. And he'd accepted her conditions with no arguments or questions. But his touch sparked something inside her. He'd filled her so completely, she wanted to beg him for more. It was his fault she'd wanted to renege on her own rules. Had he not been so skilled, so adept at knowing what she needed, she wouldn't be imagining how his lips would taste, how his tongue would feel against hers.

Sex had never been quite like this for Bailee. Passion had never threatened to overtake her common sense, or make her want to throw caution to the wind for it. Instead of rolling her eyes and preparing for the orgasmic performance of her life, she was... *Shit.* She was in trouble.

His hooded eyes clouded with lust. "You're so beautiful," he murmured, his breath soft against her face.

He trailed wet kisses up her jaw. She wanted those talented lips on hers. Except she'd told him not to. As if she was channeling Julia Roberts in *Pretty Woman*, trying to protect her heart.

Above her, his brown skin glistened with sweat. They were so in tune with each other, giving and taking in equal measure. It had been years since her body had this type of reaction to anyone.

"Let go, sweetie," he whispered against her cheek before he circled her nose with his. "Give me what I need."

Bailee could do nothing but grunt. Or was that a groan? *A whimper?* Everything about this man set her on fire. He was so hot, so virile, that she forgot to blink. Hell, she forgot to breathe. And even though he hadn't kissed her, she felt even hotter imagining it. And...*oh God*.

Her orgasm was powerful and unexpected, making her feel dizzy as it raced through her. It was good. Too good. So good tears pricked her eyes. He followed soon after, letting out a low groan.

She felt boneless, sated. This release, this man, had been exactly what she needed. He rolled over onto his back and she smiled. The need to sleep overtook her in that moment, and she allowed her eyes to drift closed. Then...

Bailee sat upright as reality dawned on her. She couldn't fall asleep. That's not what this was. In the days since she'd arrived in New Orleans, she'd agreed to let loose. Life had always been a regimented plan for her, and she wanted to do something she'd never done before.

Seeing Mr. Hottie at the bar, looking so fly in jeans and a button-down shirt, had made her decision easy. One-night stand. *Check.* It was something she swore she would never do, and she had to psych herself up for it. Giving him conditions was one thing, but she'd also given herself a short checklist of things not to do. Falling asleep after the act was at the top of the list.

Running a hand through her hair, she scanned the suite for her clothes. Apparently, they'd disappeared with her inhibitions. Her gaze drifted to the bathroom door.

"Are you okay?" he asked.

She jumped and pulled the sheet up to her chin. Nodding rapidly, she said, "I'm fine. Just... I need to go to the bathroom."

Without another word, she bolted from the bed, pulling the sheet with her. She swiped her cell phone off the dresser before stepping into the bathroom and closing the door behind her, sagging against it.

Bailee dialed her friend, and prayed April would pick up.

"Are you thoroughly satisfied, Bai?"

April had been Bailee's lab partner in Anatomy during their freshman year in college. Oddly, the two could barely stand each other during class. It wasn't until their third year of undergrad, when they both pledged the same sorority, that they became friends. Since then, they'd been closer than sisters. April was the devil on Bailee's shoulder, while Bailee played the angel on April's shoulder.

Bailee shushed April. "Be quiet. Are you alone?"

The last time she'd seen her friend was when April was leaving the bar with her vacation boo. "Unfortunately, yes. Me and my vacation boo had to part ways when he insisted on coming to Michigan for a visit. Ain't nobody got time for that."

Bailee couldn't help the giggle that escaped at her friend's words. "You're crazy."

"Hey, I can only be me. Anyway, why are you calling me? Shouldn't you be in post-orgasmic bliss with Mr. HotStuff?"

"Shh."

"You're being weird. Am I on speakerphone or something?"

"No," Bailee whispered. "But I can't talk about this right now."

"What happened? Where are you?"

"In my room," Bailee mumbled.

"Why are you whispering?" April asked. "Is he still there?"

"Yes." Bailee crawled to the other side of the bathroom, away from the door. "I'm in the bathroom."

"Judging by your behavior, I'm guessing he sucked."

"We're not talking about this. I need a favor."

"What is it? Do I need to kick the door down and save you?" April grew up the only girl in a house full of boys, and had learned a few tricks to get herself out of trouble. It had served them well over the years.

"No, you don't have to do anything like that. I just need to know how to tell him to go home."

"Wait, what?"

"How do I end this?"

"Tell his ass to go home," April said. "What's the big deal?"

"You know this is out of my depth. And I don't want to be mean. He's nice."

"Key word. Nice. He's not a killer. Just tell him thanks for the fun time, but bye."

Bailee snickered. "Tell me why I called you again? You're not helping."

"Listen." Bailee heard movement in the background, like April was walking around. "You're thirty years old. You're beautiful. You're intelligent. You can tell a man to kick rocks. It's not that hard. I'm sure he'll be just fine. He might even be relieved that he doesn't have to make that move."

"You know what? You're absolutely right. I'm a professional. I can handle this." She let out a heavy sigh. "Men do it all the time, right?"

"Exactly! You got this, Bai. I'll give you a few minutes to let him down easy, and then I'll come down there."

"Okay. Yes, I got this. Talk to you in a bit."

"Cool beans. Be direct."

"Direct," Bailee repeated. Once she ended the call, though, all the bravado she'd just mustered up seeped out of her body. "Oh, Lord, I can't do this."

Sighing, Bailee closed her eyes. This wasn't how the night was supposed to turn out, with her cowering in the bathroom in an attempt to avoid the man who had just made her see stars.

She'd had hot, amazing sex with a man she barely knew. Actually, barely was an overstatement. Good conversation at the bar, flirty banter…that wasn't knowing him. That was foreplay. But she didn't regret it because, for once, she'd lived in the moment. She'd been fun Bailee, not work-too-hard-and-asleep-by-nine Bailee. And she was okay with that. April was right. This wasn't rocket science. She could put on her big-girl panties—if she could find them—and tell him that it had been fun, but she needed to get some rest. She could tell him to beat it in the nicest way possible.

A soft knock on the door jolted her out of her thoughts.

"Hey," he called from the other side. "Are you good?"

Bailee stood up. "I'm fine. I…I need to get ready for… My friend is probably wondering where I am." She rolled her eyes at her attempt to lie.

"As long as you're okay," he said.

"No need to worry. Um…you don't have to wait. You can let yourself out," Bailee blurted. "I'm just going to take a shower and pack up."

For a minute, she wondered if bringing him back to her hotel room had been a mistake. If she'd been thinking about the aftermath, rather than his body on hers, she would have insisted on getting another room. Or going to his.

"I'll just go," he said.

Relieved, Bailee shouted, "Thanks!"

Thanks? She was worse than she thought. Not only was she rude, but she'd basically treated him like a transaction.

Bailee smacked her forehead with her palm and shuffled to the mirror. Dark circles under her eyes, smeared eye makeup and pale lips greeted her when she stared at her reflection. "Hello, Hot Mess," she grumbled before pulling the makeup remover from her toiletry bag and smearing the cream on her face.

After a few more minutes, she finally opened the door and stepped out of the bathroom. But instead of facing an empty room, Mr. Hottie was sitting on the edge of the bed. Startled by his presence, she yelped and nearly fell on her butt.

Recovering quickly, she tugged at the robe she'd put on. "You're still here."

He smirked. "What's on your face?"

"Oh no." Mortified, she ran into the bathroom, grabbed a clean towel and wiped her face. He stood in the doorway as she scrubbed her cheeks, forehead and chin. "It's makeup remover. I thought you left."

"No worries. I'll be out in a sec."

Once she finished, she dropped the washcloth on the sink and turned to him.

His gaze traveled the length of her body before meeting hers. "Unless you want a repeat."

Just the words, the promise in his eyes, made her want to take him up on the offer. But she wouldn't. She couldn't. "Uh, no. That won't be necessary. I have to go and…" She patted his shoulder as if he were simply a platonic acquaintance. "This is just… I mean, no need to pretend I like you."

"Ouch."

"I didn't mean it like that." She crossed her arms over her breasts. "I meant that we don't need to do this." *Shut up, Bailee.* "You know, the awkward promise to see each other again another time. We both know that won't happen."

He blinked.

"I just… I'm not good at this." The more she talked, the worse she sounded. And strangely, she couldn't stop talking. "I've never had casual relations. I mean, relationships."

He gripped her shoulders and squeezed. "You should stop talking now."

Bailee swallowed. "I'm sorry. I'm not usually rude."

He didn't respond to that. Instead, he stood there just staring at her with those eyes. What else was she supposed to say? Enjoy the rest of your trip? From their earlier conversation, she knew he didn't live in the city, but had traveled there for work.

Finally, he broke the silence. "I'll…" He scratched his neck. "Well, I won't see you around, but I hope you enjoy the rest of your stay here."

"I have a plane to catch in the morning. Remember, it's—"

"Your last night here," he finished for her. "I remember. Okay. Safe travels, Aries."

Bailee winced, tucking a strand of hair behind her ear. At the hotel bar, they'd agreed to keep things simple, so she'd given him an alias. Why she told him her name was Aries, she didn't know. Bailee had never been a good liar, so she'd spouted off the first thing that came to mind. He'd told her his name was Ian, which she suspected was his real name.

With narrowed eyes, he tilted his head. "Is Aries your real name?"

She couldn't even bring herself to say yes. So she simply nodded.

He shot her a disbelieving look. "Yeah…okay."

She couldn't blame him. Unfortunately, she wasn't used to giving fake names or having sex with men she didn't know and had no intention of seeing again.

Clearing his throat, he said, "Good night…Aries."

"Good night, Ian."

He turned and she followed him to the door. When he pulled it open, April was standing there, her hand poised to knock.

"Oh." April dropped her hand to her side. "I'm sorry to interrupt. I didn't realize you still had company."

Ian shot Bailee a look out of the corner of his eye. "I'm on my way out."

April smirked. "Don't leave on my account."

Bailee grabbed April's hand and tugged her into the room. "April, Ian has to go." She gave him a tight smile. "Enjoy the rest of your time here."

His gaze raked over her. "I will."

Then he was gone. Bailee shut the door and turned to April. Her friend was staring, mouth open. "What?"

April pointed at the closed door. "Girl, you're crazy. That man is even hotter up close. And judging by the way he looked at you, he wouldn't have minded staying a little longer."

Bailee tightened her robe. "Shut up." She brushed past her friend and walked into the bathroom. "What would be the point of him staying anyway? It's not like we'll ever see each other again."

"Um, because he's fine. And his arms. Those lips. That—"

"I get it, April." Bailee rolled her eyes. "He's nice looking. You don't have to give me a rundown of his finer attributes."

April eyed Bailee. "Why are you so snappy?"

Bailee didn't know why she felt so irritated all of a sudden. Leaning against the sink, she shrugged. "I don't know."

"You know what I think?"

"No, but I'm sure you're going to tell me."

"I think you're being too hard on yourself. Stop second-guessing your decision. So you let your hair down and had some fun. You're not the first, and certainly won't be the last person to enjoy a little random sex with a stranger."

Bailee let out a heavy sigh. "I know. It's just hard. I had a life, a relationship. And now I have no idea what I'm going home to. Or what I even want anymore."

"Bai, you're not an old maid. You broke up with

Brandon because you knew that he wasn't the type of man you need in your life. It's better to end things now before you end up in divorce court later. Sometimes, you just grow apart. As for your job, I still think you should move to Michigan. We can be roomies again. Fun times."

April lived in Novi, Michigan, one of the fastest growing cities in the state. It was a short twenty-five-minute drive to Ann Arbor, where Bailee's brother, Mason, lived and worked. She couldn't deny she'd thought about making the move many times over the last several months. Although she loved her hometown, there was nothing keeping her in Columbus any longer. Especially since her parents had recently moved to Fort Lauderdale to be close to her mother's family.

"April, it's not that simple. I can't just move. I have a home there."

"True. But you don't have a job."

Glaring at her friend, Bailee crossed her arms. "Really, April? You're going to throw that in my face?"

April lifted her hands in surrender. "Don't kill me, but I still think it's funny. You quit your job without another one. That's so unlike you."

"Don't remind me."

"Fine, but I'm going to need you to stop making excuses. It's the perfect time to make a move. Your place is in a nice neighborhood, and I'm sure you won't have any trouble finding a buyer."

"I guess I'm just scared."

April wrapped an arm around Bailee and pulled her into a hug. "I know."

Bailee allowed herself to relax in her friend's comforting embrace. "What if I made a mistake?"

Bailee had never rocked the boat. She'd made decisions based on expectations. Bailee chose to become a nurse because her mother thought it was the perfect way to honor her grandmother, who'd spent years in the profession. She'd bought a condo because her father told her it was important to purchase her first home at an early age, like he'd done. And she'd spent years trying to make a relationship work with Brandon, because her parents, his parents…hell, their entire community had been invested in the "B&B" wedding.

Going with the flow, doing what others expected had worked well for her. At thirty, she earned a good living and had a pretty impressive investment portfolio. Although she had a trust fund, she'd never had a reason to touch it. From the outside looking in, one might think she had a picture-perfect life.

Yet, Bailee had dreamed of a happiness that seemed just out of reach. She wanted to go to work and love what she did. She wanted to be with a man who made her smile at just the thought of him. She needed more.

"Stop. You're pretty amazing." April pulled back and met Bailee's gaze. "You've already accomplished so much. You're a freakin' DNP, for goodness sake. At thirty."

Bailee had spent the majority of her twenties in school, furthering her education. After she'd graduated from college, she worked a couple of years and then enrolled in an intensive Nurse Anesthesia–Doctor of Nursing Practice program. She'd recently completed her studies.

"Also, it took courage to end your relationship, to walk away," April continued. "I have no doubt you'll be able to flourish in another state."

"You're not going to give up, are you?"

April grinned. "Nope. I've already talked to Mason,

and he agrees. He'd be happy to have you near him. And I'm sure he can get you a job at the hospital."

Bailee's older brother, Mason, worked as a pharmacist for Michigan Medicine, formerly known as the University of Michigan Health System. "Since when do you talk to Mason?"

Her best friend and her brother had a somewhat contentious relationship. Bailee knew it had a lot to do with the little fling they'd had several years ago, against her dire warnings. Bailee knew they weren't right for each other, but neither of them had listened to her. The relationship had ended with hurt feelings and a broken heart for her best friend.

"I don't." April tugged at her ear. "Well, not really. We actually ran into each other at the mall. He was with his fiancée."

Bailee saw the flash of hurt in her bestie's eyes, and gave her a sad smile. "I'm sorry."

April waved a dismissive hand her way. "Stop apologizing. Your brother is a good guy, and he deserves to be happy. And so do you. Since you're going to be in Michigan next weekend for his wedding, you can start planning your move. Then you can come visit me when it's over."

Bailee had to admit, April's plan made sense. Breaking up with Brandon had been her first step in asserting her own will in her life. Quitting her job had been the next power move in her quest for "more."

She'd traveled on a whim to a place she'd always wanted to go, spent much-needed time with her best friend and had a one-night stand with a man who looked like sex on a stick. Bailee wasn't old. She was a woman in her prime, with her entire life ahead of her. She should be having fun, exploring life. And Bailee planned to use her newfound free time to figure out what she really wanted for her life. Instinctively, she knew a move was in her future. But she wasn't sure Michigan was the answer.

"Fine, I'll think about it." April pointed at her friend and issued a warning. "But I'm not making any promises."

April hugged her. "Yes! That's all I ask. Now, enough of the heavy stuff. Tell me all about Mr. Hot-Stuff. And I want details."

Chapter 2

Dr. Ian Jackson couldn't get out of the Detroit Metro Airport fast enough. The lure of his bed and much-needed sleep propelled him through the airport in record time. After giving up his first-class seat on the plane to a disabled elderly woman who'd struggled to make it to her economy seat, he'd been forced to entertain a little girl with stories and weird faces for the entire flight. Little Ashley with her wild curls and toothy grin had prevented his nap, but Mrs. Palmer's grateful smile made his sacrifice worth it.

He pulled his phone out of his pocket and turned it on. Five missed calls, umpteen texts. Once he'd picked up his luggage and was in the safety of the town car he'd hired to take him home, he read through his emails and text messages. Next were his voice mails.

Most were simple one-liners from his brothers, his younger sister, and his best friend, Mia. But the one from his father angered him. It wasn't so much the content of the message, but the tone. Although Ian was a grown man, a doctor, his father still felt comfortable telling him what he should or should not do.

Dr. Lawrence Jackson had not been the best and most supportive father. In fact, Ian's dad was an unbearable control freak. It hadn't been that long ago that it was revealed he had offered Ian's uncle El's girlfriend money to break up with him. Ian's oldest brother, Drake, had recently shared with him all the sordid details about his father's affair with Drake's mother.

Growing up, it was hard being the son of Dr. Lawrence and Monica Jackson. His parents weren't the loving parents his peers thought they were. They were cold and only concerned with appearances. Which was why he suspected his mother spent more time at the plastic surgeon getting Botox and the like than she did with him and his twin brother.

But his life was a cakewalk compared to those he'd seen in his volunteer work. He didn't have to worry about food or clothes or access to water. He never had to wonder how he would get much-needed medication or medical care. That was why he'd signed up to join the American Red Cross as a volunteer in New Orleans and had recently applied to Doctors Without Borders.

Unfortunately, his noble intentions would not be met with enthusiasm from his father. In fact, Ian was sure his father wouldn't be proud of his decision. Which was why he hadn't shared his intentions with him. Ian knew his father wouldn't understand, and he was tired of fighting.

With a heavy sigh, he placed his first return call.

"Ian, where the hell have you been?" Myles asked, cutting right to the chase.

"How are you, brother?"

"I'm fine. Where are you?"

Ian glanced out of the window. Hard to believe he'd been gone for six months. When he'd originally signed up to volunteer, he'd expected to be in Louisiana for three months. But he found that he'd enjoyed the work immensely and spoke with his med school adviser about extending his stay.

"I'm here, on my way home. Just landed. What's up?"

"Dad is on the warpath again. He's been asking to meet with us."

That was the last thing Ian had on his agenda. "Yeah, I'm not doing that. I have to drive up to Traverse City tomorrow anyway. The plan for the next several hours is sleep. After that, I'm going to meet my new niece."

One of the downsides to being gone for so long was Ian had missed key events in his family. His brother Drake and his wife, Lovely, had welcomed their first child. Ian was thrilled to be an uncle, and ready to spoil his little sweetie pie. They'd texted pictures of baby Zoe, and she was adorable.

"Well, he does plan to go to the wedding," Myles told him. "How will you avoid him?"

"I'll figure that out," Ian replied.

"How was the trip?"

As the town car sped down I-94 toward Ann Arbor, he noted the subtle changes in the area. Buildings were sprouting up where lush trees used to stand tall. Construction crews were working the roads, expanding them for the many commuters in the area.

"Good. We did a lot of good work. Wish you had come with me."

Ian knew Myles wasn't interested in being on the

front line. His twin was as straitlaced as they came. They were like night and day. Ian was comfortable in jeans and a T-shirt, while Myles dressed in a suit nearly every day of the week. But there wasn't much Ian didn't know about Myles, and vice versa. And Ian didn't doubt that Myles had his back no matter what. Just like Ian wouldn't hesitate to be there for Myles.

"I probably should have come down to visit, at least," Myles admitted, which surprised Ian. "I need a break from here."

"You could always ride up north early with me."

"I can't. Dad is lecturing tomorrow at the school. I told him I'd be there."

Ian shook his head. "Myles, when are you going to stop trying to fit yourself into the box Dad tries to put you in?"

"Don't start. I'm not like you, ready to leave at any moment. I need stability, and I'm happy where I am."

"Whatever." Ian checked his watch. "Let me go. I have to call Mia before she has a panic attack or something."

"What time are you going to Drake's?"

"In a few hours. Are you going to meet me there?"

Myles agreed to meet him later, and they hung up. Next, Ian called Mia.

"Ian, I hope you know that I'm killing you on sight," Mia said, skipping the pleasantries.

"Hey, Mia. Are you officially turning into a bridezilla now?"

"Ian, you're my man of honor and you haven't been here for anything. You missed my engagement party, the bridal party roundup and my bridal shower. What's up with that?"

"I've been working, Mia. And I'm a man. There's

no way I was coming to your bridal shower and eating cucumber sandwiches and dainty hors d'oeuvres, and watching you open boxes filled with lingerie. That's not what we're about."

Mia laughed. "You're silly."

"No, I'm being serious. When you asked me to stand up with you on your wedding day, I thought you meant that in an honorary way."

"Why would you think that? Stand up with me is pretty clear. Besides, you're my best friend. I need you at my side when I take the biggest step of my life."

Ian smiled. Mia Solomon had given him his first haircut—against his will. She'd made him his first mud pie and had been there through every good and bad thing in his life. Although they weren't related by blood, she was his sister, his best friend.

Ian's and Mia's fathers had been great friends, and the two families had spent a lot of time together, traveling to exotic islands and mountain villas. He'd stayed entire summers at the Solomon estate near Traverse City, Michigan, running the grounds and getting into trouble. And when they moved back to Ann Arbor from Las Vegas during his teenage years, they'd lived on the same street in a wealthy west-side neighborhood.

"You know I can be your best friend in the front row. I don't need to be in the wedding, Mia."

"You promised. It's too late to back out."

Ian didn't remember telling his friend that he'd don a tuxedo and walk down the aisle to music by himself. When they'd first discussed the wedding, she'd told him that she couldn't pick between her sisters for maid of honor. Mia was one of five Solomon women, all of them successful, all them headstrong and all of them bosses. So he could only imagine what would happen if she'd had to pick just one to handle the role.

He'd been friends with Mia long enough to know he'd never win this battle. Ian loved Mia, but she was relentless when she had her mind set on something. Sighing, he said, "What do you need, Mia?"

"How about answer your damn phone when I call you? And get up here as soon as possible. There's so much to do."

"I can't promise I'll answer the phone every single time you call. I do have a job, and a life."

"Speaking of having a life, you sent me a text about a woman the other day. Who is she?"

Ian groaned, recalling how he'd sent Mia a string of emojis when he'd met Aries at the bar. Mia had been texting him about floral arrangements and color swatches when he'd sent the text. It had been his way of telling his friend that his attention was on something else, namely an attractive and available woman.

"We're not talking about me right now, Mia," he told her. "I'll compromise and make sure my phone is on me at all times until you jump over that broom."

Mia thanked him. "I just miss you."

"I miss you, too, Big Head."

She barked out a laugh. "Shut up, Munch."

Ian groaned. "I told you to stop calling me that."

He had picked up the nickname when he was a cute, albeit chubby little boy. Mia's dad had started calling him Munch because he was always munching on food. Somewhere around the age of fourteen, Ian had demanded they stop calling him the name, and had refused to answer to it. Also around the same time, he'd started cycling and dropped his excess weight quickly.

As if on cue, Mia said, "Bring your bike. We can ride the grounds."

Aside from Myles, Mia was the only person who understood him without question. She knew that cycling was a necessary part of his life. Cycling had not only been his way to get in shape, it had also helped him get away with minimal fuss. As a teenager, he didn't have to borrow one of his father's cars to leave the house. All he'd needed was his bike. Even now, he rode his bike into work most days. The unpredictable Michigan weather didn't faze him; he could ride on the coldest or hottest days. He'd cycled across the country, through many different terrains, along the countryside or up a mountain or near the beach. He'd raced in the Tour de France and the one-day Lotoja race from Utah to Wyoming.

Ian smiled. "I knew I loved you for some reason other than your homemade biscuits."

Mia laughed. "You're crazy. Seriously, though, I really need you here, Munch. Come soon."

Something in Mia's voice gave him pause. "Are you okay, Mia? What's going on? Because if Mason—"

"I'm fine," Mia said, cutting him off. "Mason is fine. I'm just stressed. Weddings are hard work. My sisters are driving me crazy, and trying to take over."

Ian chuckled. "That doesn't surprise me, Mia. All of you think you know everything."

"Be quiet. I'm learning to sit back and observe, like you."

The Solomon family had an interesting dynamic, like his family. But Dr. and Mrs. Solomon, or Mama and Pop as he called them, beat his parents hands down in the love department. They'd always shown him nothing but unconditional love and support. When he'd mentioned his desire to go down to New Orleans to work with the American Red Cross, it was Pop's recommendation that placed him above the other candidates. Ian owed them a debt that couldn't be repaid with money. In many ways, he owed them his ability to think for himself—he owed them his life.

"Good. But, Mia, it's your wedding. No one else's opinion matters but yours. And Mason's."

His best friend let out a heavy sigh. "I needed to hear that. Lately, I've felt the pressure because Nonna is getting older, and I'm the first grandchild to marry."

Anna Maria Solomon was eighty-one years young, if you let her tell it. The family matriarch ran a real-estate development business and had amassed quite a fortune over the years. She'd adopted Dr. Solomon at age five, when his mother died. Back then, it had been a bit of a scandal for a white woman to adopt an African American child, but Anna didn't care what people said. She'd made a promise to her best friend to raise her son if something should ever happen to her, and she'd kept that promise.

Recently, Dr. Solomon retired and moved to Traverse City permanently to help his mother. Since he'd made the move, he'd opened an Italian restaurant on the outskirts of their huge estate, bringing the old recipes his mother and grandmother had taught him to the resort town.

"I get it," Ian told Mia. "But Nonna is already proud of you. You're well on your way to becoming a successful neonatal surgeon. You love your family with your whole heart, and you're giving. All things she taught you. Don't put so much pressure on yourself. I'd rather have a centerpiece out of place or a wilted flower in that arch thing than a crazed friend with bald patches in her hair due to stress."

"Oh!" Mia yelped. "I'm hanging up. You took it too far with the bald patches."

Ian laughed. "I had to make the point." The town car pulled up in front of his condominium. "Listen, I'm home. Take a long soak in the tub and go to sleep. I'll be there tomorrow."

"I love you, Munch."

"Love you, too."

Ian ended the call and hopped out.

Big doe eyes, curly black hair and a smile that melted him a little... Ian couldn't help but smile at the squirming baby girl in his arms. His niece, Zoe, gripped his index finger and tried to stuff it into her mouth.

He gently tugged his finger out of Zoe's grasp. "Nah, baby girl. Don't eat that." He gave her a pink-and-blue pacifier. "See, that's better."

"You're smitten, bruh," Drake said from behind him.

Ian ignored his brother and focused on Zoe. "Remember I'm the best uncle in the world, Zoe Bear. Don't even let Uncle Myles or Uncle-Brother El tell you anything different." Zoe let out a cute little gurgle and smiled. "That's right. I'm the greatest."

"Aw, that's so sweet." Ian's sister-in-law, Lovely, squeezed his shoulder. "You're so going to babysit. She loves you."

Ian peered up at Love. "Bring it on." He kissed Zoe's brow and handed her to Love. "I'll keep her anytime you want me to. She's beautiful."

When Ian had arrived at Drake and Love's home earlier, he'd immediately picked his niece up out of the baby swing. He'd never seen anything more perfect. Drake wasn't wrong. Ian *was* smitten.

Love smiled as she rocked the baby. "Isn't she? I can stare at her for hours."

Ian approached Love and ran his finger over Zoe's hand. "Me, too. How are you?"

Love had been part of his life since he was a kid. They'd grown up together in Las Vegas. She and Drake had been platonic best friends until a fated trip to Vegas a couple years ago. In an attempt to console Love after she'd lost a patient, Drake had taken her out to party along The Strip. The following morning, the two had awakened with hangovers and a marriage certificate. While both Drake and Love had been mortified at their drunken choice to marry, the two soon realized that they were better together and fell in love.

"I'm good. Went back to work a couple months ago, which was hard."

"You could have taken more time off, Love." Ian gave his brother the side-eye. "See, you should have gotten drunk and married me. I would have insisted you stay at home longer."

Love giggled. "You're too much."

Drake pushed Ian away. "Get away from my wife, man."

Ian barked out a laugh. "I can't help it. You're an easy mark."

"How was NOLA?" Drake handed Love a clean bib. "I can't tell you how proud I am, Ian. Despite your normal asshole tendencies, your heart to serve is phenomenal."

Drake had been the quintessential older brother in Ian's eyes, even though they were only seven months apart in age. Ian had looked up to Drake, and had followed him everywhere for years. Hearing his brother say he was proud meant everything to Ian.

"Thanks, bruh. I appreciate that."

"I mean it," Drake said. "No matter what Dad says, you're doing great work. Keep doing you."

Ian swallowed. "I've been avoiding his calls. I don't want to hear how disappointed he is in my choices."

"That's right. You're a grown man, creating your own path."

Ian wasn't the first offspring to depart from his father's predetermined field of medicine. It had all started when El, Ian's uncle, dared to become an emergency psychiatrist against Ian's father's wishes. El had been more like an older brother than an uncle to Ian, because he'd been raised by Dr. Law, as everyone called Ian's father. Drake followed El's lead when he declared cardiothoracic surgery instead of Plastics. Since then, Ian's father had been on his head about his specialty.

Working in a hospital was good, but Ian wanted to do more than breast lifts and tummy tucks. He wanted to leave an impact. There were people suffering every day who needed medical assistance, and he could provide that much-needed help. And he would. As far as Ian was concerned, working in a plush, air-conditioned building with his father and brother would be akin to dying slowly.

"Dad isn't going to be happy. But I can't open that practice with him."

Drake waved a dismissive hand. "He'll be all right. He has Myles."

Ian shook his head. "I don't know why Myles is entertaining this. He'd rather be in front of a piano, composing music."

"I'm not sure I believe that."

Ian's twin brother had spent years perfecting his skills. He'd written songs Ian was sure would be mega-hits if Myles followed through with recording them. But Myles would rather not rock the boat with their father. Dr. Law, who'd had an impressive career in Plastics performing necessary and cosmetic surgery for patients, had decided to focus solely on cosmetic surgery and open a practice in the area. Myles was set to join him.

"Well, we'll never find out, right?" Ian said. "You know how steadfast Myles is. He'll go to the grave insisting he's doing what he wants to do."

"You never know. Speaking as someone who thought I'd be living in a high-rise apartment in New York City or Los Angeles, life has a way of taking you way off course. And you know what? Living here with Love and Zoe, working at Michigan Medicine on my dream, is exactly what I need and want."

Ian nodded. "And I'd say this life agrees with you."

Love grinned up at them. "We're happy, Ian. I want you to be as happy as we are."

"He will be," Drake said. "He's on the right track. So...you never did answer my question. How was New Orleans?"

"Did you meet anyone down there?" Love asked.

Ian had thought about Aries several times since they'd spent a few hours getting to know each other intimately. The way her body had responded to his, the feel of her skin under his fingers...just the thought of her made him want to find her. But they'd agreed to one night, one time.

"Uh-oh." Love tilted her head, assessing him. "I think he did meet someone down there."

Ian blinked. "What?"

"I think you're right, baby," Drake said, folding his arms across his chest. "What's that look for, bruh?"

Frowning, Ian scratched the back of his head. "I'm ready for dessert. I saw the box of beignets on the counter. If you think these are good, Love, you definitely have to visit Café Du Monde in New Orleans." He headed toward the kitchen.

Love stood in front of him, blocking his way. "I've had them before, and don't change the subject. Who is she?"

Ian put on his best smile and looked at his sister-in-law. "I met many women in New Orleans. I'm not daydreaming about any one woman. I'm thinking about dough and powdered sugar. Trust me, there's nothing special to tell."

And Ian figured if he kept repeating that to himself, he'd finally believe it.

Chapter 3

"**M**ason!" Bailee sprinted into her brother's waiting arms and squealed when he lifted her off her feet in a tight embrace. "I missed you so much." Being enveloped in her big brother's arms made her feel safe, like she was home. And she didn't want to let go.

"I missed you, too, Bai."

When Mason finally set Bailee down, she grinned up at him. He looked the same as he looked every time she saw him. Freshly shaven, clothes crisp and eyes sincere. Mason had always been sure and dependable, and she wouldn't change him for the world.

"I'm so happy for you." She hugged him again.

Although Mason was three years older than Bailee, they'd always been extremely close. Growing up, he'd taken her everywhere, to the chagrin of some of his friends, who hated his little sister tagging along on all of their exploits.

"I'm happy, too. Mia is everything to me."

"She's perfect for you, Mase."

Bailee had had the opportunity to hang out with Mia several times over the past few years. Mia had struck her as a genuine woman who cared deeply for Mason, which was all Bailee could ask for.

"I think so, too." Mason kissed Bailee's brow. "Come on. Mom and Dad arrived last night. They want us all to sit down tonight and catch up."

Mason had met Bailee in the long, circular driveway in front of the house. As they headed toward the house, she scanned the area. "This is beautiful, Mase. Wow."

Lush greenery and beautiful flowers surrounded the huge mansion. As she drove up the private driveway, she couldn't help but gush over the expansive estate. She'd passed a huge barn, where Mason told her the ceremony would take place. Off to the side stood a smaller house, with huge white shutters and a wraparound porch. She assumed it was a guesthouse, or a pool house. A gazebo could be seen off in the distance, and Bailee imagined having coffee in the mornings out there. It was obvious the Solomon clan took care of their property.

"I passed the restaurant on my way in. It's beautiful," she said. *Anna's* was the Italian restaurant owned by Dr. Solomon, named after his adoptive mother. According to Mason, the restaurant was known for its authentic Italian cuisine and gorgeous views of Grand Traverse Bay. The stunning building was situated on a hilltop and had floor-to-ceiling windows, dark wood trim and a beautiful brick patio surrounding it. She'd noticed customers enjoying lunch outside, and couldn't wait to try the food.

"The rehearsal dinner will be there, so you'll get to

try it. We have a jam-packed week ahead of us, with activities every single day."

Mason and Mia had decided to invite their closest family and friends up to the estate ahead of the ceremony, which would take place on Saturday evening. The mission was twofold, since the Solomon clan had decided to open up the estate to other families as a wedding resort in the very near future. This wedding would be a trial run of sorts.

"I have a question, though. Where will the family stay once this place is open to the public?"

"Mia's oldest sisters, Marisa and Luna, will stay at the main house and manage it. Dr. and Mrs. Solomon, along with Nonna, have already moved into the lake house on the far west side of the estate. I'll take you on a tour once we get you settled."

"I'm excited. It's like heaven on earth up here."

They approached the door and he turned to her. "Mia's excited to see you. Maybe you can help me keep her calm until her best friend arrives."

"Why isn't her bestie here?"

"He just got back to Michigan from an extended work assignment. He'll be here today."

Bailee shot Mason a skeptical look. "Her best friend is a *he*? Are you sure you're okay with that?"

Mason wrapped his arm around her neck and squeezed playfully. "Don't worry, he's good people. You'll see."

Letting out a heavy sigh, Bailee let Mason lead her into the house. She gasped as she took in the classic decor. "Oh my God, this view is spectacular." The wall of windows offered stunning panoramic views of West Grand Traverse Bay.

They stared out at the clear blue water. "I once told Mia that she'd grown up in a northern paradise."

"You're right. It makes good business sense to turn this into a wedding resort. It can probably even be used for a family or work retreat."

"That's the plan, actually. Although the original vision was for a wedding resort, the family soon realized it could be so much more. Mia's in the kitchen. Come on."

Bailee grabbed his outstretched hand and let him steer her toward the kitchen. Inside the gourmet kitchen, Mia stood next to a younger woman Bailee had never seen before. The two were chatting in hushed tones, until Mia glanced up and saw them. Her eyes softened and she hurried over to her.

"Bai, I'm so glad you made it." After the two embraced, Mia turned to the other woman and waved her over. "Bailee, I want you to meet my youngest sister, Bianca. Bee, this is Mason's sister, Bailee."

Bailee reached out to shake Bianca's hand, but was surprised when the other woman pulled her into a quick, but tight hug. "Good to finally meet you," Bee said. "I feel like I've missed out on so much."

Bailee remembered Mason telling her about Mia's youngest sister, the fashion designer, and had heard about the gorgeous bridesmaids' dresses she'd designed for the wedding. "I'm glad to meet you, too. I'm so jealous you get to study in Milan under one of the greatest designers of our generation."

Mia smiled proudly. "She's going to take over the fashion world."

Bee waved Mia off. "I'm just me, MiMi." Turning her attention back to Bailee, Bee said, "I hear you're the best woman."

Bailee shot a wary glance at her brother. When he'd asked her to stand up with him at the wedding, she'd assumed she'd be one of the bridesmaids. But he'd quickly doused her dreams of wearing sleek dresses designed by Mia's talented sister. "I had been looking forward to wearing that fly dress you designed for the wedding party."

"I have something even better for you," Bee said with a wicked grin.

Bailee met Mia's gaze. Her future sister-in-law was practically bouncing with excitement. "What?"

"I told Mase not to tell you," Mia said. "Bee designed a slappin' tux for you to rock at the ceremony, using the measurements you sent Mason for the plain tuxedo he wanted you to wear."

Bailee smiled. "Really? Yay!"

Bee told her that they'd meet sometime today for a fitting, and she'd finish everything up before the wedding. After a few more minutes of talking about the ceremony and the week's activities, Bee excused herself to go to her parents' place.

Once they were alone, Mia turned to Bailee. "Thank you for everything you've done for us."

Bailee had always loved do-it-yourself projects and had come up with an idea for a simple, yet elegant centerpiece for the reception tables. "It's no trouble. I have everything packed away in my trunk."

"I'll get everything out," Mason told her.

"We can have the staff do that," Mia insisted. "Show her to her room first."

Mia hugged her and then rushed out of the room, calling for someone she assumed was part of the resort staff. Mason took Bailee through the house, pointing out the library, several sitting rooms and the great room. On their way up to her room, he gave her a little history of the place. It had been built in 1998, commissioned by Anna Solomon on land that had been in her family for generations. Located on Old Mission Peninsula, the house spanned eighteen thousand square feet. It had eight bedrooms, which had been recently renovated into minisuites, each with its own en suite bathroom and an outdoor balcony or patio.

"How many people are staying here this week?" she asked.

Mason ticked off the names. "Yep, we're going to have a full house. The rest of the guests are being housed at one of the hotels in town. They'll be picked up and transported here on the wedding day."

"Cool."

They stopped in front of a closed door, and Mason pulled out a key card. "This is your room." He unlocked the door and handed her the card.

Once again awed by the view, she walked right over to the huge windows and peered out at the bay. French doors opened to a balcony, and she stepped outside. Leaning against the rail, she let out a relaxed sigh. "I needed this, Mase."

He joined her and leaned against the rail. "Are you going to tell me what's going on with you?"

She eyed him. "Don't you already know?"

With a sad smile, he nodded. "He called me last week."

Brandon was one of Mason's oldest friends. They'd played basketball together in high school and had remained friends through college. "I guess he told you how unfeeling and cold I am."

"He would never say anything bad about you to me. But he did apologize, told me he wouldn't be able to attend the wedding because it would be too hard for him to see you after everything that happened."

Bailee dropped her head. "I'm sorry for that. I guess I could have waited to break up with him until after the wedding. Now you're short a groomsman."

"You know I don't care about that. I just want you to be okay."

"I'm more than alright. Mase, he wasn't the right man for me. Once I realized that, it wasn't as hard as I thought it would be to let the relationship go."

"What changed for you?"

Everything. Bailee explained how she'd woken up one day, tired of feeling unhappy and unfulfilled in her relationship. Brandon was a good guy, but he was all about what *he* wanted for them, how *he* wanted them to live, where *he* wanted to work, when *he* wanted her to quit her job and have his kids. She'd felt like an afterthought to him sometimes.

"Brandon was so caught up in appearances, and it really started to grate on me."

"Well, baby sis, it sounds like you did the right thing. You took control of your life, which is what I always wanted you to do."

"I haven't talked to Mom and Dad," she confessed. Telling her parents that they wouldn't get their high-brow Columbus wedding wasn't something she looked forward to doing. The two families had been joined at the hip for years. Their mothers practically salivated when Brandon asked Bailee to go out with him all those years ago. "I haven't answered any of their calls, because I know the Lamberts have talked to them. I just don't want to argue with Mom about my choice."

Bailee's mother was a professional nagger. She

would more than likely take on the full-time job of convincing Bailee to take Brandon back.

"She would never understand where I'm coming from," Bailee added. "And I need her to take my side in this."

"I'll talk to them with you." He pulled her to him. "We'll spend some alone time together tonight, and we'll talk. Okay?"

Bailee nodded. "Thanks, Mase."

"What else aren't you telling me?"

Mase knew her better than anyone. "April has almost convinced me to move to Michigan."

Her brother's eyes widened, and a slow grin spread across his face. "That makes me very happy. I'm glad April is good for something."

Bailee rolled her eyes. "Stop. I need you two to get it together."

"I'm just kidding." He stood and rubbed his hands on his pants. "Let's go find Mom and Dad. When I saw them last, they were headed out for a walk on the grounds."

Bailee and Mason stepped outside just as a sleek, black BMW zoomed up the driveway. From behind her, she heard a loud screech, and soon Mia barreled out of the house toward the car.

"I guess she's happy to see whoever that is," Bailee murmured.

Mason laughed. "It's Ian, the best friend."

The name Ian gave her pause, and she turned to Mason. "Ian?"

The last man she'd met named Ian had played her body like she was his own personal instrument. She'd remembered him often since they'd parted ways. The low timbre of his voice, his hair, his skin and his smell…just the thought of her New Orleans dalliance made her skin heat with a need she knew no one else could fulfill.

When Mia flung the car door open, Bailee narrowed her eyes on the familiar man who stepped out of the car. *It can't be. It cannot be.* She blinked and zeroed in on the man again, hoping that her eyes were playing a mean trick on her.

Bailee was sure her eyebrows were touching her hairline because the man talking to Mia was none other than Mr. Hottie himself. Mia's best friend, Ian, was *her* Ian—the same man who'd pleasured her so much she couldn't forget the feel of his fingertips on her skin.

Mia gestured wildly and jumped into his arms. Bailee's gaze raked over him. *Oh, shit, I'm in trouble.*

Swallowing, Bailee scanned the grounds in search of a hiding place. She needed to think. Frantic, Bailee retreated backward, her eyes still on Ian. But before she could run away, his gaze locked on hers.

He smiled. She didn't.

"Ian!" Mason shouted across the driveway. "Get your hands off of my fiancée."

Bailee shot Mason an incredulous look. Judging by the chuckle in her brother's voice, she knew he was joking. But it felt like the joke was on her. What were the odds that the same man she'd decided to have no-name sex with was the best friend of her brother's fiancée?

Ian and Mia started toward them. *Oh God.* "Mase, I'm going to… I have to do something." Before Mason could stop her, she turned and took off toward the house.

Chapter 4

What the hell is she doing here?

Ian watched Aries make a break for it into the house, and wondered why the woman he hadn't stopped thinking about since New Orleans was at his best friend's place.

Mason met them as they approached the house, a frown on his face. "I wanted to introduce you to my sister." He turned and pointed in the direction Aries had run. "But apparently she has something else to do."

Aries is Mason's sister?

Mia slipped her arm in Mason's. "It's okay, babe. They can meet later."

"I'm sorry about that, man." Mason clasped Ian's hand and shook it. "Bailee doesn't usually act so weird."

Bailee? Ian knew she hadn't given him her real name.

"Aw, maybe you should go after her," Mia told

Mason. "I'll catch up with Ian and we can get the best woman and the man of honor together in a little while."

Mason nodded and went after his sister. *Bailee.*

"Ian?" Mia called.

He blinked. "Huh?"

"Now you're acting weird." She grabbed his hand and tugged him toward the front door. "Come on. We need to talk."

Inside the house, Mia poured two tall glasses of lemonade and cut a piece of apple pie. She joined him at the breakfast bar with two forks. "You look good, Munch." Mia ate a healthy piece of pie.

A smile tugged at the corners of his mouth. "You do, too, Big Head." He glanced around the room. "The house looks great. I noticed the improvements to the barn and the boathouse on my way in."

"I know, right? All the work finally paid off. You should see the remodeled bedrooms. Each one is a suite, for guests."

Mia had told him of her parents' plan to renovate the house and turn it into a wedding resort, available to the public. He'd championed the idea, even though she'd been hesitant to accept her parents' choice.

"I told you it would be a good move on their part. They're getting older, and this house is too big for the two of them and Nonna."

"You're right. You should see the changes they made to their house. They expanded it to include a private mother-in-law suite for Nonna. She now has her own small kitchenette, and loves it. We have to force her to come out of her room sometimes."

Ian laughed. He'd missed his second family, and planned to spend as much time with them as he could before he had to leave. "She'll come out for me."

"You'll get to see everybody at the cocktail hour later. I wanted to have something to welcome the early guests."

"Good idea." *Bailee* couldn't hide from him forever. This cocktail hour was the perfect opportunity to talk to her, if he couldn't find her before then.

"So…" Mia turned her barstool to face him. "You think I forgot about the text? You changed the subject yesterday on the phone. I want to know who you met down in New Orleans that prompted you to send me that little code message."

"Mia, I always said you should have been an attorney because you've perfected the art of badgering witnesses. Come on, now. This is your wedding week. My text should be an afterthought."

"See, that's where you're wrong. I welcome anything that can keep my mind off table settings and seating charts."

"Let it go, Big Head. It was nothing." The lie rolled off his tongue as if he really believed his short time with Bailee was no big deal. "I'm here to help you get through your big day. Give me all the details."

Mia gave him the rundown of the events he'd be required to attend that week, from the cocktail hour to the summer games to the joint bachelorette and bachelor party to the rehearsal dinner, and finally the wedding and reception. Ian got tired just listening to the long list of activities.

"Will I have time to breathe this week?" he asked.

Bumping shoulders with him, Mia said, "You will. Just not much time."

They laughed, and he squeezed her hand. "You know I'm here for you. Whatever you need, okay?"

Mia leaned her head against his shoulder. "I know. That's why you're my best friend."

"I found her." Mason entered the kitchen with Bailee walking behind him.

"Babe, you're back." Mia stood, and Ian followed suit.

Bailee still hadn't met his gaze, but he'd wait for it.

"Ian, I want you to meet my sister, Bailee," Mason said. "Bai, this is Ian."

Finally, Bailee lifted her head and nodded curtly. She stepped forward with her hand outstretched. "Hi, good to finally meet you."

He raised a brow. So she wanted to play the *I Don't Know You* game. Ian would go along with it. For now. "Nice to meet you, too. *Bailee*."

Bailee slipped her hand from his grasp and wiped it on her pants. He noticed the cute flush on her cheeks and nose.

"Ian is a doctor at Michigan Medicine in Ann Arbor," Mason said. "If you decide to apply there, you'll probably see him around."

"Oh, really," Bailee croaked. "That's cool. Mia, why didn't you tell me your best friend was a hottie?" Her eyes widened once she realized her slip of the tongue, and Ian did his best not to laugh. "I mean...why didn't you tell me your best friend was a doctor?"

Ian covered his mouth to hide his smile. So Bailee thought he was a hottie? He'd keep that little tidbit in his back pocket for later.

Mia giggled. "I thought I'd mentioned it before. My bad."

"No," Ian said. "I want to hear about how hot I am."

Bailee covered her face with her hand. "This can't be happening."

Mia hugged Bailee. "Don't be embarrassed. It's cool. No big deal."

While Mia changed the subject to dinner and the arriving guests, he took a moment to catalog Bailee. Dressed in khaki shorts and a white tank, she was a vision. Casual had never looked so good. Her mocha skin was smooth, her body toned and her hair pulled back into a messy ponytail.

His slow perusal from her Converse-clad feet to the silver hoops in her ears made him want to get her alone. Again. He really hadn't had enough time exploring her in New Orleans. And look at God...now she'd dropped right into his lap. It must be fate.

"Ian?" A hard elbow to his gut snapped him out of his wayward thoughts.

Absently rubbing the sore spot, he forced his attention away from Bailee to Mia. When he met her knowing—and irritated—eyes, he knew he'd been caught. His best friend didn't miss anything. They hadn't voted her Most Likely to Solve a Crime in high school for nothing. "Yes?"

"Do you mind walking with me over to check on Nonna?"

"Of course," he replied. For the first time, he wondered what he'd missed while he'd been checking Bailee out.

"Good." Mia graced Ian with a hard eye roll before turning her attention back to Bailee and Mason. "What's this I hear about you applying at the hospital?" Mia asked Bailee.

Ian wanted to know the answer to that question, too. "Are you moving to Michigan soon?"

Bailee shrugged. "I'm thinking about it," she murmured, turning her gaze to the ceiling, to the far wall on the right, to the loose thread in her sweater, then to the floor.

"I think it's great," Mia said. "Even though he's re-tired, my father might be able to pull strings to get you an interview sooner."

Smiling, Bailee thanked Mia. "That would be awe-some."

"My mother dragged him to the spa with her today. But I'll make sure I give him the heads-up at the cock-tail party. He'll definitely want to talk to you."

"Well, it doesn't hurt to have a conversation." Bailee glanced at him before turning to Mia. "But I'm still not sure of my plans yet."

Obviously, Ian didn't know Bailee at all, but he knew a lie when he saw it. The woman in front of him was many things, but indecisive didn't seem to be one of them. He'd bet money she'd already started pack-ing for her move. "Where do you live now?" He didn't really care about the details, but he did enjoy making her nervous.

"I live in Columbus," Bailee answered, eyeing the door.

Ian shook his head and shot her a mock glare. "You better be careful around these parts." He pretended not to notice the way Mia watched him. His best friend looked from Bailee to Ian, then back to Bailee.

Mason laughed. "Whatever, man. When Ohio State beats Michigan this year, I'll be sure to gloat."

That was the one thing Ian didn't like about Mia's future husband. Even though he worked at Michigan Medicine, Mason was still a Buckeye at heart. Ohio, Columbus, Buckeye Nation and Scarlet were all fight-ing words. The rivalry between the two schools was legendary, and Ian made sure he stayed far away from

Mason during football season. No sense in ruining relationships over a game. Because Ian bled maize and blue, Michigan's team colors.

"That's right," Bailee agreed. "When was the last time you guys won a game anyway?"

"Don't start," Mia said, stepping in front of him. His best friend knew that was a sensitive subject for him. "I'm declaring this a football-free zone this week. No Wolverines, no Buckeyes. How about those Tigers?"

Ian waved a hand in dismissal. The Detroit Tigers, while near and dear to his heart, were also a sore subject for him. Especially since they couldn't win a game to save his life.

"Or those Detroit Lions?" Bailee said, a gleam in her mischievous eyes.

Mason shook his head. "Bai, please. Let's not get Ian started about Detroit sports right now. He's a diehard."

"What do you do?" Ian asked Bailee in an attempt to steer the conversation away from sports.

"I'm a nurse," Bailee answered.

"Stop playing, Bai." Mia waved a dismissive hand at Bailee. "You're totally downplaying your career."

"My sister is so modest," Mason added, with a proud grin. "She's a nurse anesthetist and DNP."

Ian tilted his head. "Ah… Impressive."

Bailee's eyes flashed to him then. A frown creased her forehead before she schooled her features. "I…um. I have to go. Mase, I'll see you in a bit." She hurried off, and once again he was left watching her retreat and wondering what she'd been thinking.

Mason turned to him. "I don't get it. I'm sorry, man. She's had some things going on. I think she's just tired. I should go find her." Mason kissed Mia quickly, and took off after his sister.

An oven mitt hit Ian in the face, startling him. He blinked, then looked down at the textured gray-and-yellow mitt. Another one whizzed past his head, and he ducked, barely missing a third one. "What the—?" Next came a matching pot holder, but he caught it. "Mia, what the hell are you doing?"

"Stop looking at her like that." Mia pointed her finger at him.

"Like what?" He had no choice but to play ignorant because Mia knew what he was really thinking. She'd throw the pot at him next.

"She's Mason's sister, a good girl and off-limits to you."

"Stop trippin'. I was just looking." Mia didn't need to know the sordid details. "Bailee is a beautiful woman."

"Whatever. Don't mess up my wedding weekend. Besides, Bailee just got out of a long-term relationship."

Curiosity piqued, Ian leaned forward, resting his arms on the countertop. "Really?" *Did Bailee cheat on her boyfriend with me?* "How long ago?"

"A few weeks, I guess." Mia shrugged, and gathered the oven mitts she'd thrown. "Mase said she just broke up with the guy out of the blue, and took off on a getaway with her best friend. I don't have all the details. Their family is really close with the boyfriend's family. Well, the fiancé."

"Fiancé? She was engaged?"

Mia frowned. "Yes."

"Hmm." Ian stretched and let out a long dramatic yawn. "Maybe I should go lie down for about an hour. I'm tired. Traveling takes a lot out of ya. Can we go see Nonna later?"

"Ian, wait—"

But Ian didn't give Mia a chance to complete her thought because he had to go. Bailee had some explaining to do.

Bailee peeked around the corner, into the kitchen. *Empty.* Sighing, she headed toward the refrigerator. She'd ducked into the massive library for a half hour, and had wound up thumbing through the impressive collection. If she'd wanted to get away, she'd found the perfect safe haven. Immersing herself in a book was her favorite pastime. She read wide, enjoying several genres, from classics to thrillers to smutty romance— the hotter and wilder the better. Fortunately for her, she'd found the perfect distraction. A romantic comedy. The flirty banter and insane sexual chemistry between the hero and heroine in the first chapter had hooked her right away.

Her plan? Grab a glass of wine and a snack and retreat to her room until it was time to meet up with her parents. Opening the sleek glass and stainless-steel fridge, she sighed. *So much food.* Decision made, she pulled out lunch meat, cheese, tomatoes, lettuce and Miracle Whip.

Bailee opened several drawers before she located the flatware and pulled out a knife. On the counter stood a bottle of red wine. *That would do for now.* It didn't take her long to find the wineglasses. She filled one with the merlot and took a sip. Next, she grabbed a plate from another cabinet.

Focused on the task at hand, she prepared her sandwich and sipped her wine. Once she finished, she didn't even bother cutting it in half. No, she simply took a bite and moaned. *So good.* Bailee topped off her glass again, swiped a few paper napkins from the dispenser and picked up her plate.

"Things would have been so much easier if you would have just told me your real name in New Orleans."

Bailee yelped, nearly dropping her plate with her sandwich on the floor. She set it on the counter with a thud. "Shoot, don't scare me like that again."

Her stomach roiled, and she closed her eyes tightly. *Maybe he won't be so hot when I open my eyes again.* Letting out a heavy sigh, she cracked one eye open. Right away, she noticed several things. Not only was he *still* hot, she'd never seen a man look so good in jeans and a T-shirt. And the tattoo that stretched from his wrist to his forearm made her want to explore his body again. She didn't remember that from their dalliance in New Orleans. *And she loved tattoos.*

Ian smirked, no doubt realizing his effect on her. *Lord, help me.* His smirk was so hot she felt naked under his heated gaze.

"Bailee."

A low groan escaped her lips. His voice was like Hennessy on ice, it was so smooth.

Bailee had thought about him so many times since she'd come home, even against her better judgment. But...*damn.* Her memories didn't do him justice. At all. Ian stood at least six-feet-perfect-inches tall, with muscles for days and a sexy, short Mohawk-style cut. Eyes the color of rich milk chocolate and a smile that seemed to melt her from the inside capped off the irresistible package.

He cocked his head, raising a curious brow. "Are you okay?"

She finished off her wine and set the empty glass

on the counter. "I'm fine. Just going to head to my room and read."

Ian stepped closer, and she fought the urge to retreat. "We need to talk," he told her.

"About what?" She tapped the granite with her finger. "There's nothing to talk about."

"How about the fact that we slept together? Or the fact that you lied and told me your name was Aries?"

She smirked. "Oh, please. You know you didn't believe that." Ian opened his mouth to speak, and she rushed on. "Besides, the whole point of a one-night stand is to remain anonymous. Right? I never thought I'd see you again."

"But you did." Ian let out a humorless chuckle. "We *are* seeing each other again."

"So? We agreed that it would only be one night." One night that had been seared into her brain. One night that she wanted to repeat.

"I didn't say that."

Bailee shot him an incredulous look. "You did! When we met at the hotel bar. It was implied we'd—"

"Bailee, that was you. You're the one who gave me a fake name and kicked me out of your hotel room."

Strangely, she hadn't remembered their interaction that way. But she dug in her heels anyway. "That's neither here nor there. The point is… Well, there is no point. No sense in talking about that night because it's in the past. And you can't tell anyone how we met."

"Why?" He folded his arms across his incredibly firm and muscular chest.

Bailee tried not to stare. She really did. But he was so freakin' hot it was hard not to just look at him.

"Better yet," he continued, "*who* do you want to hide it from? Your fiancé?"

Bailee reared back on her heels. "What?"

"You heard me. You were engaged to be married."

"Not that I owe you an explanation, but I *was* engaged, as in past tense." She crossed her arms and shot him a pointed glare. "And who told you that?"

"Does it matter?"

"Not really. But just so you know, I no longer have a fiancé or a boyfriend. I'm not a cheater."

"Good."

"Good," she repeated louder. "I'm going to my room."

His arm blocked her retreat. "Wait." She paused. "I'm sorry. I didn't mean to imply that you're a cheater. Mia told me that you'd just come out of a long relationship, that your trip happened after the breakup."

Bailee was going to kill Mason, then Mia, for opening their big mouths. "No need to apologize. I have to go."

"Bailee, how about we start over? Do you think we can do that?"

She craned her head to meet his gaze. "I'm listening."

"I won't say anything to anyone about us. But I won't pretend I don't find you very attractive. And I won't pretend that I'm not interested in exploring that attraction."

His confession shocked her to the bone and heat surged through her, burning so hot she braced herself with a hand on the counter. The ache between her legs intensified every second they stood near each other.

Time stretched out, and her gut twisted with want. They'd only been in each other's company for a few minutes, but it felt like she'd been with him forever. Neither of them said a word.

Sexual tension…two words that had never really applied to Bailee, never really had a place in the same sentence where she was concerned. But in that moment, she could cut it with a butcher knife. Something about Ian called to her on a primitive level, in a *do-me-baby-all-night-long* way. She had to get out of there, before she dropped to her knees and begged him to put her out of her misery.

He searched her eyes. She saw no flicker of amusement in his. "I can't pretend, Bailee."

"Ian," she whispered, unsure how she should respond. She was lost in his brown eyes, hypnotized by the *more* she swore she saw in his orbs. She couldn't quite put her finger on what shined back at her, but it was hot.

Their gazes never wavered, and Bailee couldn't look away if she tried. He was so close she could smell the faint scent of his soap. His eyes flickered to her lips, and his tongue peeked out to wet his own. He leaned forward. And she was so caught up in an Ian trance, she didn't back away.

Do it.

She should be alarmed by that inner voice, the devil on her shoulder that told her to let him kiss her, to let him do more than kiss her. But she wasn't. The only thing she wanted in that moment was his mouth on hers, his tongue stroking hers.

"Bai!"

Mason's voice snapped them out of their trance, and Ian dropped her arm as if she'd burned him.

Her brother walked into the kitchen, a wide grin on his face. "There you are."

Bailee smoothed her hair back with shaky hands. "Mase. What's up?"

"Mom and Dad are in the sunroom. I told them I'd come find you." Mason glanced at Ian, then back at her. "Ready for this?"

No. "Sure," she lied. Bailee brushed past him and picked up her plate. Exhaling, she stole another glance at Ian before turning to her brother. "Let's go, Mase. See you later, Ian." And without another word, she followed Mason out of the kitchen.

Chapter 5

Ian let out a string of incredibly nasty curse words. When he'd spotted Bailee in the kitchen earlier, the plan wasn't to let her get under his skin again. But she had. His intention was only to confront her on lying about her name and maybe get her to consider another night with him. But no…he'd acted like some sort of lovesick sap.

Who says *I can't pretend* anyway? Apparently, he did. And then she had the nerve to tell him it was only *one* night? That was his line. He left women hanging, not vice versa.

"How about we start over," he grumbled, repeating what he'd told her earlier.

What the hell was wrong with him? He'd never met anyone who made him feel like he had to prove himself. *Shit, I'm Ian Damn Jackson.* Dr. Ian Jackson.

Maybe he'd skip the food and crack open a bottle

of liquor. Mia would kill him, though. And this week was about her, not Bailee, and certainly not their *one* night together.

"What's up?" Myles stepped into the kitchen. "Talking to yourself?"

Ian looked up and grinned. "What's up, man?" He gave his brother a man hug. They hadn't seen each other in months. "When did you get here?"

His twin glanced at his watch. "About thirty minutes ago. You didn't answer the question. Since when did you start talking to yourself?"

"I was just thinking about work," Ian lied. "I had planned to at least check my emails when I got here, but Mia wanted to talk about the wedding."

"I ran into Mia and Mason outside. They told me I could find you somewhere in here, man of honor." Myles barked out a laugh. "Is your tux the same color as the bridesmaids' dresses? Will you have to hold a bouquet while you walk down the aisle? Line up to catch the bouquet instead of the garter?"

Myles's reaction basically gave him a taste of what he'd have to endure when El and Drake arrived the next morning. Ian glared at his brother. "Man, shut the hell up. Don't play me."

"You have to admit, it's funny. And if the shoe was on *my* foot, you would never let me live it down."

That part was true. "Well, it's a good thing you're not me."

"Sorry about last night, man," Myles said, changing the subject. "I got caught up at work."

Ian had expected Myles to stop by Drake and Love's house yesterday, but his brother had called to let them know he got held up at the hospital. Ian waved him off. "It's cool. You know I know the drill."

"I figured I'd hit the road early, though, and make the cocktail party tonight."

Ian clasped his brother's shoulder. "Good. You need some time away from the hospital."

"Tell me about it." Myles rubbed his face. "What did I miss?"

Ian debated telling Myles about Bailee, even knowing it wouldn't leave the room. In the end, though, he decided not to mention it.

"Nothing much. I haven't done much, just caught up with Mia and met Mason's sister."

"Ah, I feel out of the loop. I haven't made any of Mia's prewedding events. I had planned to go to the engagement party, but I was called to the hospital at the last minute."

"You know Mia understands. You hungry? I was just about to find something to eat."

Myles slid onto one of the barstools. "I could eat. I could also use a drink."

Without a word Ian went to a cabinet and opened it, revealing the stash of liquor Dr. Solomon had always kept there. "Glad to see some things never change," he murmured, removing a fifth of Johnnie Walker. Ian snagged two glasses, poured a healthy shot into each and handed one to Myles.

"Thanks." Myles took a sip. "Talk to Dad?"

"No. I figure I'll see him at the wedding. Then he'll be too concerned with appearances to hound me about medicine."

"That's smart."

Ian went to the refrigerator and pulled out the pan of lasagna he'd seen earlier. He warmed up two pieces. Once he finished, he joined Myles with his food at the kitchen table by the window.

"So," Myles said. "What aren't you telling me about New Orleans?"

While Ian was away, he'd talked to Myles often. He'd shared stories about the hospital he worked at, the city nightlife, the women he'd met and the work he'd done. But he hadn't told his twin about his plans. He guessed it was the "twin" thing that prompted Myles to call him on it.

Ian shrugged. "I've made some decisions."

"I know."

Dropping his fork on his plate, Ian glanced at Myles. "I applied to Doctors Without Borders."

Myles's head jerked back. "What?"

For years, Ian had felt unfulfilled within the walls of the hospital. He wanted to be responsible for bringing medical assistance to people in distress. What better way to do that than to join an organization whose very mission was to do that? Being in the field, working in areas of active conflict or post-conflict, felt right to him. He didn't have a wife, no children to make it home to. The opportunity was perfect for him at this stage of his life.

"You know I've wanted to do more for some time," Ian said. "My residency is over. Now is the time."

Both Ian and Myles had recently finished their surgical residencies at the University of Michigan. Ian had completed a General Surgery program, while Myles had done his residency in Integrated Plastic Surgery. Myles had immediately been accepted into the Craniofacial Surgery Fellowship, while Ian had chosen to take some time to determine his next steps.

Myles let out a slow breath. "Wow. That's...that's impressive, bruh."

"Thanks." It was high praise coming from Myles.

"Honestly, I don't know why I entertained Dad's visions of my career for so long. Plastics is not my thing. Now, Trauma? That's where it's at. Once I'm done in the field, I'll concentrate on that."

It hadn't taken long for Ian to realize that he didn't want to spend his life doing breast augmentation, lifts or reductions. He had no desire to contour bodies for cosmetic purposes. Working instead with trauma patients, running an emergency room or being called to save a patient with multiple life-threatening injuries appealed to him. Now he just had to tell his father that instead of applying for the three-year Plastic Surgery Residency program like they'd discussed, he would apply for the Critical Care Fellowship.

"I'm sure Dad won't be happy."

Of that, Ian had no doubt. Before Ian had decided to enter the General Surgery Residency program, he'd gotten into a huge argument with his father about his choice. He'd managed to convince his dad that having a general surgery background would only strengthen their reputation in the plastics industry.

Ian nodded, not surprised Myles knew what he was thinking. They had the twin telepathy thing down. "Well, it's not his life to live."

And that's what it boiled down to. Ian wasn't sure why their father felt the need to control their lives the way he did. Growing up, every single decision they made had to be run through Dr. Law. Nine times out of ten, what they wanted didn't matter. The family image, the family legacy and the forthcoming family practice had been drilled into them since they could walk and talk.

They sat in silence for a few minutes before Myles

told him, "For what it's worth, I think your way is better than his."

Ian turned to Myles. "*Your* way would be better than his, too."

"Ah, I'm good where I am."

The conversation about their careers always ended the same way. With Myles accepting his lot in life, like he had no choice in the matter. It bothered Ian, and he knew it bothered Drake and El. Hell, even his little sister, Melanie, hated the way Myles let their father control his path in life.

"I wish you really believed that."

"Look, just because you don't want to follow in Dad's footsteps…"

"Myles, this isn't about Dad. It's about you. But…" Ian stood up and took his plate to the sink. "I don't want to argue about this again. It's your life. Who am I to tell you whose dream to follow?"

His words were meant to have an impact, to spur his stubborn brother into action. But when he raised his eyes and met his brother's pensive gaze, he decided not to push the subject. Instead, he took his seat again. "Anyway, thanks for agreeing to play for Mia's wedding," Ian said.

It had taken a lot of encouragement from Ian and Mia to get Myles to agree to play for the wedding. His twin didn't usually share his gift with the public.

"No problem. Anything for Mia."

"Did I hear my name?" Mia entered the kitchen, followed by Dr. Solomon.

Ian grinned. "Pop, how are you?" He gave the older man a hug. "Long time no see."

"I know." Pop greeted Myles and turned his attention back to Ian. "Glad you could grace us with your presence."

"You know I wouldn't miss this."

Dr. Louis Solomon had devoted years to the General Surgery Department at Michigan Medicine. He'd been one of the first African American surgeons to hold the title of Chief of Surgery before Love's father, Dr. Leon Washington, took over the role. He was so well loved and respected by staff and patients alike, the hospital administrators had begged him to stay. In the end, the money thrown at him wasn't enough to keep him there.

Pop grabbed a glass from the cupboard and filled it with whiskey. "We've been running around like crazed chickens." Pop kissed Mia on her temple. "But I'd do just about anything for my baby girl."

Mia hugged her father. "Aw, thanks, Dad. I appreciate your support."

Ian often wondered how it would feel to have his father's support. But he'd always be grateful for Dr. Solomon. The older man had stepped into the role of father figure seamlessly. Not just for Ian, but for his brothers, as well. Every important event in Ian's life, Pop had been there with a smile on his face. The years had been good to Pop. He looked relaxed in a linen suit. His salt-and-pepper hair and beard were freshly cut.

Pop pointed at Ian. "Mom wants to see you, son. She's been asking about you all day."

"I know. I meant to go see her earlier. I'll make my way over in a few minutes."

"And you know my wife will be glad to see you, too."

"Where is she?" Myles asked.

"I left her at that high-priced spa she loves so much. I had to get out of there."

Pop told a story about his experience with his first couples massage and pedicure. The massage had been nice, but apparently, having another person "play with his toes" had crossed a line. They all laughed when Pop described how he snuck out of the place when the pedicurist went to the back to get hot towels.

"I hopped out of that chair so fast, I forgot my shoes," Pop explained. "Then I had to pay another worker to go back and get them."

"Daddy, you're funny," Mia said.

"Hey, I'm old school. No pedicures for me. I take care of my own feet." Pop finished his drink. "I have to go pick up your mother," he told Mia. "I'll see you three tonight."

"Well, I better start getting ready, as well," Mia announced before pointing at Ian. "And you better take your butt over to see Nonna."

Ian stood. "I'm going, I'm going."

"Don't let her smack you!" Mia shouted after him. "She's been slap happy lately. She'll leave a mark."

Ian wasn't worried, though. He'd take a slap from the woman who'd been like a stand-in grandmother to him. It felt good to be home, and neither his father nor any woman could change that. At the same time, he'd been in enough trouble to recognize it or even anticipate it. And as he headed toward the Solomon house to see Nonna, he had the distinct feeling that *trouble* had already infiltrated his mind—and his upstate haven—with her brown eyes, gorgeous smile and spitfire personality.

The day hadn't gone as planned. Bailee didn't get a chance to kick her feet up and read. Hell, she didn't even finish her sandwich after that talk with her parents. Once she'd confirmed her breakup with Brandon to her mom and dad, she'd had to sit there and listen to all the reasons she'd made a mistake. Exactly what she'd thought would happen.

Instead of having her back like he'd said he would, Mason had left her there to tend to his bride because some calamity had occurred with the wedding cake. It felt like she'd been chained to a desk for hours, being questioned by detectives for a crime she hadn't committed. But she'd escaped with her sanity and a tentative understanding in tow. Her mother had finally conceded that it was best to end the relationship sooner rather than later. The victory was short-lived, though, because Bailee had to agree they'd revisit the subject once the wedding was over.

Bailee stared at her reflection in the mirror. It had taken over an hour for her to get dressed for the cocktail party. It took even longer for her to find the right shoes. But—she twirled in a circle, paying close attention to her butt—she looked damn good. The little black dress fit her like a second skin, and the plunging lace bodice made her feel sexy.

On her way down to the party, she thought about Ian. For the last few hours, despite the many goings-on around her, she couldn't stop thinking about that moment in the kitchen. He would have kissed her if Mason hadn't walked in the room. The thought scared and excited her more than she should ever admit out loud. But she wouldn't let his dark eyes and hard body distract her. She had too much going on to get entangled with another man right now.

The cocktail party had already started when Bailee entered the great room. Soft jazz played through the surround sound speakers as people mixed and mingled with one another. Staff in all-black attire carried trays of hors d'oeuvres. She greeted Mason and Mia, who were standing near the center of the room, before heading to the bar.

When she spotted Ian near the piano with a model-esque woman, Bailee almost tripped and hit the floor. But she recovered quickly, grabbing the ledge of the bar to steady herself. Irritated at her clumsiness, she ordered a dirty martini, extra olives, extra vodka. *To take the edge off.* The flirty bartender slid her drink over with a wink, and she offered him a small smile in return.

Against her better judgment, she allowed herself a quick glance over at Ian—a quick glance that turned into a lingering stare. Dressed in a tailored three-piece black suit, he was too damn fine for his own good. His shirt and tie were gray, and he looked downright sinful standing there. Funny, Ian didn't strike her as a buttoned-up suit guy, though. He seemed like he'd be more comfortable in casual clothes. But she couldn't deny that he filled it out perfectly.

The woman—dressed in a revealing navy blue dress that was short enough Bailee swore she would be able to see the woman's behind if she bent over—let out an airy giggle and took a seat. Yet, even in her irritated state, Bailee couldn't deny the woman was stunning. She wore her hair loose, with long waves falling down her back, and had golden sun-kissed skin. And looking at the way Ian smiled at the woman, he seemed interested in hearing what she had to say. His behavior was akin to how he'd acted with Bailee at the hotel bar in New Orleans. Bailee narrowed her eyes on the two. It was obvious they had something going on over there. Body language didn't lie. And she couldn't stop watching them.

Ian laughed, and the two clinked their glasses together. *That jerk.* She watched him take a long sip of his drink and noted the way the woman then dropped her hand to his arm before she leaned in and whispered something in his ear.

Oh hell, no.

Bailee had never hated anyone for no reason, but she hated that woman. Because Ian obviously found something appealing about her. And it bugged the hell out of Bailee that he hadn't noticed her in the room, that his attention was solely on the long-legged woman. Especially when she'd picked her outfit specifically to drive him crazy, even if she hadn't admitted it to herself until now. Bailee looked down at her short legs and groaned. Knocking her martini back in one gulp, she chided herself for thinking, even if only for one second, how fulfilling it would be to push the woman off the chair.

Jealousy was a foreign emotion for Bailee, so when the tinge of envy wormed its way through her and gripped her tightly, it caught her off guard. Blinking, she turned back to the bartender and ordered another drink. *One, two, three...*

Okay, so counting to ten wasn't quelling the urge to turn around and walk right up to him and tell him what she thought of him. *Which is what exactly?*

Muttering a curse under her breath, she picked up her glass and brought it up to her lips. Bailee wasn't *that* woman. At least, she'd never been the jealous, crazy type before Ian. All because one night of bliss had apparently fried her common sense. No. There was no way she was going to let him win, let him think that he'd affected her. Pep talk complete, Bailee turned, determined to walk away, to not spare that man another glance.

"What are you going through?"

Bailee froze. The low, husky voice sounded like Ian's. But it couldn't be, because Ian was standing with the model on the other side of the room. Just in case, she ventured a glance over that way. Sure enough, he was still there flirting his ass off with the same woman.

"Bailee?"

She blinked. Had jealousy rendered her delusional? Or was it the martini? Sighing, she turned and yelped, nearly dropping her glass on the floor. She scanned the room, noting the curious glances from several people in attendance. A kind, older woman asked if she was okay. Bailee nodded that she was and turned to meet the amused gaze of...Ian.

"My twin."

"What?"

Ian pointed over to the man on the other side of the room. The man she'd thought was Ian. "I have a twin brother. Myles. That's him over there near the piano."

"Twins," she muttered, almost to herself. "Right."

"I'm assuming by your reaction that you thought that was me over there." He smiled then—a delicious, knowing half smile that made her sway on her feet.

She opened her mouth to speak, but couldn't. Because her mouth had gone dry. It should be a crime for a man to look as good as Ian, dressed in all black. His shirt was open at the collar, giving her a glimpse of his brown skin underneath. He looked...oh God, he looked incredible.

He leaned in. "I bet I know what you're thinking."

Bailee swallowed. For some reason, when Ian was

around, she had to remember to breathe. *Slow and steady, Bai.* She couldn't stop ogling him, imagining the naughty things he could do with his hands, his mouth and his—

"Bailee?"

His voice pulled her out of her vivid daydream. "Huh?" she managed to say.

He leaned closer and she smelled the faint hint of cognac mixed with lime on his breath. "Are you okay? You look a little flushed."

Clearing her throat, she let out a deep breath. "I'm fine. Just tired, that's all. I didn't know you had a twin. Any other siblings?"

He nodded. "Three brothers total, and one younger sister. Well, I should say two brothers and one uncle-brother."

"Uncle-brother?" she asked, intrigued by the term. "I don't think I've ever heard that before." Ian gave Bailee a brief explanation of the term, and Bailee was glad for the distraction. "So El is your father's younger brother, who your father raised as his own?"

"That's right. You'll meet him at the wedding. Actually, my entire family will be in attendance."

"Must have been really nice to have so many siblings. It was just me and Mason growing up. I often wondered what it would be like to have a sister."

"Mia can let you borrow a few of hers."

Bailee laughed then. "Right?"

"And Mia will be a great sister to you." Ian waved the bartender over and ordered another drink. "Would you like one?" he asked her.

She told him no thanks.

"So, are we ever going to talk about what happened earlier? Not just in the kitchen, but in New Orleans?"

His question caught her off guard, but she recovered quickly. "We already talked about New Orleans and agreed that we wouldn't mention it."

"Well, after that moment in the kitchen, I thought we should revisit."

Bailee didn't want to think about that almost-kiss in the kitchen, because nothing could ever come of it. So she did the only thing she could do in the moment. Pretend nothing had happened in the kitchen. "I don't know what you're talking about."

He studied her face with narrowed eyes. "Is that how we're playing this game?"

"No game. But I think it will be best if we leave New Orleans in the past. There's nothing to talk about. Like I told you earlier, it was just one night. And that's all it can ever be."

"What are you drinking?" he asked in a low, husky voice.

The change in subject jarred her, but she answered, "Dirty martini."

"Dirty, huh?" He chuckled, his gaze searing her skin with its intensity. "I like dirty."

Oh my. She knew he wasn't talking about her drink anymore, and the realization excited and scared her at the same time. The way he'd said *dirty* plummeted her mind straight to the gutter.

She opened her mouth, then closed it, then opened it again. To say what? She didn't know. He'd flustered her to the point she couldn't form a coherent sentence or even think a rational, nonsexual thought. So instead of saying anything at all, she set her glass on the bar and walked away.

Take that, Dr. Jackson.

Chapter 6

Smoky eyes. *Why the hell is she here?*

Ian gulped down his drink and ordered another. She'd rejected him again. Yet, even though he should let it go and move on, he wouldn't. Because he suspected she didn't want him to.

Bailee acted like she didn't want him, had told him to leave the past in the past. But the more she said it, the less he believed her. He just had to get her to admit it to herself.

He caught a glimpse of Bailee on the other side of the room. She was laughing with one of Mason's friends, a groomsman he'd been introduced to a while ago.

His gaze raked over her, from her head to her painted toes. Long, natural hair swept to the side. *Why is my body reacting to the mere sight of her?* Sexy, strappy sandals. *She's killing me slowly and softly.* Revealing cleavage. *Is that her breast?* Long legs that begged to be wrapped around his waist, while he—

A sharp elbow to his gut drew his attention away from Bailee. Myles stood beside him and pointed to the center of the room, where Mia shot a death glare his way. He must have missed something important. A toast?

Unable to keep his eyes off Bailee, he glanced her way again, lingered on her face. Those pouty, full lips. *Damn.*

"Ian?" Mia called, a tight smile on her face. She held a glass of champagne in her hand.

I did miss the toast.

It was absolutely Bailee's fault. And he didn't feel bad blaming everything on her distracting ass...and legs, and face, and hair. *I. Declare. War.*

Myles grumbled, "She thanked you for coming, bruh."

Ian plastered a smile on his face and nodded at his best friend. He held his drink in the air and Mia smiled, finishing her speech. She thanked everyone for attending and went over some of the itinerary for the rest of the week leading up to the wedding. The guests slowly started filtering out of the room. Dr. Solomon had graciously opened his restaurant to the guests if they wanted to grab a late dinner.

With his mind made up, Ian hung back, waited for the room to clear. Then he'd make his move. Bailee walked away from the older couple she'd migrated to during the toast, toward the door with her head down. Ian started to follow her, but stopped when Myles tapped her on her shoulder.

For several minutes, he watched his brother flirt with his Bailee. Wait, *his* Bailee? That thought alone would have sent him running for the hills a few weeks ago, but tonight he wasn't going anywhere. Not until he had her again. Not until she confirmed what he knew in the back of his mind. Not until she admitted that she wanted him just as much as he wanted her.

Irritated, Ian picked up his phone and dialed Myles.

He watched his brother glance at his phone. Myles scanned the room, a frown on his face, before he answered, "What's up—?"

"Don't say my name."

Myles put one finger up to Bailee and told her to give him a second. "Okay. Where are you?"

"Remember that time I took a monthlong punishment because you let the air out of all of Dad's tires?"

"Yeah," Myles mumbled. "Why?"

"Remember I told you I would collect on that debt one day?"

"Yes. What's going on, bruh?"

"It's that time."

Myles shoulders slumped. "Now?"

"Now. Walk away. No questions, no more flirting. Leave." Ian ended the call and waited for Myles to make up an excuse to go anywhere else. It didn't take long, either. Within a minute, Bailee was once again standing alone. She shrugged before starting toward the door again.

Ian took that moment to intercept her before she made it to the door. He pulled her into the long hallway, in a little corner, hidden from view.

"Ian?" She crossed her arms over her chest. "What are you doing?"

"We're going to talk."

"We can't," she rasped.

He took one step closer and she retreated back. "One

thing you should know about me? I hate when people dismiss me the way you did."

"Ian, I didn't dismiss you. I simply said that what happened won't be happening again."

"I don't believe you," he told her. Ian knew he was taking a chance. She could bolt at any minute, and he would be left there with that feeling that she seemed to evoke in him. One he didn't quite understand.

She blinked. "What?"

"I don't believe you," he repeated, even though he knew she'd heard him the first time.

"Ian, you're acting crazy now. What don't you believe?"

"Everything about you reacts to me." He stepped forward, grinning when she sucked in a breath and moved back a step…then two, then three. Until she pressed against the wall.

"What do you want from me?" she whispered.

Ian opened his mouth to tell her exactly what he wanted when his phone buzzed in his pocket. But he made no move to answer it. It kept buzzing.

"Your phone," she said, a smirk on her lips. "Don't you think you should answer it?"

"They can wait."

"What if it's Mia? Or a patient?"

Ian doubted it was a patient, but it could be Mia. Still, he didn't budge. Finally, the phone stopped buzzing. "I want to answer your question, Bailee. You asked what I wanted from you. I want a conversation. One that doesn't consist of you hightailing it out of the room when things get too uncomfortable for you."

She bit her bottom lip, and Ian held back a groan. The last time they'd been together, she'd insisted they not kiss. He didn't fight her on it, because he knew how intimate the act could be. Yet, standing so close to her, taking in her scent, he wanted nothing more than to press his lips to hers, to feel her tongue against his. It seemed he was in a perpetual state of arousal over Bailee, and it was a new experience for him. No woman had ever made him feel the way Bailee did.

"Just a conversation?"

"Yes." *For now.* "Are you hungry? We can grab a bite to eat at the restaurant."

"That would feel too much like a date, and that's not something I'm comfortable with."

"Fine," he conceded. "A walk?"

She assessed him a moment before nodding. "Okay. A quick walk."

Ian finally shifted to the side and allowed her to pass him. "Quick walk it is."

Outside, they walked along a brick path, toward the gazebo. They didn't speak for a while, but Ian was fine with that.

"I've been wanting to come out here since I saw it this morning," Bailee admitted.

"Really? Is that just because you like gazebos, or is it something else?"

She looked at him out of the corner of her eye, a small smile playing on her lips. "My parents had one at their house. Growing up, it was my favorite hiding place. I could escape there with a book and not go back to the house for hours."

"I saw you with a book earlier. What's your favorite genre?"

A full smile bloomed on her face. "I can read almost anything." She giggled. "But my favorite is romance."

Ian didn't bother to hide the shock on his face. "Romance, huh? What kind of romance? Contemporary, historical, erotic?"

She eyed him warily. "What do you know about it?"

"I have a sister who makes it her business to read every smutty romance novel she can get her hands on. And my best friend is a woman. I've caught her several times with her nose in one of those books. Before she met Mason, she even dragged me to the movies to see an adaptation of one of them. The one with the shy girl and the mogul who is drawn to her for some inexplicable reason."

Ian remembered that day clearly. Mia had tricked him into going to the theater, telling him that they were going to see one of those romantic comedies he couldn't stand. He'd agreed to go only because she'd cried on his shoulder for an hour over a failed relationship.

"Seriously? I'd think it would be awkward to watch that movie with your female friend."

Ian shook his head. "If you're asking if I was turned on during the movie, my answer would be a hell no."

They made it to the fully lit gazebo and she grinned up at it. "I love it. Everything about it is beautiful—the lights, the greenery, the color of the wood."

Ian watched her as she ran a hand over the railing. She was so beautiful. The way she seemed to soak in the scenery around her, the way her eyes had lit up when she peered up at the gazebo.

Bailee took a seat on the bench and looked at him. "So tell me…what's up with you and Mia?"

He frowned. "What are you talking about?"

She crossed her legs. "I notice the way you two interact with each other, and I have questions—lots of questions and some concerns."

Ian knew what was coming next. Most women he'd

dated had a problem with his friendship with Mia. He took a seat next to her. "There's nothing going on between us. We're really just friends."

"I love my brother. And if this were some kind of *My Best Friend's Wedding* type of friendship, I might have to maim you."

Ian barked out a laugh. He knew the movie Bailee referred to. It had been one of the many movies Mia had forced him to watch. "I've seen the movie. No, that's not what this is. Mia has been a good friend to me since we were kids. I've never felt anything romantic toward her."

"It just seems kind of unrealistic."

"Are you speaking from experience?"

Bailee shrugged. "Maybe."

"Well, rest assured, I won't be blurting out my repressed love for Mia during her wedding ceremony. And I won't be pulling her aside before she walks down the aisle to tell her how much I've always loved her. I'll save that for the movies."

"So nothing ever happened between you two? In all the years you've been friends?"

Ian thought about that for a moment. Not because anything had happened between him and Mia, but because he figured it was a question many people had about his friendship with Mia. "No, nothing has ever happened between us. Not a lingering glance or anything you might read about in your romance books."

Bailee laughed. "How did I know you'd find a way to bring that up?"

"It was too easy." He chuckled, and brushed a stray strand of hair out of her face. "Real talk—I guess it's not out of the realm of possibility for two friends to be attracted to each other and suppress those feelings for whatever reason. That's not me and Mia. However, my brother Drake married his best friend a few years ago."

"Had they ever dated?"

"It's a funny story, actually. But no. They went to a family reunion in Vegas, got drunk and woke up married."

Bailee covered her mouth. "Are you serious?"

"Definitely serious."

"And they're still married?"

Ian nodded. "Happily. With a new baby and everything. Her name is Zoe and I'm smitten."

Bailee's eyes softened. "That's cute. I bet you're going to spoil her."

"I absolutely plan to."

"I think that's great." Bailee shifted in her seat, adding another inch between them. He scooted closer. She stared at him and sighed. "I know I shouldn't ask you this, but I'm curious. What made you come up to my room with me?"

Ian thought back to that night. He hadn't gone to the bar to meet anyone. In fact, that was the furthest thing from his mind. A few of his coworkers had suggested a bar night after a particularly hard day at the hospital. They'd lost several patients due to a house fire, and he'd wanted a drink, so he joined them.

When Ian noticed Bailee at the bar, he'd been immediately struck by her beauty. But when he'd sparked up a conversation with her, one that didn't make him want to run the other way, he knew he wanted more. So when she'd asked him to go upstairs, he didn't hesitate. He went with it.

"I didn't want the night to end," he answered truthfully. They'd talked about everything from politics to sports. "I enjoyed talking to you."

Bailee averted her gaze. "We did have a lot in common."

"For some reason, I think you think of me as some sort of player."

She tilted her head. "Aren't you?"

He laughed. "I have been in the past."

"Okay, then. Why can't we just leave it there? Two people who connected one night, and decided to enjoy each other's company."

Ian picked up her hand and brought it to his mouth. He brushed his lips over her palm. "Because I can't stop thinking about it."

"Before you saw me this morning, or after?"

"I hate to keep repeating this to you, but you're the one who ended the night."

She pulled her hand away and stood. "Because that's what happens after anonymous sex."

Ian stood. He wanted her to ask him to stay with her tonight, tell him she wanted him, beg him to make love to her. Because he would. He wanted to. "Bailee, don't take this the wrong way, but I'm guessing you don't have random sex often."

She frowned and crossed her arms. "What is that supposed to mean?"

"It means what I said."

"Does that mean you didn't enjoy it?"

Now it was Ian's turn to be confused. "Did I say I didn't enjoy it? Obviously I did because I told you I couldn't stop thinking about it."

"Well, you never answered my question. Before or after you saw me?"

"Before *and* after. Is that a good enough answer for you?"

Bailee swallowed visibly. "Ian, I—"

Ian took another step toward her. He reached out and took her hand again, this time pulling her toward him. Her sharp intake of breath loosened something in him, propelled him to go further. "I'm not the type of man who plays games. I want what I want, and I make no apologies for it. So you tell me..." His gaze locked on hers. "Bailee, you tell me what you want me to do."

Tell me what you want me to do.

Bailee turned Ian's words over in her head. He wanted her to set the pace, wanted her to tell him what to do next. The simple fact that he'd said those words made her feel like she held the power.

The intense look in his beautiful brown orbs, the lust shining back at her made her feel unhinged. And the heady tone of his voice, the feel of his body pressed against hers, coupled with the night air and the lights of the gazebo, made for a tantalizing scene—one that could easily be written in a book.

An appropriate response to his question would have been "Thanks, but it's better that we stay clear of one another." But she couldn't bring herself to mutter those words, because she didn't believe them. She let out a slow breath, readied herself to speak. But before she could, his mouth was on hers.

It wasn't a simple, sweet kiss, either. It was hard, possessive, all-consuming. His hands cupped her cheeks, his tongue rubbed against hers, his teeth nipped at her lips. Bailee couldn't breathe, couldn't think, could do nothing but let him have his way with her mouth. Her body felt liquid, like molten lava. And he'd done that to her with one kiss? What would happen if he got her naked again? *I might die.*

Bailee wanted to cry and laugh at the same time, it

felt so good. Her senses were tuned into him. His smell filled her nose; his husky groans vibrated through her body and heat pooled between her legs.

Ian pulled back, and Bailee fought the urge to tug him to her again. His hands were still on her cheeks as he placed soft, wet kisses over her collarbone, her jawline and finally up to her ear. His hands, those lips, made her want to surrender everything to him.

Then the heat of him was replaced with a soft breeze against her sensitive skin.

Slowly, her surroundings came into view again and she registered his whispered curse. *Damn is right.*

When she met his waiting gaze, he was grinning at her. It was that same grin that made her want to lose her mind and let him have his way with her. In every position, on every single hard and soft surface in the house.

Briefly, she wondered if she should say something. But before she could think of the words, he leaned in again, grazing his teeth over her bottom lip before he sucked it into his mouth. When his tongue swept against hers again, she groaned. Then she was lost in him.

"I can't seem to resist you," he murmured against her lips. "I couldn't then. I can't now." He kissed her shoulder, sending a new wave of shivers down her spine.

She sucked in a deep breath and nearly collapsed in a heap on the hard floor of the gazebo. He was good. He seemed to know every note of her song. And she wanted more. She wanted him. But something inside her wouldn't let her say the words. Maybe it was because she knew this wouldn't end well. One of them would end up hurt, and she was 99 percent sure it would be her.

Bailee hadn't walked away from Brandon to be sucked into a different type of one-sided relationship. This time, she'd be the one pining away for a man who didn't want her the way she wanted him.

"I don't need…" She wrenched herself out of his grasp. "I shouldn't be doing this with you."

"Why?" Ian asked.

"Because!" she shouted. "I've never done this before. You were right, I don't have sex with strangers. That night in New Orleans with you was a first for me, something I did because I wanted to go with the moment for once. But the regular Bailee, the one standing here right now, is not the type of woman who can be with someone so freely. Hell, I don't go out to bars and hang out with my friends until the wee hours of the morning."

She paced back and forth in the gazebo, torn between running back to the house and finishing this with Ian. The fact that she wanted to let loose with him was doing a number on her.

"I love to read," she continued. "I'm okay with a quiet night at home with a piece of chocolate, a beer and a Netflix binge."

"Have you watched that show with the kids and the alien invasion?"

Bailee laughed at his attempt to lighten the mood. "I have. It was so good."

"I haven't seen it, but Mia raves about it."

"Ian, we're not together, and…"

"Bailee, I know we're not together. But what happened between us is still important. You're important. No matter what happens tonight, tomorrow we'll still be running around doing man of honor and best woman duties for Mason and Mia. And if you're uncomfortable with what is obviously going on between us, I'll back off."

"You would do that?"

"As much as it would pain me, yes." With his eyes locked on hers, he stepped forward. "I can see that you're really stressed about this. And that's the last thing I want."

Bailee let out a shaky breath. "Thanks."

"But I have to warn you." His voice took on a serious tone that made her tense. "This feeling you have won't just go away. Trust me. I've tried to will it away and that doesn't work."

His words stirred something inside her, but she forced herself not to think about what she wanted him to do to her body. "It will work." Her voice sounded shaky and unsure to her own ears.

"Say what you will, but your body is telling me another story."

Her breath caught in her throat, and she looked down at her body as if she would *see* what he was talking about. "Ian, please—"

He placed a finger over her mouth. "Okay. I'm done. Let's go back up to the house. We have an early football game tomorrow."

Sighing, Bailee nodded. "Sounds like a plan."

As they made their way back to the house in silence, Bailee thought about Ian's words. They had several more days in close proximity, and if tonight was any indication, she would never make it through them without wanting to explore what she was feeling for him.

Chapter 7

The next morning, Bailee woke up sweaty and frustrated. Despite her bravado the night before, Ian had affected her. She'd tried to fight it, but it didn't matter how many times she told herself to leave him alone, to ignore him; she couldn't stop her mind from wandering to his eyes, his hands, his lips, his…everything.

Last night, he'd visited her in her dreams, looking like her own personal sex genie, ready to grant her each and every wish. And he'd brought her to one delicious orgasm after another in her vivid fantasies. *Ugh.*

Bailee stomped into the kitchen and headed straight for the fridge. Swinging the door open, she pulled out the freshly squeezed orange juice. She made quick work of fixing her breakfast, which consisted of whole wheat toast, jam and a piece of ham she found in the refrigerator. When she was done, she took a seat at the small dining table in the corner of the room. She pulled out her phone and dialed April.

"Hey, chile," April answered. "What's going on?"

"April, I need to talk."

"Everything okay?"

"I know you said you weren't coming, but you will never believe what happened."

"Girl, you're scaring me. What is it?"

"Mr. Hottie, from New Orleans. He's Mia's man of honor."

"What the hell is a man of honor?"

"Dr. Ian Jackson. Mr. Hottie. You know, one-night stand guy?"

"Shut up," April said. "You've got to be kidding me."

Bailee tucked her feet under her behind and hit the button to change the call to a video chat. A few seconds later, April's sleepy face appeared. "I wish I was kidding," Bailee said. "But I'm not. He's here and looking fine as ever. If anything, he looks even hotter."

"What did you do, Bai?" April twisted the scarf on her head and sat up in the bed.

Bailee's mouth fell open. "I didn't do anything." She scratched the back of her head. "Except let him fluster me one minute, and kiss me the next."

April shook her head. "That's it? I thought you were going to say he took you in the coat closet or something. Girl, I'm hanging up. You do realize it's seven o'clock in the morning, on my day off."

Bailee giggled. "April, you have to help me."

Before Bailee started her quest to cross off several items on her bucket list, she'd sat down with April to go over the pros and cons of each. Skydiving, snorkeling, going on an African safari and visiting Niagara Falls were easy enough goals, but the anonymous sex gave her the most pause.

"Bai, get yourself together. It's not the end of the world to kiss Mr. Hottie."

"Dr. Hottie," Bailee corrected.

"It's a bonus that he's a doctor, honestly. That makes him busy on most nights. You don't have to worry about him being a bugaboo."

"Oh my God, April!" Bailee barked out a laugh at her friend. She needed it that morning. "You're too much. So I guess you won't be coming here to be my plus one?"

"There is no way I'm stepping foot in that wedding resort. Can't do it. I'll help you, though."

Bailee pouted. "Fine, help me."

"Okay, here's my advice. Let him have his way with you, girl." April grinned. "You know you want to."

"I'm hanging up. Bye, April." Bailee ended the call, but sent off a text to April with a bear hug GIF. Her friend might be crazy, but she loved her nonetheless.

Mia strolled into the kitchen, workout gear on and her long hair piled into a bun on the top of her head. She headed straight to the refrigerator and pulled out two water bottles. Bailee watched her open one and gulp down the contents in less than a minute.

"Mia?" Bailee called.

Her future sister-in-law glanced at her and smiled. "Hey, Bai. I didn't even see you sitting in here." Mia walked over to the table and sat in the seat across from her. "I just got back from a bike ride. Woo, I'm tired."

"I didn't know you rode."

"I ride occasionally. Only with Ian."

The mere mention of Ian had her sitting straight up, feet on the floor. "Oh? He rode with you?"

Mia opened her mouth to respond just as Ian jogged into the kitchen. "Over here, Munch," Mia called.

Munch?

Ian scanned the room and spotted them in the corner. He hesitated for a moment, but then approached the table.

Bailee couldn't keep her eyes off his bare chest and strong legs. As he neared her, she noticed sweat on his brow and his chest. She imagined tracing every hard inch of his body...with her tongue. *Turn away, Bailee.*

Mia handed him the extra bottle of water she had, and he twisted the cap open. Watching the two of them and the way they interacted was like watching a train wreck. Last night, he'd mentioned they were only friends, but there was a fondness there that couldn't be denied. She wondered how they had become so close. Ian was very handsome and Mia was stunning, with her dark, silky hair and topaz eyes.

"So you two ride together?" Bailee tucked a strand of hair behind her ear.

"We do," Mia answered, smiling at Ian.

"And you call him Munch?" Bailee asked.

Ian groaned. "This is the exact reason I hate for you to call me that, Big Head."

"What?" Mia shrugged. "It's a childhood nickname," Mia told Bailee. "We've called him that for as long as I can remember."

"Why?" Bailee relaxed a bit in her chair.

Mia told the story, complete with wild hand gestures and sound effects. By the time she'd finished talking, she'd shared a few other Ian adventures and Bailee couldn't help but crack up at his antics. Ian had even joined in a few times, adding his own version to the stories.

During the entire conversation, though, Ian had

acted just as she'd asked him to—like there was no connection between them. In fact, he'd barely even looked at her. And instead of making her feel better, it made her feel worse.

"Well, I need to get dressed for the football game." Mia stood. "Bai, are you joining us? It's a Solomon family tradition."

Bailee peered at Ian, who was typing something in his phone. He looked up, met her gaze, then slid off his chair. "I'm going to head on upstairs to get dressed."

She watched him walk away, then met Mia's curious eyes. "Sure," Bailee replied. "I'll be there. No problem."

An hour later, the family and their guests had gathered at an open field on the property. Dr. Solomon instructed everyone to introduce themselves. It appeared more of Ian's family had arrived. She'd met Drake and El, and their wives, Love and Avery. Bailee felt like a fish out of water because everyone seemed so familiar with each other and she was…not. Also, she quickly realized that she was surrounded by a bunch of extremely competitive people whose sole purpose was to win. And she knew next to nothing about playing football, which was pretty much a sin in her household. Basketball? Definitely. Softball? Somewhat. Football? Hell, no.

They were split into opposing teams, with Mia and Mason as captains. Mia, of course, chose Ian. Mason chose her. She almost felt sorry for her brother because she knew she would be no help to him.

After the coin toss, it was determined that Mason's team would play offense first, and she was elected to be the wide receiver.

Shocked, she turned to Mason, eyes wide and mouth hanging open. "Are you crazy? You know I don't know what I'm doing. And if I'm not mistaken, wide receivers are integral to the game."

Mason patted her shoulder lovingly. "You'll be fine. It was a strategic move. You're a runner. We need fast people on the field."

Bailee grumbled a curse. "Good luck with that."

Dr. Solomon walked among the teams, his hands clasped behind his back. "First and foremost, this is a family game. We love each other, and we won't hurt each other." The older man cut a glare at Ian. "That goes for you, son."

Ian shrugged, and met Bailee's eyes briefly before turning away. "Hey, it's a game. We're playing to win. If Myles gets in my way, I make no promises."

Bailee glanced at her teammate Myles, standing to her right. The argument between Mia and Mason that had occurred several minutes earlier still rang in her ears. The two had argued over why the twins were not allowed to play on the same team. Apparently, they cheated when they played together.

"That's if you can catch me, Munch," Myles taunted with a smirk.

"Attention on me, teams," Dr. Solomon said. "As I was saying, we're all about family here. Let's greet each other as such."

Dr. Solomon walked away, and Bailee watched as members of opposite teams greeted each other with hugs or handshakes. She looked up to see Ian in front of her. *Oh boy.*

Determined to appear controlled, even though the sight of him brought back memories of that unforgettable kiss, she reached out, intent on giving him a handshake or an awkward side hug. But when his arms tugged her forward right into his hard chest, she froze. *Don't breathe, don't react, and whatever you do, don't...*

A low moan erupted from her throat. No, it was more like a purr. He smelled like heaven, and she couldn't help but sigh in contentment. Her body was officially a traitor because it liked everything about him.

She stepped back a little and peered up at him.

He grinned. "If you're trying to act like you don't want me, you need to stop looking at me like that."

Then he took off at a jog, leaving her right where she was.

Ian considered his options. He could either go over there, pick Bailee up and carry her off the field like some sort of urban caveman, or he could throw the football and hit Myles in the head. He chose option number two, sending the ball sailing in the air. Fortunately for his twin, he missed the noggin and connected with Myles's shoulder blade.

His twin let out a loud expletive and glared at him. "What the hell, Ian?" Myles rubbed his shoulder. "Watch where you're throwing that damn ball."

"What's going on, bruh?" Drake asked from behind him.

"That's my question, too," El said, approaching them. "You hit him on purpose."

Ian tilted his head to the sky. He should have known someone would have seen his jealous display, but he'd had enough of Myles flirting with Bailee. And he couldn't stand the fact that the groomsmen were winking and grinning at her, either.

He'd tried. He really had tried to respect her wishes and keep his distance. It had been hard to ignore her at the kitchen table that morning, hard to pretend they were nothing more than acquaintances. And he couldn't deny that she felt so good in his arms when he'd hugged her earlier. That cute little purr she let out almost brought him to his knees.

"Ian?" Drake said, pushing him out of his trance. "What's up, man?"

Ian sighed heavily. "Nothing. Let's get back to the game."

Turned out Mason knew how to handle a ball quite well, and had scored the first touchdown of the game. As the other team celebrated, Ian watched Bailee jump up and down with glee. She wasn't half bad at the game. Her speed had proved invaluable to their rivals.

"Get your head in the game, Munch!" Mia shouted from somewhere to his right. "Or I'm going to replace you with Daddy."

Fighting words. Ian had never been replaced with anyone, let alone someone's father. He forced his attention back on the game, and told himself over and over again not to look Bailee's way. Of course, that pep talk lasted only a minute because he found himself staring at the way she stretched before she got into formation. She'd dressed for the game and the weather, in Ohio State leggings and a short-sleeved matching jersey. Her hair was piled on top of her head in a messy bun. Bailee Sanders was definitely the sexiest wide receiver he'd ever played against, despite her choice of schools.

The next two plays went better for his team, though, and Drake scored a touchdown. But Ian had a new target—Mason's groomsman Charles. The man had practically leered at Bailee the entire game. And she didn't seem to mind the attention because she'd been grinning from ear to ear for the past twenty minutes.

"I repeat." Drake shoved a bottle of water in Ian's hand. Mia had called a time out to make a call to the florist. "What is going on with you? You've been distracted and downright surly."

El joined them, nodding. "I agree. You're being weird."

Ian shot his brothers a side-eye glance. "I'm fine," he grumbled.

Across the field, he noticed Bailee and Charles walk off together. And when the groomsman wrapped his arm around Bailee, lifting her up off the ground and twirling her around, he clenched his hands into fists.

Drake poked his arm. "Bruh, you ruined that bottle of water."

Ian dropped his gaze to the twisted bottle in his fist, and tossed it into an empty bucket behind him. He shook his hands out and picked up the football, ready to pitch it and break up the cozy duo. But then Bailee looked his way and smiled, and he almost forgot to be mad. Almost.

"So that's what's wrong with him," El mused. "I think Munch has his eye on the beautiful Bailee, Drake."

Ian's eyes flashed to his uncle-brother. "Don't start."

Drake nodded. "I think you're right, El."

"What is El right about?" Myles asked, joining them.

El barked out an annoying laugh. "We think Ian has it bad for Bailee."

Myles turned toward Bailee and Charles, who were now talking in hushed tones. "Ah, that makes sense." Ian shook his head, knowing his twin was putting two and two together. "You're feeling Bailee. Why didn't you just say something?"

"Better yet, why are you acting like a lovesick fool over someone you don't even know?" Drake asked.

"I do know her," Ian muttered.

Three pairs of questioning eyes landed on him, but it was Myles who spoke first. "How?"

"I met her in New Orleans," Ian admitted. "And that's all I'm saying about it." Drake laughed first, followed by El. Myles joined in, and soon all of his brothers were clenching their stomachs, cracking up at his expense. "You know what? Fu—"

"Wait, wait." Myles stopped laughing. "Don't get all sensitive, bruh. We're just not used to seeing you like this."

"Especially over a woman," Drake added.

"I would appreciate it if you kept that under wraps," Ian told his brothers, even though he really didn't need to. Although they often gave each other a hard time, it was understood that anything said to his brothers always stayed between them.

El shrugged. "Why?"

Ian sighed. "Because she doesn't want anyone to know that we know each other." That admission made it worse, as his brothers broke out in another fit of laughter. Ian pushed Myles, and his brother fell to the ground still laughing. "I can't take y'all nowhere."

Drake clutched his sides. "I'm sorry, I'm sorry."

He rested his arm on Ian's shoulder. "This is how it all starts, bruh. Jealousy. Then, next thing you know, you're in love."

"You have never lied, bruh." El gave Drake a fist bump.

Mia shouted that break was over, and Ian walked away from his brothers, eager to put distance between him and his amused siblings. His team stood in formation as he barked out the next play. On the snap, he watched as Charles winked at Bailee. But when Bailee smiled sheepishly at Charles, Ian froze in his tracks. He didn't see another groomsman coming toward him until it was too late. The hit took his breath away, and he landed hard on the grass. *Sacked*.

More than a little dazed and sore, Ian groaned. Somewhere in the distance, he heard a whistle blowing and Dr. Solomon shouting, "Flag on the play!" He rolled over on his back and waited for the world to stop spinning before he opened his eyes. Standing above him were his brothers, Mia, Mason and Bailee.

"Are you okay, Munch?" Mia asked, concern in her eyes.

Dr. Solomon was on the ground next to him. "Son, you took a big hit." Pop proceeded to do a quick exam while Ian was lying on the ground. Once he finished, he stood. "Let's help him up."

Myles stepped forward and held out a hand. Ian grabbed it and let his brother pull him to his feet. "You okay, bruh?"

Ian nodded, brushing off his clothes.

"Munch." Mia reached out to touch him, but he jerked away.

"I'm fine. I can take a hit." He glanced at Bailee,

who stood with her hands covering her mouth. She stared at him with wide, sad eyes, like she felt sorry for him or pitied him. And that's exactly what he felt like— a sorry, pitiful fool. Charles stood behind her, and Ian was hit with the urge to tug her away from the man. Instead, he made an excuse to leave and walked away.

Chapter 8

The Solomon-Sanders wedding weekend officially kicked off with a joint bachelorette–bachelor party on Thursday evening. The bride and groom had already had respective parties back home, but they both wanted one last hoorah with their entire bridal party.

Bailee had kept busy the last several days helping Mia get ready for the big day. She'd run errands, accompanied Mason to his final tuxedo fitting, finished the centerpieces and eaten so much delicious Italian food she thought she'd burst—or at least have to have her outfit let out.

Most of the bridal party and several guests had arrived early Thursday morning. Dr. Solomon had reserved a block of rooms at the Grand Traverse Resort and Spa to accommodate the wedding guests. Bailee spent the day with Mia at the hotel, welcoming family and friends.

With all she had to do, thinking about Ian should have been way down on her list. Without him distracting her with his perfect body, perfect lips, perfect everything, she'd been able to finally finish that book and work on her résumé.

But, of course, he was all she could think about—in the shower, during lunch with her parents, while she chatted with Dr. Solomon about possible positions at Michigan Medicine, at the hotel while delivering the cute little welcome baskets she'd made up for the wedding guests. He'd literally taken over her thoughts. And her dreams. Ian definitely gave good dreams.

It was almost like he'd disappeared. The estate was huge, but not so big she wouldn't have run into him in the kitchen or outside. At the same time, she tried to tell herself that he had a lot to do as well to help with the wedding. He was the man of honor, after all. But when he didn't show up for the five-course meal catered by Mia's sister Daniella last night, Bailee couldn't help but wonder what—or who—he was doing. Ian's whereabouts consumed her thoughts, and she'd almost asked Mia where Ian had been. Almost. Ultimately, she'd decided against it, for obvious reasons.

Once they left the hotel, heading toward the Solomon estate to get ready for the evening festivities, Mia turned to her. "Thanks for riding with me, Bai. It means a lot to me."

Bailee smiled at her future sister-in-law. "No problem. I can't believe you're marrying my brother in two days."

"I know." Mia had a wistful smile on her face. "I love him so much, Bai. And just in case you're worried, I'd never disrespect him or mistreat him. I know how close you two are."

Mia's assurances made Bailee happy, even though they were unnecessary. "Mia, my brother has never been as happy as he is with you. I'm ecstatic that you two found each other."

"Mason told me about your breakup, and I've wanted to reach out to you since then to let you know that you can always call me if you need to talk."

Bailee eyed Mia. "Thank you. That actually means a lot to me. I always wanted a sister."

"Well, now you have one." Mia squeezed Bailee's hand. "And once you get me, you get my family, so you'll have five sisters."

Giggling, Bailee said, "That's good. I love your family."

That was true. Since Bailee had arrived, the Solomon family had been nothing but kind and welcoming to her and her family. All of Mia's sisters were sweet, genuine women. And Dr. and Mrs. Solomon had made themselves available for anything she might need. Bailee had fallen in love with Nonna, as well. The older woman was up in age, but she could think all of them under the table, and knew a lot about everything.

"So, I've been thinking." Mia bit her lip. "How would you feel about a hookup? Nothing serious, because I know you're just getting out of a relationship. But I just want you to have fun here, maybe get to know someone."

Curious, Bailee asked, "You want to hook me up for wedding sex?"

Mia laughed. "Girl, yes. That's how I met Mason."

Bailee plugged her ears. "TMI. I don't want to hear about your and my brother's sexcapades." Though she'd already heard the story. Mia and Mason had met while they were bridesmaid and groomsman for two of their coworkers. And the rest was history.

As they pulled into the Solomon estate, Bailee's curiosity got the best of her. She turned to Mia. "Who exactly are you planning to hook me up with?" She took a sip from her bottle of water.

"Myles," Mia said simply.

Bailee choked, spraying water on the dashboard. "Oh my God. I'm so sorry." She fumbled in the glove compartment for napkins. "I didn't mean to do that."

Mia put the car in Park, laughing uncontrollably at Bailee's expense. Perhaps this was why she and Mason got along so well. They both found the humor in the most embarrassing things. "I can't..." Mia held her stomach. "What the heck was that about?"

"Nothing." Bailee scratched her ear. "Went down the wrong pipe."

The lie was obvious, but Bailee went with it. The fact that Mia wanted to hook her up with Ian's twin brother was almost laughable. But she couldn't blame Mia for trying, because no one knew of her history with Ian.

Mia covered her smile with a hand. "I'm sorry. It wasn't that funny. Are you okay?"

"Other than the fact that I could have been choking on a chicken bone and you were cracking up? Sure, I'm fine."

"It's just...you're always so serious." Mia chuckled. "It's good to see you let go of decorum."

Bailee guessed Mia would think that about her. Mason had been on her to let her hair down for years. They'd argued about her penchant for oversize sweatpants and a messy bun, her lack of a social life and daily regimen of work, exercise, dinner, book, sometimes television, bed. Her relationship, the predictability of it, had a lot to do with Brandon. And she'd just fallen into it because she thought that's what she was supposed to do as a good girlfriend. But Bailee had longed to do more, to let her hair down. Shaking that stigma was the reason she'd gone to New Orleans in the first place.

"And Myles is serious, too," Mia continued. "I saw you two talking at the cocktail party the other night and thought you'd be able to connect." She shrugged. "I don't know."

If only Mia knew that Bailee had *connected* with Myles's twin. She considered confessing everything. April wasn't around, and she needed to get it out. But Ian was Mia's best friend. It would be an awkward position to put her in.

"Thanks for thinking of me," Bailee said. "I'm not sure Myles and I would get along. We might be too similar, if you know what I mean."

"Yeah, I do. Is that why you and Brandon broke up? I mean, you don't have to tell me the details, but…"

"No, it's okay to ask. Brandon and I broke up because I woke up one day and realized that I didn't love him like I should. I knew that marriage to him would slowly suck the life out of me. Not that Brandon isn't a good guy. He is. But just not the guy for me."

It was the rehearsed explanation, the one she'd told her parents and would tell anyone else who asked. The truth was a little more complicated.

"That takes a lot of courage," Mia said. "It's hard to go against what everyone else wants you to do. Ian is actually going through something similar."

The sound of Ian's name did funny things to Bailee's insides. "What do you mean?" She tried to sound uninterested, but she definitely wanted to hear what Mia had to say.

"His father is kind of dominating. Well, not kind of. He's a jerk. I've never cared for him." Mia told Bailee about Dr. Law and his impossible standards. "Ian is on the cusp of something great. He has such a good heart, a desire to help those in need. I want him to be happy doing what he's been called to do. But Dr. Law is a nightmare. Don't tell anyone I told you this, but he was so against El being with Avery that he offered to pay off her student loans if she broke up with him. And when Drake married Love, Dr. Law rigged it so Drake could win a coveted fellowship in another state, away from her."

Bailee's mouth fell open. "Wow. That's messed up."

"Right?" Mia shook her head, a look of disgust passing over her face. "But I told Ian he needs to go for what will make him happy."

"Is that why he hasn't been around?" Bailee scratched the back of her neck. "I mean, I just noticed he wasn't at dinner last night."

"No." Mia gave her a sad smile. "That hit on the football field really did a number on his back. My dad drove him to a doctor yesterday to make sure his spine was okay."

Bailee officially felt like an asshole. "Oh no. I'm so sorry."

Mia frowned. "Why are you apologizing? You didn't hit him."

Lowering her gaze, Bailee nodded. "I know. But back pain can be awful. Will he be able to go out tonight?"

"He's not coming. I told him to skip it. I need him

tomorrow and Saturday. So I'd rather he be well rested. But he's moving better today. I saw him before we left."

"That's good. I'm glad he's doing better."

"Yeah, he hurt his back in college. That's why he didn't play football for long. He probably could have gone pro if he didn't get hurt."

"That's sad. I bet he misses the game."

Mia snorted. "I doubt it. As long as he can ride his bike, he's good. He competes all over the place."

Another thing Bailee didn't know about Ian. Just one more fact about him that made her want to take April's advice and let him catch her. "You two are very close."

"Yeah, in that brother-sister kind of way. Trust me, we've never had romantic feelings for each other. That would have been tragic."

Bailee forced a laugh past her lips. "How so?"

"We'd kill each other. Anyway, I better go on in." She climbed out of the car, and Bailee did, as well. "We'll meet out here around six o'clock. The party bus will take us downtown for the festivities." Mia wiggled her eyebrows. "Look hot! And let me know if you change your mind about that hookup."

Bailee watched Mia run into the house. As a matter of fact, Bailee had changed her mind, but not about Myles. Tonight, she'd find Ian and tell him exactly what she wanted.

Bailee thought a little liquid courage would help her make her move on Ian. But she'd had one too many shots of tequila, and Mason had insisted on riding with her back to the resort so she could sleep it off.

"Get out, Bai." Mason held his hand out, and she grabbed it, using his strength to stand.

"Thanks, Mase. I'm sorry I ruined your night out. You can go back and leave me here. I'm fine."

Mason stared at her, his lips in a straight line. "I told you to lay off the Patrón, Bai. It's not even like you."

"That's the problem!" she shouted. "Maybe I want to do something unlike me. Maybe I *have* done something unlike me."

"What does that even mean?"

"It means I need to live my life. Do you know that I'm thirty years old and I can count on one hand the times I've been drunk?"

"You can add today to the list," he murmured. "Come on. I'll make coffee."

She smacked his hand away. "I told you I'm fine. I'm not even tipsy right now." Which was a lie. She was definitely buzzed. "I can walk. Go back to Mia and your friends."

Mason hesitated a little, but relented and climbed back into the bus. "Bai, call me if you need anything. I'll come back."

Bailee knew he would. He'd always been there for her when she needed him. "I'm fine," she repeated. "Go and have fun." She saluted him.

Once the bus pulled off, she shuffled into the house, her high-heeled sandals in her hand. The place was quiet. She figured the staff had gone home and that those staying in the big house were sleeping.

One heel slipped out of her hand, and she bent down to pick it up. To her right, she heard footsteps. Turning toward the sound, she spotted Ian. Dressed in low-riding sweatpants and a tank, he looked damn good.

Without thinking, she followed him through the house, careful not to make too much noise. He walked out of the back door and down a lit path. When he froze, she hid behind a nearby tree. She gave it a minute or so before she started off behind him again.

The paved path led to an outdoor patio. Her mouth fell open at the high-end structure. She stepped under the roof, marveling at the beamed ceiling and tiled floor. It was like a little hidden oasis, almost better than the gazebo they'd been in the other night. There was an outdoor kitchen, a bar, two fire pits and lots of seating. The space allowed for a wide-open view of the pool and Jacuzzi.

Ian sat in one of the cushioned chairs that seemed more like indoor furniture than the normal outdoor furniture she was used to. As she approached him, she noticed he had a book in his hand.

"Are you following me, Bailee?" Ian asked, not bothering to turn around.

"How did you know it was me?" She rounded the chair, and…*and now he's Mr. Hottie, who looks so damn hot in a pair of reading glasses*. Bailee bit her lip, taking in his long, built frame in the chair.

"You weren't being very discreet." He chuckled.

Bailee didn't know what it was. The lighting that gave him an ethereal glow, the cool summer breeze or the tequila that made her want to abandon all of her rules. She swallowed, warring with herself over her next move. There was something to be said for living like each day was your last. But taking precautions and weighing decisions was just as important.

He peered up at her and smiled.

Damn it. That one move, that one sexy twitch of his mouth, was her undoing. Because that smirk made her mind spin and her body ache with a need she'd never felt before. In that moment, every rational thought she had was overshadowed by her desire for Ian. That very second, she wanted nothing more than to climb into his lap and let him take her out of her horny misery.

Exhaling, Bailee plopped on the chair next to him. "Oh, God, this chair is so comfortable," she blurted out.

"Are you drunk?" he asked.

"No, I'm not." *Well, not exactly.*

His forehead creased. "Aren't you supposed to be out with the bridal party?"

"My brother had a fit and made me come back. He said I had one too many shots of tequila. I only had three." *Or four.* "He's so overprotective."

"Ah, maybe you should have a bottle of water." He started to stand, but she placed her hand on his, stopping him.

"Please sit." She tugged at the neck of her dress and shifted in her seat. She couldn't seem to concentrate with him so near her. He smelled like pine and musk, orange and leather. And his lips...

"Are you sure you're okay?"

"Huh?"

"I said, are you okay?"

"I'm fine. Just hot and bothered," she added under her breath.

He laughed then, and she knew he'd heard her admission. "Bailee, you're hilarious when you've been drinking."

"So listen," she said. "I've decided that we're having sex tonight."

His mouth fell open and his eyes flickered with amused surprise. "What?"

"Come on, Ian. You heard me."

The wicked grin was back, tempting her. "I'm not

sure I did. I think I need you to repeat that. Maybe a little louder this time?"

"Okay, fine." She rolled her eyes. "We're having sex. Tonight."

Chapter 9

We're having sex tonight.

Ian couldn't believe this latest turn of events. He'd spent the last two days hiding out from everyone after the football game, only coming out to eat and go to the doctor. Even though the doctor gave him a clean bill of health, noting there was no new damage to his spine, he'd decided to relax until the wedding.

"Hey," Bailee called, snapping her fingers. "Are you going to ignore me?"

Ian leaned his head back against the cushion and turned to her. She looked so innocent sitting in the oversize chair, her knees tucked under her chin. It was clear to him that she'd been drinking, but he couldn't say whether she was drunk. He'd seen her flustered and nervous, but the woman watching him was confident, resolute.

His gaze raked over her, already turning over the

different ways he could take her in his mind. Bailee wore a short black romper, with sleeves that reminded him of a kimono. She'd straightened her hair and wore a simple part down the middle. *Stunning* was the one word that came to mind when he saw her.

On his way to the outdoor living area, he'd heard her walking behind him. He knew it was her from the moment he heard footsteps behind him. It had only taken a few seconds to register the sound, but when he did, it seemed her aroma wafted to his nose. It was distinctively Bailee, summery and fresh, with a hint of mandarin. He wanted to bury his nose in her neck and inhale her scent.

Ian knew he wanted Bailee, but he hadn't realized how much until that very moment. She looked like an angel, so sweet and pure. And she'd just thrown all her cards on the table. To hear that she wanted to be with him again, especially after she'd been so adamant against sleeping with him another time, made his body buzz with excitement. It was almost too good to be true. But she'd told him in no uncertain terms what she wanted to go down that night. He'd waited for this exact moment, had awakened every morning hard and frustrated. And now...

Bailee stood abruptly, swaying on her feet a little before glancing over at him. For a minute, he thought she was going to leave. And he was prepared to go after her. She surprised him yet again when she sauntered over to him and climbed onto his lap, straddling his legs.

"Bailee," he groaned, gripping her hips with his hands to hold her steady.

"You told me you'd stay away." She cupped his face

in her hands, forcing him to look into her pretty brown eyes. "But I don't want you to anymore."

"Is that so?" he managed to ask. It was a wonder he could even formulate a sentence with her so close.

She nodded slowly. "It is. I want you."

He raised a brow. "You do?"

Bailee kissed his chin, then bit down on it. "So much." She rolled her hips, prompting him to reaffirm his grip on them. Because if her sex made contact with his growing erection, it would be all over for him. He'd have no choice but to give her what she obviously wanted.

Maybe he was going soft, but that's not how he wanted sex with her to be. They'd had hot and heavy in New Orleans. Now he wanted slow and steady. He wanted to take his time with her. And sexing her up in a chair outside in the open where anyone could happen upon them wasn't going to work for him.

"Bai?" His breath caught in his throat when she nipped at his ear. Torture. That was the word. The woman he'd dreamed about was in his lap. "We can't do this right now."

She pouted and sat back on his knees, folding her arms over her chest. "Why?" She blew hair out of her face. "You don't want me anymore?"

Ian let out a deep breath. "That's not it, baby. But you don't really want this right now. Not here."

"There's no one here!" She held her hands out wide and turned to the right, then the left, as if she were looking for someone. "Everyone is out having a good time, and I couldn't have fun because I…" She bit down on her lip. "I couldn't stop thinking about you."

The admission caught him off guard. "That's good to know. But we're outside, Bai. In the open. What if

Mason comes home to check on you? You don't really want him to find you on my lap like this, do you?"

"Mason has sex, Ian. I want to have sex. With you."

Ian chuckled. "You've been drinking."

"I'm not drunk!" she shouted. He placed his finger over her mouth, shushing her. "I know what I want."

Before he could respond, she sucked his finger into her mouth. *Shit.* "Bai, please."

Please…what? Stop? He didn't want her to stop. In fact, the only thing he wanted in that moment was for her to keep going. Her outfit was loose enough for him to make it work without baring her to the elements. But he wouldn't.

"Bailee." He slipped his finger from her warm mouth. He was impossibly hard for her, painfully hard. So hard he felt like he would burst open from the pressure.

"Ian, tell me why you don't want to have sex with me. Is it your back?"

He frowned. "No. My back is fine."

"Mia said you hurt your back." Her hands were driving him crazy. Her featherlight touch roamed over his forehead, his cheeks, his lips and down his neck. "I can help you feel better."

"Bailee." He gently pushed her fingers away from his face. "It's not my back. I'm fine."

"I didn't know you played football in high school and college. Mase played for one year in high school, too."

"I know." Mase and Ian had bonded over the love of the game the first time they'd met. They'd even formed their own Fantasy Football league, which tended to get pretty competitive. "We talked about it."

"Do you miss it?"

"No, I don't," he admitted.

The doctor had told him to relax, but hadn't put any restrictions on him. The next day he'd been stiff, but it hadn't lasted long. Dr. Solomon and Mia were just being overly cautious. He couldn't blame them, with his history. Suffering from a herniated disc had taken him out for an entire season of football. By the time he felt well enough to play again, he didn't want to. He loved the game, but his heart wasn't in it.

To the world, Ian had caught a bad break. To the world, Ian's football career had ended before it started. Michigan football fans were devastated for him; his coaches mourned the loss as if Ian had died, and his fellow players had thrown sad looks his way whenever they'd seen him on campus. But no one knew it was his decision to stop playing. Even Mia and Myles didn't know, as he'd chosen to share his decision with only two people—his doctor and Pop. Dr. Solomon had cautioned him against making decisions based on emotion, but in the end, Ian was happier for it.

"Why? I Googled you. You were good."

Her admission that she'd done a web search for information on him brought a smile to his face. "I was okay."

"No, you were good. I read several articles that lamented the loss of your prowess on the field."

When he was a kid, his father had made all of them take up a sport. It had been instilled in him for as long as he could remember that a man should have many talents. And although his father had rarely made a game, they'd still be required to participate. Bringing a second place trophy home for anything was unacceptable and grounds for a punishment.

Luckily, football came easy for him. He already

loved the game, so getting to play it in a youth league, then in high school and finally college made his days more bearable. It was also the perfect excuse to be away from the house. Myles had chosen baseball, while Drake and El both played basketball. Melanie had joined the swim team.

Bailee tapped his forehead. "Are you still here with me?" She tilted her head, searched his eyes. "You look lost in memories."

Even inebriated, she could still read him. He shook his head. "I'm here, Bai."

"You smell so good." She circled his nose with hers.

"Bailee, I—"

"No!" She sliced her hand through the air. "I just want to be with you. Why won't you let me be great?"

Ian barked out a laugh. "You're so damn beautiful." He leaned back and traced the ridge of her nose. "But you've been drinking, and as much as I want to make love to you, I won't."

Cursing, he stood and lifted her in his arms. She squealed with drunken delight, wrapped her legs around his waist. He tried to pry her tight grip from him and set her on the ground, but his best efforts didn't work. Instead, she wrapped her arms around his neck and hugged him.

Leaving his book on the chair, Ian started toward the house, grateful that he'd taken the last few days to rest his back. It took several minutes to make it to the door. Several hard minutes of her little fingers brushing over his skin and her lips sprinkling kisses over the parts of his body that were bared to her.

By the time he made it up to her room, he was on fire. Ian had never been so turned on in all his life, and unable to do anything about it. He couldn't take it. He had to get her tucked in bed, far away from him.

Ian turned the doorknob and cursed. "Bai? Where is your key card?" He hadn't seen a purse. The only thing she had when she entered the outdoor living area was one shoe. He'd spotted the other shoe along the path leading to the house. When she didn't answer, he asked again, "Bai, the card?"

"In my pocket," she murmured against his neck. "Come and get it."

Damn. "Okay, you have to get down." He attempted to set her down, but she wouldn't budge. "I can't open the door if I don't have your key card."

Bailee let out a tiny growl before she relented and relaxed her hold on him. Once on her feet, she shoved her hands in her pockets and pulled out the card. But instead of giving it to him, she held her arm up. "Are you coming in with me?"

He reached out to grab it, but she moved it out of reach. They spent a few seconds playing that game, of him trying to get the key card and her moving it away from him. Finally, he grabbed her wrist and wrenched it from her hand. "I'll tuck you in."

Opening the door, he steered her into the room, pausing at the sight of her bed. Judging by the mound of clothes on it, it had taken her a few tries to get her outfit right for the evening. He brushed past her, scooped up a pile of clothes and dropped them into an open drawer. It took him a few minutes to clear the bed, but he accomplished his task without a word. He drew back the comforter and turned to her. Her eyes were on him.

"What?" he asked.

"Nothing," she said, a somber look in her eyes.

Standing to his full height, he stepped over to her. "What's wrong, Bai?"

She swallowed visibly. "I'm sorry. I just threw myself at you. I don't know what's wrong with me. I've never done that before in my life."

Ian brushed his thumb over her cheek, enjoying the way her lashes fluttered closed. "Don't apologize. I'm glad you threw yourself at me. Now I know what you want."

"But you don't... You haven't..."

He placed his finger over her mouth again. "Bai, stop. I'm not going to make love to you when you're like this. It doesn't mean I don't want you, because I do. Very much. I would just prefer you to be sober."

"But I'm not drunk," she argued.

"You're not sober. You would hate yourself in the morning."

Her shoulders slumped. "Okay." She brushed past him, stumbled over to the bed and climbed in. "I'm going to sleep now. Will you lie with me for a while?"

Ian blinked. "Bailee, I—"

"Please? Just until I fall asleep. I don't want to be alone."

He warred with himself about the consequences of actually getting in the bed with her at that moment. If he crawled into her bed, the thin layer of control he had might snap.

"Ian?" Bailee perched herself on her elbows. "It's okay. I'm okay. Thanks for bringing me back to the room. I'll see you tomorrow." She fell back against the mattress with a low moan.

Sighing, he stalked over to the other side of the bed and climbed in with her. She rolled over to face him, a lazy smile on her face.

"You're here," she whispered. "Hi."

He laughed, turning to his side to peer into her eyes. "Hi."

"Confession time."

Ian closed his eyes tightly, steeling himself for whatever she wanted to say. He suspected it would be one more thing to endear her to him. "What is it?"

"You're only the second man I've ever been with."

Once again, she'd rendered him speechless. He stared at her, unable to respond to this latest revelation.

"I went to New Orleans to treat myself to a good time," she continued. "I haven't had many of those in my life."

"Why?" he croaked. He'd met her parents. They didn't seem cruel, or even unusual. Mason had never come across as a man who'd had a weird childhood.

She shrugged. "I've spent my life just doing what others expected of me, never rocking the boat. I met Brandon when I was five years old. He came over to my house to see Mason one day, and I fell in love at that very moment."

Ian hated hearing the words "fell in love" come out of her mouth about another man. But everything was starting to make sense. Ian was the rebound guy, the "take that" answer to her breakup. It didn't bother him as much as he thought it would. In fact, he was happy he'd been the one she'd let loose with. He wondered how this Brandon guy had hurt her feelings.

"For years I followed him around and he finally stopped running. I was a fourteen-year-old awkward kid with wild hair and braces. And he was a star basketball player and one of my brother's best friends. But he wanted me."

Ian couldn't imagine anyone *not* wanting the beauty

lying next to him. He hadn't spent any real time with her, but he already felt totally and completely drawn to her. "That's not hard to believe."

Bailee sucked in a deep breath, one he wanted to steal with a kiss. But he refrained. She smiled sadly. "I spent years with Brandon, had every first with him. He proposed a year ago, and I told him yes. I couldn't set the date, though. It didn't feel right, for some reason. It's like I woke up one day and realized that my entire life had passed me by, and I wasn't a part of it. I watched my own life from the sidelines."

A tear fell from her eyes, and he dashed them away with his thumb. "Don't cry."

She held his hand to her cheek and closed her eyes. "I'm good. I just needed to say this to someone. I've told Mason and my parents the general bits of my breakup. And I've told my best friend, April. But no one knows how this has really changed me."

"Did Brandon hurt you? Did he cheat on you?"

She shook her head, finally releasing her hold on his hand. "No. Brandon is a good man. He's kind and giving. But he's focused on his career, his ambition. He's set to take over his father's corporation, and driven to the point of pain sometimes. There were times I felt like arm candy, almost like an afterthought. And I'd given him so much of me. So much I couldn't look at myself in the mirror without wondering who was staring back."

Once again, Ian didn't know how to respond, so he remained quiet.

"Then I met you. And I made a decision based on the way we talked, the way you seemed to see inside me at the bar. It was new and different. But it was also terrifying."

"I feel the same way," he admitted.

"I know you have so much more experience with women." She smiled, a wistful look in her eyes. "But I didn't feel inexperienced with you. I felt powerful, alive. I want that again."

Ian searched her eyes, saw the truth in them. Then he made his decision. He pressed his lips to hers. Her low moan spurred him on, and he pulled her to him.

The kiss was soft, yet firm. It was everything it should have been in that moment. She needed something, and he wanted to give it to her. When he broke the kiss, he let out a deep breath and rested his forehead against hers.

"Ian?" she whispered. Her fingers swept over his neck, through his hair. "I want this. I need it."

He swallowed. "If I let you come, will you go to sleep?"

She nodded.

Without another word, Ian swept a hand up her inner thigh, under her shorts and slipped a finger inside her, moving it in and out until she was begging him to finish her off.

"Ian," she cried, rolling her hips in time with his movements and pleading with him to keep going.

Ian brushed his lips over her temple, down her nose, to her mouth, kissing her again. "You're so perfect," he murmured. "You're stunning."

With his thumb, he circled her clit at the same time he inserted another finger into her heat. It didn't take long for her to fall over the edge. She moaned his name as her orgasm pulsed through her body.

Bailee rolled over on her back, her eyes closed. She stretched and purred. The smile on her face cracked his heart wide open. If he wasn't careful, she'd be able to steal it.

"Bai?"

"Hmm," she moaned.

"I should go."

Her eyes popped open. "You're leaving? But you haven't…"

He cupped her cheeks, placed a kiss to her brow. "Go to sleep, Bai. I'll see you tomorrow." He slid off the bed and walked around to her side.

Bailee looked up at him, a lazy grin still on her lips. "Thank you," she whispered.

Leaning down, he tipped her chin up. "Don't thank me yet." He kissed the tip of her nose. "Get some sleep."

"Good night."

"Night, Bailee."

Chapter 10

"I'm so sorry I'm late." Bailee hurried down the aisle, ignoring the many eyes on her. The rehearsal had already started and she'd arrived twenty minutes late, which had been her MO all day. She'd arrived for the bridal party brunch ten minutes late, for one last alterations appointment with Bee thirty minutes late and to Mason's tuxedo fitting fifteen minutes late.

She couldn't seem to get it together. Waking up that morning and realizing she'd thrown herself at Ian the night before didn't feel as humiliating as it would have a day or two before. Because they'd shared something last night that couldn't be put into words. Yes, she'd had too much to drink, but she remembered everything about last night. She recalled the way he held on to her, the tender care he showed when he carried her back to her room, the way he'd listened to her confessions. And she remembered how it felt when he made her fall apart at the seams.

Today, when she'd seen him at the brunch, he'd watched her the entire time. But she didn't feel uncomfortable under his penetrating stare. She felt safe.

"Where have you been?" Mase asked when she stepped up to her spot beside him. "I was worried."

"I'm fine. Just moving a little slow today."

"I see," he grumbled. "I told you to stop drinking last night."

Bailee rolled her eyes. "Mase, please. I don't need your chastising right now. Mom and Dad have done plenty of that today."

Her parents had cornered her in the hallway on her way down to breakfast. Of course, her mother wanted to talk about her canceled nuptials and how poor Brandon was heartbroken and deserved a conversation. The lecture didn't stop until she'd shouted at her mother to just leave it alone, and stormed off.

The wedding coordinator announced that they would run through the ceremony again, and the wedding party headed toward the entrance of the room.

On her way, Ian stepped in beside her. "Are you okay?"

She smiled. "I'm fine. Just running a little behind."

He leaned into her as they walked. "All day?"

She froze, turning to him. "What have you heard?"

"Nothing, calm down. You were late to breakfast, and I was at the tuxedo fitting before Mason, and he mentioned not knowing where you were."

Bailee felt a flush work its way up her neck to her cheeks. "I can't exactly lie and say you're off base."

"Good, because lying is not your strong suit."

Her mouth fell open, and she shoved him playfully. "How would you know?"

"Do you even want to go there?"

Averting her gaze, she shook her head. "I don't need to. I hope I didn't…" She twisted her fingers together, trying to find the right words. "I mean… I don't want you to think I was just talking out of my head last night. I'd been drinking, but I remember everything that happened."

A whisper of a smile crept across his face. "Good. So then it won't shock you when I tell you that I didn't forget what you said, and I fully intend to finish what you started last night."

Bailee's mouth fell open, and he took one finger and tapped her chin up, closing it. But a sexy response escaped her mind at that moment.

He leaned in, his lips close to her ear. She couldn't help but scan the room, to see if anyone was paying them any attention. Surprisingly no one was. "I told you to stop looking at me like that," he said.

"Like what?" Her question came out as a breathless whisper.

The heat in his eyes made her knees feel weak. "Like you want me to pick you up and carry you out of here right now." His voice was a low growl, and it made her want to lean in for more, wedding party, wedding rehearsal, wedding ceremony and all the guests be damned. She wanted more of everything he had to offer.

"Alright, people!" the wedding coordinator shouted, pulling Bailee out of her haze. "Line up. We'll run through this a few more times before we're done."

Mia jogged over to them. "Ian, come with me."

Ian winked at Bailee before he let Mia lead him away. And Bailee grabbed hold of a chair to remain standing.

She tried to concentrate the rest of the rehearsal, to

focus. But she couldn't stop thinking about Ian. Despite
her efforts to stay far away from him for the remain-
der of the rehearsal and avoid eye contact, she found
herself glancing his way, only to find him staring at
her. He'd promised to finish what she'd started, and
she anticipated all the naughty things he would do to
her if she let him. And she would. Oh, she definitely
planned to let him.

When rehearsal ended, the wedding party and close
family and friends were driven to Anna's for a rehearsal
dinner in one of the private rooms in the restaurant.
Dr. Solomon had closed to the public for the occasion,
and the entire staff was on hand to help with the event.

Inside the dining room, place cards told everyone
where they would sit. Her seat was between Mason…
and Myles. Disappointment clouded her mind, and she
cursed herself for it. Mia had made it very clear that
she'd tried to hook her up with Myles, so she wondered
if this was an attempt on Mia's part to get them to talk
to each other.

Bailee glanced at her watch and took her seat. Soon,
Ian entered the room with Myles and an older man behind him. The pinched expression on Ian's face told her
he wasn't too happy. The three of them were standing
off in the corner, and appeared to be having a heated
argument. Myles seemed to be the peacemaker in the
situation, stepping between the two men seemingly to
keep them apart.

Bailee watched the scene unfold with rapt interest,
wondering what the conversation was about and why
Ian was so angry. And when his other brothers, Drake
and El, approached the trio, she went out on a limb and
guessed the older man was Ian's father.

"Bailee, do you mind switching seats with Bee?"

Mia whispered in her ear, drawing her attention from the corner. "She's seated next to Ian on the other side of the table. She's allergic to seafood, and the guest on the other side of her ordered the salmon. I don't want her to have an allergic reaction."

"Sure," Bailee said. She motioned to the corner of the room with her head. "Is everything okay over there?"

Mia frowned. "I can't stand him. I don't even know why he's here. He'll only put a damper on my day. I'm going to tell my daddy to step in." Mia rushed off and pulled Dr. Solomon aside.

Bailee made her way over to her new seat, and sat next to an older couple. They made small talk for a few minutes. Soon, Dr. Solomon walked over to the Jackson crew, still in the corner. In seconds, they all dispersed and Ian slid into the seat next to her.

She glanced at him out of the corner of her eye. He was focused on something beyond the table. It wasn't Myles, who'd shot her a sad look. It wasn't Mia, who discreetly dabbed at her eye with Mason's handkerchief. Maybe it was his way of centering himself, of regaining his composure. The older woman was still chatting away, but Bailee's attention was on Ian.

She fought against her instinct to touch him. Because he wasn't her problem. He wasn't even her friend really, and she didn't want to overstep. She knew more than anyone the complicated dynamics of family relationships. Especially considering she hadn't spoken much to her mother after their brief argument that morning.

Sometime during dinner, after Dr. Solomon greeted everyone and told a funny story about Mia as a child, Ian finally seemed to jolt out of his funk. He also finally seemed to realize she was sitting next to him.

Ian turned to her, and Bailee sucked in a sharp breath in an attempt to assure herself that she could actually still breathe. Her heartbeat raced faster with every second his eyes were on hers. She fidgeted under his intense stare. People chatted around them as forks clattered against plates and soft jazz played through a surround sound system. But his eyes never left hers. Swallowing, she wondered what he planned to do. At the same time, she couldn't really process what was happening around her. She couldn't think about anything but how she felt under his heated gaze, how her body opened up in anticipation.

"Bailee." His voice was low, husky.

Goose bumps pricked her skin, and her body trembled with a need that consumed her. "Yes," she said.

"I told you to stop staring at me like that."

She laughed nervously. "You started it. Are you okay?"

"I'm fine. Can I ask you a question?"

Bailee nodded. "Shoot."

Ian leaned in, so close she gripped the edge of the table. "If I were to dip my fingers in your panties, would you be wet for me?"

Her breath caught in her throat. "Oh God."

"Answer the question, Bai."

Bailee made a heroic effort not to close her eyes against the rush of warmth flooding her body right that very moment. She bit her lip, sucked in a shaky breath and turned to him. With a smirk of her own, she tossed back, "Why don't you find out?"

Ian had Bailee where he wanted her, throbbing with need for him. Seeing his father had thrown a wrench in his initial plan to get her into the coatroom before dinner started. He'd spent the first part of dinner stewing, trying to forget the harsh words his father had tossed his way. But he wouldn't spend another minute thinking about him. The only person he wanted to focus on was Bailee.

Leaning in again, he whispered, "You're already wet and ready for me, aren't you, Bai?"

"Yes," she whispered.

"You're so wet, it won't take you a minute to scream out my name."

"Yes, Ian."

His hand skimmed her thigh and she gripped it, squeezing tight and stopping his movement. When his gaze met hers, she shook her head slowly.

He looked her up and down. She wore a strapless, navy blue dress and high-heeled sandals. "You look so beautiful. So mine."

"Yes."

"Find your words, Bailee."

She turned to him. "Ian, you can't do this here."

Lust coursed through him when she let out a tiny whimper and snapped her thighs closed. He slipped his hand through them anyway, prying them open. "Just say it. Tell me you love everything about this."

Bailee stood abruptly, knocking her leg against the table, then rushed out of the room. Ian glanced at the faces around the table. Everyone was still engrossed in their own conversations. Everyone except Mia.

His best friend narrowed her eyes on him and mouthed, *What the hell are you doing?*

Ian followed Bailee out of the room. Seconds later, Mia joined him in the hallway. "Mia, go back inside."

"What is going on?" she hissed. "What did you say to Bailee? She looked spooked."

"As usual, your mind is running away from you. Bailee is fine."

"Ian, tell the truth. Something is going on between you and Bailee."

"Go back into your rehearsal dinner with your guests. I'll check on Bailee."

Mia sighed. "I've been watching you. I'm so sorry about what happened with Dr. Law."

"I don't want to talk about it, Mia. My dad is always my dad, no matter who's around."

"What did he say to you?"

Ian didn't want to relive the moment. He just wanted to find Bailee. "He found out about my application to Doctors Without Borders and basically had a fit. He called me a joke. But what else is new, right?"

Mia's chin trembled and tears filled her eyes. "I didn't want to invite him. I swear, he's only here because of my parents."

Ian squeezed Mia's shoulders and kissed her forehead. "I'm fine. I should be used to it by now."

"He's still your father. Part of you will probably always want to please him."

In less than five minutes, his father had charged into the place and knocked him off his square. And it'd pissed him off that he'd let him. "I should know better, though."

"Aw, I'm so sorry." She sighed. "Find Bailee and come back to dinner. Are you sure nothing's going on between you two?"

Ian laughed. "You're relentless, Big Head. What would happen if I told you yes?"

Mia's eyes widened with shock. "Is that what you're telling me?"

"No. I just asked a question."

"Okay, so if you told me yes, I'd wonder why and how it happened. Then I guess I would have no choice but to accept it. With a firm warning not to hurt her," she added with a growl.

"Mia, I love you. Thank you for always having my back."

"Way to change the subject, Munch." Mia winked and pulled him to her in a tight embrace. "You know that will never change. Even once I'm married to Mason." She peered up at Ian. "I love you. You're my best friend, for life."

Ian snickered. "Or until Mason tells you to stop seeing me."

Mia smacked him on the arm. "Not going to happen."

"It won't." Bailee approached them, her arms crossed over her breasts. She looked at Ian. "My brother would never tell Mia to dump you."

"Bai? Are you good?" Mia asked, squeezing Bailee's hands. "I was worried when you stood and bolted out of the room. I blamed Ian."

"It wasn't his fault," Bailee said.

"See." Ian gestured toward Bailee. "She told you it wasn't my fault, so let's drop it."

"I just had to get some air." Bailee made a show of fanning herself. "It was kind of hot in there."

Mia nodded. "I know, right? I thought it was just me. I'm going to have the staff adjust the thermostat." Mia went back in the room, leaving Ian and Bailee in the hallway.

"Bailee, I'm sorry."

"For what?"

"I didn't mean to be so forward with you."

"Ian, don't apologize. You were right. I loved every minute of it."

A bolt of lust buzzed through him, and he stepped closer to her. Tracing the hem of her short dress, he hiked it up just a little. Her eyes were hazy with desire, and pride coursed through Ian. He'd made her feel that way. He'd succeeded in his quest to drive her crazy with need for him.

The air around them crackled, even as they heard loud laughter and the clink of glasses in the dining room behind them. Ian feathered a finger over her collarbone. "Your call. Tell me what you want me to do."

Bailee's mouth fell open. "Oh," she breathed. "I…" She swallowed visibly and shifted her weight from one foot to the other before dropping her gaze.

"Ian?" Mason poked his head out of the door. His eyes lit up when he saw Bailee. "Bai? There you are." He joined them in the hallway. "I wondered where you went. You got up so fast. Everything okay?"

Bailee nodded quickly. "I'm fine. I needed air."

And Ian needed to get her alone. Now. "How about I take you back up to the house?"

"I can't leave," Bai said. "And you can't, either."

"Yeah, Ian," Mason agreed, as he took Bailee's hand in his. "Come on, Bai. Mom and Dad want to take family portrait number three thousand, four hundred and fifty-seven." Bailee laughed and followed Mason into the dining room without another word.

After fifteen million toasts, countless hugs and one too many pinches on his cheeks, Ian finally made it back to the main house. He'd spent the rest of the night dodging his father and watching Bailee smile at everybody except him. Then he noticed her slip out of the room, never to return.

"You good, bruh?" Myles held the door open for him, waiting for Ian to step into the house before he closed it.

"I'm fine. Tired."

"Is it your back?"

Myles followed Ian into the kitchen. Ian knew his brother was concerned, but he wasn't in the mood to talk to anyone about anything. The fact that Bailee had left before they could finish the very important conversation they had started before Mason interrupted them, pissed him off. And to think, the day had started off with so much promise.

"Nah," Ian said, grabbing a couple of beers out of the refrigerator. He popped the tops off, and handed a bottle to Myles.

"Dad?"

Ian waved Myles off. "No." He refused to give his father any more power over his day. Hell, over his life. "Dad is being himself. Nothing to talk about."

Seeing his father that evening, listening to the man berate Ian for daring to spend time serving the community, had cemented his desire to do just that. The more his father pushed, the more Ian wanted to do the opposite. Not out of spite, but because it was right. Life was more than galas, remote island getaways, name-brand clothes and fund-raising for the sake of appearances. The people Ian wanted to help needed more than a check. They needed someone to care enough to be there, to give their time to causes dear to him.

"I'm sorry about tonight," Myles said. "I had no idea he would even be here so early."

Ian glanced at his brother. "Stop apologizing for him, Myles."

"Yes, Myles." His father stepped into the kitchen.

"No need to apologize for me. I'm not sorry for what I said."

"Exactly," Ian agreed, taking a long pull from the bottle. "Dad has never been sorry for anything he's said."

"Look, I'm tired of being in the middle of you two," Myles said.

"Nobody told you to stand in the middle," Ian told his brother. "I'm capable of talking—or not talking—to Dad."

"Myles, I need a moment with your brother."

Ian said his goodbyes to Myles before his brother left him to face his father.

"I believe we were having a conversation before you had your unfortunate temper tantrum earlier." Ian's father stepped up beside him. "I'm not happy with your plans."

"Well, it's a good thing you're not living my life," Ian retorted.

"Watch how you talk to me, Ian." The tone in his dad's voice was unmistakable. When he was a kid, he knew that particular tone meant he should tread carefully. But Ian didn't care.

"When are you going to watch how you talk to me? I'm not sure why you even care what I do anyway. You never did before. The only time you even looked my way was when you needed me to escort a colleague's daughter to some gala or show up to one of your award ceremonies like a good little son. The fact that you're upset with me because I'm choosing to do more with my medical degree than simply earn a paycheck is ridiculous."

His father leaned forward, his hands braced on the

counter between them. "I think you better consider your next words very carefully."

"Why?" Ian had never heard his father raise his voice, but he always remembered the fear that raced through his veins at the idea that he had upset his dad. But today? He wouldn't give Dr. Law the satisfaction.

"I've worked very hard to ensure that my sons would be the best. You had the best education, the best of everything. I've groomed all of you to be strong members of the community. After everything I've done, I'll be damned if you and your brothers think you're going to disrespect me and speak to me like I'm some punk off the street. Now, you will respect me."

"Respect is earned, Dr. Law," Ian said between clenched teeth. He'd wanted to hurt his father by calling him by the name everybody else did. But his dad didn't even flinch.

"That's right. My name is Dr. Law. You would do well to remember that."

Ian snorted. "It used to upset me, how you treat us. I wondered why you made such a big deal about us playing sports, but never showed up to a game. Then I wondered why you stayed on us about our grades, but never attended a parent-teacher conference. I always knew that you thought you were better than most people. I just didn't realize that *we* were those people. You treat us like we're nothing more than the people who work for you. I'm not your assistant, I'm your son." Ian slammed his bottle onto the granite and stepped around the countertop until he was face-to-face with his father. "It would be nice if you remembered that, too." Without another word, he walked away.

Ian raced up the stairs, taking two steps at a time. In the past, any argument with his father ended with him drowning his sorrows with booze, a bike ride, food or women. It was too late to ride, the beer he'd had did nothing for his temper, he wasn't hungry and the only woman he wanted would rather smile at stupid-ass Charles than him. He rounded the corner, mumbling a string of curses about his life at that very moment when he saw her, standing in front of…*my door.* Bailee's head was down, and she seemed to be talking to someone. *Herself?*

Then she looked up, her eyes meeting his. "Ian." She twisted her purse in her hand.

"Bailee."

She tucked a strand of hair behind her ear. "I'm sorry about…" Her voice trailed off, as if she were trying to figure out what to say.

With every second that passed of her not speaking, not doing anything, Ian grew more impatient. Bailee wanted him to make the next move, and under normal circumstances he would have no problem doing so. But this wasn't a normal situation. Bailee wasn't just a random woman. And Ian wasn't in the mood to try to figure her out. He'd had enough.

"Bailee, if you have something to say, you should say it now. Because I'm tired, and I'm ready to put the day behind me." He brushed past her, pulled out his key card and unlocked his door. But before he went inside his room, he turned to her. "I'll see you tomorrow, B—"

"Ian, shut up." Bailee looked at him then, fire blazing in her brown eyes. "I'm sorry for skipping out on you tonight. I know what I said last night. I know what we talked about this morning. But, Ian…" She stepped forward, until they were nearly touching. Peering up at him, she placed her hand over his heart. His eyes flickered from her brown eyes to her full lips. "When you touched me, I lost myself again. I can't seem to help myself with you. I'm so turned on by you, so consumed with you…it scares me, honestly. At the same time, I just want to feel it."

His mouth was on hers in an instant. The minute their lips touched, he groaned. Anyone could turn down the hallway or step out of their room and see them, but he didn't care. Because she tasted like a dream. Her body molded to his like they were meant to be like this with each other. He couldn't explain it, but he wouldn't question it. Without breaking the kiss, Ian pulled her into his room and kicked the door shut.

Chapter 11

God, I can't breathe.

Ian was on the edge, dangling by a thread. And Bailee was holding the string. Everything about her was too much. Because this? Her? He'd never wanted anyone so much his body ached with need. Never before had he wanted to claim any woman. Not until Bailee Sanders came into his life. Not when she kissed him with a fire that matched his own. Not when her scent wrapped around him like a vine. She was so beautiful, and felt so good in his arms. And he wanted to give her everything he had so she'd know that no one would ever make her feel the way he did.

Her skin was so warm, so smooth he couldn't stop touching her. He ran his fingers back and forth over her neck, across her shoulders and down her arms. The way she shivered, the way she reacted to his touch by leaning closer told him that she wanted his hands on her.

Finally, breaking the kiss, he sucked in a deep breath and leaned his forehead against hers. "Damn, I need it."

Ian didn't even realize he'd said it out loud until she said, "Then take it."

He didn't need another invitation. In less than a minute, with her dress now in a puddle on the floor, he ordered, "Bra. Take it off."

Bailee let out a low moan, but did as she was told. With her eyes locked on his, she unhooked the front clasp and let it fall open, then down to the floor.

"So beautiful," he whispered.

Her nipples were hard, ready for his attention. He cupped her breasts in his hands, placed soft, wet kisses down her neck until he took one hard bud into his mouth. Her knees buckled, but he snaked an arm around her waist to hold her upright.

"Ian, you're killing me."

"Join the club," he murmured against her skin.

"What are you doing to me?"

"Patience, Bai. I'm not done touching you, tasting you." Her breath caught in her throat, and he smiled. "I'll give you what you really want in due time." Ian traced his lips over her ear before he bit down on it lightly. "You're mine." He didn't even bother to add "for the night" to his statement because he doubted he would be satisfied with one night.

"Oh," she breathed.

He stepped back and raked his gaze over her. "Panties. Take them off."

Once again, Bailee did as she was told, sliding the thin, lacy fabric over her hips and down her legs slowly.

His breath hitched in his throat at the sight of her, naked and ready to give herself to him. A low growl pierced the air, and he realized it was him. Not her.

He was so hot for her, so consumed by her beauty, he couldn't think or see straight.

"Come here," he commanded.

Bailee bit her bottom lip and approached him. "Your turn," she said, her voice low.

Ian gripped her hips, nipped her chin, her collarbone, her shoulders, as she removed his shirt. She pushed his pants and underwear over his hips.

"Now we're even." She tugged him to her, kissing him passionately.

Lifting her in his arms, he carried her over to the bed and lowered her to the mattress. He kissed his way down her body, until he was at the apex of her thighs. She squirmed under him, but he held her still. Then he darted his tongue out to taste her finally, closing his eyes at the feel of her against his tongue.

"Bailee," he murmured against her bundle of nerves. "Give me everything. Let go."

It didn't take long before Bailee stiffened, and then shuddered with her orgasm as he worshipped her with his tongue. When she collapsed against the bed, he slid a condom on and crawled up her body.

Bailee wrapped her legs around his waist and pulled him into a possessive kiss. "Now," she whispered.

He bit her chin lightly before he pushed inside her warmth, swallowing her gasp with another searing kiss. Ian could feel her muscles tense as he moved inside her. Her stomach quivered, her legs trembled, her arms flexed…every part of her responded to him, to what he did to her and how they were together. Which was good. So good. And he was close. So close to exploding inside her.

Need twisted in his spine as they raced to completion. Bailee let out a tiny little whimper, then a sexy purr right before she came, unspooling around him. She groaned his name over and over again as she climaxed. Then he was done, coming so long and hard he could hear nothing but the wild pulse of his heartbeat in his ears.

Minutes later, Ian rolled over to his back. After he discarded the condom, he climbed back in bed and pulled her against him. She burrowed into his side as if she belonged there. And, he thought, maybe she did. They didn't speak for a while, and Ian thought she might've fallen asleep.

"Ian?" Bailee traced the muscles of his stomach with her fingers.

"Hmm?"

"Thank you."

His eyes popped open, and he leaned back to peer at her face. Frowning, he said, "I'm not sure how to take that."

Bailee giggled and dropped her forehead onto his chest. "It's not what you think."

"What do you think I think?" Ian wasn't even sure what he thought she meant by her words. He just knew it didn't make him feel as good as it should have.

Shrugging, Bailee perched her chin on his chest. "I'm just glad that you didn't give up on me. That's why I'm thanking you."

"Ah, I get it now."

"I'm very stubborn. It takes a lot to get me to budge."

Now it was his turn to laugh. "I figured that out... Aries."

"Oh no. I hated that I gave you that name. It was so obviously fake. And even when you called me on it, I couldn't bring myself to let it go. See! Stubborn."

"True." He tapped her nose. "But I like that about you."

"You do?"

"Yes, I do." He rubbed her bottom lip, smiling when her eyes fluttered closed.

"Ian?" she whispered.

"Yes?" He leaned in, circled her nose with his before he brushed his mouth against hers.

"I should probably go," she said. "We have a long day tomorrow."

"Bailee?" Ian sucked her bottom lip into his mouth until she groaned. "Just so you know, I have no plans to let you out of my sight anytime soon. I'm not done with you yet."

"Oh my God."

"Bailee."

Her name on Ian's lips, in his low and husky voice, made it worse. It made her want him even more. Which was impossible, right?

"I can't," she breathed.

Bailee had already climaxed three times. There was no way she'd be able to do it again. But his touch was so gentle, his tongue was so talented, she wanted to weep.

"I meant to ask you if you finished your smutty book?"

His voice was so quiet, so muffled, she wasn't sure she'd heard him right. "Huh?"

She felt his body tremble with laughter, right before he drew her clit into his mouth.

"Oh God."

"You said that already."

Technically, she hadn't said that. But the argument died on her lips as he licked and sucked, driving her crazy with his attention, with the way he worshipped her body.

"I did finish it," she managed to say. She clenched the sheets in her hands.

"Tell me about it."

Bailee couldn't concentrate on anything, let alone a book that had held her attention a few days ago but now paled in comparison to the real deal. Because Ian was the stuff romantic heroes were made of.

"Uh, it's a friends-to-lovers book."

"What's that?"

"Oh." She gripped his shoulders and rolled her hips in time with his movements. "Uh, it's when the hero and the heroine are friends first, then they fall..." Two fingers dipped inside her. She moaned, unable to finish her thought.

"In love," he finished for her.

"Yes." She dug her fingernails into his skin. "Ian, please."

Still, he didn't stop and Bailee was delirious. In the best way, of course. And soon, she was riding the waves of pleasure over and over again.

When she came down from the high of her orgasm, she felt boneless, weak. Woozy. She could barely keep her eyes open, but didn't want to fall asleep, either.

"Sleep now," she heard Ian whisper before sleep pulled her under.

Several hours later, after an early-morning orgasm, Bailee tiptoed out of Ian's room, careful not to slam the door. She'd added a lot of things to her forgotten bucket list, but the walk of shame wasn't one of them. Bailee still couldn't believe she'd let Ian talk her into spending the night with him. Well, the lure of multiple orgasms had definitely helped make her decision.

Bailee rushed toward her suite, praying that no one

would see her. Because if someone caught a glimpse of her, they'd know what she'd been doing. She'd seen herself in one of Ian's mirrors before she walked out of his room, and "hot mess" had been the first phrase to come to mind.

"Bai?"

Shit. Bailee turned slowly, and smiled brightly at her future sister-in-law. "Mia? Hi!" That *hi* came out just a little too loud.

Mia frowned. "Where are you going?"

Bailee scrunched up her nose. "Um, to my room."

"From where? You look... Didn't you have that dress on last night?"

"Oh." Bailee dropped her head and smoothed a hand over her dress. "Well, I had to run out this morning and just threw it back on."

Mia tilted her head, her eyes narrowing. "Really?"

Nodding, Bailee said, "Yes. I had to run to my car." It was officially official. Bailee was a horrible liar.

"Were you with Ian?"

"What?" Bailee blurted out. "I mean, why would you ask me that?"

Mia sighed, shaking her head. "I'm going to kill him." She turned on her heel and started toward the other end of the hallway, where Ian's room was.

Bailee caught up to Mia and grabbed her arm, halting her movement. "Mia, wait. Please. Don't say anything to Ian."

Mia folded her arms over her chest. Her mouth was a grim line. "I told him to leave you alone."

"Seriously, Mia. I am a grown woman. And why would you assume I was with Ian? I could have been with Myles. Or any one of the groomsmen."

Mia raised a brow. "Are you really going to lie to me

after I've caught you with bed hair, smeared makeup and swollen lips?"

"Fine. I was with Ian."

"That settles it, then. I'm going to kill him."

"Mia, stop. I was hoping you'd be a sister I could talk to about things like this. I don't need another overprotective person in my life."

"Oh, Bailee." Mia's eyes softened. "That's not my intention. It's just that I know Ian."

"And you told me he was a good man."

"Yeah, he's one of the best men I know. But you're Mason's sister. If things don't work out, it will be extremely awkward."

"Why? We're not together. It's just sex."

Mia gasped. "Wow, do you really believe that? I've actually seen the way he looks at you, and the way you pretend not to look at him. It's not just sex."

"It is. So I'd appreciate it if you don't tell Mase. I don't want him to worry."

"I'm worried." Mia rubbed her face. "But…I won't say anything. Just be careful. Sometimes, even with the best intentions, things can take a turn so quickly. Look what happened with me and your brother. I didn't go to my friend's wedding thinking I'd meet my future husband."

"There is nothing to worry about, Mia," Bailee assured her. "Ian and I have an understanding." She wrapped an arm around Mia's shoulders. "Now, you have to get ready to marry my brother. And I have to get showered and ready for my hair appointment."

Bailee hugged Mia and hurried off to her room. *So much for discreet.*

Ian strolled into the bridal suite at his designated arrival time. Since he didn't need to be primped and prodded, he was told to arrive fully dressed. He draped his tuxedo jacket over a chair and headed toward the bathroom.

"I'm here," he announced, his hand over his eyes. "I hope everyone is dressed."

"It's just me," Mia said.

Ian peeked through his fingers. Once he was satisfied he wouldn't see his best friend in her underwear, he dropped his hand. "You're beautiful, Big Head."

Mia stood at the mirror, dabbing a tissue under her eyes.

"Are you crying?" Ian joined her at the mirror. "What's wrong?"

"Just emotional." Mia fanned her face. The makeup artist had already done her up, and her hair was pinned in tiny ringlets with little silver clips. The sink was crowded with various makeup containers, powder, blue sponges and white towels.

"Why are you by yourself?" he asked.

"I knew you wouldn't be late, so I asked the ladies to leave me alone for a bit."

Ian leaned against the sink, his eyes on his best friend. "You good? Need me to bust you out of here?"

Mia let out a half wail, half laugh. "No. I'm fine. Just nervous."

"That's normal, from what I hear. It supposedly goes away once you see Mase."

"Since when do you know anything about jitters?"

"Since my best friend asked me to be her man of honor."

During the rehearsal the day before, Ian had agreed to walk down the aisle like everyone else. But he'd drawn a hard line at handling the bustle thing in front of the church. Instead, Bee would take charge of that job, since she'd designed the dress. Also, he'd told Mia that he would not, under any circumstances, hold her bouquet.

Mia eyed him in the mirror. "What if I'm not a good wife, Munch? I love him so much. I want to be good for him. I want to be the wife my mother is to Daddy."

"First of all, you're not your mother. And he's not Pop. The only person you can be is Mia, the woman he actually proposed to."

She shot him a lopsided smile. "I knew you'd be what I needed right now. See? You're a good man of honor."

Ian shook his head. "Yeah, there is a first and last time for everything."

She laughed for real this time. "You're crazy."

"Seriously, you're a beautiful bride. Mason is lucky to have you, Mia."

She hugged him, and he let her. After today, things would change between them, despite what she'd told him yesterday. And he'd expect nothing less. It was time for Mia and Mason to make a life together. "Love you, Munch."

"Love you, too, Big Head." After a moment, Mia pulled away, sniffling. He handed her a tissue. "Stop crying. I'm no expert, but doesn't that make your eye shadow run?"

"You mean mascara?" She bumped into him with her hip. "You need help. Speaking of, I ran into Bailee this morning."

Busted already. Ian dropped his head. "Really?"

"Ian, what are you doing?" Mia asked.

He met his friend's worried gaze. "What do you mean?"

"She's Mason's sister!"

"So?"

"Ian, what if things don't work out between you? Don't you think it will be awkward at my baby's christening when we name you both godparents?"

"You're pregnant?" Ian asked.

"Shh," Mia said, scanning the area. "We haven't told anyone yet."

Ian smiled. "Get the hell out of here. You're having a baby?"

"Yes, why do you think I've been crying so much?"

"Hey." Ian held his arms out in surrender. "I didn't want to say anything, but I wondered why you were being a crybaby. But then I read an article about wedding jitters."

"You're the first person I've told," Mia said. "I haven't even told my sisters." Ian wondered if Mason had told Bailee, but Mia answered that question when she said, "Mase hasn't even told Bailee."

"Okay."

"So you see why I'm panicking, right?"

Ian shrugged. "No. It's not a relationship, Mia. Bailee and I are just having fun."

"Why her?"

"She's beautiful. Why not?"

"Again, she's Mason's sister."

"And? We're both adults capable of having a fling."

Mia pinned him with her *don't play with me* glare. He stepped back out of habit. "I don't think it's *just* a fling. Like I told her, I've seen the way you look at her."

He sighed. He hadn't wanted to tell Mia about New Orleans, but he did. When he finished his story, Mia gaped at him. "Close your mouth, Mia."

She snapped her mouth shut. "Oh no. You and

Bailee? She's the woman from New Orleans? You just made my point."

"How so? If anything, that should prove that we can peacefully coexist in a family situation."

"Except you didn't peacefully coexist. You took her to bed again!"

Ian turned to Mia, squeezed her arms. "I love you for caring about me. I love you for caring about Bailee. But we're fine. We both know what this is. Now, suck up those emotions and finish getting dressed. I'm getting you down that aisle no matter what." He kissed Mia's brow and stepped away from her, pointing at her. "Last chance to bail."

Mia laughed. "No bailing."

"Good to know. I'll go find your entourage."

Ian left Mia in the bathroom, and tried not to think about his best friend's warnings. Because after last night, after spending the night wrapped up in Bailee, he knew Mia was right.

There was a need in him that compelled him to go toward Bailee, to be near her. He'd told her that first night that he couldn't get enough of her. At the time, it was just something he'd said in the heat of the moment. Now he knew that it was more than that. He couldn't stop wanting her.

Which meant *peacefully coexisting* was a long shot.

Chapter 12

Mason and Mia were married at sunset, on a bluff overlooking Lake Michigan, surrounded by family and friends. The bride and groom shared personal vows that made every woman, and some men, tear up. Bailee swore she'd even seen Ian wiping a tear from his eyes. Once the pastor said, "Introducing Mr. and Mrs. Mason and Mia Sanders," the crowd erupted into loud cheers.

The ceremony was beautiful, and the little touches Mia had insisted on were well worth the trouble. The bridesmaids looked lovely in their coral gowns, and the groomsmen were handsome in navy blue tuxedos. But only one man had held her attention through the entire ceremony.

Ian commanded the room as he'd strolled down the aisle by himself. Although his tuxedo was gray, to set him apart, Mia had arranged for Ian's suit to have pinstripes. He also didn't wear a vest like the other groomsmen. He looked so good, so smooth with his swagger and his dimpled grin, she had to bite her lip to stifle the groan that seemed to always want to escape when she saw him.

Even now, as they posed for pictures, she felt her face flush as she imagined him inside her, his hands roaming her body. She wondered if he felt it, too. Was he just as aroused as she was simply from the nearness of him?

"It's driving you insane, isn't it?" Ian whispered in her ear, jolting her out of her thoughts.

Bailee bit the inside of her cheek. His scent washed over her, like fresh water and woods. She turned her attention back to the photographer in front of them. "You should probably go back to your spot. On the other side," she muttered.

"I'm supposed to be here, right behind you." He leaned forward and whispered against her ear, "I can't keep my eyes off you, Bailee. The way those pants hug your hips, the tiny glimpse of your breast in that jacket. I've never been so attracted, so hot for someone in a tuxedo before."

She fought the urge to lean into him. Smile. Click. Smile. *Oh my, what am I going to do?* "Really?" she said.

"When I saw you standing at the end of the aisle, next to Mason, I wanted to pull you onto my lap and let you ride me." Smile. Click.

His words…the way he talked to her drove her wild with anticipation. Ian hadn't even touched her yet, but she felt his fingers on her skin as if he had. She wanted him in a way that was foreign to her. No man had ever made her want to abandon her code of conduct just to get a taste of him.

Maybe it was the champagne? Or the sweet treats Mia had brought in for the wedding party to enjoy before and immediately after the ceremony? Bailee had tried them all—chocolate-covered strawberries, chocolate pretzels, chocolate almond bark, chocolate and caramel apple slices. Or better yet, it might just be the wedding effect. *Yep, that's definitely it.*

The romantic setting, the candles, the sweet floral fragrance…no wonder she seemed to be in a perpetual state of arousal. Mia and Mason had set the mood with their whimsical and romantic decor and heartfelt vows and alcohol and chocolate. Yes, it was a flimsy excuse at best, but if she kept repeating it to herself, she might actually believe it.

She sucked in a breath. Funny pose. Click. "Ian." She looked around at the other members of the bridal party, but everyone was in their own little world, trying not to look bored at the countless pictures Mia wanted them to take.

"Don't worry about them. Just focus on me. Pretend you're not wearing panties under your pants."

"I'm not."

A soft burst of air in her ear, followed by his low groan, made her want to climb him like a tree, touch him all over, shower him with kisses. "You're so damn beautiful, Bai. So sexy." His voice was raw, hoarse. His hand brushed against her behind, and she pushed back against it. She felt him then, hard against her butt, ready for her.

The photographer ordered the pairs to act like they could stand each other, and Ian snaked his hand around her waist, pulling her close to him. With his hand splayed across her stomach, she plastered another smile on her face. Click.

The feel of his breath on her skin, the brush of his lips on her ear and finally the back of her neck ramped up her arousal even more. She tried to wrench herself out of his hold, but he held her in place. "Don't move."

Weird face. Click. "Ian, you have to stop. Someone will notice." She tilted her head back to look at him. They held each other's gazes for a beat, before his dropped to her mouth. Click.

The sound of the camera drew her attention back to the photographer. And when Mia announced she wanted to take pictures with just the women, Bailee let out a relieved breath.

An hour later, they walked the lit path toward the reception area. The music was playing in the distance, and guests could be heard talking, laughing and even singing with the music.

Thank goodness for traditional head table etiquette. Bailee took her seat next to Mason, away from Ian. Dinner went by in a flash, and before she knew it, it was her turn to toast her brother and new sister.

Bailee stood, and glanced at the crowd before her. She started her toast with a funny story about the time Mason tricked her into cursing in front of her parents. And then she paid him back by telling their mom that he'd taken the car on a joyride while they were asleep one night. The guests laughed.

"Mason, I love you," Bailee said, swallowing around a lump that had formed in her throat. "We've always been there for one another. I don't expect that will change, but I'm glad that you have someone else looking out for you now. Someone who will care for you, someone who will love you through every hardship, every victory you face for as long as you both shall live. To the bride and the groom." The crowd clapped and Mason stood, pulling her into a tight hug. He whispered he loved her in her ear, and she took her seat.

Ian stood next, and told the story of how Mia and Mason had met. Bailee watched him woo the crowd and noticed quite a few women in the audience fixated on him while he gave his toast. Then his gaze softened and he smiled at Mia.

"Seriously, my life wouldn't have been as bright without you. I'm thankful that you and your family accepted me into your life and immediately treated me like I was one of your own." His eyes then focused on the table where his father sat with his family, before he turned his attention back to Mia. "If I had one wish for you, it was always for you to be happy. And I can see that Mason does that for you. Love you, Big Head. Mason, welcome to the fold." Mia wiped tears from her eyes and stood, embracing Ian. When she was done, Ian shook Mason's hand, before giving him a quick man hug.

The bridal party took the floor next in the traditional bridal party dance. Bailee fought back a smile as Ian approached her with a sexy grin on his face. He pulled her close, and they swayed to the music.

She wrapped her arms around his neck. "Nice toast. Touching."

Ian shrugged. "It was nothing but the truth."

"I have to admit, I was a little worried when I saw you and Mia interacting. But now I can see that you genuinely love her like family."

"She is my family. I'd do pretty much anything for her."

"I can see that. It's great."

"Bailee, I don't know what to do with this."

Jarred by his change in subject, she asked, "What?"

"This desire that I have to find a dark room some-where and have my way with you."

When she bit her lip, his eyes darkened. Bailee couldn't look away from the hungry look in his eyes if she wanted to. She was thoroughly under the control of his heated gaze. It went on like that for a few mo-ments, neither of them looking away. The air around them crackled with electricity.

"Where would you take me?" she asked, finally.

"There's a coatroom near the front of the building. I'd take you there. Or the bathroom toward the back of the building. Anywhere I can touch you, taste you."

Bailee wanted to tell him she would follow him wherever he wanted to go, but the song ended and Mia and her sisters pulled Ian away for more pictures. While Ian laughed with his family, Bailee took a mo-ment to speak to several of her own family members. Soon, she'd relaxed with them, reminiscing about old times and even making preliminary plans for a reunion next summer.

The DJ cooperated with her when he shifted the music from love songs to party anthems. When her fa-vorite song blasted through the speakers, she used the music to center her, to keep her mind off Ian.

Bailee allowed Charles to pull her onto the dance floor for a few songs. Mason joined them, and they spent a few minutes doing old dances and going down the Soul Train Line.

A little while later, the waitstaff served the wedding cake. Bailee snagged a piece off the tray, thanked the young waiter and immediately dipped her fork in and stuffed a fat piece into her mouth.

"You like sweets, don't you?" Ian said, taking the seat next to her, his own piece of cake in hand. But he'd grabbed a slice of the chocolate, while she preferred the white cake.

Bailee nodded. "I do."

"You remind me of Love."

She knew that Love was his brother Drake's wife, but the woman didn't look like she had a sweet tooth, let alone a baby. "Really? She's so tiny."

"Genetics, I guess."

Bailee looked out on the dance floor and noticed Drake and Love swaying to the music. "They look happy."

Ian watched them for a minute. "They are. I'm happy for them."

"Your father didn't stay long."

Earlier, Bailee had seen Dr. Law leave the reception after saying his goodbyes to the Solomon family. She'd also noticed Ian deliberately ignore his father when he'd walked out.

"He never does," Ian grumbled.

Sensing he needed a subject change, she pointed to his cake. "How's the chocolate?"

He turned up his lips. "I don't like it. Should have picked up the white cake."

"We can share." She took another bite of her cake. "If you want."

He scooted his chair closer and took a piece of her cake. "It is good," he said. "We should get another piece, don't you think?"

Bailee was either greedy or she just wanted to spend more time with Ian, because she agreed. Ian waved over a server and pulled another piece of cake off the tray.

"So," she said after a few moments. "The coatroom. Where is it?"

A slow smile spread across his face, and he pointed to a closed door on the other side of the massive space. She stood on shaky legs and made her way over, turning back for just a second to find him staring at her with his fork still in midair. She winked and then continued her journey.

Inside the coatroom, she waited. It didn't take long—Ian joined her within three minutes. He reached out, traced the opening of her suit jacket.

Bailee held out her hands. "We're here. Now what?"

He smirked. "Let's start with you stepping out of those pants and bending over. I want you to let me kiss every inch of your body. I want to hear your low moans and know that I'm the one driving you crazy, that I'm the only one who can make you feel like this"

Quite a while later, he helped her get dressed while she fixed her hair the best she could with limited lighting and lack of a mirror. They exited the coatroom and she hurried toward the restroom, hoping no one noticed what she suspected was a dazed look in her eyes, or the sated, yet cocky gleam in his.

"Superman or Batman?" Ian asked.

"Superman, of course," Bailee answered with no hesitation. "I can't stand Batman with his punk self."

Ian agreed with Bailee. Batman sucked.

"But if I had to choose comic universes?" Bailee added. "I'm shouting Team Marvel all day, every day."

Ian pointed at Bailee before giving her a high five. "That's what I'm talking about."

They'd just finished a round of This or That, and he'd learned quite a bit about her in the five minutes he had to bombard her with questions. Bailee loved horror movies and preferred beer over wine. She was a morning person, would rather listen to music than play it and shared his love of all things Marvel.

"So you were in a cotillion in high school?" Bailee asked after Ian had fed her another bite of the cake he'd boxed up from the reception. They were entangled in each other on her bed, after making love on her private balcony.

Ian nodded. During her turn in the game, he'd admitted that his disdain for formal dances had a lot to do with the annual ball his father had made him participate in during high school. "We were all forced to go. It's sort of a rite of passage for my father's set of acquaintances. They've been doing it for years, under the guise of scholarship and charity."

Every year, the wealthy African American society of Ann Arbor hosted a Beau-Debutante ball for high school seniors. The goal of the program was to develop youth transitioning from one life stage to another, and to prepare them to be contributing members of society. The organization required each participant to attend workshops on civic involvement, etiquette or social graces, and charitable activities. They'd competed in several categories, such as talent and entrepreneurship. Because his father served as a board member, Ian and his siblings were expected to participate. Ian had resented the experience, but he'd donned his formal wear and performed the waltz with his date anyway.

"And you don't believe that's the motive?" she asked.

"No, I don't."

"Why not? You mentioned scholarship was part of it. That's a good cause. So many young people can't afford to attend college."

"I know," he said. "But they awarded the big scholarship to someone who didn't need the money, to someone whose father is the CEO of a Fortune 500 company. It would have made more sense to choose someone who couldn't afford to attend a university."

"True, but it's not like there aren't other charities to support. The ball and the mission are obviously important to your father. Why else would he insist you participate?"

"My father doesn't do anything out of the goodness of his heart. He does things that benefit his bank account and his reputation." All of the charities, the surgeries and the lectures only served one purpose. Personal gain.

"That's pretty awful."

He brushed the backs of his fingers across her cheek. "He's not a nice guy."

Ian didn't know how they'd started talking about his family, but he found that she was easy to converse with. She didn't judge him, and when he talked, she listened intently. In so many ways, his interactions with Bailee reminded him of his friendship with Mia, with the added bonus of a physical attraction. It was the best of both worlds. Something that he hadn't realized he'd wanted in his life until now.

"My parents belong to a similar society in Columbus. Mason and I grew up attending the community and volunteer events. It was all about the club, as they called it." She held up air quotes when she said "club." "It's the reason I hate long, poofy dresses to this day. New season, new ball gown. I'm glad Mason asked me to be his best woman. It was cool to wear something totally different and unexpected. But don't tell him I told you that, because I gave him a hard time about it initially."

Ian laughed. "The tux you wore suited you."

"Bee is very talented." She rolled over on her stomach, and he smacked her butt.

When Ian had spotted Bailee earlier, in her suit, he'd nearly tripped on the aisle runner. The navy blue tuxedo she'd worn was simple, fitted. Bee had cut it in such a way that he'd been able to see Bailee's ample curves. Bailee had rocked the look like a runway model, in four-inch coral sandals.

"That she is," he agreed, running a finger down her spine. "But I don't think it was the suit as much as the woman wearing it."

Bailee smiled and rolled over on her back. She had on his dress shirt and nothing else. He couldn't resist pulling it open to bare her breasts to him. Leaning down, he took one pebbled bud into his mouth.

"Ian?"

He glanced up at her. "Hmm?"

"What are we doing?"

The serious tone in her voice told him he'd better stop and listen. He sat up and met her gaze. "What do you mean?"

Bailee shrugged. "This. The fact that we keep having sex like we're not leaving tomorrow."

Those two words—*leaving* and *tomorrow*—weren't ones he wanted to hear in that moment. As far as he was concerned, he hadn't spent enough time with her. Still, she had a point. The wedding was over, and he'd be making the drive back home to Ann Arbor in a few short hours.

She sighed. "We've already established that I've never been in a casual relationship. And I'm not asking you to be more," she added in a rush when he opened his mouth to respond.

"Can I ask you a question?"

She nodded.

"What kind of man do you think I am?"

"I don't know." She gestured to him. "You're Ian."

"Who do you think Ian is?"

"Initially, I thought you were a player. I figured one-night stands might not be so uncommon for you."

She wasn't wrong. He'd done a lot of playing the field in his early twenties. In the past, he wouldn't have thought twice about taking a beautiful woman back to his place and waving goodbye in the morning. But the man he was now wasn't interested in meaningless flings with women he couldn't stand in the light of day. At the same time, he couldn't say he was ready for a commitment.

"I'm not that man anymore," he admitted.

"I know." She averted her gaze. "Just in this short time, I can see that you're a man who knows what he wants, and takes steps to get it. But you're not conceited or selfish. You're not the typical trust fund baby that I've run across, rich and entitled. You don't treat me like I'm incapable of making adult decisions. I appreciate that."

"Is that how Brandon was?"

"Sort of. We grew up taking simple things for granted. But I quickly learned that life isn't easy for everyone."

"That's true."

"Brandon doesn't get it, though. He didn't learn that lesson."

"Sometimes I think that you have to take yourself out of a situation to appreciate where you were. Which is why I applied for Doctors Without Borders."

Her eyes widened. "You did? That's great."

Ian smiled at her enthusiastic response. "I think so, too. I'm excited."

"No, Ian, that's awesome. It takes a lot of guts to step outside of our comfort zone and change our circumstances. You're doing things that people just talk about. I knew so many nurses who trotted out the idea of volunteering or doing meaningful jobs, with no intention of ever sending in the application. And you've done the hard part."

"I've wanted to do it for a while. When I finished my residency, I spent some time going over my options. For a long time, I wondered if I even wanted to be a doctor. Volunteering in New Orleans, though, confirmed I do. I don't want to spend my days performing cosmetic surgeries for people like my mother."

"Ouch," she muttered.

"Enough about my parents. Back to the topic at hand."

"Right. I'm just going to be blunt."

He frowned. "Okay."

"I enjoy spending time with you. But I'm not ready for a relationship. I don't even have a job. I have no idea what I want to do with my life right now."

"Does this mean I have to get out now?"

She giggled. "No. I just felt like you should know where I'm coming from."

He cupped the back of her neck and pulled her into a quick kiss. "I'm okay with that." He patted his lap. "Come here."

Bailee straddled his lap. "So we're good?"

"I thought you said you didn't do casual relationships?" Ian gripped her thighs and pulled her closer.

"I don't. But I'm going to go out on a limb and categorize this as one moment in time. And after tonight, I think we should just be friends."

"Friends. So no regrets?"

She shook her head. "No regrets," she repeated.

He pushed his shirt off her shoulders and kissed her smooth skin. "Then we're definitely good."

Chapter 13

Bailee had spent a lot of time pretending. She'd pretended she was happy with Brandon, pretended she loved her job, pretended she didn't want to eat that glazed doughnut for breakfast instead of the cup of yogurt she ate and pretended she knew exactly what she was doing when she'd decided to have sex with Ian. Again. And again.

The bravado she'd managed to pull out of her behind while in Traverse City faded as soon as he'd walked out of her room the morning after the wedding. They didn't say dramatic goodbyes or make promises to look each other up in the future. He didn't save his phone number into her phone or even ask for hers. The sexual bubble they'd been in just popped. And her good mood flew away with it.

Telling Ian that she didn't want a relationship was the right thing to do. Even though it wasn't the complete truth. Bailee knew she needed time to be by herself, but her feelings weren't as clear-cut as she'd like them to be. Ian understood her in a way no one had before. He got her. And that made him even more attractive to her.

Giving voice to her true feelings wasn't something she had been prepared to do at that point. So she'd decided to play it cool and *pretend* she could do casual with him. She'd chosen to settle for the physical connection between them. And now she was left with an ache in her stomach that couldn't be soothed. Not with a doughnut, not with a book and not with her vibrator.

"Girl, I told you to eat that damn doughnut." April yanked her earbuds out and jogged in place, waiting for Bailee to catch up to her. "You look pitiful."

It had been a week since her brother and Mia tied the knot. One week since Ian had made love to her so hard, so good that she couldn't remember sex before him.

Bailee bent over, sucking in several deep breaths. "I'm not pitiful. You're running too fast. I told you I ate a lot last week."

"I call BS. All the sex you had last week should have burned those calories right off."

"Shut up." Bailee shoved her friend playfully. "It wasn't a lot of sex."

"Seriously. You have to get your head back in the game, Bai. Your interview is in three hours."

With the decision made to finally move to Michigan, Bailee had spent the last several days cleaning out her house. She'd hired a property management company to handle the rental contract and maintenance on the condo, and rented a storage unit to store her furniture and other items. Bailee had arrived on April's doorstep, suitcases and boxes in tow, last night. And her

best friend had showed her to the guest room where
Bailee would stay until she found her own place, and
then demanded details on the wedding week and Ian.

"I still don't understand how you ended things with
him," April said. "You just chucked up the deuces and
kicked him out of your room?"

Bailee finally plopped down on a nearby bench.
"April, we're not a couple. We talked about it and
agreed to leave our fling in Traverse City."

"And New Orleans."

Bailee glared at her bestie. "You make me sick."

Shrugging, April bent and stretched. "What happens
when you see him again? Especially now that you're
here and applying for a job at his hospital."

Bailee had thought about what she'd say when she
saw Ian again. The only strategy she could come up
with was to treat him with respect and try not to climb
him like a tree. "I'm not worried about that," she lied.

When April arched a brow, she knew her friend
didn't believe her. "I'm going to let you keep telling
yourself that. Do you think you'd want to have sex
with him again?"

Bailee would like to say no and mean it. But who
was she kidding? Of course she wanted to be with him
again. Just the thought of him made her want to take
off her clothes and let him have control of her body.
The real question was, *would* she be with him again?

Standing up, Bailee took off at a run. Anything to
avoid more questions from April. Or maybe she was
simply trying to outrun her feelings.

Later, Bailee arrived at the hospital thirty minutes
early for her interview. Dr. Solomon had arranged for
her to meet Love's father, Dr. Leon Washington, who

was also chief of surgery at Michigan Medicine. As a favor to both his daughter and his friend, Dr. Washington had agreed to meet with her today. According to Dr. Solomon, the interview was a formality. She pretty much had the job if she wanted it. Which she did.

I guess.

Michigan Medicine was one of the largest healthcare systems in the country, and was owned by the University of Michigan. Bailee had visited the hospital before with Mason, but the impressive renovations made it seem like a different place. She'd read up on recent additions when she wasn't busy moving or daydreaming about Ian. They'd done a lot to improve the patient experience, including bringing in cutting-edge medical equipment and updating patient floors.

The only thing she didn't like was the horrendous parking situation. It had been a nightmare driving onto campus in the middle of the afternoon, and even worse trying to find a spot in the crowded parking structure. After driving around every single floor, she'd given up and used the valet service. Now she was cranky and sleepy and pissed off. Not a good combination if she wanted to remain composed and professional at the hospital.

When she arrived on the surgical floor, she felt a little better. The candy bar she'd grabbed on her way up helped. The walls were painted with warm, bright colors, not the drab gray or white walls she'd seen at other hospitals. Bailee tucked her leather binder under her arm and approached the desk.

"Hi, I'm here to see Dr. ..." Her voice trailed off when she spotted Drake to the right, talking to Myles and Ian. She took a moment to watch their interaction, noting the ease they shared with each other, the genuine smiles on their faces. The brothers looked relaxed, happy to be around each other. And Ian...

She drew in a shaky breath as she cataloged every single detail about him she could make out. Ian in regular clothes was fine, but Ian in dark scrubs? *So damn hot.*

Even though they hadn't been together in days, she still felt his kisses on her mouth. She couldn't stop thinking about his lips, his tongue on hers. She wanted him; she needed to feel that again. Decision made, she started toward him. But then she stopped in her tracks when a stunning woman joined the fellas.

The woman had on the same color scrubs as Ian and Drake, so Bailee figured she was a surgeon. Ian wrapped an arm around the woman and grinned at her. It was the same, sexy grin he'd shined on Bailee only a week ago.

"Excuse me?"

Bailee jumped at the voice behind her. When she turned, she met the cool eyes of the receptionist and realized she hadn't even told her who she was there to see. Had the woman been trying to get her attention this whole time? Bailee swallowed, and tried not to glance over at Ian again. "I'm sorry. I'm here to see Dr. Leon Washington. I have an appointment with him at two o'clock."

The lady gave her a curt nod, before giving her directions to the doctor's suite, where his administrative assistant would let him know she was there. Bailee spared Ian another glance. The woman had disappeared, but the brothers were still there. And Ian was looking right at Bailee.

Taking a deep breath, she walked toward them. She greeted Myles and Drake with a sincere smile and hugs.

Then she turned to Ian and gave him a plastic, stiff embrace. He smelled good—like the sun and the beach and mandarin.

"Hi, Ian," she breathed. Her voice sounded foreign to her own ears. Her gut twisted as she awaited his response.

"Bai," he rasped.

Vaguely, she heard movement behind her, felt the breeze of someone passing her. But her eyes were only on his. Until she remembered the woman and the dimpled smile he'd thrown at her. Anger simmered in her gut. Not at Ian, but at herself for being *that* woman. Bailee had never been the jealous type. Why the hell did she even care who he talked to anyway? Ian wasn't her man. They'd only shared a couple of hot and heavy sexcapades. No promises. No expectations. *Ugh.*

Ian held out his arm when she tried to walk past him, effectively blocking her movements. "Hey."

"Move, Ian."

"You're just going to walk away from me like that?"

Bailee met the curious gazes of Myles and Drake, scanned the area and noted a few nurses watching the scene unfold. "I'm not doing this with you right now. I have an interview." At that moment, the beautiful doctor he'd been talking to earlier breezed past them and waved. "Why don't you go talk to your little friend over there. Maybe she'll scratch that itch you always seem to have."

Without a word, he gripped her arm and steered her into an empty exam room. Whirling around, he pointed at her. "Seriously, Bai? I don't date women I work with. That's a surefire way to lose my job. And what the hell is your problem? *You* told me that we should just be friends."

She snorted. "And I bet you couldn't wait to get your flirt on with the next available woman."

"Are you crazy? Did you forget you're the one who said you didn't want to be in a relationship?"

"I didn't forget, okay? But this is the reason I said that."

"You're killing me. Make up your mind. One minute you're acting like you're cool with the boundaries *you* set. Then next week you're acting like you caught me cheating on you."

"Listen, you said you don't date people you work with. I'll be working here soon enough, so that should solve the problem."

She brushed past him, yanking the door open and hurrying down the hall.

Ian pounded his fist into the wall. *Ouch.* He shook his hand out. He couldn't believe what had just happened. Not only did she accuse him of messing around on the job, but she'd walked away from him. Again.

He thought they'd moved past the BS in Traverse City. They'd parted on friendly terms, even though Ian didn't need another friend. Mia was enough. Thoughts of Bailee had followed him all week, on his bike rides to work, during rounds, at lunch and especially overnight.

When he'd seen her in the lobby, looking so beautiful in a black pencil skirt and silk blouse, he'd wanted to march over to her and brand her. Because she was so damn fine—all golden and tight and serious. Everything that had never been attractive to him before, and now he couldn't stop thinking about her—in his bed, on his floor, in the car or even in a tree. He'd take her any way he could, anywhere she'd let him.

Stalking toward the door, he froze when it swung open and Bailee stood in the doorway. "Bailee, you—"

She entered the exam room, a shy smile on her face. "I'm sorry. I...I was a maniac."

Ian closed the distance between them, pulling her into a deep kiss. "You were," he said when he broke the kiss. "But you're forgiven."

Bailee sighed. "I have to go to my meeting with Dr. Washington. I just couldn't walk away without telling you that."

She backed away from him, but he yanked her forward, groaning when her body crashed against his. "Have dinner with me."

"Just dinner?"

Desire, lust and something else he couldn't name surged through him. Ian wasn't naive. He recognized his dilemma. He'd known everything was different when he got home from Traverse City and realized he missed her. He wished he could say it was just the mind-blowing sex that he missed, but he knew it was more than that. It was their connection, the way they seemed to fit together in ways that went far beyond the physical attraction.

"A date." He placed a kiss to her cheek, then her mouth. "Whatever that entails."

Bailee shot him a lopsided grin. "You want to date me?"

He peered up at the ceiling, pretended to think over her question. But when her fingers grazed his arms as she clenched his sleeve, he looked down at her. "Yeah, I do. I know we agreed to just be friends, but—"

Bailee placed her index finger over his mouth. "Newsflash. We've already passed the just friends stage. I don't even know why I said that because, like I told you, I don't do casual relationships."

"Good." He kissed the tips of her fingers. "Because we're doing this." He gripped her shoulders and stepped away from her. "You better go. I'll pick you up at seven."

"Don't you need to know where I'm staying?"

"Text me your address."

With a frown, she said, "I don't have your phone number."

"Yes, you do. I wrote it on the little piece of paper you used as a placeholder in the book you borrowed from Dr. Solomon."

Before Bailee had left the Solomon estate, she'd borrowed a book from the library—one she'd wanted to read for quite some time.

Bailee giggled. "You didn't."

"I sure did. I guess you haven't finished it yet."

"I haven't had time."

"Well, you better get to it. Talk to you later."

She beamed. "Okay. Later."

Dinner consisted of Caribbean food at Bahama Breeze Island Grille in Livonia, Michigan. Ian had chosen the spot because they played live music on the deck, and he knew from their time together that Bailee enjoyed reggae. He'd ordered the Jamaican Jerk Chicken, while Bailee picked the Braised Short Rib & Oxtail entrée. At some point—he wasn't sure when—Bailee had stolen a piece of his chicken.

He dropped his gaze to his plate, then brought it back to Bailee.

She bit into the piece of chicken she'd taken and moaned. "So good."

Ian tried to be mad, because he really wanted that last piece. But the way she did a little dance while she ate was too cute. She'd dressed in ripped jeans, a tank and one of those sheer kimonos he'd seen his sister, Mel, wear from time to time. Her hair fell wild and free, which he liked.

"If you weren't so damn sexy, I might be a little upset that you took my last piece of chicken."

Bailee stopped dancing. He hooked his foot around the leg of her chair and pulled her closer to him. When she was next to him, he picked up the hand that was holding the pilfered piece of chicken and took a bite.

She let out a shaky breath. "Hot," she breathed.

He raised a brow. "The chicken?"

"The man," she admitted.

Ian sucked the sauce off one of her fingers. "So good."

"The sauce?"

"The woman wearing it." He grazed her thigh with his other hand, traced the skin between the tiny rips in her jeans.

"Ian." She bit her lip as her gaze dropped to his mouth. "Just so you know, I don't put out on the first date." His eyes snapped to hers, and he caught the hint of a smile in them. Then she outright laughed. "You should see your face right now."

He joined her, chuckling. "You got me."

"Seriously, though." She leaned back, peering into his eyes. "I spent a lot of time in a relationship that wasn't good for me. I don't want to make any drastic decisions or jump into something so blindly. But there's something about you that makes me want to rip out every page in my rule book."

He thought about his response, tried to figure out

how he could say what he felt without really saying it. Ian knew what she meant, though. He couldn't remember the last time he'd wanted to take a woman on a date. But he'd found himself worrying over the details. Did she like casual or fancy, Italian or steakhouse? In the end, he went with his gut. Bailee came from money like he did, but she wasn't pretentious. She was down-to-earth and appreciated the small things in life, like a good book or a turkey sandwich. She loved to be outside and eat dessert. And he wanted to give her those things. He wanted to give so much more.

But he wasn't sure he was ready to tell her how crazy he was about and for her. He didn't think it was the right time to tell her that he hadn't felt so consumed by another woman. Ever. After all, this *was* only their first date. They hadn't discussed anything other than the fact that they wanted to see each other, that *he* wanted to date her. That was a huge feat in and of itself. Ian didn't date, or have girlfriends. Not because he was a jerk or a player, but because he didn't have the time to devote to another person. He'd never met a woman who made him want to make the time for her. Until now.

So he did something that shocked the hell out of him. He told her the truth. "I think we should take our time with this. I don't expect you to do anything that makes you uncomfortable. I just want to get to know you, to take you out." He brushed his thumb over her chin, then swept the back of his hand down her neck, enjoying the way her eyes fluttered closed. "I've never met anyone like you before."

"And you never will again." She winked at him.

He chuckled. "I don't doubt that."

"Ian, I hope you know I didn't mean what I said

about not putting out. I think it's pretty obvious how this night is going to end."

"Does this mean I get to take you home?"

"Only if you let me set the pace. It's my turn to drive you wild."

Bailee liked to be in control of her emotions. That was very obvious. Which was why he'd relished the act of seducing her. But he wouldn't mind giving her control over his body. In fact, he wanted her to take it.

"Really?" he asked.

She leaned in closer. "I want to touch you everywhere. I want to taste you on my tongue. All of you."

"You do?"

Nodding, she said, "I do. I want you naked and ready for me." She dropped her hand to his erection and squeezed.

Damn. Ian scanned the restaurant, spotted the waiter near the register and waved him over. When the man in the yellow tropical shirt had made his way to their table, Ian told him, "Check, please."

Chapter 14

Bailee had enjoyed the last month getting to know Ian. They'd spent most nights together, reading, eating, sitting outside on his patio. They'd talked about anything and everything, gone to a jazz club with Drake and Love, attended a movie premiere with El and Avery. Mia and Mason had invited them over for barbecue and beer last Sunday.

She'd learned about his obsession with chess, how Dr. Solomon had taught him the game. Ian had been in the chess club in high school. He'd taught her how to play, and even let her win sometimes. Bailee discovered her daring side when they went and got tattoos together. He added to the elaborate design on his back, while she decided to get a tiny daisy behind her ear. It hurt. But he'd held her hand the entire time, and rewarded her for her bravery later with his tongue. Ian had taken her on bike rides and she'd cheered him on at his last race. Bailee had gladly taken his one hundred dollars when she'd beat him in a swim challenge.

And now she knew what it meant to be totally and completely enamored by another person. Ian was funny, generous and caring. He'd sat through a marathon of her favorite rom-coms without even complaining. He'd even admitted—reluctantly, of course—that Tom Hanks and Meg Ryan won the contest for best couple in *You've Got Mail*, her favorite movie.

And sometime between the late dinners and the games of chess, she'd fallen in love. And every day, she fell a little more. At this point, he could do just about anything and she would think it was adorable.

The realization that she loved him made her feel sick and elated at the same time. Sick because they hadn't defined what they were to each other or made any promises. Elated because she felt better with him near her, and she slept better beside him.

Bailee was a planner, though, and it had started to bother her that they still hadn't talked about his plans for his career, or their plans for each other. Ian wasn't content working in the hospital. He wanted to be out in the field. She loved that about him, but she wasn't sure if his goals aligned with hers.

Dr. Washington had offered her a job at Michigan Medicine, but Bailee had turned it down. Instead, she'd applied for an Adjunct Professor position with the university. Unbeknownst to Bailee at the time, she'd met the Dean of the Nursing School at Mason and Mia's wedding. The older woman and Mrs. Solomon were close friends. Mason's in-laws pulled a few strings to get her an interview, and she was awarded the position. She would start her new appointment in August. Being off work during the summer had allowed her time to

enjoy Michigan. She'd put down a deposit on a condominium in Ann Arbor and was just waiting on a close
date. In hindsight, having her mini–midlife crisis on
her thirtieth birthday was just the thing she'd needed
to get her life together. She only hoped her heart didn't
ruin it for the rest of her. Because if things didn't work
out with Ian, she knew it would wreck her.

Tonight, they were at a pregnancy reveal party for
Mia and Mason. Her brother and new sister-in-law were
ecstatic to become parents, and had planned the reveal
for the start of Mia's second trimester. The news that
she would soon become an aunt had shocked Bailee,
but Ian didn't seem all that surprised. She'd figured
Mia had told him beforehand.

Her brother's backyard had been transformed for the
intimate dinner party, complete with a long table under
a tent, lots of lanterns and plenty of food. For the reveal,
Mia and Mason gave everyone gift boxes wrapped in
pretty pastels. Everyone opened their box at the same
time, and the room erupted in loud cheers. In Bailee's
box, there was a picture of Mia and Mason's joined
hands holding tiny little booties and a T-shirt that said
Auntie's Baby. Happy tears had pricked Bailee's eyes
as she embraced her brother and Mia, and whispered
her name to her nephew or niece.

The news was a welcome surprise, and Bailee enjoyed hanging out with her friends and family. Even
April, who was out of town for work, texted several
happy dance GIFs when Bailee had shared the good
news with her. Now Bailee was seated on a lounge chair
watching everyone mingle and laugh. Four people were
playing Spades at a card table, her parents had flanked
Mia and Mason to iron out plans to travel to Michigan
once the baby was born. And Ian…he looked so ador-

able playing with his niece, Zoe. He'd spent several minutes flying the cutie-pie around the backyard and making airplane sounds. He'd played patty-cake and talked baby talk. And Bailee felt her heart open up a little more and her body react to the scene before her.

She couldn't stop ogling him, and she knew she should because they were in public. Her parents were mere steps away, for goodness' sake. But she couldn't help it. She wanted him. It was his fault, really. He'd started it in the car on their way over, with his dirty, filthy words and his roaming hands. And he'd continued it over the course of dinner, with his whispered promises of cake and orgasms later.

Bailee just needed to get his attention. She needed him to walk over to her and say the two words she wanted to hear.

"Profiterole, ma'am?" A waiter held a tray full of assorted cream puffs in front of her.

Those aren't the words.

Bailee nodded and took the offered dessert. She bit into the tiny pastry and moaned at the burst of cream that filled her mouth. *Yum.*

When she looked up, Ian was staring at her, a hungry look in his eyes. He handed his niece to Drake and walked over to the wine table. As he poured her a glass, he looked her up and down. The heat in his eyes took her breath away, and she felt arousal pool between her thighs. Would she always want him like this? Would her fingers always itch to touch him? Would the sound of his voice, the feel of his eyes on her always make her feel weak and strong at the same time?

She sat up straighter, watching him as he stalked toward her. A slow smile spread across his face, lighting up the room and squeezing her heart. He had a beautiful, genuine smile. One that made her want to hold on to him forever.

Ian leaned down once he'd closed the distance between them. "Stop looking at me like that." His voice was a low rasp, almost a whisper. "You should know better by now."

Bailee swallowed, and held out her dessert. "Cream puff?"

He took a bite, chewing slowly, his eyes never leaving hers. Bailee swore she was about to go up in flames. He was so close she felt his breath on her lips, smelled the cream filling on it. She wanted to lick him. And he hadn't even touched her yet. Which was a good thing because if he did, she might explode. In the middle of the pregnancy reveal party. In front of everybody.

Ian kissed her bare shoulder. Then her neck. Then her lips. She let out a whimper when he took her mouth like there was nobody else in the room. She remembered the first time he'd kissed her in public. They'd spent the day on the Detroit River with his brothers, and listened to Boney James as he played to the crowd at Chene Park, an outdoor concert venue. And as the saxophone pierced the night air, they'd danced on the deck. When Ian had leaned down and placed a sweet kiss to her lips, she'd frozen. But that didn't last. It never did when his mouth was so close to hers.

Pleasure wrapped around her spine, then moved down to her core. She wanted nothing more than to have him inside her, making love to her the way only he could. Bailee cupped his face in her hands, giving herself to him. She didn't care what anyone had to say. She just wanted his lips on hers.

"Bai?" he said when he pulled back. "Let's go."

It was a good thing that Ian's house was literally

seven miles away from her brother's house. Because she was wound tight, burning with need and yearning to be touched. Once they made it to his place, it took only seconds for him to strip her bare, lay her on the bed and sink inside her.

Pure bliss. Two words, so much meaning. Bailee didn't know how she would get over how it felt when he filled her, when he made love to her. Each and every time felt new, like he was completing her puzzle, providing a missing piece of her that only he had. It was so good, so hot.

As if he'd read her mind, he grumbled, "It's so good. I can't stop wanting it."

"Yes," she breathed.

It didn't take long before she cried out her release. It felt like he'd stolen her breath, almost like he'd pushed her over the edge without her realizing it. He fused his mouth over hers, sucked on her bottom lip until she whimpered. Then his fingers dug hard into her hips and he was coming, too, groaning her name over and over again.

Bailee fell back against the mattress, sated. She turned to Ian, who was lying next to her, staring up at the ceiling. He reached out to her and pulled her into his arms.

"I don't know what I'm going to do with you." Ian kissed her brow.

"Keep doing this." She stretched, and hooked a leg over his waist. "This is good."

Bailee had never been with someone she could have fun with. For the first time, she didn't feel weird about being silly, or simply enjoying the moment. She'd never smiled as much as she'd smiled with Ian.

He shifted, turning to his side. "Doctors Without Borders emailed me."

Bailee's heart dropped. "Really?"

"They want me to fly out to New York for an interview."

"Oh." They'd talked about his application before. She knew how much an opportunity like this meant to him. But it felt like a ticking time bomb ready to explode.

He wrapped his hand around the base of her neck, kissed her nose. "This is the first step in the hiring process."

Bailee knew that. She'd read up on the organization herself. Once he was accepted to the program, he would have to go through a rigorous training in a faraway destination. Then he'd wait until they placed him somewhere. A typical assignment could last from nine months to one year.

"That's good," she said, trying to sound supportive and happy for him. "You've worked so hard for it."

Ian rested his head on her shoulder. "Yeah, I have." He pulled her close to him, wrapping his arms around her tightly.

Bailee swallowed rapidly as her heart pounded hard in her chest. She should probably say something else, but she couldn't bring herself to talk, sure her voice would betray her. It felt like Ian wanted to say something, too. Something important. Was it so much to hope for that he felt the same way as her? As happy as he probably was to get the call, could he be regretting the timing, too? Several moments passed, and Bailee's loud thoughts threatened to unravel her.

But then Ian pulled back, peered into her eyes. "Come with me to New York."

Relief surged through Bailee as she searched his face for a sign. His brown orbs pleaded with her to say yes, but they were also filled with something else. It felt like hope, and maybe even more than that. *Love.*

She nodded. "Sure. Let's do it."

New York City was one of Ian's favorite places to visit. He'd spent a lot of time there during college, making little weekend trips with Myles or Mia to explore the city. So he was surprised Bailee had never been to the Big Apple.

They'd arrived early in the morning the day before his interview. Although the organization offered to pay for his travel expenses and hotel stay, he'd opted out. Because once Bailee had admitted she'd never experienced Manhattan or Brooklyn or Harlem, he knew he had to make this trip count. He'd splurged on first-class tickets, and had reserved a suite at the Four Seasons.

The money he'd spent, the plans he'd made, the favors he'd called in were all worth it to see the smile on Bailee's face when they stepped into the gilded lobby of the hotel that morning. And she'd shouted with glee and jumped into his arms, showering him with kisses, once she'd seen their suite. The Central Park Suite featured oversize windows that offered panoramic views of the park. The suite also included a separate living area and a private terrace with outdoor furniture.

Ian had arranged for room service to deliver breakfast, and they'd enjoyed pancakes, fresh fruit, thick bacon and mimosas on the terrace. Then Bailee had pulled him into the room and let him make love to her for a few hours.

The hotel was situated in Midtown Manhattan, so there were several sites he wanted to show her. Since he'd listened to her when she'd told him about her favorite romantic comedies, he figured he'd surprise her and take her on a tour of the places she'd only seen in her favorite movies.

He'd started with a cab ride to the Empire State Building, and more specifically, the eighty-sixth floor Observation Deck, where his boy Tom Hanks won Meg Ryan's heart in *Sleepless in Seattle*. That's when Ian had discovered Bailee was just a little bit afraid of heights and wouldn't get too close to the railings.

After they left the Empire State Building, they'd visited the 91st Street Garden, where once again Tom Hanks revealed himself as Meg Ryan's online suitor and sealed the deal with a kiss. And because Bailee was such a huge *You've Got Mail* fan, she'd nearly cried when the Uber dropped them off in front of the park.

"Oh my God, Ian. This is awesome."

They'd stopped right in front of the sign where her favorite on-screen couple pledged their love for each other.

"I can't believe you did all this for me."

Ian shrugged. It wasn't rocket science. The only thing he'd done was listen to her. He'd spent time getting to know her, learning what made her happy, what made her sad and what made her want him.

"You deserve it, Bai." He stepped into her, traced her lips with his finger before he kissed her. "Haven't you figured out that I'd do anything for you?" Because Ian didn't have any control over his actions or his heart.

Tears filled her eyes. "Ian, this is…everything."

He kissed her cheeks where the tears fell. "Don't cry."

"I can't help it. No one has ever done anything like this for me."

In the back of his mind, he realized this interaction was eerily similar to the one in the movie she loved so much, which was corny and so not him. But in that moment, he didn't care. Seeing her so happy made him happy. Bailee had shared a lot of things with him over the last several weeks. He couldn't believe Brandon had never spoiled her, never made it a priority to make her smile. *Punk.* There was no excuse for Bailee to not have been to New York or Hawaii or Jamaica or Paris.

"I still can't wrap my brain around that," he said. "Did I tell you he was a punk?"

She giggled, leaning her forehead into his chest. He wrapped his arms around her. They swayed to silent music as he contemplated how to tell her what she meant to him. Although he hadn't officially given her the title of girlfriend, he felt like she was his. And he'd acted accordingly. He hadn't seen anyone else, or even wanted to see other women. He knew that she wasn't dating anyone else, either. But with Doctors Without Borders looming over his head, he didn't want to make a promise he couldn't keep.

Long-distance relationships worked only sometimes. Ian didn't want to hurt Bailee, and he didn't want to be hurt. And he didn't want to ask her to wait for him, especially after everything she'd gone through with the punk. She'd finally taken control of her life, made lasting changes that she was happy with. He didn't want to throw a wrench in any of that.

He loved her. It was real and all-consuming. It was everything. A lump formed in his throat when she pulled back and graced him with her perfect smile.

They held each other's gazes. She traced the line of his jaw, sending sparks straight to his heart. His veins hummed with a need to claim her. But he'd stick with his plan for the night.

"Where are we going?" she asked.

"What if I wanted to surprise you?"

She groaned. "I've had enough of surprises. I want to know what you have planned for me."

"Tickets to *Cats* the musical."

Her eyes lit up with glee, and his heart opened up a little more. She wrapped her arms around his neck and kissed him. "Ian, you didn't."

"I did."

Bailee had told him that her father had promised to take her to see the musical when she was a kid. She'd held out hope for the day she'd be able to see the play, but the tour ended and her father had forgotten. Mr. Sanders had been apologetic, had even taken her to see *The Lion King* in Chicago, but it wasn't the same.

Ian had called in a favor from a friend who worked as a real-estate developer in in the city. Cedric came through at the last minute with excellent tickets. Ian wanted her to meet his friend, so they'd decided to get together for drinks before the show.

He set her down on the ground and she beamed at him. "You're spoiling me." She grabbed his hand and pulled him out of the garden. "I might have to keep you."

Her words stirred something inside him. Tugging her to him, he asked, "Might?"

She stood on the tips of her toes and kissed him. "I'll amend that to say I will definitely keep you. As long as you keep giving me what I want."

"Ah, I get it. You'll keep me around as long as I keep making you scream my name?" Her smile...*damn*. He sucked in a deep breath, because breathing seemed to be a chore right then.

"Something like that," she said with a wink.

Ian wanted to say more. He wanted to tell her he loved her and he wanted her to be his forever. But the loud blare of a horn scared her, ruining the moment.

Later, Ian and Bailee met Cedric and his date for cocktails at Ty Bar, off the main lobby of the hotel. They enjoyed bar bites and Hudson Bourbon, which was created specifically for the bar. Bailee had surprised him when she'd ordered the bourbon neat, instead of one of her preferred fruity cocktails. Ian loved watching Bailee step outside of her comfort zone more and more.

Surprisingly, *Cats* the musical was good. Ian enjoyed the show. Bailee held his hand the entire time, squeezing it when the actors jumped out of the shadows. When the show was over, he took her to a dessert bar Cedric had recommended.

Back at the hotel, they were barely in the room before Bailee tackled him. Clothes flew off, her skirt behind his head, his shirt behind hers. She unbuckled his pants and pushed them down. He fumbled with the ties of her blouse, tempted to rip it to shreds to get to her.

Bailee steadied his hand. "You better not rip my shirt, Ian. It's my favorite."

Ian growled, hooking his hands under her butt, lifting her in his arms and carrying her to the bedroom. He dropped her on the bed and crawled on top of her. He savored the way they fit together, like she was made for him. Their lovemaking wasn't hot and fast. Instead, it was slow and tender. And when they finished, coming in tandem, he knew he'd never love anyone the way he loved his Bailee.

* * *

After his interview the next day, they spent time in Central Park. They visited Bethesda Fountain, walked The Mall like another couple in one of her favorite movies, *Brown Sugar*, played chess in the Chess & Checkers House and rode the Carousel. On Saturday, they lazed around the hotel suite until dinner. He took her to Dinners in the Dark at Camaje, where they enjoyed dinner blindfolded.

"Where did you come up with that idea?" Bailee asked once they were back in the suite. She was curled up in his lap on the terrace.

He shrugged. "One of the doctors talked about it at work one day, and I figured why not."

"I loved it."

The idea was to enjoy dinner without sight, which was supposed to heighten other senses, like smells and textures. "It was intense."

"Sensual," she agreed. They watched the skyline for a few minutes before Bailee hopped up.

He gripped her wrist. "Wait, wait, wait…where are you going?"

She bent down and brushed her lips over his. "I'll be right back." True to her word, Bailee was gone only for a few minutes. When she returned, she held a box in her hand. He opened his arms and she climbed into his lap again. "I got you something."

Ian took the offered box. "What is it?"

"Open it."

He lifted the top off the Tiffany Blue box, and wondered when she had time to go and purchase something from the jewelry store.

"I ordered it online, and picked it up while you were gone on your interview yesterday."

He eyed her as he pulled the white ribbon and lifted the top off the box. His heart tightened in his chest when he pulled the silver key chain out. It was a rook.

"It's stupid, but I thought it was cute."

He ran his finger over the metal, touched by her thoughtfulness. Although it was small, the fact that she'd listened to him, that she'd thought of him, made him love her even more.

She bit her lip. "Do you like it? I remember when you were teaching me how to play chess, you mentioned the rook was your favorite piece."

Ian remembered the conversation. He'd spent some time explaining each piece and its role in the game. And when he got to the rook, he'd confessed that he loved how the piece had simple movement, but it played an important role in game play. The rook threatened the king, supported the queen and sometimes sacrificed itself for a bishop or knight. And in the end, rooks were often the last pieces standing, aside from the kings.

He'd often equated chess to real life. Pop had taught him many lessons while they'd played—focus on the board and not the opponent, be creative, don't read more into other players' moves, be flexible, look after the little guys because they matter, and think three moves ahead. Most people liked the queen, because it was the most powerful piece on the board. But the rook represented the value of support and sacrifice, giving of himself for others.

"Thank you, Bai. I love it." He pulled her into a kiss. *I love you.*

Chapter 15

Bailee started her job and moved to her new condo the same week. It was now the end of August, and she'd settled into her new life in Michigan. Classes would start after Labor Day, and Bailee was enjoying the preparation. She'd thrown herself into lesson plans and presentation materials. She wouldn't say she'd never go back to nursing full-time, but she liked the idea of training the next generation of nurses.

Tonight, Ian was coming to her place for the first time before she flew down to Florida for the holiday. They'd watch movies and chill, preferably naked. After their trip to New York, they'd grown closer, spending lots of time together. Still, they hadn't made a commitment, although she'd never dream of dating someone else. She was hopelessly in love with Ian. She wanted him, and only him.

Bailee stirred the meat on the stove. Steak and

shrimp fajitas were on the menu because Ian loved them. And he deserved to be spoiled since he'd single-handedly coordinated her move. Last week, they'd rented a truck and driven down to Columbus to pick up the rest of her things. And he'd insisted on unpacking everything in one day. Then he'd helped her set everything up.

"Bai?" Ian called from the front of the house.

"In here!" She dropped the onions and peppers in the pan just as Ian rounded the corner and entered the kitchen. Her heart pounded in her chest at the sight of him in his scrubs. *So fine.* And a sight for sore eyes. He'd just worked two days in a row, and the only inter-action they'd had was several flirty—more like dirty—texts and a hurried video chat. She smiled when she noticed the tiny smirk that formed on his face when he saw her.

"Hey, beautiful." He massaged her shoulders. "Smells good in here." He kissed the back of her neck, then her jaw, then her lips.

"You know I had to hook you up, to thank you for everything you've done."

He sat down on one of the barstools. "No need to thank me." He yawned.

"You look tired."

"I am. But I'm hungry, too."

"Dinner is almost ready. Why don't you go relax on the sofa?"

"Sounds good." He gave her another quick kiss and disappeared a few seconds later.

Once the fajitas were finished and his plate was made, she took it to him in the living room. She chuck-led at Ian curled up on the couch—fast asleep. She set the plate on the coffee table and pulled a blanket over him.

His eyes popped open. "I'm up."

"No, you're not. Go back to sleep."

Ian gripped her wrist, pulling her down on the sofa with him. He wrapped his arm around her. "Stay with me. I just need a quick nap, and then we can eat and watch a movie."

She turned in his arms, ran her fingers through his hair. "The food will be here when you wake up."

"I'm sorry," he muttered.

"Don't apologize."

"Is this going to stop you from doing me? Because if so, I'm up. I feel great. So good I could run a marathon."

She laughed. "Ian, go to sleep. I'll be here when you wake up."

"I missed you." Then he buried his face in her neck and promptly fell back to sleep.

An hour later, Ian woke up and smiled. Bailee set her book down. "You're up." She stood. "Ready to eat?"

"I'm hungry, but not for food." He waggled his eyebrows.

"You're silly." She shoved him playfully.

"I'm serious." He grabbed her ankles and tugged her forward.

Bailee cracked up when he pulled her pants and shirt off. "You're crazy."

"About you," he murmured before he kissed her. His phone rang and he groaned. "I hope it's not the hospital."

"It's fine. Answer it." She scooted off the couch and walked into the kitchen to reheat his food. A few minutes later, she came back with his plate. "Hey, are you okay?" He was sitting on the couch, staring at a spot on the wall. "Ian?" She sat next to him. "What happened?"

He looked at her then. "That was Doctors Without Borders."

Bailee swallowed. "Okay. Did you get accepted?"

Ian nodded. "Yes. They want me to fly out for training next week."

"Next week?" she repeated. "Wow."

Knowing he'd applied for a position was one thing. But being faced with him actually going away was quite another. His eyes bored into her, waiting. For what? She didn't know. If he was waiting for her to ask him to stay, he'd be waiting forever. Because she couldn't do that. She couldn't tell him not to go.

"I don't know when I'll actually be assigned a post," he said. "It could be two weeks, or two months."

She nodded. "I know."

"I don't even know how long the assignment will be."

"At least nine months," she said.

"Can we...?"

She looked at him then. "I'm excited for you. We need to celebrate."

"Bai? Don't you think we need to talk about this?"

"Why? There's nothing to talk about. We both knew this was coming. The interview was just a formality. Your résumé is impressive. I knew they'd hire you." But she was ashamed to say she'd hoped they wouldn't. Because even though they'd spent so much time together and it felt like they were on the same page, she knew they weren't ready for long distance.

Bailee stood, but he grabbed her hand. "Sit."

She sat.

"You're going to tell me to leave and not give us options?"

Shrugging, she said, "What options? It's not like we're together." His face fell, and she knew she'd hurt him. She forged ahead anyway. "Ian, we didn't make any promises."

"Is that it?"

"What else is there?"

"Bai, I can't even believe you're saying this to me after everything. I'm supposed to walk away like what we have doesn't matter to me? And be okay with it? I can't do that."

Glancing at him, she asked, "Why?"

"Because!" He stood and paced the floor. "You're my... You're mine."

His admission had simultaneously filled her heart with joy and trepidation. "Ian, you're leaving. And I want you to go because I know it means so much to you."

"You mean something to me, too. I didn't expect it. I definitely didn't plan for it."

"Me, neither." Her voice broke, and she squeezed her eyes closed. Tears wouldn't help the situation. "But it's not like you'll be gone forever. You're going to come back. Look, Ian. The way I see it is our timing just sucks. And that's life."

"Is it because you don't trust me to be gone and not cheat on you?"

Her gaze snapped to his. "No."

"I would never hurt you like that."

"I believe you. But sometimes getting hurt is inevitable. Especially when a situation is hard. I'd rather walk away now than invest more time and effort into a relationship that won't work."

"Straight up? How do you know it won't work?"

"I doubt that it will. It's only been a few months. I

stayed in a relationship for over fifteen years waiting for things to get better. Or accepting that they sucked. I don't have it in me to do that again. What if you go away and love it? What if when you get there, they love you so much they want you to go on more assignments? Where does that leave me?"

"Okay, so you're scared. That's understandable."

"I'm not just scared, Ian. I'm being realistic. Why don't you just concentrate on your new job right now? Because this is probably confusing things for you."

"Don't tell me how I feel, Bailee," he snapped.

"How about I tell you how I feel, then?" She folded her arms over her chest. "I already care so much about you it feels like I'll burst open from the intensity of these feelings. Being with you like this took a lot for me."

Hurt flashed in his eyes. "So you regret being with me?"

Her shoulders fell. "No. Ian, I've loved being with you." *I love you.* "But you're me in this situation."

Ian looked thoroughly confused. "What?"

"You're at a crossroads in your life. You have to go with a clean slate. Without me and expectations and commitments that don't align with the vision you have for yourself. Because if you don't—if we try to make this work—one day you might realize you've wasted time trying to make a relationship work that was doomed from the beginning."

"That's the craziest thing I've ever heard!" he roared. "You left Brandon because he was a selfish punk who didn't put you first."

"I left him because I wanted more for my life. And you want more for yours. So go. We're good. We can be friends."

Ian stepped back as if she'd slapped him. "Friends?"

"Yes." She turned on her heel and walked into the kitchen. *What am I doing?*

The same thing they'd bonded over was the thing that could tear them apart. Their ambition, their need to be understood, their desire for something more. When she'd started this, she never expected to love him. Hell, she didn't even feel like she could love anyone after Brandon. What had happened between Bailee and Ian was anything but casual, and more serious than she ever anticipated. Yet she wouldn't change a single thing.

Doubt clouded her mind, and panic welled up inside her. How was it even possible to be a wreck over Ian when she hadn't shed a single tear over Brandon? *Because I love him.* Ian was right. The situations were different. He wasn't Brandon. And she wasn't Brandon's Bailee anymore.

Bailee wanted Ian, more than anything. "Ian," she whispered. Bolting out of the kitchen, she called his name as she entered the living room. But he was gone. She opened the door just in time to see him speed out of the subdivision.

Closing the door, Bailee leaned against it and sunk to the floor. Burying her face in her knees, she finally let loose the tears that had been threatening to fall.

It had been only two hours since he'd left Bailee's house, but Ian felt like he'd been thrown into hell. The conversation replayed in his mind on a continual loop. Even the whiskey he'd downed hadn't dulled the ache.

"Why didn't you just tell her how you feel?" Myles asked as he refilled Ian's glass.

"Right?" Drake said, glaring at Ian. "That doesn't even make any sense."

"Oh, shut up." Love smacked Drake on the arm. "Like you haven't made stupid decisions before?"

After he'd left Bailee's house, Ian drove to El and Avery's place. One look at him, and El called in reinforcements. His siblings had descended on the house in minutes.

"You should have fought for her," El said.

"Says the man who didn't fight for me," Avery deadpanned.

"Hey," El said. "This isn't about me."

"I thought we were building something," Ian said. "And she was so flippant about it. Then she called us friends. I'm not her freakin' friend."

"Listen, Ian," Love said, squeezing between Drake and Ian. "I'm not going to tell you that you did the wrong thing. We all know that Doctors Without Borders isn't a death sentence for a relationship. I'm sure even Bailee knows that. But she's scared, so she said some things I'm sure she's regretting right about now."

Avery plopped down on the other side of him. "Love is right. Sometimes we women can be a little hasty."

"Exactly," El chimed in.

"As I was saying," Avery said, blowing El a kiss, "she messed up. And she'll realize it. Sooner rather than later. Have faith, brother. And stop drinking so much."

"And when she does come to you," Love said, "tell the girl you love her. Jeez. Get it together. I'm not sure why you haven't told her before now."

"That's what I said," Myles said, jumping in. "It was pretty obvious to us. Since when do you spring for extravagant vacations in New York City for anybody? I can barely get you to buy me dinner, and we were in the womb together for nine months."

And that was when Ian finally laughed. "You're dumb as hell. But thank you. I appreciate the support."

When Ian got home later that evening, he was surprised to find his father waiting for him inside. How he got a key to Ian's place, he'd never know. He dropped his keys on the table next to the door.

"What are you doing here?"

"I heard you were accepted into the program," his dad said.

"Is this when you tell me you won't support my decision? Or when you let me know how disappointed you are in me?"

His father sighed. "I don't want to tell you any of those things, son. Our conversation has played in my head many times since the wedding."

"And you're just now coming to clear the air with me?" He'd gone practically the entire summer without seeing his father. Ian knew Dr. Law's schedule was generally packed, but he also knew his dad had been in town for weeks.

"I figured you needed time."

Ian stared at him incredulously. "Really? Almost three months?"

"Look, son. I'm an asshole. What can I say?"

"How about I'm sorry?"

"I'm sorry."

Ian stared at his father in disbelief. An apology was the last thing he'd expected from his father. "What?"

"I apologize. You were right. I should be proud of the man you've become. I *am* proud of you. Of all my children, you're the one most like me."

As far as Ian was concerned, that wasn't a compliment. "I'm not sure what to say about that," he grumbled.

Then his father laughed. It had been years since he'd seen his dad smile, let alone laugh. "You've never backed down from a fight with me. Not even when you were a little boy. You go after what you want. That's something to be proud of. It's something to respect. The fact that you're willing to lose momentum in your own studies to give back to communities in need is commendable. And something I've never had the courage to do."

Ian was speechless. And since he didn't know what to say, he walked to the fridge and pulled out a bottle of water. "Did you want something to drink?"

His father nodded. "I'll have a beer."

A beer? Ian had never seen his father drink anything but bitter scotch. But he grabbed a Modelo out of the refrigerator, popped the top and slid it across the table to his father. They sat for a few moments, him guzzling his water and his father sipping his beer.

"That woman," his father said. "The one you've been hanging out with? Where is she?"

"Again, how do you know what I've been doing?" Ian laughed. "I haven't seen you." It seemed his father knew everything.

"I've seen you."

"Bailee," Ian said. "Her name is Bailee."

"That's right. Mason's sister."

"Yeah. We broke up."

"Really?" His father took another sip from the bottle. "I actually like her."

"How do you even know her?"

"I ran into her when I was leaving the Solomon estate. She told me it was a shame I couldn't see what a good son I had. Then she said I should spend more time supporting you instead of tearing you down."

That was news to Ian. Bailee had defended him to his father. Damn, he loved that woman.

"When do you leave for training?" his father asked.

"Next week, after the holiday. The recruiter told me they wanted me to start as soon as possible because they're short on qualified doctors."

"Good." Dr. Law stood. "I better get home." He clasped Ian's shoulder. "You'll do well, son." His father walked to the door. "Oh, before I go." He pointed to a box on the coffee table. "That was sitting outside when I got here."

"How did you get a key to my place?"

His father laughed. "Good night." Then he was gone, without answering Ian's question.

Ian picked up the box on the table and opened it. A new chess set, the one he'd told Bailee he wanted weeks ago, was inside. But it wasn't just a chess set. It was hope. He picked up the card and opened it.

Ian, I had planned to give this to you tonight. I hope you love it.

Ian did love it. Even more, he loved her.

Chapter 16

Pregnancy reveals, gender reveals… Ian knew Mia was going to take this being-a-mother thing too far. His best friend had texted him while he was in Montreal at training, and let him know that she'd scheduled the reveal so that he could be there. But he had no idea it would be on the day he'd returned from training.

The moment Ian walked into his best friend's house, Mia screamed and ran over to him, pulling him into a tight hug. "You're here. Thank you for coming."

"Did I have a choice? Because I could have sworn I got a message on my phone threatening me if I didn't make an appearance."

Mia laughed, shoving him lightly. "Fine. So you didn't have a choice. I'm just glad to see you. How was Montreal?"

Ian spent a few minutes telling Mia about training. It was rigorous, but he'd loved the challenge. Except for the nights when he'd tossed and turned, missing the feel of the woman he loved next to him. Every time he closed his eyes, he saw her. Every time he breathed, he smelled her. She lingered on him as if she'd doused him in her essence. Being away from her shined a light on how incomplete he felt without her. He missed her. He missed the sound of her laugh, the way she bit her lip when she was concentrating on something or when she was turned on. He missed her smile. He missed the feel of her in his arms, the warmth of her body against his.

Bailee had left for Florida the morning after their argument, and then he'd left for Canada. He'd sent her a few texts while he was away, which she'd responded to. But the things he'd wanted to say to her couldn't be said over text or on a phone call. He needed to see her.

"Is she here?" he asked.

Mia smiled. "She's out on the patio."

Ian kissed his friend on the cheek and headed for the patio door. Bailee was sitting outside, a beer dangling from her fingers. She wore black jeans and a T-shirt. Her eyes were closed. *Perfect.*

"Bai?" Her eyes popped open and she whirled around, nearly falling out of the chair. He rushed over to her and held the chair steady. "Are you okay?"

"Ian?" She jumped up, shook her hand. "I spilled beer on my jeans." She grabbed a paper towel off the table next to her chair and wiped her pants, growling in frustration. "Shoot, these are new jeans." Then she looked at him and smiled. "Hi."

"Hi."

"When did you get here?"

"Just now. Mia told me you were out—"

"I'm sorry," she said, interrupting him. She inched closer to him. "I'm so sorry, Ian. I was so wrong.

There's so much I want to say to you. Things that couldn't be said over the phone."

"I know," he said.

"Do you want to sit?"

"Let's go to the gazebo."

She smiled, and they walked toward the structure Mia had recently added to the backyard. Inside, she leaned against the rail, peered up at the sky. "It's a beautiful night."

He stared at her. "Yeah, beautiful."

She shot him a shy smile. "How was Montreal?"

"Can we talk about that later?" He picked up both of her hands. "I hate the way our last conversation ended. And I'm partly to blame. Because I didn't tell you how I really felt. I didn't communicate what was on the line for me. I left without letting you know how much I love you."

Bailee gasped.

"That's my fault. I won't make the same mistake again. I love the idea of Doctors Without Borders. I enjoyed learning and training to go out in the field. But being up in Canada, not knowing where *we* stand, was a special kind of torture. Because you mean more to me than any job, any opportunity."

"Oh, God," she breathed.

"What?"

"Can we back up just a little bit?" She let out a shaky breath. "Because you love me?"

He pulled her to him and kissed her. She tasted like beer and cookies, and something distinctly Bailee. When he broke the kiss, he pressed his forehead to hers. "Of course I love you. Isn't that obvious? I love you so much I can't even think straight." Ian was a transformed person when she was in the room. It didn't matter who was there; Bailee commanded all of his attention. "And I couldn't go another day without telling you."

Grinning, she brushed her thumb over his bottom lip. "I love you, too."

He closed his eyes and let her words wash over him. He cupped her cheeks and brushed his lips over hers.

"Does this mean you accept my apology, that you forgive me for tripping out?"

"There's nothing to forgive." He grabbed her hand, led her over to a nearby bench and pulled her down on his lap. "I need you to know that we can make this work. Because I—"

"Ian, I know. I won't pretend that I don't hate that you'll be so far away, but that's what planes are for. And vacations."

He chuckled. "Bai."

She babbled on about frequent flyer miles and Marriott points before she asked, "Do you have an idea of when you're going to be assigned to a post?"

He sighed. "Next week, but—"

"Aw, I won't get much time with you." She gave him a lingering kiss. "But it's okay. We'll make the most of the time we have now."

"Bai, stop." He pinched her mouth closed. "If you'd let me get a word in edgewise, I could tell you something very important about my assignment."

She nodded.

"My assignment is in New Orleans."

Come to the hotel bar. I'll be waiting.

The text had been short, but Ian's words had stoked a fire in Bailee. Her arousal was at a tipping point by the time the town car pulled up at the luxury hotel, the same one she'd stayed in all those months ago, the same hotel where she'd met him. Bailee thanked the driver and slid out of the vehicle.

It had been a month since Bailee had seen him, and she was anxious to lay eyes on him. They'd talked nearly every day since he'd left, sharing their days with each other via video chat. He'd told stories of long days working in the inner-city hospital and on the streets. The latest hurricane, a category three storm, had devastated the city. But everyone on his team had been working hard to help rebuild the medical system. He worked hard, but always made sure to check in with her, even when he was exhausted. Sometimes he'd even fall asleep while they were on the phone, and Bailee listened to his soft snores, taking comfort in the sound of his breathing in her ear.

The technology at her fingertips helped, but she'd missed the face-to-face contact. She'd missed his touch, his lips. Every minute of the day, she'd been aware of his absence. She was so gone over Ian.

Memories of sweaty sex, slow or fast lovemaking with Ian only made her cranky. Dirty texts and phone sex paled in comparison to the real thing, even though Ian was good on the phone. Last night, Ian had sent her a five-word text saying, Get on a plane. Now. A minute after she'd received the text, her phone buzzed with another notification—an email. He'd sent her a gift card for the airline. So she did as she was told, booking a flight and throwing a few outfits in a carry-on. She couldn't get a flight out that same night, but she'd found one for the next day.

Bailee pulled out her phone once she stepped into the lobby and made one call. To April.

"Guess where I am?" she said when her best friend picked up.

"Where?"

Bailee hadn't told anyone she was leaving, since she'd be back in two days. "I'm in New Orleans."

"Get out. When did you leave? And why didn't you tell me?"

"It was a last-minute thing. Ian sent for me."

"You are so spoiled," April said. "I'm jealous."

"Don't be. You're pretty spoiled yourself." For the last month, April had been happily dating one of their college friends, and had even admitted she might love him.

"Right? I can't believe it."

"I have to go, but I just wanted to let you know that I'll be off the grid for two days. We'll do lunch when I get back, so we can catch up."

"All right, Bai. Love you. And don't come back here with child."

Bailee laughed. "Shut up. Goodbye." She ended the call and sent a quick text to Mason, letting him know she was with Ian. Then she turned off her phone and walked into the hotel bar. She spotted Ian right away, sitting at the end of the bar, a drink in hand. Her eyes narrowed when she saw a woman cozy up to him. But then her heart soared when he shook his head and sent the woman away.

She slid onto the seat next to him and gestured for the bartender. When the man asked for her order, she told him to bring a bourbon for her and another for the gentleman next to her. Once her drink was in front of her, she took a sip, enjoying the smooth taste.

"Thanks for the drink," Ian said.

Bailee swiveled her bar seat around so she could

face him. He was dressed in dark jeans and a white button-down shirt. She was sure he could feel her gaze, but he didn't acknowledge her or even react to it. But that was okay. She could play this game, too. "Come here often?"

He arched a brow, shot her a sideways glance before turning to face her. His eyes traveled over her body, like he was memorizing everything about her. "No. But I needed a drink and figured I'd try it."

She crossed her legs and watched his gaze drop to her bare legs. Bailee had chosen a wine-colored strappy-back skater dress that showed just enough skin to drive him crazy. Bailee tipped her head up to the ceiling, noticed the little touches she hadn't noticed before. "I just flew in for the weekend," she told him. "To see my *friend*."

"Must be a good friend for you to wear a dress like that to see him."

Smirking, she nodded. "The best."

"Is he, now?" He slid off the seat. Ian inched closer to her and gripped the edge of her seat, caging her in with both arms.

"Yes," she breathed, staring into his eyes—eyes that seemed to see inside her, eyes that made her want to give in to the burn that worked its way through her body.

"What's your name?" he asked.

"Aries." He dropped his head to her shoulder, chuckling softly. "What's yours?"

"Ian. And this game is over." He traced the V of her dress with one finger. "I missed you, Bai."

"I missed you, too. Now kiss me."

Leaning in, he whispered, "You're bossy." But then his mouth was on hers, and she was lost. His kiss was full of need, and when his tongue slid between her lips, she moaned.

Too soon, he broke the kiss, and Bailee felt desperate for more of him. "I need you."

He brushed her knee with his thumb, and slid his hand up her thigh slowly. The feel of his fingers on her skin almost made her forget where they were. Almost.

Bailee snapped her legs closed. "What are you doing?" she asked. "We're in a public bar."

She knew Ian had chosen this spot at the bar purposefully, because it was off to the side, and hidden from most of the customers. But still...

He pressed a kiss to her shoulder. "Staking my claim," he murmured against her skin. "I wouldn't want your friend to come back and think he has a chance with you."

"Are you jealous?"

"Are you mine?"

Bailee raised a brow. "What do you think, Ian?"

"I want you to say the words, Bai." He nipped at her earlobe before pulling it into his mouth. "Your hands." He kissed the palms of her hands. "Your mouth." He pressed a soft kiss to her lips. "And your body." Ian slipped his hand under her dress and it wasn't long before tips of his fingers grazed her sensitive core. She gasped. "Tell me, baby. Tell me you're mine." He slipped his thumb under the band of her panties.

"I'm yours," Bailee whispered. She couldn't take it. His touch lit a fire in her that wouldn't be doused.

"Good. Now, tell me that no one makes you tremble or shiver or tingle the way I do."

"Nobody. Only you."

"You're mine." His voice was a low, husky growl.

"Yes."

"Not only is your body mine, but your mind is mine and your heart is mine."

Bailee shuddered. "Everything, baby. Everything is yours. And you're mine," she added.

"All yours." He caressed her cheek with his other hand.

"Ian?"

"Hmm?"

"Take me to bed."

It took less than five minutes for them to get to her room. Ian nearly tore the door off its hinges when the key card didn't work at first. Finally, the door clicked and he pushed it open. With hands roaming, lips nipping, they undressed.

"Get on the bed," he ordered. "Now."

Bailee didn't need to be told twice. She ran to the bed and jumped on it, laughing when he followed suit. Soon, they were in the throes of passion, moving together, giving and taking.

Ian gripped her hips, sinking all the way into her. "I'll never stop," he whispered. "I'll always make you feel this way."

Her orgasm burst through her with a fury, so intense it felt like she'd split in two. And he joined her soon after, moaning her name.

When Bailee came down from her orgasmic high, she opened her eyes to find Ian staring at her. He circled her nose with his. She loved his tender side. She loved how he took care of her, how he made sure she was always good.

Bailee kissed him, pouring her heart and soul into it. And when she pulled back, her breath caught at the love shining back at her through his eyes. "Ian." She traced his jaw, peppering kisses over his face. "I don't ever want to lose this feeling."

"We won't. I promise. Because of you, I know how to love."

Tears filled her eyes. "Stop making me cry, man."

He kissed her tears away. "My poor Bai. Don't cry. I love you."

"I know. Love you, too."

Chapter 17

Eight months later

Bailee waited outside the Detroit Metropolitan Airport. Ian's flight was due in any moment. The last two days had been a nightmare of flight delays and missed phone calls. But she'd finally received the call she'd been waiting for that morning. Ian told her to be there by eleven o'clock.

She glanced at her watch. It was now eleven thirty. No Ian. Grumbling a curse, she rested her forehead against the steering wheel. She yelped when someone knocked on the passenger-side window. Bailee jumped out of the car when she realized it was Ian. She ran into his waiting arms, into a delicious kiss.

When he set her down on the ground, she wiped her gloss off his lips. "You made it."

"Finally." He hugged her again. "You look good, baby."

"So do you."

Ian had shipped most of his belongings ahead of time, so he didn't have to carry so much luggage. It had been a long eight months of weekend visits, phone calls, emails and FaceTime. She'd visited him in New Orleans several times, and he'd flown home for the birth of Mason and Mia's baby.

When his assignment ended, Ian had turned down the opportunity to extend his employment and booked a flight home. He hadn't even told her about the offer until he'd purchased his ticket to come back to Michigan. His explanation had simply been, "I'm coming home. No more questions. I love you."

Ian tossed his bag in the trunk and hopped in the driver's seat, and soon they were on the road. He made a quick stop at his house to read his mail, eat and make love to Bailee. Then they hit the road to Traverse City. Dr. Solomon had planned a huge birthday celebration for Nonna, and Ian hadn't wanted to miss it.

They arrived at the Solomon estate early in the evening. It was still as beautiful as it had been the first time she'd seen it. And she couldn't wait to spend time there with Ian. When she entered the house with him right behind her, she was thrilled to see the Solomon family, the Jackson family and the Sanders family had already arrived. And...April?

"April!" Bailee exclaimed, hugging her friend. "What are you doing here? I thought you had a work thing this weekend."

Her bestie shrugged. "Mia invited me. Who turns down a minivacation at a beautiful resort?"

More hugs were exchanged, high fives were given,

cheeks were pinched and kisses were planted on foreheads.

Bailee's heart swelled in her chest at the love in the room. Everyone had taken time out of their busy schedules to gather and enjoy one another. She'd never grow tired of this. She eyed Ian, who was swinging Zoe in his arms. He looked incredible, with his tanned skin and bulging biceps. And the happy toddler in his arms loved her uncle "Een," as she called him. He met her gaze and winked, before he continued to make buzzing sounds against a delighted Zoe's belly.

Once they were settled in their room, the same suite Bailee had stayed in during the wedding week, they gathered for dinner in the outdoor kitchen. Dr. Solomon barbecued pork ribs and ribeye steaks, while Mrs. Solomon and her mother zoomed around, readying the table with the settings and dishes full of corn on the cob, macaroni and cheese, greens, fried potatoes and coleslaw. All of Bailee's favorite dishes.

Bailee snuck a cream puff from the dessert table before taking her seat next to Ian. There were tiny boxes on each place setting that they were all instructed not to open until after dinner. She wondered what type of reveal they would be treated to tonight. Mia was a new mother and Avery had recently announced her pregnancy, so it couldn't have anything to do with them. Love could be pregnant with Zoe's little sister or brother, but Bailee didn't think so. They'd recently had a conversation about babies, and Love had made it very clear that she wanted more time between the babies.

While Ian had been away, Bailee had grown very close to the Jackson clan. Even Ian's sister, Mel, had become a dear friend to her. It was Bailee who had encouraged Mel to follow her heart and attend business school instead of medical school like her father and brothers. And Bailee had been there when Mel broke the news to Dr. Law that she was moving to New York City next year to attend Columbia University. He'd taken the news surprisingly well, but that was likely because he didn't believe Mel would follow through— he had said as much. Yeah, he was still Dr. Law.

Dinner was served, and she piled her plate with tender ribs, a small piece of steak and a little bit of everything else. "This is so good." She cut into her steak and popped a piece into her mouth. "So tender."

Ian eyed her, a gleam in his eyes. "Yeah, except that's not your steak. You think you're slick."

Bailee giggled. She'd swiped Ian's steak off his plate a few minutes ago, while he was making funny faces at Zoe. "I'm sorry. I should have grabbed a bigger piece, and now it's all gone."

He smiled at her. "It's fine."

Once all the plates were cleared and everyone was full, Mia announced that it was time to open the gifts. Bailee picked up her box and shook it. It couldn't be a T-shirt because the box was so small. Maybe it was a key chain? Or a trinket from Nonna? A souvenir from Dr. Solomon's trip to Florence?

Everyone tore open their boxes, and Bailee watched for reactions. Except everybody's box was empty. Frowning, she finally opened hers and gasped. Inside her box sat a beautiful, clear, sparkling diamond. A ring. "Oh my God." She turned to Ian. "What is this?"

Ian turned to her. "You told me that you didn't want an out-of-the-ordinary proposal. But—"

"Did I tell you that?" Bailee thought proposals

should be intimate, either between the man and the woman or with a small gathering of close family and friends.

"You did. And stop interrupting me while I'm trying to be sincere." He mimicked the act of zipping up lips, before he pulled her chair closer to him.

Vaguely, she heard some "Aws" and "Oh my Gods" somewhere around her. But she couldn't look at anyone else but the man sitting in front of her.

Ian picked up the box—her box—and pulled the ring out. "I didn't need months to tell me that I want to be with you for the rest of my life. This past year, getting to know you and love you, has been the best year of my life. I don't regret taking the opportunity to serve my community, but I've also realized that being so far away from you for an extended period of time doesn't work for me."

Tears streaked down her cheeks, and he gently wiped them away with a tissue.

"I know beyond a shadow of a doubt that my life is nothing without you," Ian continued. "I love you so much, Bai. I want you to be Mrs. Jackson. Will you marry me?"

Bailee didn't need to think about it. She already knew what she wanted, so she shouted "Yes!" before climbing into Ian's lap, wrapping her arms around his neck and kissing him. She heard the applause and cheers, but Bailee couldn't stop kissing her future husband.

Soon, she heard the clearing of throats and realized she might have set the record for the longest kiss at a semipublic proposal. She pulled away and whispered to Ian, "Your hand is on my butt."

Ian chuckled and kissed her nose, then her chin. "I know." Then he smacked her butt for good measure. "I love you, Bai."

She traced his jaw with her finger. "I love you, too."

* * * * *

WHEN I'M WITH YOU

DONNA HILL

Big thanks to all of my readers new and old that have made The Lawsons of Louisiana series such a success. I couldn't do it without you.

Chapter 1

"Your sisters are planning *our* wedding," Avery said as she loaded the dishwasher.

Rafe handed her the glasses from the table. "Yeah, they can be a bit enthusiastic," he said chuckling. He came up behind her, bent over her body and grabbed her waist. "The main thing is we're going to be legal, official, permanent."

Avery straightened and turned to face him, leaned against the dishwasher. She looked into his eyes, and as always a flood of heat flowed through her. Being in the same air space with Rafe always did that to her, made her hungry for him, weak to his will. But this was *her* wedding, *her* day. She splayed her hands against his chest. "Look, babe, I know it's your family, and I don't want to cause any rifts, but...I need some space."

Rafe's simmering gaze slowly moved over her face, the way it did whenever he was trying to see beneath the surface of her words. She shifted her weight under his close scrutiny.

"I'll talk to them, okay," he said softly.

Avery pressed her lips together and nodded her head.

"Come 'ere." He pulled her tight against him. "All I want is for you to be happy. Just tell me what you want and I'll make it happen."

Avery rested her head against his chest, soothed by the steady beat of his heart. Her temple suddenly pounded and a flash of sharp pain shot across her eyes. Her body tensed.

Rafe eased back and looked down at her taut expression. "You okay? Another headache?" He stroked her cheek.

Avery let out a slow breath. "A little. It'll pass."

Since the explosion in Paris and the concussion she sustained when she'd rescued Rafe's father, she'd intermittently suffered from mild to severe headaches. The doctors assured her that they would lessen and then eventually disappear with time.

"Maybe we need to get the doctor to run some more tests."

"No." She shook her head. "It's only been a little over two months."

"Yes, but you go back to work next week. The doctor has to clear you. You have to be on your A-game, darlin'. You said so yourself."

She leaned up and kissed his lips. "And I will be." There was no way she would see any doctors and tell them what was really going on with her. They'd never clear her to return to duty. And if so it would be desk duty. She did not work her way up the ranks of the Secret Service to sit behind a desk. Plus, she was up for promotion. No way would she blow it. Two Advil. End of story. "I'm fine." She turned the dial on the dishwasher and it hummed to life. Another morning of domesticity.

After leaving Paris, Rafe took Avery to the Lawson compound to recuperate from her injuries before returning to Avery's place in Washington, DC. Rafe easily made her townhouse his second home. Their pseudo "living together" arrangement was easier than she'd imagined.

They were a natural fit with each other, as if living under the same roof was something they'd always done. Rafe was attentive, but gave her space. He possessed chef-like skills in the kitchen, a penchant for neatness—she never had to step over discarded clothing, or clean up after a meal—and above all he was a master in the bedroom who made her see heaven on a regular basis. This man was going to be her husband. Sometimes when she looked at him or held him tight between her thighs, she couldn't believe that Rafe Lawson was hers. What she wanted was just the two of them, but marrying Rafe was marrying his large, controlling family.

"You sure you'll be okay until I get back from 'Nawlins?" He wiped off the countertop with a damp cloth.

She shimmied onto the barstool at the island counter and extended her hands to Rafe. He took two long steps and was in front of her. He raised her hands to his lips and kissed the insides of her palms.

"I'll be fine, and right here when you get back." She leaned in to kiss him.

"Hmm, I can change my plans," he said against her cheek, "and stay here, which is what I'd rather do." He caressed her hips.

Avery giggled. "Me, too, but you've been gone long enough. Take care of your business."

He stepped deep between her legs. "Business can wait." He threaded his fingers through the hair at the nape of her neck, dipped his head and kissed her collarbone.

Avery sucked in a breath of desire and instinctively tightened her legs around him. "You're going to be late," she whispered.

He brushed his lips along her neck, nibbled the lobe of her ear. "Privilege is the perk of owning your own plane. Can't leave without me." He covered her lips with his and drew her tongue into his mouth.

Avery untied the belt on her robe and then looped her arms around his neck. "Thank you for perks," she said, as Rafe lifted her from the stool. She wrapped her legs around his waist while he walked them into her bedroom.

Rafe eased her down on the bed and braced his weight above her. "Say the word, darlin'," he whispered in her ear while he stroked her hip and then lifted her left thigh and draped it over his arm, "and I'll stay." He nuzzled her neck, dipped his head down to suckle the peaks of her breasts.

Her heart raced. "Rafe…" she moaned.

"Tell me what you want." He slid his hands beneath her and pushed deep inside.

"Ahhh…" She clung to him. "You…only you."

"You got me. Always," he said from between his teeth and let his body prove it.

"I can drive you to the airport," Avery dreamily offered as she stretched her naked body beneath the twisted pale blue sheets.

Rafe glanced over his shoulder, lifted the sheet and peeked underneath. "Naw, darlin', this is how I want to remember you while I'm gone." He lightly swatted her lush bottom and pushed up off the bed. "Gonna shower and dress. Want anything while I'm up?"

"Hmm," she moaned. "Nope." She tugged the sheet up to her chin and closed her eyes.

Rafe chuckled and padded off to the bathroom.

Avery distantly heard the rush of shower water, soon followed by Rafe's rendition of The Temptations' "My Girl." She smiled and burrowed into the overstuffed pillow.

How would she manage without Rafe? They spent their days talking, debating, laughing, investing in each other's happiness, and their nights consummating their love. This would be the first time they'd be apart...since Paris...

The scent of smoke filled her nostrils. Her heart raced. *Blackness. Screams. Pain. Sirens.* The sheets clung to her damp body. Sinking. She was sinking. Falling. Had to get out.

"Avery!" Rafe gently clasped her shoulder and sat next to her on the bed. "Cher..."

Her eyes flew open. Her body trembled.

Rafe gathered her up in his arms. "Sssh, just a dream, cher." He rocked and held her until the shaking stopped.

"I'm ok-aay." She forced a smile and pushed her damp hair away from her face.

"No, you're not. And I'm not going anywhere. Not leaving you."

Avery pushed herself into a sitting position. "I'm fine, Rafe. Really. Just a dream—like you said. The doctors said to expect flashbacks. That's all it was. Period." She took his face in her hands. "If it will make you feel better, I'll ask Kerry to stay over until you get back."

A deep line etched itself between sleek, dark brows. "No. Kerry has to work. You'll be alone all day."

"Rafe, it's just a headache and some bad dreams. I'm not an invalid."

"I'll go on one condition only." He looked hard into her eyes.

She folded her arms and pouted. "What?"

"You stay at my house in Arlington. Alice is there. She can get you whatever you need, keep you company."

"You mean keep tabs on me," she said with an arched brow.

"Well, yeah. That, too," he conceded with that slow smile.

Avery huffed, pondered the offer. "Okay. If that's what it's gonna take to get you on that plane."

"That's exactly what it's gonna take. I'll call and let Alice know to stock up. Make a list of anything special you want and I'll let her know." He pointed a finger at her. "List. Pack." He winked and then turned to get his clothes and dress.

By the time he'd finished dressing, Avery was ready to get into the shower. She'd left a list on the bed. Rafe grinned. Martini mix and taco fixings. He placed a call to Alice and let her know company was coming. Alice was delighted that Avery would be staying at the house and promised to take great care of her while he was gone.

"Got everything?" Rafe asked while he carried her bag to the door.

Avery stood in the middle of her living room and took a slow, deliberate look around. She drew in a deep breath. Every move that she'd made since she graduated high school was to establish independence. After she lost her mother in her teens and spent almost the next decade eating her way through life, before she hit her own near-life-or-death moment, she finally turned all her energy into gaining control over every aspect of her life—from healthy eating to religiously exercising, to a laser focus on rising up the ranks of the Secret Service. She cherished the life that she'd built for herself, *by herself*, even as her father worked tirelessly to keep her reined in.

This packing up and going to stay at Rafe's place, under his direction, went against every instinct of self-preservation that she had. She gritted her teeth. "I think so," she finally said. She hiked her oversize zebra-print tote over her shoulder, snatched up her keys from the table by the door and walked out. "What about my car?"

Rafe opened the passenger door to his Navigator and

froze when he caught the look of panic in her eyes. He cupped her cheeks in his hands. "Cher," he crooned, "we'll take your car if you want, and leave mine here. I'll take a cab to the airfield."

The burn of tears threatened to spill. She blinked rapidly and nodded in agreement. "Thank you," she whispered.

He leaned down and gently kissed her lips. "I know, darlin'," he said in his easy drawl. "This isn't what you want. But I promise, it's going to be all right. Trust me." He lifted her chin and looked into her eyes. "Trust me."

Avery swallowed over the dry knot in her throat. "I do."

"Good." He shut the passenger door of his Navigator, took her keys, walked around and opened her car door.

Avery tossed her tote on the back seat while Rafe stowed her bags in the trunk and then got in behind the wheel.

"Listen…" He buckled his seat belt. "I know you crave your space." He reached across the gearshift and took her hand. "All I want is to make sure you're okay. That you're safe. I'd make myself crazy in 'Nawlins worrying about you. I want to take care of you, cher. Let me," he added gently.

Avery leaned in and lightly kissed him. "I know…thank you…really."

He gave her a reflective look as he caressed her chin with his thumb. Then he turned the key in the ignition and pulled off.

Less than an hour later, Rafe eased Avery's car down the driveway of his Arlington, Virginia, home. He shut off the engine, just as Alice pulled the front door open and stepped out. She hurried over to the car.

"Mr. Rafe. So good to have you home. And Ms. Avery." She wrapped her arms around Avery in a motherly hug and buzzed her cheek with a kiss. "Come, come. Let's get you settled. Are you hungry?"

Avery giggled. "I'm fine, Alice. Thanks."

"I have everything all prepared. You can stay in the guest room, or Mr. Rafe's room," she added with a wink and then led them inside. "And I made a tray of snacks just in case," she tossed over her shoulder.

Rafe glanced at Avery. The smile on her face eased the knot of tension in his gut. He slid an arm around her waist and they walked inside.

Avery held Rafe's hand that rested on her hip. "Thank you for this," she said.

"Nothing to thank me for." He squeezed her hip. "I want you to be taken care of. Anything you need, let Alice know." He grinned. "She loves taking care of people."

"Your car is here!" Alice called out.

"See." He grinned and kissed her forehead. "Sorry, darlin'. I need to get going. Want to beat this weather."

Avery looped her arm through his, and they walked out of his bedroom, downstairs and out to the car that waited to take him to the airport.

"I'll call you when I get in."

"Fly safe."

"Always." He kissed her lightly. "Love you." He glanced past her toward the house. "Take care of my woman," he called out to Alice, who stood on the front steps. He gave Avery one last hug. "Call you tonight."

Avery nodded and stepped back as he got in the car, before taking a quick look at the overcast sky.

The car door slammed, and the car slowly eased down the driveway and out to the street. Avery felt a rush of emptiness open inside her. A warm arm slid around her shoulders and held her close. Alice smiled knowingly up at her.

"Mr. Rafe will be fine, and back before you know it. Come inside. You must try my jambalaya! Just a little taste," she teased with a sparkle in her eyes.

"I'd love some."

"Oh. My. God. This is sooo good," Avery gushed, finishing off another mouthful.

Alice beamed. "Have as much as you like. There's plenty." She pulled out a chair and sat opposite Avery at the circular wrought-iron and reclaimed-wood table.

"I am so happy that Mr. Rafe finally settled down."

Avery glanced up from beneath her lashes.

"His heart was so broken…after Janae." She slowly shook her head. "I didn't think he would ever be the same." She turned her palms up. "And he's not," she said succinctly. "He's better." She wagged a finger at Avery. "Because of you."

"What…was he like after…"

Alice's open expression grew somber. Her brows tightened. She spread her palms down on the table. "Rafe was always a little wild and reckless, especially with that motorcycle of his. But after Janae, whatever piece of himself that kept him halfway grounded broke. On the outside, he was the same—that easy smile, the charm, the chivalry. But there was a darkness that settled inside him. He took crazy chances, went from relationship to relationship, in constant conflict with his father—more than usual. I was afraid for him. Every time he got behind the wheel, or on that bike or up in that plane of his, I prayed." She made a quick sign of the cross. "Because I knew, under that smile, he didn't care about his own life anymore."

"I had no idea," she murmured.

"I'd been with the family for years, but when Rafe decided to take over this house, I came here. He needed someone to look after him since he wasn't going to look after himself. Back in 'Nawlins, he has his sisters and brother."

"The move had to be hard on you."

"I've been taking care of Mr. Rafe and his family since they were running around in shorts. He's like a son to me." She lowered her voice as if she feared being overheard. "Always was my favorite." She winked.

Avery grinned.

"Then he met you and the light came back to his eyes. His laughter is real again and that…thing that drove him to be so reckless seems to have stepped into the background. He wants to be around for you."

Avery's throat tightened. "How'd you know I needed to hear this today?"

Alice patted Avery's fisted hand. "I haven't spent half my life taking care of people without being able to spot need in someone."

"I'm glad he has you in his life."

Alice pushed up to her feet. "Now that you're part of the family, I'll be looking after you, too. And I think you could use a hot bath, a fluffy robe and a good movie."

Avery tossed her head back and laughed. "You read my mind. Alice, can I ask you something?"

"Of course." She collected the plates.

"How do I get Dominique, Desiree and Lee Ann to… let me have my own wedding?"

Alice pursed her lips. "Hmm, those three sisters together are like a hurricane, with Dominique at the center of the storm." She turned on the faucet in the sink, rinsed the plates and put them in the dishwasher. "They adore their brother, and they're so thrilled that he's happy again—they want to orchestrate every detail of the occasion for him." She dried her hands on a black-and-white striped towel, blew out a breath. "One piece of advice I can offer, you don't want to get in between Rafe and his sisters. If what they're doing is too much, talk to them. Make sure you're part of the plans and decisions. All of you women love him, so do it together."

Avery bobbed her head. "Thanks." She got up. "In the meantime, I'm going to take your advice and sit in a hot tub for a while."

Avery went upstairs. She searched the cabinet beneath the sink and located the bath beads that she'd brought over the last time she was here. She poured a handful into the water rushing into the tub from the jets. Although she took a shower earlier, the bath would be therapeutic. Almost immediately the scent of soothing lavender filled the room. She stripped out of her clothes, turned off the faucets and sank into the steamy, scented water.

Every muscle sighed in pleasure. She leaned her head back against the lip of the tub and closed her eyes. Alice's words of advice played softly. She didn't have the time or opportunity to go down to Louisiana to do a face-to-face with Rafe's sisters. She'd figure something out. She'd find a way to get them to accept that it was time to let Rafe go and that she would be part of his life and their family.

Chapter 2

Rafe disembarked from his Cessna. Flying always filled him with an awesome sense of invincibility. High above the clouds was a feeling that he could not describe. The only thing more thrilling was being with Avery. He smiled. He'd barely been gone three hours and he missed her already.

He thanked the crew, hopped on his motorcycle that he'd left parked at the landing strip and sped home. As he rode with a controlled abandon, the landscape of his life spread out before him. He'd spent years doing just this, racing through life, not taking the time to really see what was in front of him. Sure, there were good times to be had, and he'd never want to go back and change them. But he'd done it all while running on empty. For all the travel, the music gigs, the successes—and failures—and the women, there was a space inside him that none of those things could fill. He was starting to feel whole again from the inside. All the bourbon, reckless behavior, and even the fights with his father were all part of trying to fill the emptiness.

He maneuvered around a slow-moving minivan, resisting the urge to lean in and press the gas all the way down to the blacktop of the highway. He smiled beneath the tinted visor that shielded his face. It was all Avery's fault. She was the one responsible for his reincarnation.

Rafe signaled for his exit, dutifully followed the flow of cars up the ramp and out into residential traffic. After a short ten-minute ride he pulled into the driveway of his two-story townhouse. The garage door whirred open. He parked his bike inside and entered the house through the door that led to the kitchen. He set his helmet on the granite countertop, tugged off the black leather gloves and tossed them there, as well.

He walked through the kitchen and into the living space to be greeted by the pile of mail that had been slid inside the mail slot of the front door. Scooping up the stack of bills, newspapers and subscription magazines, he absently sorted through half of them, deciding what to keep and what to toss, before dropping them on the end table. And then he headed upstairs to his bedroom.

He wanted to change his clothes first. After that he would get in touch with his producer to set up a meeting about the new tracks, and then check in with Quinten and try to twist his arm into coming to the Big Easy to sit in on a set. He'd bribe him with gumbo. Tomorrow he would go to the office. Although he'd put together a solid team for his foundation, he still needed to show his face and be a presence. Besides, there was something intangibly fulfilling about walking into a building and into rooms he'd envisioned that were now a reality. But it was the good work the RBL Foundation did for the young people of the community that was immeasurable. For all the crazy bull that he'd done in his life, the Foundation at least put a fresh coat of paint over it, and it was certainly an endeavor that he could be proud of.

He pulled on a pair of well-worn gray sweatpants and a T-shirt and then went back downstairs in search of food. Passing through the living room he grabbed the mail he'd tossed on the end table and took it with him to the kitchen.

Although the Lawson family always had a housekeeper, each of the Lawson siblings learned how to cook. And if Rafe had to say so himself, he was pretty damned good. He tugged open the fridge. Milk, eggs, a half roll of salami and something in a plastic bowl that he didn't recognize. The trick of course was to remember to shop. He pulled open the vegetable bin and grinned with relief at the sight of a green and a red pepper that still had life in them, along with a package of shredded cheddar cheese. Omelet coming right up.

While he wolfed down his omelet, he snapped open one of the major New Orleans newspapers that he received via delivery service. He started at the back of the paper, in the sports section, worked his way forward and nearly choked on his omelet when a picture of him and Avery—taken when he had no idea—with the caption "Rafe Lawson, New Orleans's most eligible bachelor, engaged to Avery Richards." There was a short paragraph that followed, announcing the engagement and that Avery was the daughter of Senator Horace Richards. It went on to state that the marriage of Lawson and Richards will redefine the political power couple. The nuptials are scheduled for early summer. No date has been set.

With every word, the knot in his stomach tightened. First of all, where the hell did anyone get their picture? Were they being followed? And most important, who gave the damned newspaper information on his and Avery's engagement? He slapped the paper down on the counter. Had to be one of his sisters, and he would bet money that it was Dominique. It had her signature all over it.

"Shit." He pushed back from the table with such force that the stool toppled backward, hit the floor and rolled. He gripped the paper in his fist and stormed upstairs to get dressed. His visit to the family home was going to be sooner rather than later.

Friday nights when the family was in town they generally turned up at the family home at some point. Hopefully tonight would be no different, which would help him avoid having to make a round of house calls. More than likely Lee Ann was in DC with Sterling. And he didn't think the announcement in the paper was her doing, anyway.

Rafe opted to drive his Audi. As furious as he was he didn't want to get on the road with his bike. He checked the trunk to make sure his small duffel bag with his "on the road" change of clothing was inside. He unzipped the bag and did a quick check of the contents. Satisfied, he slammed the trunk shut and got in behind the wheel. He had a very strong feeling that tonight would be a three-bourbon evening and driving would not be an option.

Halfway between his home and the family residence Rafe used the voice-activated phone feature and called Avery.

"Hi, darlin'," he said the moment the call connected.

"Hi." She yawned.

"Everything good? Sounds like I woke you."

"Hmm, I guess I really did nod off. Alice fed me and insisted I take a hot bath." She yawned again. "I thought I was reading," she said over light laughter.

Rafe chuckled. "Not going to keep you. You need your rest. Just wanted to hear your voice and let you know I got here okay."

"Sounds like you're outside or something."

"Yeah, I'm on my way to the family house."

"Oh."

"Plan to talk to my sisters…about the wedding." No reason to tell her more than that. He'd deal with the mess in the papers.

Alice's advice rushed to the forefront. "Rafe…babe, I was being overly sensitive. I'm not going to put you in between me and your family. When I come down there next month I can talk to them myself. I know they mean well."

Rafe ran his tongue across his bottom lip. He couldn't let it go. It wasn't in his DNA, but he wasn't going to upset Avery. "Whatever you want to do, darlin'. As long as you're happy and stress-free. To me, that's what's important."

"Thanks. Well, say hello to the fam for me."

"I will."

"Love you."

"You, too, cher. I'll call you tomorrow."

"Okay. Have a good evening."

"You, too."

The call disconnected. Rafe frowned. He didn't want to slip into a habit of lying to Avery. Even though what he told her wasn't an out-and-out lie, it was a lie by omission. If he could stomp out the newspaper reports, then she wouldn't have to know. His line of reasoning was thin to say the least. What he needed to do, in the meantime, was set his sisters straight. The last thing he wanted was for Avery to get bombarded with her face plastered on the tabloids and splashed across every Louisiana paper's gossip section. He was used to it. He grew up on the receiving end of razor-sharp pens and intrusive flashbulbs, lived much of his adult life as a "trending topic" and grew immune to seeing his face on the pages of the news or covers of magazines. But that wasn't Avery's life. He had to do everything in his power to protect her. She may carry a gun and have security clearances, but both were useless against vigilant and determined journalists.

Rafe made the turn onto the private grounds where the Lawson mansion stood, glad to see some lights on, signaled right and eased his vehicle down the winding road that opened onto the sweeping green landscape that braced the eight-bedroom, six-bath family home. Growing up, it was nothing to play hide-and-seek in the massive house, peek into the formal dining room to see the famous faces of those that most only saw on television, slide down the mahogany bannisters, race for hours across the grassy lawn, attend the best schools or skip rocks along the pond that ran behind the house. For him and his siblings, and cousins that frequented the home, it was all pretty normal. But his father and his uncles drilled into them from the time that they were old enough to sit still and listen that the life the Lawsons lived was a privilege, not a right, and as such they owed society a debt, and that debt was to pay it forward. Each of his siblings, minus himself and Dominique, embraced the Lawson mantra. As the two rebels of the family, Rafe and Dominique were hell-bent and determined to do whatever was necessary to tick their father off. Their track record in that regard was impeccable. Dominique should have been his twin instead of Desiree's. He and Dom were true sibling soulmates. However, that pesky thing called love swept through the Lawson clan like a summer storm and took each of them out one by one, Dominique included. Rafe remained the last holdout—until Avery.

He parked on the side of the house, used his key to open the front door. The aroma of backyard barbecuing mixed with laughter beckoned him. He followed the lip-smacking scents and was met by the wide-eyed surprise of his aunt Jacqueline, his brother Justin and his fiancée, Bailey.

"Rafe!" Jacqueline greeted him, her smile wide. "I thought you were in DC, baby."

"Hey, big bro," Justin said, raising a bottle of beer in salute.

Rafe rounded the white wrought-iron table, leaned down and gave his aunt a hearty kiss on the cheek. "Hey, Aunt J, good to see you. Where's Ray?"

Raymond Jordan had long been his aunt's freelance photographer. They'd traveled the world together, chasing that elusive story in some of the most exotic and often dangerous places on the globe. Finally they realized that what they needed—beyond the excitement of the next assignment—was each other. More than that, Raymond was instrumental in seeing his aunt through one of the most difficult times in her life. As much as her brother Branford's bone marrow saved her body, Raymond's love saved her soul. Now that the Lawson children were either married off or working on it, the house for the most part was empty. Jacqueline and Raymond decided to return to Jacqueline's childhood home and finally put down some roots.

Jacqueline laughed at her nephew's question. "Down in the wine cellar. He swears he's a wine expert now."

Rafe chuckled and went to bear-hug his brother. "Hey, bro. Didn't expect to see you here. When did ya'll get in?"

"Came in from New York this morning. Just for the weekend."

Rafe turned to his sister-in-law-to-be. "Bailey, woman, you still hanging out with this guy," he teased and buzzed her cheek.

Bailey giggled. "No other choice. He's stuck with me."

Justin draped his arm around Bailey's shoulder and winked up at his brother.

"You two keep it up and somebody's gonna write a book about you," Rafe playfully warned.

"Very funny," Justin groused. "But I see you're still in the headlines." He lifted his chin toward a magazine tossed on top of the side table.

Rafe's eyes narrowed and zeroed in on the magazine.

"My man," came a hearty greeting from behind Rafe.

Rafe looked over his shoulder. Raymond stepped out onto the veranda with a bottle of wine in each hand.

"Now it's a party," Raymond joked and set the bottles down on the table.

Rafe grinned. "Was just asking about you. Looking good, man."

"Other than the snowcaps," he said, running a hand over his head and then stroking his tapered goatee, "I'm feeling good." He patted his chiseled belly. "Gotta keep up with my gorgeous wife."

"How's Avery doing?" Bailey asked.

"She's good," Rafe said on a breath. "Heading back to work next week."

"So soon," Jacqueline said with a frown. She held out her flute, which Raymond filled with chilled red wine. "Seems like that mess in France was just the other day," she softly said and mouthed her thanks to Raymond, who took a seat next to her. "Your father is still recovering. Still needs a cane to get around and rehab once per week."

"Dad's injuries were a little more severe, Aunt J. He had broken bones, *and* he's no kid."

"Still…" She sipped her wine. "As long as she's better."

The headaches, the nightmares… The family didn't need to know all that. "Yeah, me too." He stepped around his brother and pulled up a chair from the back end of the veranda.

"Beer's in the cooler," Justin offered.

"Thanks." He flipped open the cooler and took out a can and then reached for the magazine. His jaw tightened. There was a picture of him holding open a car door for Avery, with the caption "Louisiana playboy Rafe Lawson a person of interest to Secret Service Agent Avery Richards." He muttered a string of curses under his breath. "You wanted to know what brought me here," he ground out, flashing a look at his aunt. "That's why." He tossed the offending magazine onto the table.

"Guess you haven't seen the local daily paper," Justin said with a raised brow. "Big spread."

Rafe's jaw tightened.

"Rafe," Jacqueline began, her tone soft and entreating. "You know how this works, especially with our family."

"*I* do. But Avery doesn't."

"Maybe not, but unfortunately when she agreed to marry you it came with all the Lawson baggage. Media has been tracking your every move since you were a teenager."

"Gotta admit, big bro, you always give them plenty to feed on," Justin added.

And now Avery was paying for his wild ways. Rafe pushed out a breath and plopped down in the available chair, stretched his long legs out in front of him. He snapped off the top of the beer and took a long, deep swallow. "Yeah," he muttered in reluctant agreement. "Pictures are one thing, but giving details is something else."

"What do you mean?" Bailey asked.

"Announcements in the papers about our engagement. Someone had to tell them, and it wasn't me."

Everyone got quiet.

Rafe looked from one averted face to the next. "Dominique," he said for all of them. He shook his head.

"You know Dom," Jacqueline offered, stretching out

her hand to cover his. "She's so happy for you and Avery. Making the announcement wasn't done to hurt you."

"I know."

"Your wedding is all she talks about."

Rafe sighed. He knew his family was sincerely happy that he was finally settling down, that he'd found someone to fill the space in his life. After Janae, he'd gone on a buck-wild, non-stop binge of reckless living. When he met Avery, his world finally came into focus and his nonchalant attitude shifted. He finally, for the first time in years, wanted more than the thrill of the moment. He wanted a forever. His aunt and brother were right, of course. He'd lived his life, along with the rest of his family, under the glare of the spotlight. However, it was a part of his reality that he didn't want for Avery, especially when the glare of the spotlight was intentional. Add the zeal of his sisters into the mix, wanting to have their hands in every aspect of the wedding, and it was a blowup waiting to happen. As much as he may not have a problem with his sisters planning his wedding, his first obligation now was to Avery. She was the only one he wanted to make happy. Dominique was going to have to take a step back. Two steps.

"Dom coming by this weekend?" Rafe asked.

"Probably," Jacqueline said. "I was planning Sunday dinner. She usually drops by."

Rafe nodded. He pushed up from the chair and stood. "In the meantime, what's a brotha gotta do to get some of that barbecue?"

The tense air filled with relieved laughter.

"That's what I'm talkin' 'bout," Raymond said.

Rafe walked over to the stainless-steel grill that was set up outside of the veranda. *Sunday couldn't get here fast enough*. He loaded a plate with ribs and a side of salad to take the edge off. He and Dominique were going to have a serious chat.

Chapter 3

Avery slipped on the pale peach satin robe, which Rafe purchased for her on one of their spontaneous vacations, and went downstairs to the kitchen.

"Good morning!" Alice greeted her with a broad smile. "You look rested."

"Good morning. Yes, I am. Hmm, something smells delicious."

"Cheese grits, maple-dipped bacon and light-as-a-feather eggs. I wasn't sure when you would be getting up. But everything is in the warmer. Fresh coffee and juice. Take as much as you want. I need to run some errands in a bit, but I should be back in an hour or two."

"Sure. Go."

"Do you need anything?"

"No. I'm fine. Thanks." She pulled out a chair from the breakfast nook and sat down, while Alice slipped out of the kitchen and took care of all the magic she created in the house. The silver warming tray, and a glass bowl of chopped fresh fruit was in the center of the table. Avery lifted the oblong cover of the warming tray and smiled. She had to admit, it would be really easy to get used to this kind of life. She scooped eggs, bacon and grits onto her plate and added fresh fruit.

A copy of *The Washington Post* lay neatly folded at the end of the table. She pulled it closer and then poured herself a mug of coffee.

The front page was plastered with raw images of the devastation across the Caribbean islands and Puerto Rico that were still recovering, months later, from a series of catastrophic hurricanes that ravished the areas. A wave of sadness swept through her. She could not begin to imagine what the people continued to go through. Meanwhile, here at home, the country was not being torn apart by outside forces, but from those within.

She slowly chewed her food and flipped the pages, scanning the headlines, from international news to arts and entertainment. She choked at the shock of seeing her face staring back at her from the paper and then grabbed a glass of juice to wash down the bacon.

Avery's pulse quickened. It was a picture of her and Rafe at that outdoor café they loved in DC. Beneath it was a caption and a short paragraph, announcing their engagement and pending summer wedding. They were at that café shortly before she went off on detail to Paris, *before* the engagement. Her thoughts turned in circles. *She* certainly wasn't anyone a journalist would be interested in. If anything, because of her work she remained as low-key and inconspicuous as possible. She dropped the paper down on the table. It wasn't her they were photographing; it was Rafe, and she was swept up in the tide of his notoriety even outside of Louisiana. Collateral damage.

Having his sisters orchestrate her wedding was difficult enough to navigate, but this kind of publicity could jeopardize her job, more important, put at risk the people she was sworn to protect.

"Dammit!" She pushed away from the table. This was going to turn into a nightmare. She felt it in the pit of her stomach and she had no idea what to do about it.

"I just saw it," Kerry said into the phone. "Are you okay?"

"I don't know, girl. I'm stuck between stunned that the rest of the world gives a damn who I marry, to furious that the rest of the world gives a damn." She pushed out a breath of frustration. "It was bad enough when my own father had me followed when me and Rafe first started dating. At least I could get him to stop with his craziness. This is a whole other story and I have no idea how this is going to play out at work."

"Hmmm, yeah, there's that. But, hey, no way is the Secret Service going to allow photographers to trail around, taking pictures."

Avery let her head flop back against the cushion of the couch. "I guess," she muttered.

"If it helps any I haven't heard any whisperings or gossip here at work."

"That's good, and I want it to stay that way."

"Listen… I know how you are about privacy. It's part of our job, but it's also part of who you are. I know you. If you could move through the day without having to give over anything of yourself, you would. I get that your self-imposed isolation is a defense mechanism. If no one can get close, no one can hurt you. But now there's Rafe."

Even the sound of his name made her heart tumble in her chest.

"What you have going with Rafe is a whole new world for you. You're going to have to find a way to deal with it, sis, if you want to marry him."

"I know," she whispered. "I just wish…it was the two of us, ya know. He has this big-ass family…"

"Try to look at it this way, you'll finally have not only a husband but a *real* family, Avery, with sisters and brothers and cousins. You won't be that motherless, only child anymore. Embrace it, instead of trying to keep it like a side chick." They both laughed at her comparison. "You deserve a family," she added softly.

It was true. She did deserve a family, although she had no idea what being part of one even meant. After her mother died, with no siblings or extended family, it was her and her father, Horace. Rather it was *her*. Horace Richards turned his entire life toward building his career in politics. She was on her own. Kerry was the closest thing to family that she had…until Rafe.

"I'll try," she conceded. "Anyway, stop by when you get off."

"His place is out in Arlington, right?"

"On second thought, I need to get out of the house. Why don't we meet for dinner? I can drive in."

"Sounds like a plan."

"Seven?"

"Works for me."

"Let's meet up at Baldwin's. We haven't been there in a minute." Baldwin's, named in honor of literary icon James Baldwin, was renowned for its excellent cuisine, but especially for the literati who frequented the establishment, often reading from their new works, performing spoken word or just chilling. The vibe was stimulating while simultaneously relaxing.

"Perfect. See you there."

"Bye." Avery disconnected the call and set the phone down on the table. She glanced around. What was she going to do with herself for the rest of the day? Maybe she'd go for a run, burn off some of her pent-up energy, clear her head.

She pushed up from the couch and went into the bedroom to change clothes.

"Alice," she called out from the front door. "I'm going for a short run. Be back soon."

"Sure." She peeked her head out from the kitchen. "Should I fix lunch?"

Avery opened the front door. "Only if you promise to eat with me."

Alice smiled. "Okay."

"Great. Be back soon—in about an hour or so."

Avery stepped out into the bright afternoon. A light breeze blew, perfect for running. She did a few light stretches, started off and never noticed the car parked across the street.

Baldwin's, as always for a Saturday night, sizzled with energy. Music from the house's jazz band played their rendition of "'Round Midnight," beckoning every customer who walked through the door to bob his or her head to the rhythm.

Avery could see from peeking around the tinted windows that separated the seated guests from the hostess station, that there were barely any empty tables. There were two sets of customers ahead of her and Kerry waiting to be seated: a couple and a party of four. Hopefully the wait wouldn't be too long.

Baldwin's, beyond the cultural significance of honoring the author, activist and icon James Baldwin, held a special place in her heart. On one of several visits when Rafe visited her in DC, Baldwin's was one of the venues where she heard him play. Was it that night that she fell irrevocably in love with him when he played Coltrane's "Love Supreme" to a standing ovation?

Kerry nudged her.

Avery blinked. "What?"

"What are you grinning about?"

"Oh," she laughed lightly, amused that she was caught in her daydream. "Just thinking about one of the nights I was here with Rafe."

"Table for two?" the hostess asked.

"Yes. Thank you," Kerry answered.

She took two menus from the holder on the podium and handed them off to a waitress. "Mia will show you to your seats."

Avery and Kerry walked several steps behind Mia as they wound their way around the dark circular tables, which were topped with white linen and illuminated by votive-candle centerpieces. The space, which was reputed to be one of the Underground Railroad passages, was rife with alcoves, thick cedar-wood rafters, plank floors and carvings in the wood walls, which urban legend claimed are the names and dates of slaves who had escaped—a testament to their passage. Each area of the two-story restaurant was designated as music, art, science, law, literature and named after a noted black figure, like Sojourner Truth, Nat Turner, Thurgood Marshall, Toni Morrison, Dr. King, Malcolm, Ida B. Wells, Gil Scott Heron, Sonia Sanchez, of course Baldwin and many others. Periodically, the management would switch out a namesake and replace it with another noted figure. On the tabletops, along with the candles, were tent cards with writings from the icons. Coming to Baldwin's was always an experience, as well as a mini lesson on the wealth of black history.

Tonight, Avery and Kerry were seated in the Thurgood Marshall section, which was off to the right of the stage, but still with great views of the comings and goings of the space.

Avery and Kerry settled in their seats and Mia took their drink orders, promising to be back shortly.

"I've been looking forward to this all day," Avery admitted. She flipped open the menu. "Yes, crab cakes!"

Kerry chuckled but then suddenly stopped.

Avery glanced up from the menu and landed on Mike, who was walking toward their table. She laid the menu flat.

"Avery...my God." His dark brown eyes widened in genuine surprise, followed by a smile that was actually warm. He took it upon himself, pulled out the extra chair and sat. He leaned in toward Avery. "How are you?" he asked, his voice low and insistent.

Tonight, Avery desperately wanted to get away from everything that reminded her of Paris and what happened. Mike was a big reminder. They were both on duty the day of the explosion. When she came to, debris and bodies were everywhere. Mike was hurt during the blast. Her training kicked in and she began aiding the injured, one of them being Rafe's father, another was Mike, among the dozen or so others. She and Mike had their standoffs during their time at the Secret Service, both personal and professional, and were both up for the same promotion. Ironic that Mike should be right as rain and she was...

"Good to see you, too, Mike," Avery finally said.

"Word on the street is that you'll be back this week. True?"

"True."

He nodded. "It'll be good to have you back, Avery. Really."

"Thanks, Mike."

"Well, good to see you. You, too, Kerry."

Kerry umm-hmmed in her throat.

"Enjoy your evening." He got up and walked away.

Kerry reached across the table and covered Avery's fisted hand with her own. "You okay?"

Avery nodded. "Fine." She pushed out a breath. "Going to have to get back to dealing with Mike sooner or later."

"I still can't believe that with all you went through, the heroics not to mention the injuries that you sustained, that Mike is even in the running for the promotion." Kerry shook her head in disbelief.

"You know as well as I do that this is an old-boys' club. The fact that women are part of the club at all, *and* rising up the ranks, still ticks off a lot of the establishment. If they can find anything to disqualify me, they will."

Mia returned with their drinks and took their dinner order.

Kerry raised her glass. "To kicking butt and taking names."

Avery tapped her glass against Kerry's. "All day." She took a long sip of her frozen strawberry margarita. She would not let anything or anyone stand in the way of getting what she rightly deserved, even if that meant lying to the doctors. No way would she stand down and let Mike walk in the shoes that should be hers. She picked up the tent card and read the inscription. It was a quote from Thurgood Marshall. "A man can make what he wants of himself if he truly believes that he must be ready for hard work and many heartbreaks." Exactly, and she was ready.

Chapter 4

Even after all the time that had gone by, and Miami, Florida, had become her home for the past sixteen years, she still kept up with the news from Louisiana and DC, and of course New York City, from her online subscriptions. It helped in her ongoing recovery to read about things that were once so familiar to her. There were still, even now, parts of her life that she could not distinguish between reality or a false memory. But the one thing she knew for certain was that she had been deeply and irrevocably in love. Now *he* was in love with someone else, marrying someone else.

His smile still made her soul shift, her heart beat just a little faster. She ran her finger across his face on her computer screen. He looked happy, truly happy...without her.

She lifted her hand and touched the scar that ran the length of her forehead, which she covered with bangs or innovative hairstyles. The burns she'd sustained on her legs had healed well, and were barely noticeable anymore. Some days when the pain was really bad she used a cane, but most of the time the medication the doctor prescribed worked.

She tilted her head to the side, studied the image from an angle. His fiancée was beautiful in an understated way. A part of her knew that she needed to let him and the past go. But the part of her that remembered what her life had been like with him wouldn't let her. He was the only thing from that time that she truly remembered. Them. The two of them against the world. The memory anchored her, kept her from losing the last vestiges of herself and falling into a dark hole of a manufactured past.

Sixteen years is enough time to move on. Rafe clearly did. She had for the most part. It was best—at least that's what her parents had told her. She'd believed them even though much of what their relationship had been was more mist than substance. The fact that she'd survived at all was a miracle, the doctors said, and memory loss was the price that she paid for her survival. She'd done years of physical therapy, rounds of plastic surgery, seen countless specialists, but most of her life prior to that day was hazy at best. Except for Rafe Lawson. He was the only constant.

She longingly studied his picture before closing the cover of the computer. Much of what her life could have been was ripped from her, her body altered, her memory stolen. For years she'd been at the mercy of doctors and therapists and her parents, and bit by bit she began to create a new life. But she had to go back into the past. She owed it to herself and to Rafe. He loved *her* first and seeing her again would make him remember.

Chapter 5

Rafe returned to his Louisiana home, soothed somewhat by his aunt's calming words. She'd pulled him to the side shortly before he left to remind him that Dominique was his reflection and could have been his twin instead of Desiree's. Dom lived for excitement, upsetting the status quo and making a splash. Add in the fact that she adored her big brother and it was no surprise that she wanted the world to share her joy. Not to mention that Dominique Lawson thrived on attention, even if the attention was vicarious. He grabbed his go-bag from the trunk and carried it inside, thankful that he didn't have to use it. He shut the house door behind him, picked up the pile of mail he'd left on the table and turned on the lights against the overhanging gray of a new day. His aunt J was right. He and Dom were two sides of the same coin. He tugged off his jacket, tossed it on a side chair in the living room and dropped the mail on the couch, before turning on some music. Truth be told, the announcements and the pictures didn't really bother him, but they bothered Avery. So, somehow, he was going to have to get Dom to put a halt to her personal public-relations campaign, and for his sisters Lee Ann and Desiree to loosen the reins of wedding planning. And he had to do all that without starting WWIII. *Lucky me.*

He crossed the living room to the bar and fixed a shot of bourbon and then flopped back on the couch. He took a deep swallow, leaned his head back and closed his eyes. On Sunday he would get with Dominique and straighten things out. End of that story. But he still had plenty of other business to handle now that he was home, and he intended to make a quick pit stop to New York to get with Q, since it was unlikely that he'd bring Muhammad to the mountain, before returning to Virginia.

A lot had been put on hold since Avery's and his father's injuries from the bombing in Paris. Even though his nightclub and his foundation had good people at the helm, he kept his hand in. Lack of oversight was the downfall of too many businesses, and he had no intention of letting his become a statistic.

He finished off his drink and went through a mental checklist of everything he needed to take care of in the next few days. One thing that nagged at him, and something that he and Avery never really discussed, was where they would live. His businesses were in Louisiana, but her job was in DC. He supposed it was an unspoken understanding that he would be the one to relocate. It was easier for him, of course. Didn't mean he had to like it.

He blew out a breath and stretched his arm to gather up the mail he'd dumped on the other end of the couch, flipped through the envelopes and relegated each to either take care of or ignore. He stopped halfway, tossed everything else aside as he stared for a moment at the embossed return address of which he was very familiar with—the family attorney. Or rather his father's attorney that the family used. How had he missed this?

Frowning, he turned the envelope over, ripped it open and pulled out the thick sheaf of folded papers. His head jerked back as he read the first page for the second time.

"What the hell…" His eyes ran over the words in utter disbelief and rising fury.

His father had always tried to control the lives of his children no matter how old they were or how far away they moved. But this! He hurled a string of expletives, picked up his phone to call his father but stopped. This conversation deserved a stare-you-in-the-eye sit down.

He shoved the pages back in the envelope, got up and put it in his go-bag. After he took care of his business here at home and in New York, his father's office in DC would be his next stop. He pulled out his cell from his back pocket and swiped to his phone calls. He pressed the phone icon, leaned back and waited.

"Hey, darlin'."

"Hi! I'm just walking in the door."

"Oh. Okay. Go get settled. We can talk another time."

"No. It's fine."

He heard a door close. "Everything good?"

"Yes. Kerry and I went to Baldwin's tonight."

He chuckled. "Love that place. Who was on set tonight?"

"House band. What about you? How was your visit?"

"Went well." His gaze drifted to his bag and the envelope that stuck out. "Anyway, cher, you get yourself together. We'll talk tomorrow. I'm kinda beat."

"Okay. Tomorrow, then." She paused. "I love you."

"Love you, too, cher. No matter what. Rest well."

"I will."

Rafe pressed the icon to end the call and tossed the phone toward the far end of the couch.

Chapter 6

Generally, after talking with Rafe, she always felt better, secure, uplifted, everything but what she felt now. She slipped out of her robe, turned back the sheets and crawled under the covers. Something was wrong. She felt it in the tone of Rafe's voice. It wasn't what he said, but what he didn't.

Had he brought up her concerns about the wedding and it didn't go well? Had he gotten into it with his sisters? She should have told him not to say anything. She was a big girl and didn't need her husband-to-be running to her rescue. She was skilled in dealing with insurmountable obstacles. How difficult could three sisters be?

She turned on her side and switched off the nightstand lamp, but it was hours before she finally fell into an exhausted sleep.

* * *

Alice was busy in the kitchen when Avery wandered in close to noon.

"Well, well, there you are." She wiped down the counter with a damp cloth. "You were up late."

Avery plopped down on a counter chair. "Couldn't sleep after I got in last night. Thought watching television would help. Sorry if I kept you up."

"Not at all. I'm a night owl. Came down to make some warm milk and I saw the television light on under your door." She came to stand beside Avery's hunched form. "Are you feeling okay? You don't look like yourself."

Avery forced a smile. "Who do I look like?" she teased.

Alice placed a comforting hand on Avery's stiff shoulder. "Like a woman who needs to talk." She sat down.

Avery blinked rapidly. She lowered her head and then glanced briefly at Alice. The only female in her life that she'd confided in was Kerry. Growing into womanhood without her mom, there was a reluctance inside that kept her from forming any female bonds for fear that the bond would be broken, taken from her like her mother was. She had no frame of reference for mothering, even as she desperately craved it.

Tears, unbidden, slid from her eyes. Instinctively, Alice gathered Avery in her arms and held her close, let her cry. Tenderly she stroked her back and cooed soft words into Avery's hair. "Let it out," she soothed. "It's all right."

"I'm s-orry," Avery whispered and sniffed.

"Nothing to be sorry for. We all need a good cry every now and then."

Avery sniffed harder, wiped her eyes with the back of her hand and lowered her head.

Alice eased back but kept her hands planted on Avery's shoulders. "Want to tell me what's bothering you?" she gently asked.

Avery pushed out a long breath. "I don't know how to handle being in this family, any family. I've had to go at it on my own for most of my life. Then there's my career. It's all about orders and following instructions, being on alert, suspicious." She sighed. "In my life outside of work it's the only time when I can pull away from the straitjacket of my everyday life. Now, with the wedding and Rafe's family…all of those mixed feelings and experiences tumble all over each other and I don't know how to deal with it."

Alice patted Avery's thigh. "When you spend hours out of your day being on alert, looking for shadows in every corner, it's got to be hard to let that go, to trust that there are folks that ain't the boogeyman, that don't intend to hurt you, that only want to get close because they really do care. Rafe loves you and you love him, and he's not going to see you struggle against the weight of his overbearing family." She wagged a finger. "At the same time, you gonna have to dig deep and find a space that you can open." She smiled. "Burdens and troubles ain't so heavy when you have help." She tipped her head to the side. "How many weddings you planned?"

Avery's eyes widened. Her mouth opened a bit but then closed.

"Hmm. Those girls, if they know nothing else it's how to put a wedding together." She chuckled. "Give them and yourself a chance. I understand the ties that bind you at work. You don't get to speak up, only take orders, and it's hard to break old habits. But…how 'bout this. Next time, *you* initiate the get-together. *You* call Dom or Desi and tell them your thoughts. One step at a time?" Her right brow lifted with emphasis.

Avery pushed out a breath. "You're right. This is all so new to me."

"As much as those Lawsons may fuss and feud with each other, the love and the bond that they have is unbreakable." She squeezed Avery's hands. "They want you to be part of that. And if you give it a chance, you might find what you've spent your life looking for."

Avery wiped away the remnants of her tears and offered up a wobbly smile. "I'll try."

Alice winked. "Good girl. Now," she planted her hands on her hips, "hungry?"

She smiled for real this time. "Starved."

Chapter 7

Avery finished her late breakfast, took a shower and went for a short run. She pushed through the stiff breeze wrapped in muggy air. Before she'd gone a little more than a block her skin grew damp and a line of perspiration dribbled down the center of her spine. Her limbs pumped. The fuel of adrenaline rushed through her veins, and clarity pushed through the cobwebs of her thoughts.

She loved Rafe. There was no doubt about that. Yes, she was overwhelmed by the rush of family, even a little scared. But if what Alice said was true, they wanted her to be part of who they were. She'd never had that before, but because she wanted a life with the man of her dreams she would find a way to work through her issues.

Avery rounded the corner and headed back to the house. Just as she slowed in front of the walkway, a car door opened and a man got out, blocking her path.

"Avery Richards, right?"

Her senses leapt to high alert. Instinctively her hand flew to her waist, where her gun would have been.

"Whoa!" He held up his hands. "Reporter."

She frowned. "Reporter? What do you want?" Her nostrils flared.

"I was hoping I could get a statement from you."

"I don't give statements." She tried to move, and he stepped into her path.

Her body flexed. "Step aside."

"I was hoping you would give me a comment about your engagement to Rafe Lawson. Your father is Horace Richards, right? Senator Richards."

Her head snapped to the right. "What did you say?" She took a step toward him and he flinched.

"Look, all I want is an exclusive for the paper. Playboy Lawson and heir to the family jewels hooks up with a senator's daughter—a Secret Service agent—that's news."

"Get away from me." This time she shoved him out of her way and started up the walkway.

"Are you staying here now? Have you moved in?" he shouted to her back.

Avery quickened her step, a beat short of a jog until she reached the front door. She took a quick look over her shoulder. The reporter snapped her picture. She opened the door and shut it solidly behind her. She leaned her back against it, felt her heart hammer in her chest.

Alice was walking toward her with a blue cloth shopping bag in her hand. She stopped halfway. "What is it?"

Avery vigorously shook her head. "Nothing. That run took more out of me than I thought."

Alice hurried over. "Go in and sit down. I'll get you some cold water."

Avery forced a smile. "Thanks. That's probably what I need."

Alice went off to the kitchen. Avery pulled herself together and walked out onto the back deck. Now she was
being followed by reporters? How in the hell did they know
where she…of course, the papers announcing the engagement. She pushed out a breath of frustration and squeezed
her eyes shut for a moment. This was not good. The last
thing she needed was to be followed around by reporters
or photographed while she was on duty. Dammit!

Alice pushed open the screen door to the deck. "Here
you go, sweetheart." She extended the glass of ice water
toward Avery.

"Thanks, Alice." She took several long swallows before
setting the glass down on the circular wrought-iron table.

Alice studied her for a moment. "Feeling better?"

Avery nodded. "Yes. Thanks."

"Okay. Well, I have my daily errands to run. Shouldn't
take too long. Need anything while I'm out?"

Her thoughts swam. "Um, no. Thanks, Alice."

Alice turned and went back inside.

Avery lowered herself onto one of the lounge chairs.
What was she going to do? Rafe felt it best that she stay
in his home so that she wouldn't be alone. But clearly his
house was being staked out. If there was one reporter,
eventually there would be others. Going home might not
be a better option. They probably knew where she lived.

She headed up to the bedroom, pulled out her suitcase
and began to pack. Then she called Kerry.

Chapter 8

Avery checked the bedroom. Satisfied that she hadn't overlooked anything she shut the door and pulled her small rolling suitcase behind her. She made a quick stop in the kitchen to leave the note she'd written for Alice.

She took the extra set of keys that Rafe gave her and locked the door behind her. When she'd insisted that he drive her car to his house, it was more a matter of trying to maintain some sense of control. She turned the key in the ignition. Now it was her method of escape.

A little more than a half hour later she pulled up in front of Kerry's house and parked on the street. She stared at the house. What was she doing? She wasn't a runner. She didn't run from problems to avoid confrontations. Guess there was a first time for everything. What she needed was some space to think. The very idea that she was being watched creeped her out in a way that being followed by her father's private hire when she'd first started dating Rafe didn't. This was different. She turned the car off just as Kerry's front door opened, and she stepped out.

Kerry walked to the car. Avery got out.

"Hey, girl." She opened her back door, pulled out her suitcase and came around to the sidewalk, where Kerry was standing. They hugged.

"You good?" Kerry asked, the concern etched between her brows.

"Yeah," she said on a breath. "Thanks for letting me stay here."

"Girl, please. Come on in." She draped her arm over Avery's shoulders and they walked inside.

"Can I get you anything?" Kerry asked once they were settled inside.

"No. Thanks. Just want to sit here for a minute."

Kerry plopped down in the side chair opposite Avery, just as her cellphone rang. Avery took the phone from her back pocket. "It's Rafe," she mouthed to Kerry, who eased out of her chair and walked away.

Avery dragged in a breath and pressed the talk icon. "Hey."

"Avery, what's going on? I got a call from Alice. She said you packed your bag and went to Kerry's."

"I got here a little while ago."

"Why!"

"I went for a run this morning. When I was on my way back to the house, I was stopped by a reporter who wanted to know had I moved in. He wanted me to comment on our engagement." She heard his muffled expletives. "I can't be a target, Rafe. Especially now when I'm getting ready to go back to work."

"I know," he ground out. "I get it. Look, I'll take care of it."

"I really don't see what you can do. This is the media.

You know better than anyone they can be relentless, and if one of them is following me, there will be others."

"Every media storm has its moment. This is going to disappear the minute something more interesting happens." He paused. "Darlin'... I'm sorry. I don't want any of this for you."

"I know that. It's not your fault. But I have to do this for now. I need you to understand that."

"I don't like it, but I get it. My only concern is you."

She sighed softly. "How is everything back home?"

"So far...okay. I'll see the family tomorrow. You'll see the doctor on Monday, right?"

"Yes. I don't have a choice if I want to go back to work." She would do whatever she needed to do to get cleared. Even if it meant lying about what she was still going through.

"And the headaches?"

Avery closed her eyes and as if conjuring a spell the lie slipped over her lips. "I'm fine."

"You *would* tell me, right?"

She hesitated a beat. "Of course."

Rafe blew out a breath. "I'll be back in about a week. Sooner if I can get everything tied up here. I need to fly up to New York, get with Quinten."

"Can't wait."

"We're gonna get through this, darlin'—walk down that aisle and into forever. Me and you."

Her heart always shook loose from its anchor when he talked like that...about them, forever. She smiled. "'Kay."

"Talk to you tomorrow."

"Absolutely."

"I love you, Avery. No matter what."

"Love you, too. Bye." She disconnected the phone and wondered what he meant by "no matter what" again?

* * *

He had to get away from his thoughts at least for a little while. He went down to the garage and fired up his Harley. Not long after, he was racing along the blacktop with the thick Louisiana air whizzing around him.

The early Saturday-evening traffic was relatively light, allowing him to hopscotch across the three lanes at will. Beyond the ribbons of white and yellow lines, rooftops and spires, the sun took its final bow, stretching its fingers of orange and gold across the horizon in a last-ditch effort to cling to its illuminating power. Sunset always had a calming effect on him. As a kid, whenever he'd gotten into trouble at school or was feeling misunderstood, his mother, Louisa, would take him out on the back porch and they would watch the sun set over the lake that ran behind their home. His mother would remind him that the end of the day was the time to put all the happenings of the day to rest. It was the time to think about tomorrow and how to do things better or different. Funny he should think about that now.

Rafe bore down on the accelerator the moment there was an opening. He flipped down his tinted visor against the glare, leaned into the bike until they were one unit of flesh, bone and metal. Together they rode into the wind that pushed against him, tried to hold him back. This was what he did, who he was, even as the counsel of his mother still flowed through his veins. He pushed through the obstacles that tried to hold him back, whether it was his controlling father, who wanted to mold him into his image, a relentless media that chronicled his life and made up the rest, or the laundry list of wannabe matchmakers and conniving women that wanted nothing more than to claim the Lawson name. It was true that a bunch of what was in his way was a result of his own creation. He laughingly told his siblings that he had a "rebel gene" that compelled him to buck the status quo at every turn.

But in a few months he would be a husband, and if he wanted his marriage to last, he was going to have to permanently shake off the tentacles of his past and find a way to quiet, if not silence, the rebel in his soul.

Chapter 9

Avery couldn't seem to shake Rafe's cryptic comment when they last spoke. If there was one thing that she'd learned about him in the time they'd been together, it was that Rafe Lawson was *never* vague. He said exactly what he meant, and the world be damned. It was one of the many qualities that she loved about him. His honesty and exactness made her feel secure, knowing that whatever he said, whatever commitment he made, it was for real. This was the first time she didn't feel that way.

She stuck her feet in her flip-flop slippers. Kerry was on duty, doing a double. She had the house to herself until at least nine, and the emptiness of the two-bedroom condo echoed the sentiments of her stomach as she walked down the hallway to the kitchen. She passed the rows of framed black-and-white photos that hung singularly and in groups, telling the story of Kerry's growing-up years with her two older brothers and sister, the vacations, holiday gatherings, her handsome exes. She stopped in front of one photo that captured the image of Kerry at her college graduation, flanked by her parents, who gazed at their daughter with unabashed love and pride.

The image of her own college graduation day took its place in front of her eyes. She saw herself, unsmiling with her father standing next to her, his stiff arm draped ceremoniously across her shoulder. She realized with a pang just how different she was from her best and only friend, how her life and family were so very different from Kerry's. Different from Rafe's. She longed for what they had and at the same time was terrified of it. She stroked the outline of Kerry's photographed face. When you had *all that*, there was more to lose. She could take the singular loses. She was expert at that. But the love of a family…

A searing razor-edged pain sliced through her skull, bringing her to her knees. She reached out to break her fall but took several of the photos crashing to the floor with her. Hot tears sprang from her eyes, clouding her already hazy vision. Her stomach roiled from the pain. Down on her hands and knees she drew in long, deep breaths, until the pounding lessened and her vision began to clear. She drew her knees up to her chest and leaned against the cool off-white wall, and this time the tears weren't from the pain but from fear.

She lost track of how long she'd sat huddled against the wall. When the pain subsided enough for her to attempt to push herself to a standing position, the photo of Kerry and her family lay cracked at her feet. The metaphor didn't escape her, but her next problem was explaining what happened to Kerry.

Kerry wouldn't flip about the cracked glass of the framed picture, but rather what caused it. Her worry would be about her friend.

Slowly she picked up the photographs that had fallen and gingerly returned them to their rightful places on the wall, except the one she'd damaged. She took that one with her into the living room and set it on the table.

The pain in her head lessened to a dull throb and a steady beat behind her right eye. That was a good thing. She'd get through this episode. She put one foot in front of the other, returned to her room for her medication and crawled back into bed, where Kerry found her hours later curled in a fetal position.

"There you are," Jacqueline greeted as Rafe walked out to the back patio on Sunday afternoon. The family, extended and immediate, were in various stages of lying back. "Started to think you weren't coming."

"Wouldn't miss it, Aunt J." He kissed her cheek. "Jackson, good to see you, man. It's been a minute." He shook his brother-in-law's hand.

Jackson rose with the handshake and clapped Rafe heartily on the back. "Looking good, bruh. Life must be treating you lovely."

Rafe chuckled. "Can't complain." He beamed at his younger brother Justin. "Yo, bruh." The brothers embraced, clapped each other on the back.

"Hey, beautiful lady." He leaned down and kissed Bailey's cheek.

"Hey," she said with a smile, and squeezed Rafe's hand.

His sister Desiree was glued to the hip of her husband Spence, who had a protective arm around his very pregnant wife.

"You look like you're ready to pop any minute, sis." He squatted down next to her. He playfully rested his ear against her belly. "Sounds like you have a football team in there, girl."

Desiree swatted his arm. "That's 'cause I'm hungry," she said over her laughter.

"Right," he teased. "Spence, long time, man. How are you?"

The two men shook hands.

"Can't complain. It's all good. How's Avery? Recovering okay?"

"She's doing well. Ready to go back to work."

"Glad to hear that. Give her my regards."

Rafe bobbed his head in agreement.

The back door swung open and Dominique stepped out with a platter of seasoned chicken for the grill. Her diamond-shaped face and long-lashed eyes lit up. "Rafe!" She set the platter down on the table and threw her arms around her brother. "So good to see you," she said against his chest and then looked up at him. "Glad you came. I have so much to tell you. Is Avery coming? Is she here?"

"Good to see you, too, sis," he said. "And no, Avery's not coming. She's in Virginia. Goes back to work tomorrow."

Rafe worked on keeping his expression impassive but was pretty sure he'd failed when he saw Dominique's bright smile dim. She knew him well. "We need to talk," he said low enough so only she could hear.

Dominique pursed her polished lips. "Sure." She sauntered over to the table where she'd deposited the tray of chicken and walked with it over to the grill.

Jacqueline shot Rafe a warning side-eye, to which he responded in kind and smoothly moved out of her line of fire. His aunt Jacquie was definitely not one to play with, but she also hated scenes. She wouldn't intentionally do anything to publicly put him or his sister on blast.

He moved toward Raymond, who was refilling the cooler with bottles of beer.

"I'll take a cold one," he said, coming up behind Raymond.

"You got it." He pulled a bottle from the bottom of the cooler.

Moisture ran down the sides of the bottle and made the golden contents shimmer in the afternoon sun.

"Thanks, man. How's it going?" He grabbed an opener and popped off the cap.

"Taking it easy today. Actually, I head out next week on an assignment. Trying to spend 'quality' time with my wife before I go," he said with a toss of his head in Jacqueline's direction.

"Where to this time?"

"Afghanistan. Getting imbedded with the army. Three weeks."

"I don't know what I'm supposed to do for three weeks," Jacqueline said, before slipping her arm around her husband's waist.

Raymond chuckled, leaned down and kissed her forehead. "Woman, when have you ever not had something to keep you busy, and we have Paris to look forward to when I'm done."

"Yes," she cooed and turned fully into his embrace.

Rafe gripped the beer bottle tighter. Paris had been a city that he'd loved, visited many times for business and pleasure, but after the bombing and almost losing Avery and his father, Paris would never be the same. He tossed his head back and took a long, deep swallow of the icy brew and then followed the path to the grill.

"You plan to help or stand around looking cute?" Dominique teased while she continued to place the seasoned wings on the grill.

"So you *do* think I'm cute?" he tossed back and came to stand next to her.

"Hmm." She looked him up and down. "You'll do. Hand me the sauce in that bowl, please."

Rafe retrieved the bowl and started brushing the wings with sauce. "We have a problem, sis."

"I figured as much." She turned to him with her hand planted on her hip. "What?"

"The wedding. Avery feels like you and Desi and Lee Ann are making it more ya'll's than hers."

Dominique's neck jerked back. "What? Why?"

He gave her his you-know-damn-well-why look.

She pursed her lips and huffed. "I just want your wedding to be everything, Rafe." She pressed her palm against his chest and fluttered her lashes.

Rafe refused to give in and held back a smile. "Don't try to work me, D."

"Me? Work you?" She closed the cover to the grill and then turned back to her brother. "None of us want to take over the wedding. And we certainly don't want Avery to feel that she's not a part of the planning. I guess we...*I* got carried away. This is a big deal. You? Married?" She flashed him her dimpled smile. "We never thought it would happen...after Janae," she said softly.

His jaw clenched. *Janae.* "It is kinda crazy." He pushed out a breath and shoved his hands into his pants' pockets. "But it's a little more complicated than just wedding planning on steroids."

"What else?"

"I know you were in your zone when you made the announcement to the papers..." He explained Avery's reaction, right up to her being accosted on the street by a reporter.

"Damn," she whispered. "I had no idea."

"Yeah. Me either. For us the media is like a regular

Tuesday, but not Avery. And she has concerns that it could affect her job."

"I never thought of that." She looked up at him with wide eyes. "I am so sorry, Rafe. I swear. I'll fix it," she added quickly, and Rafe could see the wheels turning in her head.

"Slow down. I don't want you doing anything else. Got it?" he said with a warning glare. "We'll keep a low profile, and hopefully they'll latch onto something more interesting."

Dominique folded her arms. "Fine."

More than any of his other siblings, he and Dominique were the closest, even more so than Dom and her twin sister. Like his aunt Jacqueline said, they were kindred spirits. She was the one who would nurse his wounds after one of his fights or tumbles from his motorcycle and took his side even when she kinda thought he was wrong. They shared hurts and secrets, and other than Quinten, she was the only one who came close to understanding how losing Janae totally changed his DNA.

He kissed the top of her head the way he did when she was a teenager and would get busted sneaking in late, and she'd cry on his chest about how her latest punishment was going to ruin her life. But they weren't kids anymore. This was the real deal. Dom had to realize that her actions had consequences. Like him, she was driven by raw emotion. He released her, and when she looked up at him, he knew they'd make it all work; they always did.

"Promise me that you'll let me handle it," Rafe said.

Dominique pursed her polished lips. "Fine. But I'm here when you need me."

"I know that." He draped his arm around her shoulder and pushed out a breath. "Enough of all this. What I really want to know is, where's your etouffe? You know I can't come home and not get my favorite."

Dominique giggled, and for the moment all was right at the Lawson house.

"How are you feeling today?" Kerry asked. She lifted her mug of mint tea and brought it to her lips.

"I'm fine. No after-effects." She lathered her everything bagel with a dollop of cream cheese.

Kerry put down her mug and rested her forearms on the wood tabletop. "Avery... I know you want to power through this, but I saw you yesterday."

Avery glanced up from beneath her lashes and then quickly focused on her bagel. "I'm fine."

"You're not fine, A! What if you're on duty and you have an episode? Are you willing to risk the safety of your assignment and yourself for a point of pride?"

Avery lifted her chin. "As long as the doctor clears me, I'll come back. If not... I'll have to follow his instructions."

Kerry studied her friend, heaved a sigh. She held up her hand. "Fine." She pushed back from the table. "Want to ride in together, or are you taking your car?"

"I'll take my car. No telling how today will turn out."

"Look, even if you're not approved for full duty, at least you'll be back in the office, even if it is desk duty."

Inwardly Avery cringed. They may as well take her badge and gun if she was going to ride the desk. That was not what she trained and worked so hard for. Whatever she needed to do to ensure that she was fully back on the job, she would do. The problem was she wasn't sure who would be harder to convince, the doctor or Kerry.

"I'll cross that bridge when we get there." She wiped her mouth with a paper napkin and put her plate in the sink.

"Do you want me to go with you? Moral support? I can call and let them know I'll be late."

"No. Not necessary. I'll be fine. Ready?"

Being back at the Agency was the shot of adrenaline she needed. For the first time in months, she felt energized. Walking through the doors, seeing the familiar signposts of plaques and portraits, she knew she was home again. This was where she belonged, what she'd worked for, deserved to be.

"Agent Richards, welcome back," the security guard at the check-in station greeted. "Great work in Paris," he added.

"Good to be back. Thanks." She swiped her ID, placed her weapon and badge in the plastic bin and walked through the metal detector.

She gathered her belongings on the other side and walked toward the elevator. The doors slid soundlessly open. Avery walked to the back of the elevator and pressed her back against the wall as other agents and staff boarded, floor by floor.

For days leading up to her exam she'd refrained from taking any medication. She needed to be able to show them that the meds were no longer necessary. The doctor gave her a full exam, took some blood and urine samples and asked her a laundry list of questions, from her eating to sleeping habits. He'd focused for quite some time on the headaches and how she'd been able to wean herself off the medication.

She'd practiced long and hard on the lie that she would tell, and looked him right in the eye when she told him with a straight face that she'd been pain-free for weeks—episodes over.

He'd nodded as he listened and took notes. Finally, he

looked up and smiled. "As long as the tests come back with no problems, I can give you medical clearance. They should be in by the end of the week. In the meantime, I'll call over to headquarters and let the director know that you can be returned to limited duty until the tests come in." He'd stood. "Welcome back."

She'd breathed a major sigh of relief, shook the doctor's hand and walked out, confident that she'd gotten a part of her life back.

The elevator doors opened on her floor. Her heart suddenly began to race. Her right temple throbbed. She sucked in a lungful of air, put one foot in front of the other and walked off. She would get through this. She had to. She plastered a smile on her face as the pain intensified.

"Good morning, Agent Richards. Welcome back. You can go right in. The director is expecting you."

"Thank you." She straightened her shoulders and walked toward the director's office. She knocked on the closed door.

"Come in."

Avery stepped inside. Director Fischer stood when she entered. "Agent Richards. Come in. Come in. Have a seat."

"Thank you, sir." She focused on sitting in the chair and not the pounding behind her left eye. She linked her fingers together on her lap.

"So…how are you?"

"Good. Feeling great. I'm confident that the doctor will give me a clean bill of health."

"He's already called. His preliminary report will be here in the morning, but from what he told me, you're cleared for limited duty."

"Thank you, sir."

"You do understand that limited means no fieldwork for now."

"Yes, sir. I understand."

"Good." He slapped his palm on his desk for emphasis and stood. He extended his hand, which she reached in and shook.

"I'll get back to work," she said with a smile.

"Yes, and set up with my assistant your firing-range review and field physical."

"Of course."

"And…as you know your name is still in the running for the assistant deputy director position. We put everything on hold while you were recovering. Of course, going forward, much of the evaluation will hinge on the final medical report and your field physical."

"Yes, sir. Of course. I understand."

Director Fischer gave a short nod. "Welcome back."

"Thank you, sir." She turned to leave, forcing herself to put one foot in front of the other. The top of her head felt as if it would explode. She needed her medication and she needed it now before she passed out. "I'll call to make the appointments," she managed to say to the director's assistant and then hurried down the hall to the elevator.

She smiled and waved, made brief cursory small talk to the colleagues that greeted her en route to her office. Once inside, she quickly locked the door. Her vision began to blur. She breathed in deeply through her nose while fumbling in her purse for her pain medication. Her hands shook as she tried to twist the childproof cap off. She shoved two tablets into her mouth and swallowed them dry.

Still leaning with her back against the door, she shut her eyes and imagined the calming waters of the Caribbean ebbing and flowing toward white, sandy shores. She saw herself drifting away toward the horizon, carried along by the soothing blue waters.

By degrees the intensity of the pain lessened. She

squinted against the light coming in from the window
behind her desk and slowly crossed the room. No sooner
had she sat down, her desk phone rang.

She reached for the phone and slowly brought it to her
ear. "Richards."

"Hey, girl. Didn't want to call your cell in case you
were still in the middle of things. How'd it go with the
doc and Fischer?"

"Perfect." She gave Kerry a quick rundown.

"Whew. That's a relief. Well, I know you need to get
settled and up to speed. I'll see you later at the house. I
have off-site work today."

"Okay. See you later."

Avery hung up the phone, leaned back against the head-
rest of her chair. The pain meds were starting to kick in. It
worked. She should be happy. This was what she wanted.
But at what cost? Her eyes filled. At what cost?

Chapter 10

Rafe checked in his desk drawer for the keys to his silver Lexus. It had been a while since he'd taken his birthday present to himself out on the road. Although the car was more than a year old, it barely had eight thousand miles on it and still had that brand-new leather smell. He'd treated himself to the luxury automobile to celebrate the success of his foundation landing a major grant and, of course, his thirty-fifth birthday. Cars, clothes, travel, money were abundances that were commonplace in his life. He didn't grow up worrying about his next meal or if he'd get ragged at school for not having the latest Jordans. The Lawsons traveled in the rarified air that most black folk only dreamed about. But "all that stuff" never meant much to him. It was just the way things were. But as he traveled across the country, he came to understand the adage, "to whom much is given, much is expected." It took him a minute to find his way, but he did when he launched his foundation. They were making real progress, and this year would be the first that the foundation would be able to award three full college scholarships for musicians of color. His father did it his way through politics, and Rafe would make his mark with music.

He grabbed his black, hip-length leather jacket from the hook by the door and walked out to the garage through the kitchen.

For all the cities he'd visited there was always something special about his hometown of New Orleans that drew him back. The rich, dark history and culture of the city of New Orleans exuded an energy that went beyond the parties in the streets, sticky pralines, spicy gumbo, Anne Rice's vampire novels, Mardi Gras, impromptu street performances and iconic structures. It was the people that made it magical—with their big hearty smiles and the swag in their step within their multi-colored milieu, even in the midst of despair and abject poverty. The city, like blood, flowed through his veins, and each time he returned home, he was transfused.

Behind the wheel, the thought of permanently moving away gathered speed in concert with the Lexus. It was a bridge that he and Avery would have to cross. But as he drove through the streets that ranged from palatial estates tucked behind professionally manicured gardens and wrought-iron gates to the trailers and prefab homes occupied by the survivors of Katrina, to the lull of the mighty Mississippi, he was no longer sure that he'd be willing to give it up.

He exited the I-610 and took the main streets into downtown. His office was located on Canal Street, once the pathway for horse-drawn carriages for the wealthy, while others rode the streetcars that withstood the test of time and the upriver boundary of the French Quarter. Street parking was at a premium along this stretch that was peppered with luxury hotels like the Ritz Carlton or the Astor Crowne Plaza, which were converted from their historic predecessors, the high-end stores—Maison Blanche, Godchaux's and D.H. Holmes—and theaters and restaurants that overflowed with residents and tourists at all hours of the day and night.

Rafe drove past his office and the Joy Theater, went around the block to the lot. He maintained a monthly account for days like this. Walking back to the building where his office was housed, he was pleasantly assaulted by the live music floating from the opened doorways of restaurants, followed by low- and high-pitched laughter and the unmistakable 'Nawlins twang.

Tourists strolled wide-eyed, laden with bags, and in awe of the assault on the senses from every direction, while the residents reveled in the ordinary everyday-ness of their lives.

Rafe pulled on the vertical silver bar handle of the glass door and stepped into the refreshingly chilly air, a respite from the wooly weight of humidity, a hallmark of Louisiana weather.

He took the elevator up to the tenth floor, which housed the suite of six offices and a conference room. For now the space was large enough to accommodate the needs of the RBL Foundation, but Rafe knew that, as his vision continued to expand, so would the need for more space.

"Halle, how are you?" he greeted his receptionist, before he plucked a rose from the vase that held the dozen he'd sent her like clockwork each week. He handed it to her with a bow.

Halle's laughter, which always sounded like runs on a Steinway piano, filled the reception space with her ever-ready joy.

"Why, Mr. Lawson," she purred, lowering her long lashes over rum-colored eyes and slowly dragging the bud of the rose beneath her nose, "how gallant of you, kind sir."

Rafe grinned. "I can only try. What do I need to know?"

Halle easily shifted back to full business mode. "The board members should be here in about an hour. I've ordered lunch from Creole House, and Danielle said she wanted to see you as soon as you arrived."

"Thanks. Danielle's in her office?"

"Yes." He started off but then stopped and turned back. He pointed a warning finger in her direction. "Tell whoever it is that keeps sending you flowers that I'm a very jealous boss," he teased with a wicked glint in his eyes.

She shook her head and laughed at their inside joke. "Will do."

Rafe strode down the carpeted corridor, passing the five office spaces that occupied the spine of the space. Along the soft white walls hung framed photos of the galas, the political and fund-raising events, and the staff and members of the board. He turned left at the end of the hall, away from the conference room, and stopped at Danielle's office, which was across the hall from his. He knocked on the closed door.

"Yes. Come in."

Rafe eased the door open and poked his head through the gap. "Busy? Halle said you needed to see me."

Danielle whipped off her designer glasses—today they were blue rimmed—and placed them on the desk, which was stacked on either side of her with folders. "Hey." She waved him inside. "Come on in."

Danielle had been with him from the beginning. They'd met through his sister Dominique's business, First Impression. Danielle had been instrumental in promoting Dominique's dream to the general public. But her skills extended beyond publicity. She had an MBA with a specialty in finance, was detail-oriented, great with seeing the small things in the big-picture world of Rafe Lawson, could run numbers in her head at lightning speed, knew what he needed before he needed it and, at the drop of a hat, she could stand in for him at any venue. When he took all that into account, he knew he was making the right decision and was confident that the board would agree.

She leaned back in her chair, rubbed the bridge of her short, slender nose. "How are you? It's been a minute." She tucked her shoulder-length, bone-straight hair behind her ears.

Rafe came around and sat in the overstuffed paisley-print chair opposite her desk. He draped his right ankle across his left thigh. "I know." He blew out a breath. "Lot going on, but I knew I had you holding everything down. Anything I need to know before this meeting?"

She reached into her desk and pulled out a red folder and handed it to him. "Basic notes on where the scholarships stand, list of donors, quarterly projections and an outline for the summer fund-raiser."

Rafe flipped open the folder and quickly scanned the very detailed notes. He bobbed his head. "Thanks. Anything else?" He closed the folder and rested it on his thigh.

"The scholarships are a big deal, Rafe. Three full rides." She beamed in delight. "That was no small feat. So the roll out and the event have to be larger than life. I've already started the plan, secured the venue. I did want to sit down with your sister Desiree. With her being on the city council, it can only help to bring in more support with her connections."

"Not a problem. We want big-ticket donors at the event, along with the presidents of the universities."

"On my list."

"I want to personally sign all of the invitations."

She nodded and made a note. "I've asked Halle to put together a list of caterers."

"No. I'll get my brother-in-law Spence to handle the menu. His staff is big enough to handle it."

"Got it." Danielle tipped her head to the side, her dark chocolate eyes locking on Rafe. She put her notes aside. "How are you…really? And how is Avery? I've seen the papers lately."

Rafe's brows rose and fell. He pushed out a breath and brought Danielle up to speed.

She linked her slender fingers together, and Rafe wondered as he spoke how she was able to be so productive with her long embellished nails.

"If there's anything I can do, you know you only have to say the word," she said once he was done.

"'Preciate that." He pushed to his feet. "See you at the meeting."

"Yep."

He left and went to his office across the hall.

As much as he would like to take total credit for the foundation and its mission, the idea was originally Janae's. She planted the seed of the idea years earlier, when they were on a weekend getaway to Aruba as part of her social-work studies. They visited several schools on the island. After talking with many of the students, they were both moved by the students' love of learning and desire to go to college one day. Unfortunately, that would not be a reality for many of them. Janae said that, back home, so many students were faced with the same fate, and with the Lawson family name, connections and wealth, they could make a difference—offer scholarships to deserving students. He let the idea sit, not sure if he was really the one to take on that role.

Still, it wasn't until years after he lost her, after no longer caring about much of anything, that her vision took root again. He knew that if he was ever going to find his way back to some sense of normal, he needed to find a purpose in his life that went beyond satisfying his own needs. With the legal help of his brother Justin, he formed the foundation. He sat behind his desk and looked around at the plaques and framed citations on the wall. He shook his head and smiled in bemusement. Had someone told him ten years ago that this was where he would be, he would have laughed in his face. Now, he couldn't see otherwise.

He leaned back and exhaled as a melancholy smile shadowed his mouth. Janae would be proud. Her spirit was part of the success of the foundation. Whenever he spent time here, he often wondered what things would be like if Janae was with him. His smile widened, sure that Janae's "save the world" mantra would be imprinted on all their endeavors. That's why it was going to be hard to let the board know that he was turning the reins over to Danielle so that he could take a back seat. The notion that he would possibly have to relocate to DC was already difficult, but if he could set things up so that the transition would be smooth, that's what he would do.

He frowned, stroked his smooth chin. Funny, if Janae was here, this would not be on the table. Reflexively his jaw tightened. But she wasn't. He pushed back from the desk, pulled the lower drawer open and pulled out a striped tie—part of boardroom décor, which he always bucked against. But wearing a tie on today of all days was the least he could do.

Rafe took his suit jacket from the hook and slipped it on. Hopefully Danielle would take the announcement well, since he'd chosen to hold his cards close to his chest until this meeting. Harder for her to say no.

* * *

"You blindsided me," Danielle said, staring across at Rafe. Her palms were planted on her desk, her body tense. "Why? And why the hell didn't you say something?" She held up her hand. "No. Don't bother. I know why you did it…so that I wouldn't say no."

Rafe's attempts to look sheepish didn't move Danielle.

"There's that," he admitted and slid his hands into his pockets. "Look, there's no one more qualified to run the foundation." He slowly paced in front of her desk, his head lowered in thought as he spoke. "You do it anyway." He turned to face her. "You deserve the title of CEO and the perks that go along with it. I'll still have my hand in— you know that. But you'll officially run the day-to-day."

Danielle looked directly at him. "I don't know what to say." She paused. "Thank you for the confidence you have in me. I won't let you down."

"I know that." He gave her that half grin. "So…we good?"

"Did you give me a choice? Yes," she said with a conceding smile, "we're good."

He loosened his tie, pulled it from around his neck and then stuck it in his pants pocket. "Let me know when the invites are ready for my signature, and have Halle draft up a press release with the announcement." He winked. "Talk to you soon."

His next stop was his club on Bourbon Street, centered in the heart of the French Quarter, renowned since the mid-1800s as the hot spot for Mardi Gras. He could have chosen any number of locations for a nightspot in New Orleans, but the energy, the history, the thrill of the Quarter was visceral. There was no place like it in the world. Although his club was one of many, what he offered was a menu prepared by a chef who trained under Emeril himself. Pair that with his highly skilled bartender who created a one-of-a-kind version of the infamous Hurricane for weekend guests, and Lawsons was *the* place to be. It didn't hurt that he often played a set and used his connections in the music industry to bring in some of the top-named jazz musicians.

His co-managers, Marcus and his wife, Antoinette, ran Lawsons like a well-oiled machine. The staff was happy, the customers were thrilled and business boomed.

When he popped into the club the lunch crowd had dwindled down to those who struggled with the reality that they had to return to work. His club was fashioned after the clubs he'd visited in Europe; although large in space, they were designed with a feeling of intimacy. Circular tables that seated no more than four and private banquettes for larger parties were situated on gradient levels. The dark wood walls were adorned with signed black-and-white photographs of film, television, athletic and musical stars. Every seat in the house had perfect views of the stage, and the dim, recessed lighting provided the perfect ambiance.

"Mr. Lawson!" Antoinette walked toward him from the back while wiping her hands on a towel. "I didn't expect you. Everything okay?"

Rafe leaned down and buzzed her cheek, lightly squeezed her shoulder. "In town for a few days."

"Congratulations on your engagement."

"Thank you." He took a quick look around. "How's everything going?"

"Busy," she said on a breath and with a full-bodied smile. "We had to hire two more wait staff."

"Whatever you need to do. Who's on the entertainment lineup?"

"Thinking about sitting in?"

Rafe chuckled. "Never know." He folded his arms and leaned against the bar.

She gave him a rundown on the upcoming performers.

"Real tempting," he said, nodding his head in appreciation. "Probably on my next visit. Tryin' to get Quinten Parker to come down."

"Now, that would be fantastic."

"Flying up to New York in the morning. Gonna twist his arm."

"Make sure you do. Me and Marcus will make it *the* event."

"I know ya'll will. Anyway, I'm out. Just wanted to stop in and see how things were going. I'll be back in town in a few weeks. But anything come up before then, you know you can always reach me."

"Marcus will be sorry he missed you," Antoinette said while they walked toward the front door.

"We'll catch up next time. Let him know the new website for the club is fire! The shots of the interior, menu, photos of the performers—perfect. Brotha got skills."

Antoinette laughed. "All those classes he took are finally paying off."

"For sure." He pulled the front door open. "Thank you for all your hard work. Lawsons is a success because of you and Marcus, and I appreciate ya'll."

"That means a lot."

"I'm only a phone call away. Whatever you need." He wagged a finger. "And I'm gonna get Quinten down here."

"I know you will," she said with a smile. "Safe travels."

"Thanks." He stepped out into the late afternoon and was embraced by the meaty arms of heat. He muttered a useless curse under his breath and walked to his car. If he was going to have to pull up stakes and relocate to DC, at least he knew that his enterprises were in capable hands.

Chapter 11

"I'm going back to my place after work," Avery said as she and Kerry walked into a staff meeting.

"Are you sure? You know you can stay as long as you want."

They found two seats in the back of the room, which was already filled with about thirty agents by the time they arrived. The agents would always joke that if all of them were in one room, who was guarding the hen house?

"Thanks. I appreciate it, but I think the dust has finally settled. Like Rafe said, the reporters will find something else to write about." She shrugged. "I guess they did. And it's time for me to put all the pieces of my life back in place, and going home is one of them."

"Okay. But you have a key if you change your mind."

"'Preciate that."

"Say no more. Do you, sis."

The director took to the podium and went through his

mind-numbing update. Fisher had about as much warmth and personality as an empty plastic bag, but he was good at his job. He was not a nurturer like his predecessor. He didn't groom his agents; he simply expected them to rise to the challenge.

Avery let her mind wander while Director Fisher spoke. She'd been back at work for almost two weeks. She'd passed her field test and her labs were clean. Today was her first day back on detail—late luncheon gathering for the senators and donors at the Watergate Hotel. She was assigned to Senator Kevin Banks, a Republican, but she wouldn't hold that against him. Briefly she glanced around the room, taking in her colleagues. They were all nondescript. They could be anybody or no one, and she fit right in with her well-fitted dark blue suit, hair pulled back into a tight knot at the nape of her neck, dark shades at the ready and underarm holster hugging her agency-issued Glock. She was a part of something bigger than herself, but without the emotional commitment. Maybe that was why this line of work suited her in ways that relationships didn't. If one of her colleagues were…lost, there would be one nearly identical to replace that person. That wasn't true of relationships when feelings and desires were involved. Here you weren't allowed the luxury of "feeling" anything. You did your job.

She shifted in her seat, crossed her legs. Things were finally returning to a life that she understood, where she was in control. She only took the pain meds when the pain became unbearable, and no one was the wiser. She got her job back, and she was determined to get the promotion that she deserved.

"Not as boring as usual," Kerry whispered as everyone began to file out.

Avery blinked away her musings, smiled and stood.

"Thank goodness." She checked her watch. "I'm on duty in thirty minutes. What's on your agenda?"

"I'm stationed at the Capitol. Easy day for me."

"I'll give you a call later." She patted Kerry's shoulder and headed off in the opposite direction.

The standard black Chevy Suburban was parked in front of Senator Banks's townhouse in Reston, Virginia. Avery and her partner for the evening, Agent Brian Halstead, were stationed and waiting.

"Good to see you back on duty, Richards," Halstead said.

"Feels good to be back." She scanned the area and adjusted her headset.

"I hear you're in the running for a promotion."

Senator Banks's front door opened. Avery and Brian moved in unison toward the front door and then escorted Senator Banks and his wife into the vehicle. Senator Banks was the chair of the Foreign Relations Committee and a ranking member of the Judiciary Committee.

"In the meantime," she said, taking a last look around before swinging into the front passenger seat, "I still have my job to do."

She slid open the partition that separated the security team from the passengers. "ETA is twenty-five minutes, sir."

"Thank you."

Avery shut the partition and focused on the road and the afternoon ahead. Tonight she would sleep in her own bed, move one more step toward normalcy.

Agents were accustomed to the press hovering, jockeying for position to get a shot or shout out a question. They took it in stride, remaining focused on their assignment and protecting those under their care.

When Avery exited the car to quickly check the scene around the entrance to the hotel, nothing could have stunned her more than to hear her name shouted out from the clutch of reporters huddled nearby.

Her heart rate escalated so quickly that her breath caught in her throat. Instinctively her head swung toward the sound.

Senator Banks and his wife stopped in mid-step.

"When is the wedding, Agent Richards?"

"Has Rafe Lawson stopped his playboy ways?"

"Are you still going to work after the wedding?"

"Does Senator Richards approve?"

Oh, my God. Her stomach seesawed.

Brian Halstead threw her a look of alarm and quickly guided the senator and his wife inside. Avery drew in a breath and followed the group inside.

"What the hell was that?" Senator Banks demanded the instant they crossed the threshold.

"Senator… I apologize. Everything is under control."

He frowned. "It doesn't appear so, Agent Richards." He turned to Agent Halstead and spoke to him in hushed tones.

Halstead nodded. "Yes, sir." He turned to Avery, and said in an undertone, "The senator wants you to wait here to be replaced by a backup agent. I'm sorry, Avery. I gotta make the call to headquarters."

Numbly she nodded, knowing that it was protocol if an agent was compromised. She felt sick. A million thoughts raced through her head. How could this be happening?

"I'm going inside with the senator and his wife. Backup will be here in ten. You'll take his car back to Central," Halstead said, returning to Avery after his call.

Avery swallowed. "Of course."

Agent Halstead turned and walked away.

Avery felt as if she was standing outside of her body. The feeling was surreal. She paced the lobby floor, and like clockwork her replacement arrived in exactly ten minutes. Her day only grew worse when she saw that Mike was her replacement.

"Director wants to see you when you get back."

"I'm sure," she managed to say.

Mike handed her the keys to the Suburban he'd driven to the Watergate.

She clenched her teeth to keep from screaming, gripped the keys in her hand, turned and walked outside, hoping that she wouldn't lay eyes on the reporter and be tempted to run him over.

Chapter 12

"Hey, Aunt J. Everything all right?"

"I…don't know how to say this."

Rafe opened the car door. "What is it?"

"I got a call a little while ago. On the house phone…the woman said she was Janae."

The air stopped in his chest. "What?" He gripped the side of the car door.

"That's what she said. She said she was Janae and she was trying to reach you."

Every muscle tensed. "No. That's not possible." He tried to move but couldn't. "Janae is dead, Aunt J. Dead."

"Sweetheart, I know. We all know, but she told me things that only Janae would have knowledge of."

The pulse in his right temple began to pound. He shook his head in denial. "What could some imposter possibly have to say to make you think it was Janae?" he snapped. Pure adrenaline pumped through him, sending fire through his veins.

"She told me about the family photo that we took the summer before...everything happened in New York...and how she didn't feel right getting in the picture, and that you and Dominique insisted. How would this woman know that, Rafe?"

His thoughts swung back to that summer day. A family reunion cookout. Everyone was there—all his siblings, significant others of the time, his father, cousins, uncles, and his grandfather Clive presided over the festivities. Melanie Harte, the diva of soirees and matchmaking, was in charge of organizing the family shindig, from sending out the invites to the decorations, to the never-ending menu. He remembered how reluctant Janae was to join in the family photo and how Dominique told her that she was the closest thing to permanent that had ever come into Rafe's life and she "betta" get in that photo and act like it.

There was no way that some stranger would know that specific detail.

"Rafe, are you there?"

He blinked the past away. "Yes," he said in a bare whisper.

"Sweetie, what do you want to do? She left a number. It's a Florida area code."

The knot in his gut tightened. "Florida." He'd never met her parents, who lived in Chicago, while they dated. "She always told me her parents wanted to relocate to Florida," he said, in a faraway tone of disbelief. He heard his aunt's sharp intake of breath.

"Rafe...could it be...after all this time?"

"I don't know how. But if what she says is true, why turn up now?"

"She said she saw the announcement of your engagement on one of the entertainment channels and knew she needed to reach you."

Rafe squeezed his eyes shut. His jaw tightened. He muttered a string of expletives. "Text the number to me."

"All right. And Rafe…"

"Yeah…"

"This isn't Dominique's fault. And whoever this woman is, if in fact she is Janae, you need to find out for certain."

Rafe blew out a breath. "Send me the text when you get a minute, Aunt J."

"I will." She paused. "Listen to me…be easy, Rafe," she gently warned. "I know you…"

"I'm fine." He disconnected the call, pulled the door fully open and slid in behind the wheel.

His head was all over the place. He couldn't get his thoughts to slow down long enough for them to make sense. How was this possible? He gripped the wheel. Janae Harper was dead. She was one of the countless souls lost that day in the World Trade Center disaster. True, her remains were never discovered, but no one, her family included, believed that she was alive. He'd spent the next two years after the tragedy doing all that he could to find some sign of her, all to no avail. Over time he'd shoved his feelings way down inside and tried to move on.

For the most part he did keep his feelings and those memories at bay, but there were still those moments when he was alone, or heard a song, or caught a whiff of the perfume Janae used to wear that he'd stumble backward to that horrid day, and all that terror and soul-wrenching heartache would implode.

His phone chirped. The text was from his aunt, with Janae's number.

Rafe stared at the number until the image began to blur. Janae's face floated across the windshield. His temple throbbed.

He put the car in gear and somehow made it to his family home without getting into an accident. Shaken, he entered his home like a stranger. Nothing looked familiar. He blinked, shut the door behind him and walked inside. He went into his father's study.

Alive. He wouldn't believe it until he heard her voice for himself. He squeezed the cell phone in his palm. He walked over to the bar and poured a tumbler of bourbon, downed the liquid in two long swallows and poured another. He moved over to the easy chair and flopped down. The 407 area code of Florida burned behind his closed lids.

The bourbon was making fuzz around the sharp edges. But he needed a clear head. A clear head, 'cause this mess didn't make sense. It didn't. This was some b.s.—had to be. He pushed up from the couch, paced, thirsted for another drink but stopped himself.

Instead, he scrolled through his messages and stopped on the one from his aunt Jacqueline. He ran his tongue along his bottom lip, pressed his thumb on the number on the face of the phone. The call connected.

Each ring sent a shockwave through his system, but nothing could have prepared him for the sound of the voice on the other end.

"Hello?" the familiar voice said into the phone, piercing through his fog.

Rafe cleared his throat. "I was given this number—"

"Rafe! You called."

The knot in his gut hardened, expanded until it filled his chest. "Janae." The name stumbled across his lips.

"I wasn't sure you'd call, that you'd believe it was really me."

The voice was the same, the soft Southern lilt still there. "I'm still not sure…after all this time." His voice rose. "How? We—everyone believed you were killed in the towers. All this time," he repeated in disbelief. "You were alive all this time and you—"

"Please, I know this is hard, but let me explain."

"Explain! You let me believe you were dead. How do you explain that?"

"It's complicated. My injuries…were severe."

He felt as much as he heard the hitch of pain in her voice, and his anger instantly tempered. Slowly he sat down. This wasn't about him.

"There's still a lot I don't remember about that day. They told me when they pulled me out that I'd been buried under a lot of rubble. Broken bones, burns, dehydration… I was in a coma for over two months. When I finally woke up in the hospital I didn't remember anything, not even my own name."

Rafe felt sick. He struggled to imagine what she had endured. "But when you remembered…your family…why didn't someone tell me that you were alive?"

"I didn't remember. I only knew what I was being told. Through a bunch of tests and calls they finally found my parents. I didn't recognize them. They *told* me they were my parents and I believed them. I stayed in the hospital for almost six months…surgeries, rehab. When I was stable and strong enough to leave they took me to Florida."

A knifelike pain twisted in his chest. He struggled to process what she was telling him, tried to connect the dots. She'd had no memory. Two people claiming to be her parents took her back to Florida. How could he be sure that this was Janae and not someone who'd been led to believe that she was? Yet deep in his soul he knew the truth. He knew her voice. Whatever else may have changed, that did not. He'd heard her voice in his dreams for more than a decade.

"When pieces of my memory began to come back, the only thing that was ever clear was you."

The jolt of her words hit like a punch in the gut.

"Not everything…at first. In the beginning it was only images. I'd see your face, your eyes, your smile. It was my only constant. Over time I remembered more, but never about any other part of my life except with you and me."

Rafe listened in numbed silence while Janae told him about things they'd said to each other, places they'd been. She told him about the first time she asked about the scar on his right shoulder and he told her it happened in a motorcycle accident. Whatever reservations he may have had dissolved with every passing moment. This was Janae.

"But you still haven't told me why you never let me know you were alive."

"My parents made all the decisions. I asked them about you. They told me that bringing you back into my life wouldn't be fair to you. That it was best if you thought I was dead." She uttered what sounded like a sad laugh. "When I looked at myself in the mirror, when I had to be helped out of bed, when the pain would be so bad on some nights that I wanted to die… I believed them. Why should I burden you?"

"God, Janae. If you know me like you say, you'd know better than to think that. We were in love. Young, but in love. You were my world. When I woke up in that hotel room and found you gone—then saw the towers come down." His voice broke. "A part of me died that day, too!" He slammed his fist against the wall. "Months and months and no word. I thought I'd go crazy. I blamed myself. If I hadn't taken you to New York—"

"Don't, please don't. You couldn't have known. No one could. How could either of us know that me taking a morning jog would change our world?" She paused. "I'm so sorry, Rafe."

He paced and ran a hand across his face, surprised that his eyes were damp. "Why now?" he asked quietly. "Why contact me now?"

"I never stopped loving you. Loving you kept me alive. I want to see you, Rafe."

"See me! Now you want to see me?"

"Rafe…please. At least think about it."

He swallowed over the burn in his throat. "I'll think about it."

"Thank you. I'll wait to hear from you. Goodbye, Rafe."

Rafe disconnected the call and squeezed the phone in his palm as if he could break it in half. His tense shoulders slumped.

"Hey, Rafe. I thought I heard someone talking. What are you doing here?" Dominique asked, coming from the kitchen. He turned to face his sister. Alarm widened her eyes.

"What the hell?" She rushed over and grabbed his arm. "What's wrong?"

Rafe lowered his head a moment and then looked at his sister, debating whether he should tell her. "I…something's happened…"

"Oh my God, Rafe…but… I can't believe it. All this time. What the hell? Alive! How could she do this?" Her gaze of fury landed on her brother. Her tone immediately softened. "How are you though? I can't imagine what you're going through." She drew closer, looped her arms around his waist and rested her head on his chest. "I am so sorry."

"Nothing for you to be sorry about, sis. I'll deal with it."

She leaned back and looked up at him with astonishment widening her eyes. "Deal with it! How the hell do you deal with someone coming back from the freaking dead? This is some *Days of Our Lives* b.s."

If the situation wasn't so dire, he would laugh. Dominique was a true whiz at one-liners.

"Yeah, feels like a soap opera. Unreal."

Dominique dropped her arms and stepped back. "Have you told Avery?"

He shook his head slowly. "No. Not yet." He paused. "I'm going to Florida, first."

"Rafe..."

"I need to see her for myself."

The siblings stared into each other's eyes, understanding more than any words would convey.

Dominique nodded and gripped Rafe's upper arm. "You need me to fly shotgun, let me know. I'm there."

Rafe halfway grinned. "I'm good, sis. I can handle it. 'Preciate the offer."

Desiree waddled in from the downstairs bedroom. "What are ya'll gabbing about?" She yawned, looked from one to the other before lowering herself into the nearest seat.

Dominique flashed Rafe a questioning look. He gave a short nod.

"You're not planning to have my niece or nephew anytime soon?" Rafe quizzed, stalling for time.

Desiree looked up at him with her brows drawn together. "Huh?"

"Something you should know, but I don't want you getting yourself all worked up. Promise?"

"Don't play with me." She propped her arms over her belly and began tapping her right foot, picking up the pace by the second, a sure sign that she was getting agitated.

When Dominique was on the verge of imploding, she

started running her mouth, punctuated by perfectly placed cuss words. Desiree, on the other hand, would start with the pose and then foot tapping, eye-rolling and the barrage would follow. She hadn't gotten to the eye-rolling phase yet.

"Aunt J got a call…from Janae…" Rafe began.

By the time he'd finished bringing Desiree up to speed, her eyes had filled with tears of despair for her brother.

"Rafe," Desiree said with a catch in her throat. "My God, I don't even know what to say." She turned to her twin, who mirrored her distressed expression. "What about Avery? What did she say about you going to see Janae?"

"She doesn't know," he confessed.

"Rafe! You have to tell her," Desiree insisted. "How are you going to explain all this *after* the fact?"

"I'll handle it, Desi."

She reached out and took his hands. "You have to."

Rafe blew out a breath. "I will."

Desiree rubbed her belly and said, "Are you going to tell Justin?"

Rafe nodded. "Plan to. Might as well bring the whole family in on it. This…Janae thing affects all of us one way or another."

The trio walked back over to the veranda, where the rest of the family was intently listening to Raymond's story about one of his trips to Nigeria. All eyes turned in the direction of the three somber faces that approached.

Rafe stepped up onto the wood decking of the veranda and leaned against the railing. "I got some news," he began and gave his aunt a quick look…

The media and Janae. How long would it be before they latched onto *that* story? He had to tell Avery, but he needed to put his own eyes on Janae before he would really believe what he already knew. New York would wait; seeing Janae in Florida would not.

He walked over to the small desk tucked away in a corner of his bedroom, opened the cover of his laptop and signed in to the travel website that he used and booked a flight for Wednesday morning. He'd arrive in Miami at noon. That would give him the better part of the day to make sense out of this bittersweet nightmare.

He leaned back in the chair, gazed up at the ceiling and linked his fingers behind his head. What the hell was he going to do? Janae's parting words echoed in his head. She still loved him. But what about him? He was engaged to Avery. He loved *her*.

Frustration whipped through him, propelling him out of the chair to pace the bedroom floor. He wanted to see her again, desperately. What did that mean? What did that say about his feelings for Avery? He'd lost count of the nights he'd dreamed of Janae. There were so many versions of how he'd been able to save her. In some dreams they never made it to New York, but went to Atlanta instead. The only way to keep himself from losing his mind was to push her out of it. His stomach clenched. Admitting it, even to himself, only amplified his guilt. So, he did all he could not to think about Janae at all, what they'd had and the day that changed everything. He'd gotten good at it, good enough that he found space in his soul for Avery. Now…

He sat on the edge of his bed, looked across the room to the black backpack that held his things for his short trip to Florida. The Lawson clan vowed to be there for him for whatever he needed, whatever he decided. But they all emphatically agreed that he could not go to Florida before he spoke to Avery.

He knew they were right. That wasn't the issue. The issue that he'd been unwilling and unable to speak aloud was his unresolved feelings about Janae. He'd thought he'd finally put them to rest when he met Avery, but hearing her voice, knowing that she was still alive... He turned the phone around in his hand, ignored the knot of apprehension in his gut and placed a call to Quinten.

Chapter 13

"Yo, wait…what do you mean she's alive?" Quinten barked into the phone.

"Q, a woman claiming to be Janae called the house phone yesterday. Left a number for me to call in Florida. Knew stuff that only Janae would know. I called. I talked to her. It's got to be Janae."

"Damn," Quinten dragged out. "Whaddaya gonna do?"

Rafe paced the kitchen floor. "I booked a flight to Florida."

"What about Avery?"

Rafe ran down his plan.

Quinten sputtered an expletive from between his teeth. Momentary silence hung between them.

"Hey, no way around it, bruh. Gotta know for sure," Quinten said. "And when you do, you will deal with things between you and Avery."

"Yeah. I know."

"Say the word and I can fly down there to ya. No problem."

"Naw. I'm good. I'll take care of it. See what she…has to say. Figure it out from there."

"I'm here if you need me."

"Thanks. I'll let you know what happened. Say hey to Rae for me."

"Will do. Easy, man."

"Yeah. Later."

"Damn, girl," Kerry whispered. "How in the world did they know where you were going to be?" She poured them both a glass of wine.

"Who the hell knows?" She paced her kitchen floor and vacillated between anger and defeat. She ran both hands through her hair. "This is my damned job, my career they're messing with! The director all but told me that I'll be on desk duty indefinitely. He can't risk my personal life jeopardizing the people I'm assigned to protect. He even suggested that maybe I should take a leave of absence." Her eyes burned with tears of fury.

Kerry muttered a curse. "This might not be the right question, but have you spoken with Rafe?"

She tossed her head back and laughed bitterly. "Rafe! Rafe! Him and his family are the reasons why this happening."

"I'll take that as a no," she muttered.

Avery cut her eyes in Kerry's direction. "What…you think I should call him, that he's going to ride in on his white horse and fix this mess?"

"No. But I do think he needs to know what's going on."

Avery plopped down on the kitchen chair. She gazed off into the distance. "He said he was going to take care of it, that all this would pass," she said, her voice weighed down with disappointment.

"I'm sure if there was anything that he could have personally done, he did, A."

Avery sighed heavily. "I don't even know anymore." She turned her pained eyes toward her friend. "I was totally humiliated today."

Kerry reached across the table and covered Avery's clenched fists with a comforting hand. "It's gonna be all right, girl. Ya'll love each other. You'll get through it together."

Avery sniffed, blinked back tears and reached for her glass of wine. "Yeah, until the next shoe drops."

"But until it does, which more than likely it will— simply because that's life—you need to talk to him and let him know what's going on."

Avery took a sip of her wine. "I will."

"Good." She pushed back from her seat and stood. "I gotta run. Date," she added with a half smile.

"Enjoy. I'll be fine. I promise I won't walk out into traffic." She forced a laugh.

"See you tomorrow."

"Okay. Thanks for coming by."

"I got you." She gathered her things and left. "I'll come by after. I can tell already that it's going to be an early night. Leave the key."

"You don't have to do that."

"I know." She pecked her cheek and left.

Avery stared at her cell phone. Once she'd finished her glass of wine, she reached for her phone. It rang in her hand.

Chapter 14

"Hey, darlin'," he gently greeted. "I need to talk to you…"

After he'd spilled his guts about the reappearance of Janae and his plans to fly out to see her, Avery was quiet for so long that at first he thought she'd hung up, until he heard what sounded like muffled sobs.

"Avery…cher…please don't cry…talk to me."

"What do you want me to say?" she finally managed. "You're stunned…confused…whatever. I get it," she said. The fire returned to her voice. "That's not what's killing me inside. What's killing me is that you lied to me, Rafe. You *knew* you were planning to see her and even if you didn't know for sure, you never said a word. I could tell something was wrong when we talked, but I convinced myself it was my imagination. You were going to let me believe you were going to New York. From everything you've *decided* to tell me, if it wasn't for your family, you might not have said a damned word! How am I supposed to marry a man that would lie to me? But the real question, the question that is turning my stomach is, why? Why would he lie to me? And none of the answers that I've come up with have me and you working out."

His whole body jerked in alarm. "Avery. Wait a second. Listen to me."

"No. I've heard enough. Have a safe trip. I hope it's everything you want it to be. Goodbye, Rafe."

The sound of the dial tone vibrated in his ear. He dialed her back. The call went to voice mail. He tried three consecutive times with the same result.

"What are you going to do?"

Avery propped her bare feet up on the circular ottoman and took a sip from her glass of wine. "Go to work tomorrow," she said and stared off into space. "Try to salvage what's left of my job."

"You know what I'm talking about, A," Kerry said.

Avery blew out a slow breath. "I can't marry a man that would lie to me. I can't marry a man that's still in love with someone else." She sniffed as tears threatened.

"Who says he's in love with her? Did he tell you that? Come on, Avery. What would you have done in the same situation? No one could have been more blown away about the woman coming back from the dead than he was. You know why you're doing this," she said softly.

"Doing what?"

"Running."

Avery turned her face away from the truth. "I'm not," she said without much conviction.

"You figure if you can cut ties first you won't be the last one standing. You stay in control."

Avery pressed her fist to her mouth.

"Do you love him?"

"You know I do!"

"Do you believe he loves you?"

She hesitated. "Yes," she whispered.

"Tell him that. He probably needs your support now more than ever."

"But what if he realizes that he's still in love with her?"

Kerry gave a sad shrug. "There's nothing that you can do about anyone else's feelings. If it's meant to be, Rafe is gonna come back here and marry you, just like the plan."

Avery swiped at her eyes. "And what if he doesn't?"

"You'll deal with it. You've never been a woman that needs a man to define her. None of that is gonna change, with or without Rafe Lawson."

Avery lowered her gaze and studied the remnants of her wine. This was something out of a novel, not real life. Her life was orderly, foreseeable. She was trained to spot trouble from yards away. She'd missed this one by a long shot. What would she do if Rafe told her that he was still in love with Janae? And was she really angry at Rafe for his deception, or angry at herself for the lie that she was perpetrating to everyone in her life?

The question trampled through her mind. Was she really willing to simply give up, let go of the man of her dreams and fold like a three-legged table? Kerry was right. Deep inside, part of her wanted to be the one to walk away, to end it. Love was the one challenge she was never able to conquer. Her love couldn't save her mother. Her love couldn't soften her father's heart. The two most important people in her life were lost to her. Their loss carved a hole in her spirit, made her believe she was unworthy and that love only led to hurt and emptiness.

Loving Rafe was so blinding, like looking into the sun. It consumed her, tricked her into believing that love could bring happiness and fulfillment. But in the end, it would end. It always did.

Kerry rubbed sleep from her eyes and robotically fixed a pot of coffee. When Avery's bell rang she thought she was hearing things, until it rang again. Early morning visits and late-night calls were always trouble.

She tightened the belt on her robe and went to the door. She peeked through the blinds on the window next to the door. Her mouth dropped open. She glanced over her shoulder, back at the door and unlocked it. She pulled the door open and stood like a sentinel.

"Kerry."

"What are you doing here?" she demanded.

"I need to see Avery."

"Really? *Now* you need to see her?"

"Kerry, is she here?"

She folded her arms in defiance. "You have no idea what you did—what you did to her."

"That's why I'm here, because I do know," he said quietly.

Kerry's chest rose and fell. She glared at him for a moment longer and then stepped aside and let him in.

"Thank you."

The door shut behind him. "Have a seat. I'll go—"

They both looked toward the stairs.

Avery gripped the bannister. When he looked into her eyes in that way that flipped her heart, for a moment she forgot what was wrong, all the crap that happened in the last twenty-four hours, and all she wanted to do was run to him. But she didn't.

"You want me to stay?" Kerry asked.

"No. It's okay." She came down the final step and walked into the living room. "Why are you here, Rafe?"

"I needed to see you, cher."

Her insides shifted. She bit down on her bottom lip, crossed the room and sat on the side chair to keep him from sitting next to her, so that she could think—breathe.

Rafe was not going to make it easy. He came to her, knelt in front of her and took her hands in his.

"Forgive me."

She blinked rapidly against the burn of tears that threatened to fall.

He squeezed her hands, lifted one to his lips and kissed the inside of her palm. "Forgive me, cher. I never wanted to hurt you, deceive you. Never. I should have told you everything that I knew when I knew it. Yes, I planned to go and see her without telling you. Not because I wanted to lie to you, but because I wanted to be sure before I brought my baggage and asked you to unpack it." The ache in his voice reached his eyes as they moved inch by inch across her face and dipped down into her soul. "I love *you*. You."

She would put an end to all this, and tell him it was too late, that he should leave. *Now*. But she needed something different for herself. She needed to stop being afraid of tumbling into love, and allow it into her heart. For real. If there was anyone she could take that big leap with, she believed it was Rafe Lawson.

Slowly she nodded her head, wiped at her eyes. "I love you," she said in a shaky whisper.

"That's all we need." He rose from his knees and gently pulled her to her feet, took her face in his large hands. He lowered his head and covered her lips with his.

Her sigh mixed with his moan of relief and need.

"I'm sorry, cher," he whispered against her mouth before dipping his tongue into the sweetness of her mouth.

Her arms looped around his neck, and his clasped

around her back and waist and pulled her fully against his rising desire.

"Come home with me," he said, his voice hot with desire.

She leaned back to look into his eyes. "New Orleans?"

"Arlington."

She held onto the smile blooming on her lips. "Oh." She tipped her head to the right side. "And what would we be doing at your home in Arlington? A girl has to get to work in the morning." Such that it was. But they had enough to deal with. She'd deal with her own issues.

"I'll make sure you get to work and ready to take on all the bad guys." His thumb brushed her bottom lip. "Say yes. I want you. Can't you tell?"

His slow easy grin ignited the smoldering flame in her center to a four-alarm blaze.

"You are a charmer, Rafe Lawson," she purred. "I finish at five. I can be to you by six."

He hung his hands on her waist. "I'll send Alice home and fix dinner myself."

"Okay."

The loud clearing of Kerry's throat had them both turn in her direction. She was fully dressed and leaning against the frame of the archway.

"I can only conclude that whatever needed to be worked out got worked out. But…" She focused on Avery. "You're going to be late."

"Oh no. What time is it?"

"6:15."

She looked at Rafe with apology written all over her face. "I'm sorry. I've got to get ready."

"Yeah, yeah. Go. I'll see you later." He kissed her one last time as if they were the only two people in the world. "Six." He released her and walked toward the front door.

"Thanks," he quietly said to Kerry as he passed her. The door closed softly behind him.

"All is forgiven I take it?" Kerry asked, turning toward Avery.

Avery blew out a breath, still wrapped in the essence of Rafe. "I...we'll see." She looked at her friend. "I want to try. I need to."

"Did you tell him what happened at work?"

"No. I'll figure it out on my own. Like you said, it'll work out."

"Good. But, girl." She turned her head toward the closed door. "If that man came for me, I'm going with him. I'm just saying. Humph."

Avery burst out laughing and draped her arm across Kerry's shoulder. "I know that's right."

Even though she was temporarily stuck behind a desk, it wasn't as awful as she'd thought. There was plenty to keep her busy. At least she had something wonderful to look forward to at the end of her shift. The director had reassigned her to scheduling—from detail assignments to training and mapping where every agent was and with whom. It was one of those detail-oriented assignments that she was actually quite skilled at.

Toward the end of the day she was summoned to the director's office. She braced herself for more bad news.

"Come in and have a seat, Agent Richards."

Avery sat. Was this the other shoe? She lifted her chin and focused on the director.

"I've had an opportunity to consider what transpired at the Watergate. I'm fully aware that it was not of your making. You're a damned good agent. One of our best. But what happened could have seriously jeopardized the safety and security of your charge."

"Yes, sir." She continued to look him square in the eye. "There is no easy solution."

Her heart began to race.

"For the next month I want you off detail. You'll work in-house. Give the vultures time to set their sights on something else. When I feel it's appropriate I'll see about getting you back out into active field duty."

She swallowed. "Yes, sir."

Director Fischer linked his thick fingers together on top of the desk. "We should be making a decision on the promotion in the next month or so. Keeping you out of the headlines will help in that arena." He cleared his throat. "I will be honest with you, Agent Richards, the hiring committee is very concerned that with you marrying someone of such high profile, it may be a major liability. We're weighing all the options."

She kept her expression neutral. "Thank you, sir."

He nodded solemnly. "Keep doing a good job, Agent Richards."

"I will, sir. Thank you." She rose, turned and left. She tried not to let her anxiety show on her face as she passed several colleagues in the corridor. She was still being considered. At least that was something. She beat down the ugly feeling of resentment. Why should falling in love possibly cost her everything she'd worked for? One thing that she could count on was that Rafe would make her forget all the things she didn't want to think about.

When Avery arrived at Rafe's home, neither wasted any time. Rafe greeted her with a kiss that weakened her knees, plied her with a chilled glass of wine and then lulled her to a scented bath. He took great pleasure in undressing her, of rediscovering the rose-petal softness of her skin before he helped her into the deep jet tub.

He knelt down next to her as she sank into the steamy, scented water. She sighed, her body and mind succumbing to pure bliss. Rafe took the blue sponge and gently washed her back, squeezing the hot, sudsy water over her shoulders and down the rise of her breasts, which peeked out above the water. He leaned in and kissed her on the back of her neck. "Want some company?" he whispered. He nibbled her ear while his free hand wandered across the swell of her breast, before diving down into the water between her legs.

Avery drew in a quick breath as his thumb brushed across her swelling clit. "I'd...love it."

Rafe stood and tugged his fitted black T-shirt over his head, tossed it aside. He pulled on the string of his gray sweatpants and let them pool at his feet.

Avery's breath stopped in her chest, awed as always by the sheer perfection of his milk-chocolate body coming into full view. Her teeth taunted her bottom lip while she watched him, over her shoulder, step into the tub and ease down. His long, muscular legs straddled either side of her. She felt his growing erection press against her lower back.

Rafe lifted the thick, wild spirals of her hair from her neck and placed hot kisses there and down along her spine. His arms looped around her waist, fanned out and separated her thighs. "Bend your knees," he whispered in her ear. "And lean back against me."

She glanced at him over her shoulder and caught the glint of fire in his eyes. She bent her knees and leaned back.

His large hands slid up and down the inside of her thighs, the water making the path smooth as silk. His fingers spread across her belly and up to the underside of her breasts before sliding back into the water to brush and tease her exposed clit.

Avery whimpered. Her body trembled ever so slightly.

Rafe eased her further down toward the faucets. He cupped her breasts and teased the taut nipples until her moans rose in shuddering bursts.

Avery rested her head against his chest, closed her eyes and succumbed to his pleasuring.

"Rest your heels on either side of the tub," Rafe ground out.

Avery followed his instructions.

He eased her forward a bit more until she was spread wide and vulnerable. He clasped her tightly around the waist and turned on the jets. The warm water gushed out and felt like a million massaging fingers. The intensity of the onslaught of rushing water against her fully exposed, totally stimulated clit made her see stars.

"Ohhhh!"

"Hmmm, relax…enjoy," he cooed, holding her in place.

Rafe reached around and held her thighs firmly apart. The water pulsed steadily against her. Her limbs trembled. Her moans turned to whimpers. She gripped the side of the tub. Her breathing escalated as mind-altering pleasure whipped through her.

"Go with it, darlin'," he whispered.

She struggled to breathe as the first wave crashed against her. Her cry mixed with the steam-scented air. Rafe slipped two fingers inside of her, and lights burst behind her eyes.

"Ahhhh, ahhhh!" Her hips rose and fell, thrashed against his hand and the power of the water as jolts of pleasure roared through her veins. Shudders ran up and down her body as wave after wave of release erupted until she was weak.

Avery smiled as she listened to Rafe singing in off-key splendor in the kitchen while she tugged the sheets off the bed and straightened up his bedroom the following morning. She shoved the sheets inside of a pillowcase and went to the walk-in closet to get a clean set, and nearly tripped over what Rafe called his "go-bag." She picked it up to put it on the shelf, out of the way, and a folded set of papers fell out on the floor. She reached down to pick them up and noticed the lawyer letterhead. She didn't consider herself a snoop in the sense that she went around looking for things, but her instincts kicked in and she opened the papers.

She frowned as the words spilled out in front of her. The more she read, the more furious she became. A prenuptial agreement! She couldn't believe that Rafe would do something like this—to *her*. Did he think she was some kind of gold digger who was only after him for his money! What the hell.

Her temple began to pound.

"Hey, cher, I whipped us up some—"

"What is this?" She waved the papers in front of him. "A damned prenup, Rafe. Are you kidding me?"

Rafe held up his hands. "Take it easy."

"Easy! Easy! No. I won't take it easy." She paced in front of him. "Isn't it enough that your family tried to hijack the wedding and, for all intents and purposes, I've been demoted to desk duty because of the damned press following me around. That's my life, my career that I built. On hold. And let's not forget your ex-lover that has risen from the dead!" Her eyes filled with tears. "And now this!" She shook the pages violently in the air and then threw them on the floor. She slowly shook her head. "I'm the one that has had to adapt, change, give things up. Me." Her chest heaved with emotion. "I can't do this." Her throat clenched.

His countenance tightened. "What are you saying?"

She faced him. Tears ran down her cheeks. "I can't do this… I can't marry you."

"Avery." He took a step toward her. She held up her hand to halt him.

"Marrying you… I'd gain a husband but lose myself. Between your family and that," she pointed to the papers on the floor, "and…my career going down in flames…" She swiped at her eyes. "I can't." She looked down at the diamond blazing on her finger. She twisted the band and slid the ring from her finger.

Rafe stared at her. Stunned. Hurt. But shock was quickly replaced with anger. "I should have known better. I should have kept living my life. *My* damned life! Whatever made me think that this would be different?" He snorted a sound of disgust. "Well, you got your wish. This is what you wanted all along—a way out. You got it." He stared at her hard. "Keep the ring." He whirled away, stormed down the hall and out.

The door rattled in its frame. The next sound she heard was the roar of his motorcycle.

She stood under the arch of the closet door, gripped the diamond in her palm, slipped to her knees and wept.

Dazed, spent, she finally pulled herself together, gathered her things and left Rafe's home. She couldn't go home, didn't want to. She went to Kerry's place in DC, instead. She was numb as she moved through the space like a ghost—disembodied from the real world.

What had she done? Rafe was right. She had been looking for a way out and he provided her with all the ammunition she needed. Her secret, her fear of what might really be wrong with her, drove her decision. If she was honest with herself, she knew that to be true. Rafe had been down the road of losing someone before and it nearly broke him.

She couldn't do that to him again. It was best this way. Her head pounded. She pressed the heels of her palms against her eyes. Her shoulders shook as sobs overtook her again.

When Kerry came home several hours later she was beyond surprised to see her friend curled up on the love seat.

"Hey there, I didn't expect you back." She tossed her purse on the couch. "Where's Rafe?" She pulled off her jacket and added it to the couch.

Avery curled into an even tighter knot on the love seat.

"A, what's going on?"

She slowly lifted her chin from her chest. "It's over. The wedding is off."

"What are you talking about?" She plopped down on the side chair. "What happened?"

In bits and pieces Avery told Kerry about the prenup, the fight and her declaration. For quite some time after she'd finished, Kerry sat in silence. Finally she spoke.

"What is really going on, Avery? This isn't about a piece of paper."

"Yes, it is," she insisted.

"Don't b.s. me. I'm your friend. You love that man. And he loves you. You were willing to go the extra mile when he explained about Janae. But you freak out over a piece of paper. Are you serious?"

"It's not going to work." She shook her head. "There are too many obstacles and we aren't even married yet."

Kerry covered her face with her hands and groaned as if in agony. She pulled her hands away and jumped up from her seat. "This is nonsense."

"No, it—"

"Yes, it is, and you damn well know it." She huffed out a breath. "Do you love him?" She stared at her friend, daring her to lie.

"Yes."

"Do you believe he loves you?"

Avery swallowed. "Yes."

"Does he make you happy?"

"Yes." Avery lowered her head, linked her fingers together and studied her bare feet.

"Do you know how lucky you are? You have a man that adores you, a family willing to make you a part of it—something you've never had. Not only does that man love you, he's smart, talented, gorgeous, sexy *and* rich."

Avery sniffed. She drew in a long breath, pursed her lips and released the truth that she'd been battling with for months.

"There's something I need to tell you…"

Chapter 15

Rafe was blind with hurt and fury. He tore through the streets of Virginia like a man possessed. Avery had no idea all that he'd given up for her, everything that he was willing to change for her. He'd opened his heart and his soul, something he'd vowed never to do again. He could have told her that the prenup wasn't his idea and that he'd planned to confront his father. But why should he have to try to convince the woman who was supposed to love him that the man she'd decided he was could never be the man that he knew himself to be? No.

He raced by an eighteen-wheeler to the blare of angry horns and screeching tires. He'd thought they'd gotten over the biggest hurdle thrown at them—Janae—or at least someone claiming to be her.

Janae would have given him a chance to explain. Janae listened. She always listened. *Avery…* He pressed down on the accelerator, cut across two lanes of traffic and zipped onto the exit to downtown DC.

He parked his bike in front of the only available space on the street. He looked up at the awning. *Baldwin's*. He snorted a disgusted laugh at the irony—the beginning and the end.

Rafe pushed through the doors of Baldwin's and the quick flow of memories rushed at him. He went straight to the bar, determined to wash the images away.

The club, generally packed in the evening, was loosely occupied with early lunch goers who flocked there for the midday slider special, which was fine with him. He wanted to be by himself but not totally alone. He knew how quickly he could sink into that dark place, and being at home with nothing to distract him would take him there via express.

"What can I get you?"

Rafe looked up. *Pretty* was his first thought. "Bourbon."

"Straight up?"

"Yeah, thanks. Make it a double. Please."

He slightly swiveled his head to follow her movements. He felt like he knew her from somewhere but couldn't quite recall. She returned moments later and set the short tumbler of bourbon in front of him.

"Can I get you a menu?"

He gave a short shrug. "Sure."

She reached beneath the counter and pulled out a menu. "Take your time. Let me know when you're ready." She went to tend to another customer.

Rafe lifted the glass to his lips and took a deep swallow. The liquid heat hit his empty belly like a splash of lava. He breathed in deeply, let the warmth flow through his limbs. He wrapped his hands around the glass and stared off at nothing in particular. The light chatter of the customers and activity of the staff faded around him.

He'd truly believed that Avery was the one. After years of running, hiding from commitment after Janae, he was ready to let go of the past hurt and loss and begin a life with Avery. But even from the beginning, as much as he believed she cared for him, there was a part of her that he never seemed to reach. But he'd chalked it up to his own battle with personal demons. He finished his drink. Obviously, his instincts were right.

He wasn't sure what was driving the rage inside him: the idea that it was so easy for her to throw everything they had away, or the idea that she somehow believed the worst of him.

Probably best. He signaled for a refill. Maybe Janae's resurrection was more than bad timing, maybe… Naw, he wouldn't go down that road. Until he put his own eyes on her, he couldn't be sure of anything. That was the craziest part of this ugly day. Avery seemed willing to understand about Janae, and his need to see her, but was ready to toss everything out the window over a prenup that he had nothing to do with.

"Here you go. Ready to order?"

Rafe's dark gaze lifted to settle on her face. Recognition nipped around the edges, but would not come full bloom.

"I used to work with Bailey at the Meridian," she said with a knowing half smile. "Addy. I worked your grandfather's birthday party last year with her, too."

Rafe snapped his fingers. "That's where!" His smile slowly dissolved. *The night he met Avery.* "Was racking my brain trying to place you. What are you doing here?"

"Got married six months ago and we moved here for my husband's job. He teaches at the University of Virginia."

"Nice."

"How's Bailey?"

"She's great. Saw her last week, when I was back home."

"We kind of lost touch when she moved to New York with Justin."

Avery wouldn't have relocated to New Orleans for him, even though he'd been willing, much like his brother Justin, who uprooted his life for the woman he loved. He finished off his second drink as the dark clouds loomed closer.

"You're a long way from home yourself."

"Here on business." His jaw tightened. "How 'bout another refill." He held up his empty glass.

"You know we have the best crab cake sliders this side of the Mississippi. Why don't I bring you a plate with that next drink?"

He half grinned. "Sure thing." He grabbed a handful of mini pretzels from the glass bowl she'd subtly put in front of him, and tossed them in his mouth. He chewed thoughtfully, thinking about relationships that were his examples: his sisters and their husbands, his aunt Jacquie and Raymond, Justin and Bailey, and even his father and mother, when she was alive. They were all willing to sacrifice a part of themselves for the person they'd committed themselves to. That's what he'd been willing to offer Avery, beyond his body, his soul, his fortune. Obviously she didn't feel the same way.

Addy returned with his food and his refill. "Need anything else, let me know."

"Wish it was that easy, darlin'," he said into his glass. "Wish it was."

Addy made sure he was good and sober before he left Baldwin's nearly three hours after his arrival. He could tell the drinks had grown weaker as the pretzel bowl grew larger and was topped off by two cups of coffee.

"I want to thank you for a very pleasant afternoon," he said after paying his tab. "I'm pretty sure you're the reason I won't be a stain on the street."

"You just be careful out there, and I hope whatever is bothering you works itself out."

He pushed to his feet. "I'm sure it will one way or the other. Always does." He winked.

"Take care."

"You, too."

Addy walked to the other end to serve a customer. Rafe reached into his pocket for his wallet, returned his credit card and took out a hundred-dollar bill. He wrote "thank you" and placed it under the pretzel bowl.

He stepped out into the late afternoon sunshine, glanced back at the awning. Baldwin's. He shook his head, hopped on his bike and revved the engine. Hopefully Avery would be long gone by the time he returned. He needed to get ready for his trip to Florida and finally clear his plate of the distant and soon-to-be past so that he could move on.

Chapter 16

"I'm listening," Kerry said while she settled on the paisley printed side chair.

"I haven't been honest…about my health."

Kerry sat straighter. "What are you talking about? You said the doctors cleared you."

"Only because I haven't told them what's been going on with the headaches."

Kerry frowned.

"They haven't gone away. Sometimes they are almost blinding." She paused. "I stopped taking the pain meds for a while before my physical so there would be no drugs in my blood."

Kerry hung her head and then looked across at her friend. "Why?" She held up her hand. "Don't tell me—because of this damned job." She blew out a breath of frustration. "Are you crazy! Over a job. Seriously? What good is it going to do if you pass out or worse?"

Avery worried her bottom lip with her teeth. "My job, my career—it's everything that I've worked for. Can't you see that?"

"What I see is someone willing to sacrifice their health and maybe their life for a job that will replace you in a heartbeat with a plaque on the wall. Not to mention that you could be putting everyone around you in jeopardy if you have one of those episodes on duty. I know how important this promotion is for you. It's a chance to prove something to your father."

Avery looked away.

"But, girl!"

"I was scared. I *am* scared that it's something more than the after effects of the explosion." She blinked slowly. "It's the real reason why I broke it off with Rafe."

"What? What are you talking about?"

Avery curled up tighter in the chair. "Rafe has already lost so much. Everyone in his family told me what losing Janae did to him."

"Yeah, but apparently she ain't lost," she snapped.

"That's not the point."

"Then what is? 'Cause I don't get it."

Avery dropped her bare feet to the floor and leaned forward. "If something is really wrong with me…something serious, I can't saddle him with that. I won't."

"You're being very…*Avery*. Stubborn and single-focused. That man loves you. You love him."

"It's not enough."

"Hell if it ain't. Sickness and in health."

"*After* the 'I dos.'"

"You don't even know what's really wrong. For all you know, it could be the medication, or your recovery time is just longer than they thought. It could be a bunch of things."

Avery wiped a tear away.

"I can't let you do this. You're going to the doctor and let them run whatever tests they need to run. And we'll deal with whatever. As for Rafe, that part is up to you, but going to the doctor is not up for debate. I'm going with you."

"Okay," she conceded. "As long as you come with me."

"Not a problem. Make the appointment." She stood. "You're staying here tonight."

Avery nodded.

"I'm going to see what's in the fridge, or we can order." As she passed Avery she squeezed her shoulder. "It's going to be okay."

Avery stared off into the distance. What if it wasn't?

"Please stow away any electronics, put tray tables up and ensure that your seat belt is locked. We will be landing in the Sunshine State shortly, where the weather is a balmy 80 degrees."

The flight attendant's announcement clicked off. Rafe gazed out the window as the landscape of Florida began to break through the puffs of white.

He'd barely slept the night before, leaving his mind and body on edge. When he'd returned home, there was a space in his soul that wanted Avery to be there to fill it. But the larger space, that dark hole that had begun to spread, was glad that she wasn't.

The plane bumped down on the tarmac and cruised to the gate. Rafe unsnapped his seat belt, got up and retrieved his carryon from the overhead, and then helped a young mother who was trying to juggle a sleeping baby and two bags.

"Here, let me help," Rafe offered and gently took the bags and draped them over his shoulder.

"Thank you so much," she breathed in relief. "I think

my son must have gained five pounds while he slept," she joked. She peered down at the baby's innocent face.

"He slept the whole trip," Rafe commented, walking down the aisle, behind the woman.

"He is an angel. Never gives me a minute of trouble and he loves to travel." She laughed lightly and kissed the baby's forehead.

They exited the plane and walked out into the arrival terminal.

"Do you have luggage?"

"No, but my husband is meeting me in baggage claim."

"So, you live here?" They walked side by side through the throng of travelers.

"Yes. About five years. Originally from New York. My husband's mom got ill so we relocated here. You?"

"Visiting. From New Orleans."

She smiled. "I thought I heard a little twang," she teased.

Rafe chuckled. "I should have picked up on the New *Yawk*."

She wagged a finger and grinned. "I told my husband that we may have moved South but I was keeping my New Yawk accent."

They entered the baggage claim area and headed for the exit. She peeked over heads and between bodies and then suddenly her face lit up. She raised her arm and waved.

"There he is."

A tall, medium-built man in a white T-shirt and khaki shorts came toward them, but it was clear that he only had eyes for his wife and son.

The instant they were close enough his fingers threaded through her Angela Davis afro and pulled her in for a long "find a room" kiss.

Rafe lowered his gaze until the couple reluctantly separated. Their son was wide awake now and apparently just as happy to see his father as his mother was, as he began to bounce in his mother's arms and reached for his father. The man lifted his son into his arms.

The scene in front of Rafe was simple, happened every day, but for him it hit his gut in a way that saddened him. This was what he'd hoped for—to have his own family to come home to. Maybe this kind of life wasn't in the cards for him. That realization broke something inside him.

The woman turned toward Rafe. "I am so sorry. Sweetie, this nice man helped me with my bags. I didn't even ask your name."

"Rafe Lawson."

"Thanks, man," the husband said and shook Rafe's hand before taking the two bags from him. "Glen Dawkins, and you've met my wife, Selena, and our son, Gabriel," he said, sliding his arm around the waist of his wife.

"Pleasure."

"Thanks again," Selena said. "Enjoy your stay."

Rafe offered a tight-lipped smile, gave a short nod to the couple and walked away. He couldn't imagine that enjoyment would factor into his visit.

Once outside, he called for an Uber, and a half hour later, he was in his hotel room at the *W*.

Rafe sat on the side of the king-size bed that faced the beach. From the panoramic window of his fifteenth-floor suite the pulsing expanse of Miami Beach spread out before him. Any other time he would be planning his night out on the town; instead he was mulling over the inevitable. He stared at the face of his cell phone, used his thumb print to open the screen and scrolled for the number stored for Janae. He looked at it, tossed the phone across the bed. Not yet.

Rafe stood, walked to the window and opened the terrace doors. He leaned on the railing and inhaled the scent of ocean air.

Why put off calling Janae? It was the only reason he was in Florida. But to see her, confirm for himself that the voice on the phone was truly Janae, would upend everything he'd believed and grown to accept all these years. Where would that leave him—them?

He turned away from the setting sun and returned inside. He picked up the phone from the bed. This time he dialed her number.

"Hello?"

"It's Rafe."

"Hi," she said with that same sweet inflection that he remembered.

Rafe closed his eyes for a moment. "I'm in town. Only overnight. I thought we could meet tomorrow."

"Yes," she said almost before he could finish.

"Where?"

"You can come here if you don't mind."

"Text me the address. Noon work for you?"

"Fine. I'll see you then."

"Tomorrow, then."

Rafe disconnected the call and realized that his pulse was racing. He dragged in a breath, looked at his screen again, swiped for his messages and snorted a derisive laugh. Nothing from Avery.

His phone chirped with an incoming message. *Janae's address.* He slid the phone into his pocket, picked up his room card key from the dresser and went in search of the bar.

Chapter 17

"Ready?" Kerry asked while she checked the contents of her purse.

"As ready as I can be."

"I'm just glad the doctor was able to see you on such short notice."

"Guess he heard the low-level panic in my voice. He wants me to go straight to the diagnostic center for the CAT scan, then come to his office."

Kerry walked over to where Avery stood, putting on her jacket. She put her arm around the shoulder of her friend. "I know you're scared, but it's going to be okay. I feel it. But you have to believe it, too. And no matter what the doctor says, we'll deal with it. I'm here for you."

Avery's luminous brown eyes welled with tears. She pressed her lips tightly together and nodded her head.

"And you're going to talk to Rafe. Tell him the truth. He deserves it."

Avery glanced away, took her purse from the hall table. "I'll think about it. Rafe is busy reconnecting with his lost love."

"You know that's not what's going on. It's what you want to be going on so that you have a way out—blame him so that you won't have to tell him that you've been lying to him."

Avery jammed the straps of her purse over her shoulder. "I know what I'm doing," she snapped and walked to the front door.

"No, you don't," she muttered.

Avery tossed her a "not today" look over her shoulder. Kerry stuck out her tongue.

"I carry a gun too, ya know."

Avery huffed and stifled a chuckle. Kerry knew her better than she knew herself and always had a way of making her see the light, even when she didn't want to.

"I'll call him," Avery said, barely above a whisper, once they were seated and belted in Kerry's Honda.

Kerry lifted a brow. "Good."

"*After* I get the results back." She held up her hand to stop the retort she knew was coming.

Kerry put the car in gear and pulled out of her driveway. "Fine."

Avery didn't realize just how frightened she was until the nurse told her to get undressed and put on the gown, and that the doctor had ordered an MRI rather than the CAT scan. She knew instantly that the reason for the change was the doctor was concerned that something was missed on her earlier CAT scans. MRIs produced much more powerful images that revealed issues deep in tissue and bone.

She wanted to run out and just say the hell with it. But she knew she couldn't go on this way. She wanted her life back, free of pain and fear. Besides, she'd never get past Kerry, who was sitting in the reception area, waiting for her.

She hung up her clothes and put on the gown. A few moments later the nurse came to take her to the exam room. The tube-like contraption looked like something out of *Star Wars*.

The technician helped her onto the table and positioned her.

"This will take a while," the technician said. "And the noise can be unsettling, but I need you to remain as still as possible. We don't want to have to do this a second time." He made some adjustment to the panels on the tube and then left the room.

Moments later she heard the voice of the technician. "Ready to begin. Please don't move."

Avery closed her eyes, tried to tune out the rhythmic metallic bang of the machine and said a prayer.

Chapter 18

Rafe crossed the expansive lobby of the W hotel and stepped out into the blazing sunshine and pulsing energy of Miami. The Audi convertible rental that he'd picked up at the airport was driven to the front door of the hotel by the valet.

"Your keys, Mr. Lawson," the valet said.

"Thanks." He took a twenty from his wallet and pressed it into the young man's hand.

"Thank you, sir. Thank you."

Rafe gave a quick lift of his chin in acknowledgment and got behind the wheel of the Audi. He adjusted the mirrors and the seat to accommodate his height, punched in the address on the GPS, put the car in gear and drove off.

He'd been to Miami a few times over the years, mostly to party along South Beach, which is known for its glamorous nightspots and celebrity-chef eateries. He'd lost track of high-end stores and indie fashion shops he patronized that lined the shopping strip on Lincoln Road Mall. So, between the parties at night and the beach during the day, he really didn't pay much attention to street signs and landmarks. But from what he could recall, not much had changed since his last visit.

The streets, even before noon, were teeming with a montage of revelers, many of whom looked like they were coming in from the night before and others just getting started.

Rafe took Ocean Drive to the A1A. According to the GPA, he should arrive at Janae's place in twenty minutes. Staying focused on the building traffic helped to keep his thoughts off what he was heading toward. But every time traffic slowed to a halt, a flash of Janae would jump in front of him.

He was so torn between simmering anger at the deception that had gone on for more than sixteen years, and the unresolved feelings he'd buried that had begun to bubble to the surface.

Her house was less than five minutes away. He took the next exit and drove along Orchard Road and began checking addresses. Number 5856. He slowed and turned the car onto the short driveway and pulled up to the single-story home. The large bay windows wrapped around either side of the front door, which was covered by a portico. The lawn looked freshly mowed and the shrubbery clipped with precision. A single towering palm stood sentinel.

For several moments Rafe sat behind the wheel, gripping it with both hands. The house didn't look like anything he'd ever imagine for Janae. But then again, he no longer knew *this* Janae. He turned off the engine. There was no turning back. Whatever happened on the other side of the door, he'd deal with.

The front door opened in concert with him stepping out of the car. For an instant the world stopped spinning. It was her, in the flesh, and not her at the same time. His heart hammered so hard in his chest that it was difficult to breathe. And then she smiled. It *was* Janae. He would never forget the smile that lit up every corner it touched.

Caught in the surreal moment he slowly walked down the rest of the driveway and stopped at the bottom step.

"Rafe…"

Her hair was long now, framing and hiding her face at the same time, not like the short twists she once wore that showcased her wide eyes and high cheekbones.

He came up the two steps to stand in front of her. "Janae."

"Thank you for coming."

He jammed his hands in his pockets.

"Come in." She stepped aside and held the screen door open.

Rafe eased by her and entered the small foyer that opened on either side to the sitting room on the left and kitchen to the right. From where he stood he could see straight out to the back that boasted a small pool—a staple of Florida living.

"We can talk in here," Janae said, extending her arm toward the sitting room.

He followed her and couldn't help but notice the slight limp as she walked. Inwardly he winced for her pain. He took a quick look around. The room was small, but cozy and a bit overstuffed with knickknacks and memorabilia that took up the mantel, glass cabinets and end tables. Framed photos of Janae with her parents hung on the walls.

Rafe turned to face her. He unbuttoned the single button on his navy-blue sports jacket, revealing the brilliant white open-collared shirt.

"Can I get you anything? Something to drink?"

"No. I'm fine. Thanks." He sat in the armchair near the window.

Janae took her time and sat opposite him. A circular table separated them.

"Where do I begin?" she said softly.

"Anywhere. Tell me something that makes sense, Janae. When you remembered something, anything about us, why didn't you let me know you were alive? How could you do that to someone that you claimed to love?" He leaped up out of his seat and began to pace, rubbing his hand across the back of his neck. He whirled toward her.

"It was *because* I loved you that I didn't call," she said, so quietly that it sounded like a prayer. "I had so many physical struggles after what happened—still do. Memory pretty much gone, scars, nightmares." She sucked in a breath. "I didn't want to burden you, and my parents—my caretakers—convinced me that it was best for everyone that I stay away."

"Even if I was to accept that then, why now? Why come back now and ruin my life all over again?"

"I still love you, Rafe." Her deep bronze gaze pierced the protective coating he'd submerged himself in.

His gut shifted. Slowly he shook his head in denial. "It's not that simple anymore, J. I had no choice but to move on." His throat clenched while he slowly lowered himself into the chair. He rested his forearms on his muscled denim-clad thighs and leaned forward. "I can't even imagine everything you've been through, Janae. Sometimes I think that what I imagined was even more horrific—simply because I didn't know!" He linked his fingers together and looked into her eyes. "Maybe there's a part of me that understands all your reasons, but it doesn't take away all the damage that not knowing has done. In sixteen years, it was hard, but I moved on, Janae. I had no choice if I was gonna survive. Losing you...nearly destroyed me. I had to find my way without you, push into the back of my mind all the plans we made, the things we'd hoped for." He dragged in a breath. He thought about Avery—his second chance—and their last conversation. His jaw tightened. He wouldn't give in and let go again.

"Janae... I know I'll always love you, too." He breathed deeply. "But what we had is the past. I can't go back. *We* can't go back."

Janae lowered her head to hide the tears welling in her eyes. "I hoped..." She sniffed. "But I understand. I only want you to be happy, Rafe."

They were quiet for a moment. "What about your parents?" he gently probed.

She blinked rapidly. "They passed away. A year apart from each other about three years ago. I always believed they hung on to make sure that I was okay."

"I'm so sorry, Janae. Really."

She pressed her lips together and nodded slowly. "Thank you."

"So...you're here alone?" He studied her face and noticed for the first time the slight discoloration of her right cheek that looked as if it might be the result of burns.

"In the house, yes. But I have friends and my work. I do intervention at the local high school for at-risk students and double duty as guidance counselor."

He smiled, remembering her passion for social work. "That's great. I know you're amazing."

The stiffness of her shoulders seemed to finally relax, and a true smile lit her eyes. "I love my students. So many of them have it rough. I mean really rough." She looked right at him. "Not like how me and you grew up. We thought a hard time was not going to a concert, or the car not starting." They both laughed at the memories they shared. She glanced down at her hands, covered the left that was scarred. "I found my place. That part is good. I've made friends and have pieced together my life one day at a time." She swallowed. "There are still things that I don't clearly remember." She shrugged lightly. "I've grown to accept it and don't fight with myself about it anymore. It took time and a lot of therapy." She smiled, the way he remembered.

As he listened the hardened shell that he'd wrapped around that part of his soul that contained all things Janae slowly softened, and he allowed himself the briefest of moments to remember what it felt like to love her, but also the emotional work that it took to move on.

"I'm happy for you. I can't imagine your struggle, but the woman that I remember was always a fighter."

He stood. Janae's gaze rose with him. He came to her, took her hand and brought it to his lips. "Thank you for finally closing the space in my life, Janae. Knowing that you survived…" His throat tightened.

She stood, wrapped her arms around him and rested her head on his chest. He stroked her back and for a moment all the years and uncertainly slipped away. He stepped back. "Take care of yourself, Janae." He kissed her cheek, turned away and didn't look back.

Chapter 19

"We should have the results back from the radiologist in a day or so," the doctor said. "The pain, in the meantime, can be managed. I'm going to write you a new prescription. But you must take the medication."

Avery nodded. "Are there any side effects?"

"Well, it can make you groggy. You shouldn't drive for up to two hours after you take it."

"That's going to interfere with my job. I have to drive and be alert."

"Ms. Richards, I need you to understand that we can't ever be too cautious with head injuries. Most times they heal on their own, but sometimes they don't. I need you to be prepared for that. Hopefully, that won't be the case."

"Are you saying that I might be on some kind of medication for the rest of my life?" she asked, panic rising in her voice.

"It's possible. But let's not go down that road until we

get the results back," he said, patting the air with his hand. "I'll give you a call as soon as I get the results. We'll go from there." He turned to his computer and tapped in her information. "The prescription is being sent to your pharmacy. It should be ready by the time you get back home." He folded his beefy hands on top of the desk. "Do you have any more questions for me?"

Avery lowered her head and shook it slowly. "No." She looked across the desk at him and then stood. "Thank you, Dr. Ryan."

Kerry popped up from her seat the moment Avery exited the doctor's office. "What did he say?"

"The results should be back in a day or two. Got a new prescription and was told that this may be my life," she added morosely.

"It's going to be okay. I know it will." She hooked her arm through Avery's as they walked out.

"Yeah," she murmured.

"Are you going to talk to Rafe?"

"Not now. Not yet."

Kerry used the key fob to disengage the car alarm. "Hungry?"

"No. If you could drive me home, that would be great."

"Are you sure? You know you can stay with me as long as you want."

"I'm sure. I need to sleep in my own bed." She opened the passenger side door.

"I won't get offended, but the offer is good if you change your mind." She opened her door and got in. "What about work? Are you going in tomorrow?"

Avery snapped her seat belt in place. "Have to. I've barely been back and already had to take a day off. I don't need to add to Director Fischer's doubts. He said the promotion is still out there. Hopefully the media interest in me and Rafe has died down—especially since there's nothing to write about," she added and turned her head to stare out of her window. Not to mention that she didn't need her father getting wind of what was going on before she had a chance to tell him herself. It was only a matter of time before he found out. But she needed to steal as much of it as she could for now.

Kerry didn't comment. Avery would work it out. She always did.

After a stop at the pharmacy to pick up her prescription, Kerry dropped Avery home and promised to call later.

Sitting in a tub full of bubbles, surrounded by low lights and the unwinding aroma of lavender, Avery leaned back against the lip of the tub and closed her eyes. Steam wafted around her. She missed him. From the depths of her soul she missed him. Her insides twisted and unwound. Rafe was the man she wanted. But what if she would never be well? What if she decided to try to work it out, but he was still in love with Janae? Her heart tightened. She had to be all right. Rafe *had* to choose her. But if she was always going to be a semi-invalid, living on pills and stuck behind a desk or worse, she knew she would be a horror to live with, to love. And she'd grow to resent Rafe and he'd eventually resent her for ruining his life—*again*.

She opened her eyes and stared up at the white ceiling. It was best to let go now.

Rafe's flight landed in New Orleans shortly before six. The travel time between Florida and Louisiana was barely two hours. He wished it was longer. He wished he could stay up in the air, let the clouds separate him from the reality of firm ground for a little while longer.

Seeing Janae shook him more than he was willing to admit. Feelings for her still simmered under the surface. Being with her brought back a tidal wave of memories and raw emotions. But he had to reconcile with the reason why he was facing her for the first time in sixteen years. She'd deceived him.

He got it. He understood why she'd stayed away. In some macabre way she was trying to protect his feelings, and her parents were trying to protect her. But Janae honestly believed that he would have walked away.

That's what unsettled him the most. How could she say that she loved him if she believed that he wouldn't have loved her enough to stay—no matter what? How do you love someone and allow him to believe that you're dead, allow him to wallow in the guilt of loss?

Would he have stayed in Florida and tried to figure it all out without the *possibility* of Avery? The question plagued him as he drove home from the airport. He needed to see Avery, be with her and settle things between them. She was going to listen to reason.

He instructed his phone to dial his aunt Jacquie while he drove.

"Rafe. Sweetie. Are you back?"

"Yeah. Actually, I was hoping you were home."

"Coming by?"

"Yeah. Should be there in about forty minutes."

"I could use the company."

"See you soon."

When Rafe arrived, Jacqueline took one look at his face and wrapped her nephew in her arms. For several moments she held him like she did when he was a wild rambunctious child who had been punished for his antics by his father and sought out his aunt to hear his hurt and grievances.

Reluctantly Jacquie released him, slid her arm around his and ushered him into the house.

"I just turned off the pot."

Rafe grinned. "Smells like a jambalaya party."

"Comfort food. Come on."

Rafe shrugged out of his lightweight brown leather jacket and hung it on the back of the kitchen stool.

Jacquie busied herself at the oven. She took out a tray of rolls and placed them on the marble island counter.

"Hot damn, Aunt J." He snatched a piping-hot, home-made roll from the tray and popped it back and forth between his fingers while he blew on it.

She glanced at him over her shoulder. "If you'd wait a second you wouldn't have to do all that," she said with laughter in her voice.

Rafe blew on the perfectly browned, butter-lathered roll and took a bite. His long lashes lowered over his eyes as he hummed in satisfaction.

She took two large ceramic bowls from the cabinet and set them on the table along with cutlery. Rafe jumped up with his mouth filled with a roll and took the stainless-steel stew pot from the stove and set it on the warming tray in the center of the counter.

"Did Raymond leave yet?"

Jacquie blew out a breath. "This morning. Guess that's why I started cooking." She looked at her nephew. "Comfort."

He patted her hand. "He's gonna be fine, Aunt J."

"I know. It's just hard being sidelined. You know I'm not used to that," she said and puttered a sad laugh.

Since his aunt's near-death diagnosis two years earlier, and her brother Branford being her savior, she'd scaled back on her travel, especially extended travel. Jacqueline Lawson was a renowned photojournalist whose work was featured in magazines and museums around the world. Her partnership with Raymond only solidified her cache and his. But the doctors wanted her to give her body another six months of high nutrition, rest and follow up, and then she would be one hundred percent back to herself.

Fortunately, she had a husband like Raymond who was strong enough to withstand the Lawson wrath when she fought tooth and nail to go against doctor's orders and chase the next story. He'd put his foot down and let her know that there was nothing out in that world that was more important than what they had together, and they would be nothing without each other. He had no intention of losing her over some job, and if she loved him as much as she claimed, she'd realize the truth in what he said. The lioness purred.

Jacquie ladled heaps of the mouth-watering jambalaya into Rafe's bowl and then hers. She took a seat next to him, waited for him to break the silence.

"She's the same but different," Rafe finally began slowly, and took a spoonful of food. Thoughtfully and at times with difficulty he recounted his meeting with Janae.

Jacquie listened with patience, never interjecting her thoughts or opinion, only from time to time lovingly patting his hand.

"I've been back and forth in my head," he said on a breath of confusion. "Avery pretty much ended things between us. Janae was willing to start over." His cheeks puffed, he blew out a slow breath, turned and looked at his aunt. "Why are women so difficult?"

Jacquie chuckled. "You askin' the wrong woman if you check with my husband. But, seriously, we're nurturers at heart, always wanting to take care of others, even by sacrificing ourselves in the process." She clasped his fisted hand. "You, Rafe Lawson, bring out that quality in women in spades. They all want to take care of the bad boy, tame his heart, tend to his wounds."

"So, I gotta be a bastard to women? Is that the answer?"

"No, of course not. What I'm saying is you need to be aware that when women love, they protect. Janae was trying to protect you, as hard as that is to digest, and I firmly believe that Avery is trying to protect you from something, as well." She stared directly into his questioning gaze.

"If you're ever going to find some peace inside yourself, whatever you decide to do about Avery, you need to find out what she thinks she's protecting you from. You see the aftermath of how that belief can go terribly wrong," she added.

He focused on the contents of his bowl and churned his aunt's advice over in his head. He turned to her and offered up that heart-stopping half grin. "Plan to."

"Sounds like a toast is in order." She hopped up from her seat, went into the living room and returned with a bottle of bourbon, which she held high like a trophy. She poured for them both.

Rafe lifted his glass. "To the wisest aunt a nephew could have."

Jacquie grinned. "I'll drink to that."

Rafe and Jacquie talked and laughed and ate long into the night. When he woke the following morning, he knew exactly what he had to do. After a long, hot shower and a change of clothes that he kept in his go-bag, he met up with his aunt in the kitchen. She was totally absorbed in the newspaper while she sipped on a cup of espresso.

"Mornin'. Sleep okay?" she asked, looking up as she absently tucked a wayward lock back into the high twists on her head.

"Yeah, I did actually," he said on a breath.

"Coffee?"

"To go. I'm heading out."

She turned halfway on the stool and looked at him. "Where?"

"DC."

She smiled and then turned back to her paper. "Good. Thermos in the cabinet over the sink," she added, hooking a thumb over her shoulder.

Rafe poured coffee into the thermos and then came up alongside his aunt. "Thank you for listening, Aunt J." He leaned down and kissed her soft cheek.

"And you make sure you do the same," she said, wagging a warning finger.

He winked and walked out. Keeping an open mind was the plan, but he'd seen many of the best laid plans fall apart. He was willing to listen if Avery was willing to talk honestly.

Chapter 20

Avery was at her desk, working her way through her mind-numbing assignment of determining which agents were up for new detail assignments. Although the in-house policy was to keep the agents with the same clients, periodically, for a variety of reasons an agent was reassigned. At least she still had her job, such as it was.

She lived for being in the field. She relished the uncertainty, the level of focus needed no matter how mundane an assignment may appear to be. Sitting behind a desk was not what she'd worked and trained for. It was not what the previous director saw in her.

Heaving a sigh, she made a note next to an agent's name when her cell phone began to vibrate on her desk. She snatched it up and the air hitched in her throat. "Hello…"

"Hey."

The smooth sound of his voice enveloped her like a warm blanket. "Rafe."

"I didn't want to be too presumptuous and pop up at your job without calling."

"You're here? In DC?"

"Got in about twenty minutes ago. Still at the airfield. Didn't know if I was going to have to turn right back around. Do I?"

Her heart raced. "No. I...want to see you."

"When are you free?"

"I'm off at six."

"I'll come to you around eight. You are back in your place, aren't you?"

"Yes."

"Everything been okay...reporters bugging you?"

"No. It's been quiet."

"Good." He paused a moment. "We have a lot to talk about, Avery. Lot to straighten out."

Her stomach clenched. "I know," she said softly.

"I'll see you at eight."

"How long will you be in DC?"

"That depends on how the night goes. I'll see you later."

Rafe picked up his car that he kept parked at the landing strip and drove to his Arlington home for a quick change of clothes before meeting his father for a late lunch. He'd half expected his very busy father to be unavailable or out of town, but was oddly surprised that not only did he agree to meet with his son, but invited him to lunch at the club where the politicians on the Hill gathered for meals and to cut deals.

As much as he disliked wearing a tie, he'd don one for the occasion, knowing that if he didn't, it would be the first bone of contention on the long list between him and his father. He chose a custom-tailored, slim-fitting charcoal-gray two-piece that he had made at the renowned Martin Greenfield's Clothier during one of his trips to New York.

He surveyed the row of shirts hanging in his walk-in closet and finally settled on a pearl-gray shirt. He paired it with an obsidian tie with barely perceptible maroon stripes.

Dressed and as mentally ready as he could be, he took the prenup from his go-bag, stuck it in the inside pocket of his suit and then headed out. He tossed his bag into the trunk of his Benz and headed out of Virginia to DC.

His father made reservations at Charlie Palmer's Steak House on Constitution Avenue. It was his father's favorite place. At any given time an array of who's who could be found huddled over the linen-topped tables, or sequestered in the private dining room. His father always said the service and the food was impeccable and that that was the real reason he went there. But Rafe knew better. The steaks reminded Branford Lawson of home and the atmosphere reeked of the power that Branford Lawson wielded in Washington.

He pulled up in front of Charlie Palmer's and a red-vested valet came to take his car. When he walked inside the tables were filled with suited men and women, waiters were balancing trays of wine and expensive liquor, and crystal flutes and tumblers gleamed beneath the chandelier lighting.

"Reservation?"

He blinked and focused on the young woman in front of him. "Yes. Lawson."

"Oh, yes, the senator is here already. I'll take you to your table."

Rafe walked behind her and spotted a few familiar faces on their way to his father's table—the two hosts from MSNBC, the speaker of the house was holding court in back, and he was pretty sure he spotted the junior senator from New Jersey in an animated conversation with his senior counterpart from New York.

His father had a private table by the window.

"Dad."

Branford lifted his gaze from the sheaf of papers in front of him. "Son." He extended his hand to the seat opposite him. "You look well."

"Thanks." He pulled out a chair and sat.

"I ordered for both of us. Save some time."

Of course he did. He signaled for the waiter. "Bourbon." He linked his long fingers together and focused on his father. "I got the papers from your lawyer."

"Good. The firm is very thorough, made sure you were protected."

"Protected? From what, Dad?"

Branford leaned back in his chair and surveyed his son from above his half-framed glasses. "You never fully understood the vastness of the Lawson fortune."

"Don't you get it? I don't care about all that. I'm building my own fortune, my own legacy."

Branford snorted a laugh just as the waiter arrived with the meals.

"Thank you, Ralph. Looks great as always."

"Of course, Senator."

Branford unfolded a white linen napkin and tucked it in his collar. He pursed his lips. "Food is excellent." He lifted a steak knife toward Rafe. "Eat up."

Rafe tossed back his drink and then set the glass down on the table.

Branford cut into his steak and put a piece in his mouth. He chewed slowly. "What this family has, who we are, didn't just happen with your granddad Clive." He rocked his jaw.

"What are you talking about?"

"Your great-grandfather Raford worked the land."

"I know that. He married MaeJean Hughes."

"They were barely more than slaves. Worked for the Fontaines."

"Dad, what does any of this have to do with *you* writing a prenup for *me*?"

"That land that old man Fontaine left to your great grandfather wasn't just any land. It was the seed for everything we have. The land birthed a string of small businesses, employed half the black folks in the area, multiplied and spread." He paused, looked Rafe dead in the eyes. "Son, we own all of St. Mike, Everett, Joe and Montgomery parishes. All the land and businesses running along the south bank of the Mississippi, straight down to the delta."

Rafe listened in stunned silence, trying to absorb the enormity of it all. "Why…didn't we ever know this?"

"You're the eldest. The heir. Your uncles know. Grandpa Clive told each of us when we married. The eldest sons are told when they marry." He leveled his gaze at Rafe. "The legal arrangement wasn't meant to control you—no one can do that—" He laughed lightly. "It was to protect our legacy and ensure that it would continue for the next generation. You're the one that everything will fall to. You'll be responsible for the prosperity of the businesses, the lives of employees, homeowners, the rest of the family, your siblings." He leaned forward. "It's why I've been so gotdamned hard on you, son. I needed you to be ready."

"Why didn't you just tell me, Dad? Talk to me."

Branford nodded. "You're right. I should have. When you got engaged to Avery, I knew it was time. This," he waved his hand between himself and Rafe, "isn't my forte. Pretty sure you know that." He turned his attention back to his steak.

Rafe put down his knife and fork. "There's something I need to tell you, too."

* * *

"All this time…" He stared at his son with astonishment. "Son, I am so sorry."

Rafe nodded.

"What are you going to do?"

"There's no going back. That much I know for sure. I'm going to see Avery this evening. Talk. Work it out."

"Make her listen. She's the right woman for you, son."

Rafe angled his head to the side. "Oh, really?"

"I like her."

"Yeah, me, too."

Branford raised his glass. Rafe did the same. The two talked and ate and drank while the lunch crowd disappeared and the early dinner customers arrived. The walls came down. They allowed themselves to be seen in ways they had not in the past, and it felt really good.

By the time they left the steak house, the sun was beginning to take a dip. They stood together in front, while Rafe's car was brought around. Branford's driver pulled up, as well.

"Dad, you had him waiting all this time?"

Branford shrugged. "I had food sent out and told him I'd call when I needed him back."

Rafe chuckled. "You're getting soft in your old age."

Branford grumbled in the back of his throat.

The valet arrived with Rafe's car. He turned to his father, extended his hand for a shake as they usually did. To his surprise his father pulled him in for an embrace and patted him solidly on the back.

"You work things out with Avery, and we'll talk more about the future."

Rafe's throat tightened. He looked into his father's eyes. "I'll call you."

"I'd like that."

The valet handed Rafe his keys. He gave a final glance at his father, got in the car and drove off.

As he drove home it took all his concentration to focus on the road and the blooming evening traffic. His head was spinning with everything his father revealed to him. The Lawson family was not just well-off. They were beyond wealthy. They wielded the kind of wealth that shaped the landscape, government, altered the narrative, determined outcomes. He drove through large swaths of land, past buildings and homes, and realized for the first time that he was the steward over all of this and more. The magnitude of it was humbling and unsettling as he struggled to wrap his mind around it all. Then of course, there was his own businesses to run.

He pulled into his driveway and went inside. As much as he hated to admit it, the prenup made sense. Although he didn't believe that Avery would ever take advantage, it was to protect her as well as the family.

He tugged on his tie and jogged up the stairs to his bedroom. It was nearly six thirty and he had every intention of getting to Avery's at eight on the dot, and he wanted to stop on the way and pick up a bottle of the wine that she liked.

After a quick shower and change of clothes, he repacked his go-bag with fresh clothes and toiletries, along with the prenup. He exhaled. He seriously hoped that Avery was up to and willing to talk. They had a lot to hash out, but it was going to take a real commitment from them both to make it work. He could only do so much by himself.

Chapter 21

Avery checked the time—again. It was ten minutes later than the last time she'd checked. Her stomach was in knots and her heart kept thudding. The last thing she wanted was to get herself worked up and usher in an attack. She looked at the bottle of medicine on her dresser and debated taking a tablet, but decided against it. She needed to be clear and focused and since she had not taken these new meds before, she had no idea how her body would react.

She'd debated with herself ever since Rafe's call whether or not she would tell him everything that was going on with her physically. She understood Kerry's rationale that she should be up-front and honest—that he deserved to know the truth. He'd already endured being the recipient of a lie perpetuated by someone he loved.

Janae. He'd seen her by now. Too many questions about what happened between them trampled through her head.

Images of them together, reunited, taunted her. What if he was coming to tell her…?

The doorbell rang and her entire body jerked in alarm. She drew in a long breath, hoping to slow her racing heart. At the door, she paused for a moment with her hand on the knob, neutralized her expression and then pulled the door open.

"Cher."

The soft single word of endearment was like a love song to her ears. Her soul filled with only the kind of joy that Rafe could bring.

He took a step across the threshold, reached out to her and she found herself enveloped in the strength of his arms. She inhaled deeply, filling her lungs with the renewal of his scent, and listened to the pounding of his heart, and the doubts that plagued her slipped away.

Rafe leaned slightly back. Avery looked up into his eyes an instant before his mouth covered hers. His fingers threaded through the soft tangle of her curls, pulling her into the heat of his kiss.

She sighed into his mouth as he kicked the door closed behind him and in the same motion pinned her against the wall.

The heat of their need for each other fused their bodies together.

"I've missed you crazy," he groaned into her mouth.

She tugged at the hem of his Oxford shirt, pulled it out from the waist of his jeans and slid her fingers up and along his chest before loosening the buckle of his belt.

"Here?" he murmured, and suckled her neck.

"Yes. Yes."

Rafe needed no further invitation. His hands knew all her secret places and found them while incrementally baring her warm skin to his hungry eyes. Her shorts and black panties pooled at her feet and the slight pop freed her breasts from the black bra, and he feasted on them as a man starved.

Avery's moans spiraled while Rafe plied her with hot, wet kisses traveling downward until he was on his knees. She gripped his shoulder and bit down on her lip as his tongue separated her folds and awakened the epicenter of her desire with flicks of his tongue.

Rafe cupped her round behind in his palms and pulled her to him, suckled, kissed, licked her until her inner thighs trembled and her belly fluttered. Gently he drew the swollen bud between his lips and teased, stopped, teased some more. Avery whimpered and dug her nails into his shoulders. Her toes curled as a shiver raced up the back of her legs, spread through her limbs and shook her body with explosive jolts of release.

"Oh, god! Rafe..." Her knees weakened as another wave swept through her.

Rafe slowly rose draping her long legs over the bend of his arms. She wrapped them around his waist as he found his way inside her, pushing the air out of her lungs. She gasped as he filled her, moved hard and fast inside her—over and over and over until there was nothing he could do to hold back the jettison that flooded her.

Shaken and breathless they slid to the floor, limbs tangled, bodies wet.

"Up against a wall...two feet from my front door," Avery managed to say with breathless laughter ringing in her voice.

Rafe braced his palms on the floor behind him and looked at her through the half slits of his eyes. "A testament to your power ovah me, darlin'...which isn't totally satisfied." He rocked inside her and his still stiff erection was unmistakable. "What are we gonna do about this?"

Avery smiled mischievously, pressed her hands against his chest and pushed him onto his back to straddle him.

"Naughty girl." He cupped her breasts, which overflowed his palms as she rolled her hips and rode them to ecstatic release.

Wrapped in a single light blanket, curled on the couch with soft music in the background Rafe and Avery sipped wine between kisses and light touches.

"We really should eat something," Avery said dreamily. She rested her head on his chest.

"I don't feel like moving. Just want to hold you."

Avery snuggled deeper against him, hummed softly under her breath. She wanted this time to last as long as possible to avoid the hard facts they still needed to deal with.

Rafe stroked her hair away from her face, kissed the top of her head. "It's over," he said quietly.

She lifted her head to look at him. "Janae?"

"Yes."

Her heart thumped.

"How…how was it, seeing her again?"

"Hard. Unreal. Sad."

She stroked his chest. "I…need you to tell me about it."

Rafe drew in a breath. "I went to her house…" He told her in bits and pieces what they'd talked about, her reasons for staying away.

"She still loves you." She hesitated. "Do you still love her?"

Rafe leaned his head back and stared up at the ceiling. "I'll always love her, love what we had, but I'm not in love with her. I know that. And I know that there's nothing in me that wants to go back."

Avery was quiet, taking in what he'd said. She could not imagine the agony that he'd experienced that day and all the days that followed. He'd found a way to piece his life together and found love again—with her. She didn't want to do to him what Janae had done. If they were going to build a life together, it had to be on a foundation of trust.

"I need to tell you something," she began.

"Baby…" He angled his body to face her. "You could have told me. You've been dealing with this and we should have been dealing with it together. Don't you get it? I'm in this one hundred percent. All in." He hugged her tighter. "I'm going with you to get the results. End of story." He cupped her cheeks in his hands. "Whatever the deal is we'll handle it together. I need you to hear me on this. No damned job is more important than your health and your life. Nothing is more important to me than you. Period. You got that?"

She nodded. A tear slipped down her cheek.

"No more secrets. I don't need you trying to protect me from the truth. Ever." His aunt's words echoed in his head. He kissed her softly, tasted her tears. "It's going to be all right, baby." He brushed the damp tracks on her cheeks away with his thumb.

She sniffed.

He sat up. "Now I'm starved. And we have a lot more to discuss."

"What?"

"Let's order something first and talk over dinner."

Chapter 22

They ordered two large pizzas, one with sausage and pepperoni for Rafe and the other with extra cheese and broccoli for Avery. Each of them were halfway through before they came up for air.

"Guess we were hungry, huh?" Avery giggled over a mouthful of food.

"Hmm. Umm." Rafe washed down his pizza with a long swallow of red wine.

Avery tucked her legs beneath her. "So…what else? The suspense is killing me." She leaned back and sipped on her glass of wine.

"It's about the prenup." He watched her expression tense. "I know what you said and how you feel. First of all, I didn't get it written up."

Avery frowned. "You didn't. Then—"

"My father did it. But you didn't give me a chance to explain that part of it."

"Rafe… I… I'm sorry. I just thought—"

"I get it. I would have figured the same thing, unless you know my father. He likes to have his hand in everything."

"I of all people should understand that. I'm the poster child for the controlling parent." She reached out and touched his cheek. "I'm sorry. I shouldn't have jumped to conclusions." She pushed out a breath. "Honestly, it was just an excuse."

"Huh?"

She took his hands. "This whole being in love and devoted and committed to someone or something other than myself and my career is unchartered territory for me. I got scared. And I stupidly figured that if I found a way out I wouldn't be around to be hurt or…to lose you."

"Woman! I'm not gonna hurt you. I'm not leaving and you're not losing me."

"Promise?"

"Yeah." He grinned, but the seductive smile slowly dissolved. "There's more."

Avery set down her glass.

"I went to see my father today. About the prenup."

"Okay."

"He told me the real reason why he had it drawn up."

Her tapered brows drew together. "The real reason? What are you talking about?"

He refilled her empty glass and handed it to her. "Take a sip. You'll need it."

"You're scaring me." She slowly reached for the glass.

"Darlin', scared is putting it mildly."

He got up, crossed the living room to the glass cabinet and took out the bottle of bourbon, poured a short glass and returned to the couch.

Avery's eyes widened in growing alarm. "Rafe…what the hell is going on?"

He stood in front of her. "Well…you kinda knew that my family was well-off."

"Yes, and?"

"We're a little more than well-off." He tossed back the drink and his eyes squeezed shut as the heated liquid slid down his throat. He sat next to her and began at the beginning with his great grandfather.

Avery listened in numbed silence. The enormity of what he told her stretched the bounds of her comprehension. She tried to envision him as this magnate with near-limitless power and resources at his disposal. She knew power, saw it in action and how it had the ability to make or break a person. Too much power corrupts. The state of the country was a testament to that.

But Rafe was to be her husband, the man she'd spend the rest of her life with. She watched his expression shift from awe to excitement to humility. This was not a man that would let the elixir of power poison who he was.

Rafe looked into Avery's eyes. "The prenup is not set up because of a trust issue or that I'd ever not want you to have whatever was mine. It's to protect you in case anything should happen to me. You would not be responsible for all of the entities in any way."

"First of all, nothing is going to happen to you." She sighed. "I get it. I do. When I saw it I understood what I wanted to understand. Not to mention that I had no idea…"

"Yeah, me either."

"So now what?"

"Nothing really changes, at least not yet. I come into my inheritance when I get married. Dad said after the wedding—*and* honeymoon—" he winked "—the learning curve will begin."

"And what about your businesses? The foundation? Your music?"

"About that. I didn't get a chance to tell you." His tone softened. "Before everything kinda blew up with us I'd already begun to put some changes in place, shift the management of things so that I could confidently relocate to DC—for you. I know how important your career is and your career is here."

Her throat clenched. She lowered her head and bit down on her lip. "Oh, Rafe." She looked up, her eyes clouded with tears. "I...you are the most amazing man I've ever known." Her gaze combed his face. "To have you love me is the greatest gift and my gift to you is my heart, my soul, my undying love and commitment." She leaned in and kissed him long and slow. "We got this," she said against his mouth.

"That's what I've been trying to tell you, darlin'." He tossed the blanket to the floor.

"So, does this mean I can get my twenty bucks back for the pizza?" she teased as he moved between her thighs.

"Whatever I have," he ground out, easing inside her, "is yours."

"You want me to drive you to work?" Rafe asked while he finished shaving.

Avery came up behind him and slid her arms around his bare waist. "No. Not necessary. You know I like to have access to my own car."

He turned, leaned down and kissed her, leaving shaving cream on the tip of her nose. "Yes, ma'am."

"But I'd love to find you here when I come home." She grinned up at him.

"I might be able to arrange that. I have some business to take care of today. Won't take long, and I need to stop by my place, pick up a few things."

"Good." She whirled away.

"You should hear from the doctor today about the results and when you need to come in, right?"

Avery stopped mid-step. "Yes." She turned back around.

Rafe walked toward her. "It's going to be fine. We got this."

She leaned on him for a moment. "I'm going to be late fooling around with you." She pushed against his chest and walked out into the bedroom. But she couldn't turn her back on the fear that churned in her stomach.

Every time her phone rang, her whole body jerked. This time the call was from Director Fischer, who wanted to see her right away.

"Damn," she muttered when she hung up. She slid her cell phone in her pocket, turned off her computer and locked her office door behind her. A million thoughts ran through her head as the elevator ascended to the executive floor. Had the director gotten wind of her visit to Dr. Ryan? More fallout from photographers? She couldn't see a good outcome to the impromptu request.

The doors slid open and she all but slammed into Mike.

"Richards. How are you?"

"Good. Thanks."

"Congratulations are in order. Maybe we could celebrate over drinks." He stepped onto the elevator and the doors closed before she could respond.

Avery continued down the corridor and stopped at the director's administrative assistant's desk.

"Agent Richards. Go right in. The director is expecting you."

"Thanks." She tugged down on the hem of her dark blue jacket and walked toward the director's office. She tapped lightly on the door.

"Come in."

"Good morning, Director Fischer."

"Agent Richards, please come in and have a seat. I'll get right to it," he began before she barely was in the chair. "I know that you were up for the assistant deputy director, and you would probably do a damned good job at it. In fact I know you would."

Here it comes.

He folded his hands and leaned forward. "However, something has come up that I believe your skills and experience are a perfect match. An opening in the Joint Terrorist Task Force has opened. As you know, our agency works in partnership with the FBI on this task force."

Avery nodded. "Yes, sir."

"Your name was put forward to fill the position of special agent in charge."

She blinked rapidly. "What?"

Director Fischer offered a rare smile. "The assistant position here at the agency is a good one, granted, but it's really a glorified desk job with perks. That's not where your skills lie. You speak multiple languages, your IQ is off the charts, you're one of our best in the field and your investigative abilities are stellar. Not to mention that you're somewhat of a hero around here."

"Thank you, sir."

"I have to admit I did have some concerns about the incident with the reporters while you were on duty. But everything else about your service to the agency outweighs any reservations I may have had. You're not a paper pusher, Agent Richards. You don't have the temperament to be bogged down in bureaucracy and that's a lot of what that assistant position would be."

"I don't know what to say."

"I'll give you a day, two at the most, to get back to me with a decision. I hope you'll seriously consider it. You'd be the first woman in the position," he added to sweeten the pot.

Avery pushed out a breath and stood. "Thank you, sir." She extended her hand, which he shook. She turned and walked out. Her heart was racing. It took all she had not to do a screaming happy dance down the austere corridors of the agency.

She rushed back to her office and the first call she made was to Rafe. It went to voice mail and she was sure she sounded like a crazy person, but she didn't care. Next she called Kerry, but she was talking so fast that Kerry simply hung up and showed up at Avery's office door moments later.

"What the hell is going on?" she demanded as she burst through the door.

Avery paced as if the rug was on fire. "Sit. Sit." She twirled in a circle. "I just got offered to be special agent in charge with the Joint Terrorist Taskforce," she blurted out.

"Say what?" Kerry leaped up out of her seat.

"Yes!" she screeched and pressed her fist to her mouth. "I just came back from the director's office."

"Avery... Oh. My. God. This is major. Girrrl!" She came over and hugged her tight and then stepped back and squeezed her shoulders. "You are going to take it, aren't you?"

"I don't know. I mean it's going to mean travel, long hours. I'm getting married in four months."

"Wait." She held up her hand. "When did this happen again?"

Avery sat on the edge of her desk. "Rafe came by last night." Her cell phone vibrated on her desk. "One sec." She reached behind her and picked up the phone. "The doctor's office."

"Answer it."

Avery swallowed, pressed the talk icon. "Hello? Yes. Sure. Okay. Thank you." She set the phone down. "The results are back."

"And?"

"He wants me to come in this evening to talk about the findings."

"I'll go with you."

"Thanks, but Rafe insists that he go with me."

"Not a problem. And speaking of Mr. Wonderful, what happened?"

"So much. I don't even know where to start."

"You can start from the good part—the great makeup sex, and work back from there."

Avery cracked up laughing. "Girl, girl. Humph. No words," she said, her cheeks burning with the memories.

"Since I've been replaced as your wingman, let's meet up for lunch. Catch me up."

"Sounds like a plan."

"One good for you?"

"Yep. Meet up in the lobby."

Kerry turned to leave. "See you then."

Alone the whirlwind events of the morning took their toll. Slowly she sat down, rested her elbows on the desk and her chin on her fist, and tried to process everything. She and Rafe were back on track. She would be marrying one of the wealthiest, most powerful men in the country. She'd just been offered a dream job. And her doctor wanted to see her about the diagnosis that he wouldn't discuss over the phone. That was the hard reality that could negate everything else.

She spun around in her chair only to face the wall. Ironic? She turned back and took up her phone, dialed Rafe. This time he answered.

Chapter 23

Rafe held Avery's hand as they listened to the doctor explain Avery's diagnosis.

"What you have is what is called PCS or post-concussion syndrome."

"What is that?" Avery asked. Rafe squeezed her hand.

"Post-concussion syndrome has various symptoms, such as headaches and dizziness that you've experienced. They can last for weeks and sometimes months after the injury that caused the concussion. You display the full array of symptoms—headaches, dizziness, fatigue, irritability, anxiety, insomnia, loss of concentration, ringing in the ears, blurry vision."

"Are you saying this is going to last forever?"

"I know the diagnosis sounds frightening, but the good news is the scans show no damage, no fractures, no clots. In other words, you will be fine. It may take a little while longer. But you will be okay. For some reason that science has yet to figure out, women seem to be more susceptible to PCS than men."

"So, I have to live with it."

The doctor nodded. "There are some schools of thought that believe post-concussion symptoms are related to psychological factors, since the most common symptoms are headaches, dizziness and sleep problems. They're similar to symptoms that people that have been diagnosed with depression, anxiety or post-traumatic stress experience."

"So, I'm crazy on top of everything else?"

"No. Not at all. But you did experience a traumatic event. The main thing now is to manage your stress as much as possible. Get as much rest as you can. Take the medication only when needed. But I'd say in another month or so you should be feeling much better." He opened his desk drawer and took out a card, slid it across the desk.

Avery reached for it. "A psychologist?"

"A suggestion. If you feel that you need to talk to a professional about anything that happened during the explosion."

She drew in a long breath and put the card in her purse.

"Do you have any questions for me?"

"What if I'm not hundred percent in another month?"

"Then I would want to see you again and I'd insist that you see the psychologist, because the problem would not be purely physical."

Avery pursed her lips.

"What can I do?" Rafe asked.

Dr. Ryan smiled. "Make her life as easy as possible and make sure that she doesn't overtax herself. Be supportive."

Rafe looked at Avery and winked. He turned to the doctor. "Not a problem."

"Well, that's it. Any questions that come up later, call me. However, if for any reason the symptoms become worse, increase or the medication does not work, contact the office immediately."

Avery nodded and stood. "Thank you, Dr. Ryan."

"Of course. Take care of yourself."

Rafe shook the doctor's hand. "Thanks."

Rafe had taken an Uber to meet Avery at work since she'd insisted on driving her own car. When he opened the passenger door for her, he half expected her to object, but she slid in without a peep.

"The doctor said a mouthful, baby, but the news was good."

"Eventually good."

"Better than *never* good."

She angled her head toward him and shot him "the look."

He threw up his hands in mock surrender. "Sorry." He turned on the car and put it in gear. "The doc did say irritability was a symptom," he mumbled only to receive a punch in the arm. "He left out violence," he added over his laughter. "Let's go get some dinner."

Avery folded her arms and pretended to pout. "Just keep in mind that I may be a little bit crazy."

"About me, I hope."

Avery groaned. "Baldwin's."

"You read my mind, darlin'."

"That's incredible, sweetheart," Rafe enthused. "You deserve it." He took her hands from across the table and brought them to his lips. His voice lowered to a husky whisper. "Nothing sexier than a badass sister with power and a gun."

Avery's cheeks heated. "So you think I should take it?"

"You're damned right. Why wouldn't you?" He released

her and sat back. "What did Kerry say?" he asked, knowing that of course she talked it over with her best friend.

"We had lunch today. She said I should take it and that I'd be a fool if I didn't try to work things out with you."

"I knew I liked her."

She pushed her shrimp scampi around on her plate with her fork. "I'd work crazy hours."

"Me too."

"A lot of travel."

"Me too."

"It could be dangerous at times."

"That's the sexy part." He licked his lips. "Look, I get it. If anyone does I do. We'll make it work."

"When would we ever see each other?" Her brows drew together.

"Don't you know who you're marryin', woman? I can make things happen, be where I need to be, wherever you need me to be."

Her eyes danced lovingly across the smooth sculpture of his face. "Why are you so freaking amazing?"

He feigned confusion, shrugged. "I've been told it was in my DNA, or maybe in all the bourbon I've tossed back over the years," he joked.

"I love you, man," she whispered with a smile beaming across her mouth.

"Love you right back, darlin'." He picked up a sticky barbecue rib and tore off a piece of sauce-drenched meat. "Eat up, 'cause you're gonna need all your energy."

She tipped her head to the side and looked at him from beneath her long lashes. "And why is that, Mr. Lawson?"

He wiped his hands on the cloth napkin, leaned forward. "'Cause I fully intend to make crazy love to you until you beg me to stop."

Avery leaned in. "If you know nothing else about me, know that I'm not the begging kind of woman."

That slow simmering grin that set her soul on fire moved across his lush mouth.

"Let the games begin, darlin'."

The month of February, already short, was flying by but Avery and Rafe were pretty much inseparable, making the most of the time they had together. Rafe's time was his own. During the day he worked on his music in his studio at his home in Arlington while Avery went through the rigors of processing and training for her new position. At night they had each other, and Rafe made sure that the only thing Avery had to do at the end of the day was absolutely nothing.

He drove her to work—she'd stopped protesting—and picked her up at night. On most nights they stayed at his place and Alice treated them like high-priced hotel guests. They lounged, they talked, watched old movies, listened to Rafe's compositions, held marathon phone and Skype conversations with his sisters about the plans for the wedding, and made love like crazy.

Rafe turned on the fireplace and he and Avery snuggled under a blanket on the couch with their feet up and munched on an oversize bowl of buttered popcorn. The forecast was for a light dusting of snow and from where they sat, they watched the flakes sparkling like liquid diamonds as they passed through the street lights.

"Do you really have to leave tomorrow?"

"My father has been insisting that I sit down with the lawyers. Go over some things. He has the meeting scheduled for tomorrow afternoon."

She rested her head on his shoulder.

"Dominique really wants you to come on down to 'Nawlins and go over some things in person. Whatever those things are." He scooped up a handful of popcorn. "I can't hold her off much longer. My physical and mental well-being are at stake."

Avery tossed her head back and laughed. "Oh, be a big boy." She patted his thigh. "But seriously, I want to go, but things are too crazy at work right now."

"You can come down and join me this weekend. Fly down on Friday and come back Sunday night. Bring Kerry along for backup."

She chuckled. "She is my maid of honor. Fine. I'll come down on the weekend if Kerry can get away."

"Good. Make it happen. I don't want to be away from you too long." He slid his hand beneath the blanket and played a piano riff along the inside of her thighs. "Both of you can stay at the house. I'll arrange your airfare."

Avery closed her eyes and sighed when his fingers maneuvered around the elastic of her panties.

"I'm going to drop you off in the morning, then head to the strip." He leaned closer and nuzzled her neck. "But I'm going to need an extra special send-off."

She turned into him, looped her arms around his neck. "Whatever you say, baby," she whispered before locking her mouth with his.

Chapter 24

Avery dragged herself into the house and shut the door and the exhausting day behind her. It had been non-stop between meetings and hours of training; she'd barely had time to blink. Fortunately, it was the start of the weekend and she could relax. She dropped her laptop bag and purse in the foyer and her keys in the glass bowl that sat on the small circular table near the door. She shrugged out of her white wool coat and scarf, hung them on the coat rack and walked into her empty house.

This would be the first night in weeks that she'd spent alone—without Rafe. The first day in weeks that she'd had to drive herself, going and coming. She laughed. *I'm definitely getting spoiled.*

She headed straight for the kitchen and immediately wished that she'd find Alice busy whipping up one of her fabulous meals. Instead she opened a fridge that boasted a half container of milk, apple juice, leftover Chinese—

that was suspect at best—and a bag of spinach. She shut the door and pulled open the drawer where she kept her menus, selected one from the Mexican restaurant that she liked and then went to retrieve her phone from her purse.

When she took out her phone and turned it on for the first time in hours she was shocked to see five missed phone calls, and realized with a groan that she'd been so crazy busy all day that she hadn't had a minute to check her phone. Probably Rafe wanting to let her know he'd arrived and check on her, although he usually texted.

She smiled, tapped in her code and pulled up her phone messages. Her heart began to race. It wasn't Rafe's number. It was a Louisiana exchange. She swiped on the number and listened to the frantic voice on the other end. Desiree. Dominique. Jacquie. "Please call as soon as you get this."

No. She couldn't catch her breath. Her thoughts scrambled in a million directions, none of them good. Her finger trembled as she pressed the call-back icon next to Dominique's name. The phone was answered on the first ring.

"Avery?"

"Yes. What's going on?"

"It's Rafe…"

Avery reached behind her for the chair. A flash of heat roared through her. "What is it?"

"He never arrived. He never made it to the meeting. No one has heard from him and…he went off radar somewhere over the Potomac."

She was going to be sick. "No. That's not possible. He left this morning. He had a meeting at one. He told me." She could hear her own voice rising in pitch, but couldn't stop it. "He told me!" she screamed.

"Avery, they're searching for him now."

"Oh, God." Tears spilled from her eyes. She held her chest as if that would keep her heart from leaping out.

"Lee Ann, her husband and Dad are there in DC. They want to send a car for you and bring you to Lee Ann's house. The rest of the family is booked on a flight first thing in the morning." Dominique paused. "We're going to find him. You know Rafe." Her voice cracked. "He's too crazy and badass to let anything happen."

Avery sniffed, swiped at her eyes.

"Avery?"

"Yes," she managed.

"A car will be there for you in about an hour. All right?"

"Okay. Yes."

"It's going to be okay, Avery. I know it is."

"It has to."

"See you tomorrow, sis."

For several moments after the call ended, Avery sat frozen in place. She knew she needed to get ready, but she couldn't get her body to react. *Rafe.* Her heart twisted in her chest. The sudden ring of her phone jolted her like a bolt of electricity, snapped her out of her malaise. She snatched up the phone. "Hello!"

"Hey, it's me. Didn't hear—"

Avery broke down.

"Avery. What the hell? What's wrong?"

"Kerry…it's Rafe…his plane."

"I'm on my way. Ten minutes."

Kerry answered the door for Avery, who hadn't moved from her curled position on the couch since Kerry arrived.

"Hi. I'm Kerry, Avery's friend."

"Preston Graham. Lee Ann's husband."

"Any news," she mouthed.

Preston shook his head no.

Kerry led him into the living room.

Avery drew in a sharp breath when Preston walked in. She rose halfway out of the chair. "Any word?"

"No. I'm sorry. Not yet."

"It's dark and so cold." She blinked back tears.

"We're going to find him. The thing now is for all of us to be together, stay strong and positive."

Avery bobbed her head and finally rose to her feet. "My bag is in the hall." She walked out.

"If it's okay, I'd like to go along with you."

"Not a problem."

"I'll follow."

When they arrived at Lee Ann's home in Silver Spring, Maryland, Lee Ann and Branford were gathered in the family room, along with two men in dark suits who looked very official.

Lee Ann came over to greet her, gathered her in her arms. "It's going to be all right," she hummed in Avery's ear before she released her.

Avery pressed her lips tightly together and nodded. "This is my best friend, Kerry."

"Hi, Kerry. Glad you're here. Come in. We're waiting to hear back from the coast guard."

Avery's stomach churned. "Does anyone have any idea what happened? Did he make a distress call, anything?"

"Aviation recorded a distress call, but it was garbled and then cut off."

She squeezed her eyes shut.

"Come. Sit." Lee Ann ushered her into the family room.

Branford was getting off the phone. He turned to talk to the two men in hushed tones. They nodded in unison. Branford noticed Avery.

She walked over to him. "Senator Lawson."

"How are you, dear?"

"Terrified," she confessed.

He placed a large comforting hand on her shoulder. "Rafe is a survivor."

Her throat clenched.

"Lee Ann, let's get her a drink."

"We have food in the kitchen," Lee Ann said. "Let's get you both something to eat. It may be a long night." She led them into the kitchen.

The long countertop was lined from end to end with chicken, shrimp, rice, salads. Alice entered from a back room with a stack of plates.

An odd feeling of relief flowed through her. Seeing Alice made the nightmare not seem so real. "Alice."

Alice put down the plates and hurried over to Avery. They hugged tightly. "How are you, sweetheart?"

"I don't even know, Alice. Oh, I'm sorry. This is my friend Kerry."

"I've heard good things about you," Alice said.

"You, too. Good to finally meet you."

"Wish the circumstances were better. Come. Get something to eat. There's tea and coffee."

It was the longest night of her life. She slept in fits and starts, jumping at every sound. At some point she fell into a restless sleep. When she finally woke, for a moment she didn't know where she was and then reality hit her and her pulse raced. She grabbed her robe from the foot of the bed and slipped it on.

The sun was barely visible. The sky was overcast with threatening gray clouds. With gritty eyes and aching bones, she went downstairs, following the sound of the television.

The muffled sound of the television was coming from the den. The door was partially opened. She peeked in and stopped in her tracks. Rafe's father was seated in an over-size Chintz chair. The images on the screen showed the icy Potomac and two coast-guard vessels. The announcer was saying the search continued for Rafe Lawson, son of Senator Branford Lawson. Lawson's single-engine Cessna had gone down somewhere over the Potomac. So far, parts of the plane had been found, and the rescue efforts contin-ued for the senator's son.

Avery pressed her fist to her mouth to keep from screaming. But then she heard the soft sobs of Rafe's fa-ther and her heart nearly broke in half. She quietly pushed the door open and went to kneel in front of him. She took his hands before he could resist.

"He's going to come home," she said with an assur-ance that she wasn't sure she felt. "He's tough. You said so yourself. He found a way to survive this. He's coming home." She squeezed his hands between hers. "We have to believe that."

Branford glanced up from their clasped hands and looked into her eyes. "He loves you deeply."

She swallowed over the knot in her throat. "I know."

The sound of voices traveled to them from the front door. His children had arrived. Branford straightened and cleared his throat.

"Our little secret," he intoned, referring to his momen-tary lapse. "Can't have them thinking the old man is get-ting soft."

Avery offered a tight-lipped smile of agreement.

Branford took her hand and they walked out to meet the Lawson clan.

"Dad! Avery." Dominique hurried over and hugged them simultaneously, followed by Jacqueline and Justin and Bailey.

"Any news?" Dominique asked, slipping out of her mink coat.

"Nothing yet," Branford said.

"Desiree would have come but the doctor said she's too close to term to fly," Jacqueline said. She focused on Avery. "How are you holding up?"

"One minute at a time."

Alice appeared in the doorway. "Coffee is hot, and I'll get some breakfast started."

The group trouped into the kitchen and found seats at the table and island counter.

"I just don't understand. It's been almost twenty-four hours," Dominique cried. "And all anyone has found is debris." She sniffed hard and wiped her eyes. "That's my brother, dammit. They need to do more! Dad. You have to be able to do something." She blinked rapidly.

"Everything is being done. The coast guard, divers. Helicopters."

Avery's belly knotted.

"It was below freezing last night," Jacqueline said morosely.

"'Morning, everyone." Kerry shuffled into the kitchen, gave Avery a hug and took a seat at the kitchen table. "Any news?"

Avery shook her head no.

Moments later Lee Ann and Preston joined the assemblage.

Alice brought a pot of coffee and set it on the table, tugged the belt on her robe and turned toward the fridge. She took out eggs, bacon, sausages, green and red peppers and shredded cheese. Soon the kitchen was filled with the comforting aroma of frying maple bacon, sausages and biscuits.

"Anything I can do, Dad?" Justin said, coming over to put his arm around his father's shoulder.

"I'm just glad you're here, son." He reached for the remote and pointed it at the television mounted on the wall but left it on mute.

The local news anchor was in the field where fires ravaged the West Coast, while the scroll at the bottom of the screen noted *the search for the downed plane of Rafe Lawson, son of Senator Lawson, is still underway.*

"It's all over the news," Dominique said and poured a cup of coffee. "Somebody had to see something."

Avery felt trapped in some kind of nightmare that she couldn't wake from. She couldn't reconcile her mind with what was actually happening around her. As she looked from one face to the next it was as if she was witnessing someone else's life, nothing that she was part of. Yet to her horror she was part of it.

This time yesterday she was with Rafe, talking and laughing and making plans. Any minute she expected him to come bursting through the doors, taking up all the energy in the room and telling them some crazy story about what had happened.

Lee Ann's voice of assurance pierced her fog.

"Rafe is tough. He's been through his share of near misses. He'll come through this one," Lee Ann insisted and rested her head on her husband's shoulders.

Alice put a platter of bacon and sausage on the table, followed by an enormous tray loaded with a fluffy western omelet. Justin pulled up the rear and set the biscuits on the table.

Avery dared to lift her eyes to the television screen. Her heart leapt at the words emblazoned on the screen: *Breaking News.* "Please turn it up! Turn it up!" She pointed frantically toward the screen.

Dominique snatched the remote and bumped up the volume at the same time that Branford's cell rang and his security darted into the kitchen holding up a phone. In the background the reporter was saying, "Search and rescue has located Rafe Lawson, found clinging to the rocks. He is being rushed to Georgetown University Hospital. His condition is unknown at this time…"

"Oh, my God," Avery screamed.

Branford waved his security over while answering his phone. "Yes. Yes. Thank you. Right away." When he looked up at the wide-eyes of expectation from his family it appeared that ten years had been shaved off his face. "They found him." His voice shuddered with emotion. "He's alive, but unconscious." He took the secured phone from his agent. "Yes, we just heard," he said to the caller. "Heading to the hospital now. Thank you."

Avery trembled with relief as hugs and tears were shared all around. Branford held her the longest.

"Go, all of ya!" Alice instructed. "I'll pack this up."

Everyone heeded Alice's directive and darted off to get dressed.

Chapter 25

Nearly two hours later the head nurse came in to advise them that Rafe had been moved to ICU. However, only one person could visit at a time and only for ten minutes.

"I know if it was me in there," Justin said, looking from one to the other, "not that I don't love ya'll but I'd want to see Bailey." He put his arm around her shoulder and kissed the top of her head.

"He's right," Dominique conceded. "You should be the one to go, Avery."

Avery pushed to her feet. "Are you sure?" She looked to Branford and he gave her his blessing with a nod of his head. Avery exhaled, offered a tight-lipped smile to the family and followed the nurse out.

"I don't want you to get upset when you see him," the nurse said as they entered the corridor leading to the ICU. "There are tubes and machines and he's pretty banged up."

She pushed through the swinging doors and it was as

if they'd entered a whole other world—something out of a sci-fi movie. Large monitors were mounted strategically throughout. The main nursing station sat in the center manned by four nurses, all in front of computer screens that monitored every patient in the wing.

Behind every glassed room, they passed patients connected to some kind of machine, who appeared ghost-like beneath the white sheets. The only indication of life was the hiss of breathing machines and the eerie beeping like an alien pulse that vibrated through her.

The nurse stopped in front of room 807. "Ten minutes," she said before turning away.

Avery gathered a cloak of strength around her and gingerly approached. She'd seen plenty of bed-ridden patients, some like her mother, sustained only because of machines. This was different. This was her love.

Slowly she approached the bed. The nurse was right. The sight of Rafe, bandaged and bruised, connected to wires and tubes, broke her heart. She heard her own whimpers mix with the hum and beep of the machines.

She pulled up a chair and sat next to him, took his hand in hers. "Baby, I'm here," she whispered. "The whole family is down the hall, waiting to see you." She stroked his hand. "We were so scared. I…don't know what I would do if I lost you, not after all that we've been through. You're going to get better, baby. You have a wedding to attend." She wiped tears from her eyes, glanced at the machine that tracked his heart and pulse. "We have plans, and I can't do them without you. You promised me forever, and I'm holding you to it." She sniffed, leaned over the bedrail and kissed his hand. "Come back to me," she whispered. "If you can hear me, come back to me. I love you so much."

A nurse came in to change the bag of warm saline.

"I'm sorry but you're going to have to leave now," she said softly. She hung the new bag and checked the tubes.

Avery nodded numbly and slowly stood and then leaned over and whispered to him, "I'll be back as soon as they let me. Rest. Heal." She kissed his bruised cheek. "Love you, darlin'," she said using his term of endearment.

Throughout the day, the family took turns visiting with Rafe. The doctor advised them that his temperature had returned to normal, his vitals were strong and all they could do now was wait until he woke up.

Avery was sitting next to the bed the following morning, talking softly to him about the new job and all the training she had to go through when suddenly his fingers moved. She jumped up. "Rafe. Rafe. Can you hear me, baby?"

His eyes fluttered open. It took several moments before he was able to focus on Avery. "Who's Rafe?" he asked in a hoarse whisper.

Oh, God, no. Avery's hand flew to her mouth, and then that slow simmering smile moved across his. "Hey, darlin'."

Her heart thundered so fast she could hardly catch her breath. "You! How could you do that?" she screamed, more elated than upset. "Rafe. Oh, baby." She leaned over to hug him and he winced. "Sorry. Sorry. Nurse!"

The nurse came running in.

"He's awake!"

She came around to the side of the bed, took his pulse, checked his pupils and the readings on the monitors. "I'll get the doctor. Welcome back, Mr. Lawson."

Chapter 26

"Do you remember what happened?" Avery asked while he wolfed down a cheese steak she'd brought him. Great hospital, he'd said, but the food was lousy.

"Most of it. One minute I was in the air and the next..." He shuddered. "They just came out of nowhere. A swarm of damned birds. Knocked out the engine. I lost control." His jaw clenched as the images and the fear that engulfed him that night filled his mind. "You know how they say your life flashes before your eyes?" He snorted a laugh. "It's true." He turned to Avery. "All I could think about as that plane was going down was you—all the times we were together, the love we made, the promises, our wedding. I didn't want you to see me in pieces."

"Babe..."

"When the plane hit the water..."

Avery squeezed her eyes shut.

"I blacked out I guess," he said slowly as if searching

for the words. "When I came to it was freezing. I was so fucking cold." He threw his head back. "It was pitch dark." He frowned, tried to concentrate. "I must have been thrown clear. I don't even know. I found a piece of debris and clung to it. The next thing I remember was waking up in the hospital and seeing you." Janae's words flitted through his head. She'd told him that he was the only constant in her life, the one thing she clung to, the memory. Now he understood, because he'd lived his own version.

"I heard you talking to me."

Avery blinked back tears and held his hand. "You did?"

"I swore I heard you. It was like you were pulling me up out of the water, out of the dark. I knew I had to get to you. Let you know it was gonna be all right."

"It will be. It is," she said and leaned in to kiss him long and sweet. She moved back and stroked his forehead. "Might leave a scar." She lightly ran her finger along the butterfly bandage over his left brow. "Gives you a rugged look," she teased.

"As soon as I can, I'm going to show you rugged, darlin', believe that." He reached up, cupped the back of her head and drew her in for the kiss he wanted. Just to make his point.

"Get a room."

They turned to see Quinten in the doorway, chuckling.

"We already have a room, bro. Folks just won't leave us alone," he joked.

Quinten came in and gave Avery a warm hug. "How you doing, lady?"

She grinned as if she'd won the lottery and shot Rafe a quick look. "Doing real good. Listen, fellas, I'll leave you two alone. I have a few errands to run." She leaned over and kissed Rafe. "See you later, baby."

Avery walked out, warmed by the sound of their laughter. She couldn't wait to get him home. They'd have to devise some innovative techniques until he was completely healed, and she couldn't wait to start experimenting.

The press was camped outside of the hospital the day that Rafe was released more than a week after he was brought in. Lee Ann had suggested that it would be best if Rafe gave a statement to the media, suggesting that it would slow the feeding frenzy and then he could recuperate in peace.

Rafe talked it over again with Avery while she helped him get into his shirt.

"Whatever you need to do," she'd said. "This is Lee Ann's arena down here. If she thinks it's the right move I would take her suggestion."

He winced, held his side and slowly sat down on the one chair in the room.

"You okay?"

"Yeah, yeah. Gonna take a minute."

She got his sneakers from the closet and put them on his feet. "Not much that can be done for cracked ribs. Rest."

"Funny how things happen."

"What do you mean?"

"Couple of weeks ago I loosened the reins on all of my businesses. Now it's good that I did. Got all the right people in place and I don't have to worry about it while I recuperate."

Avery leaned to the side and put her hand on her hip. "I really would have preferred that you found some other way to make space between you and your businesses. Next time you want to make major changes in your life give me a heads up."

"Yes, ma'am."

The nurse arrived with a wheelchair.

"Your chariot, Mr. Lawson," Avery teased. "The family is downstairs."

Avery walked alongside the nurse's aide who pushed the chair down the hall. She bent down to whisper in his ear. "Be your sexy, charming self so I can get you home—alone."

"Naughty girl. I'll talk fast."

Lee Ann, Dominique, Justin and their father met Rafe and Avery in the lobby of the hospital.

"The car is right out front," Lee Ann said. "Plenty of reporters out there. You have a feel for these things," she said, pressing his shoulder. "Say as much or as little as you want."

He glanced up with a lopsided grin. "I got this, sis. Not my first rodeo with these folks."

"Don't we know it," Dominique quipped.

"Very funny," Rafe responded. "Okay, let's do this."

Branford opened the glass exit doors and Justin took over for the nurse, pushed the wheelchair down the ramp and the media descended.

Immediately Avery's protective instincts and training kicked in. Her first reaction was to block him from the crowd that approached and scope out any potential threats, anyone out of place who didn't look right. There was the general array of print and television media, many faces that she recognized from her various details, and of course there were the curious bystanders who stopped to see what was going on. Her gaze continued to scan the crowd while keeping within inches of Rafe.

Slowly he rose to his feet. Avery watched him contain the pain as he came to his full six-foot-three-inch height. He still sported the bandage over his eye and his thigh was thickly bandaged under his gray sweats, his ribs taped beneath his Tulane University hoodie, and Avery couldn't describe how utterly edible he was.

"How are you feeling, Mr. Lawson?" one reporter shouted.

"Like I'm getting over being in a plane crash," he said with his patent roguish smile.

The crowd chuckled.

Rafe held up his hand. "But seriously. I'm very lucky to be here. My family, the coast-guard team never stopped looking for me. I had the best doctors here at Georgetown who patched me up—pretty much brought me back from the dead. And I want to thank everyone involved."

"Planning on getting up in a plane again?" another reporter called out.

"Soon as I can." He started to sit back down and Justin grabbed his arm to help.

"Senator Lawson! Senator Lawson, any comment about your son's miraculous rescue?"

"I'm very grateful, and I think my son has said the rest. Thank you all very much." He walked ahead and got into his Suburban.

"Senator Lawson, do you think that you being the chairman of the Homeland Security Committee had anything to do with your son's plane crash?"

Branford stopped halfway in and halfway out of the door of the Suburban. He turned toward the reporter. "Unless terrorists can command bird strikes I doubt it very seriously." He shook his head in annoyance and got in the car.

"How does your fiancée feel about you wanting to fly again?" another reporter tossed out to Rafe.

Avery inwardly flinched, second-guessing her decision to be present. The last thing she needed was to get tossed back under the spotlight.

"Ya'll know I'm a true Southern gentleman and one who

never tells. Thanks, ya'll." He sat down, and Justin pushed the wheelchair toward the waiting SUV.

Avery bit back her smile. He was right. He knew how to handle the media like a pro. The whole family did.

As Rafe was wheeled past the phalanx he caught a flash in his peripheral vision. "Wait." He suddenly gripped Justin's hand.

"What's wrong?"

Avery stopped short, as well. "What is it?"

Rafe looked again. His gaze raced over the crowd. "Nothing." He frowned. "Sorry. Thought I saw someone. Let's go."

Avery studied the faces and the bodies of the dispersing crowd, while Justin helped Rafe into the SUV. Something spooked him. But what? She waited until everyone was in the SUV before she got in, taking one last look before shutting the door.

Branford returned to the Capitol. Lee Ann, Dominique and Justin came by Rafe's home, made sure he was settled and then went back with Lee Ann to her home in Silver Spring. Dominique, Justin and Bailey were booked on flights to leave in the morning. Jacqueline would return to New Orleans at the end of the week and promised to help Alice out during the day while Avery was at work.

"Alone at last," Rafe said and stretched his arm out for Avery.

She eased down next to him on the couch and gently adjusted the pillow under his elevated leg. "Need anything?" She pressed her palm to his chest.

"Just you." He brushed his thumb across her bottom lip, turned as much as his cracked ribs would allow and leaned in to kiss her.

Avery melted against him, physically needing him with a ferocity that swirled with hurricane force inside her. She moaned into his mouth as the tip of his tongue pressed and danced with hers. A match of desire lit in her belly, the warmth spread to her limbs, intensifying when Rafe slid his hand beneath her blouse. As much as she wanted to feel him inside her, she knew for the time being that second base was as far as they could go.

"Get undressed," he ground out and then sucked on her bottom lip with his teeth.

Avery's lids fluttered open. She reared her head slightly to look him in the eyes. "Rafe…we can't…"

"Get undressed," he said again. "I need to see you."

She drew in a shaky breath and slowly stood in front of him.

Rafe rested his head against the cushion of the couch and watched, with growing lust, the show unfolding in front of him.

Avery unbuttoned her starched white blouse and let it fall to the floor. She reached behind her and unfastened her black lace bra, slid one and then the other strap off her shoulders and tossed it aside. Rafe's eyes darkened. A groan rumbled in his chest. "Keep going."

There was only one time she'd ever felt shy and uncertain with Rafe, and that was during the very first time they'd made love. But he'd made her feel not only beautiful and desirable but invincible. She knew that however she felt, weak or strong she could be those things with him and it would be okay. This moment was different. She felt like she was readying herself to be with him for the very first time.

"Everything," he insisted.

Her fingers trembled ever so slightly as she unzipped her slacks and slid them down. She stepped out of them and repeated the act with her panties. She'd never felt more vulnerable in her life. But when she witnessed the look of love, admiration and heat in his eyes, her insecure moment evaporated.

"You're so beautiful," he whispered.

Her entire body heated. She stroked her lip with her tongue.

"Come here."

She took the few steps, but he stopped her when she was close enough to reach out and touch. He languidly caressed her hip, her thighs.

"Put your foot up here." He patted the space on the couch next to him.

Her breathing escalated. Rafe stroked the inside of her thighs until she began to moan. His fingers teased her slit, which grew slippery and wet with an invitation that he willingly accepted. She gripped the back of the couch to steady herself and gasped when his finger slid inside her.

"Closer," he urged.

Her head spun.

"Closer," he said again, and then his mouth was on her, his tongue in her.

"Ahhhh!" Her fingers dug into the couch. She cupped the back of his head and gave herself over to him.

His mouth was magic, casting an erotic spell that she wished would last forever. His tongue flicked and teased and licked until she was weak. The pit of her stomach fluttered. She heard her cries rise above her pounding heart as the first wave of release whipped through her. Rafe gripped her rear and squeezed in rhythm with the pulse that throbbed within her wet walls until she was spent.

She slipped down onto the couch, mindful of not tumbling on Rafe while she pulled herself back from the heavenly ride he'd taken her on. She rested her head on his chest and closed her eyes. What they'd just done played behind her lids. An unbidden moan slipped from between her lips.

Rafe twisted a lock of her hair around his finger. "You good, cher?"

"Hmm, umm," she murmured. Her hand drifted down his chest past his bandaged ribs and inched beneath the elastic waistband of his sweats until she wrapped her hand around his thickening erection.

He sucked in air through his teeth. "Naughty girl."

"Returning the favor…"

Chapter 27

Rafe's eyes fluttered closed and then opened halfway. "I think you took advantage of me in my weakened state."

"I'd have to say that you rose to the occasion. Pun intended."

He winced from the pain when he laughed.

"You want to take a pill?"

He shook his head no as he settled in bed. "I'll ride it out. Not too bad."

"What about your leg? Coming up the stairs…"

"Nothing I can't handle, darlin'."

She leaned over and kissed him. "I'm going to let you get some rest." She adjusted the pillows and pulled up the comforter. "Alice fixed a bunch of food. I'm going to see what I can heat up."

He yawned. "Sounds good." His eyes drifted close. "Nurse…maybe you could give me a sponge bath later."

Avery burst out laughing. "You are terrible. Get some

rest." She turned out the light next to the bed and tip-toed out.

When she checked the double-door fridge, she had no idea one woman could cook so much food. Every shelf was stacked with food—rice dishes, potato salads, fried chicken, rice and beans, crawfish, steamed vegetables, shrimp and even a large container of lobster bisque. She shook her head in astonishment. Every plastic container was labeled. "This woman needs to open a business." She took out a container of shrimp and one of red beans and rice. She took down a plate from the cabinet, spooned on food from the containers and then popped the plate in the microwave. She had a pretty good feeling that Rafe was fast asleep, but she was starving.

While she waited for the food to heat, she turned on the television. The local news was on. She was going to surf past it to MSNBC when the familiar backdrop of George Washington University Hospital filled the screen and the Lawson family leaving the hospital.

"Earlier today, flanked by family and security, Rafe Lawson, son of Senator Branford Lawson, was released from GW Hospital after more than two weeks, following a near-fatal plane crash. The younger Lawson has built a reputation on his daredevil lifestyle and his array of beautiful women. Most recently he's been paired up with Senator Horace Richards's daughter, Avery Richards, with a wedding date set for late spring. When asked today what his fiancée had to say about him flying again, this was his response…"

They played the clip of Rafe's very gallant response.

Avery smiled. He was born to be a star. The camera loved him. A real natural. Then suddenly his open, engaging expression tensed, as if he'd seen a ghost. She looked closer. That was the moment he'd stopped the wheelchair.

He saw something in the crowd. She only assumed it then but she knew for certain now.

The microwave dinged.

Commercial.

Avery stood over the bed, watched him sleep. She should leave it alone. He said it was nothing, but her antenna pinged, and she wouldn't rest until she knew for sure. She turned away and went to take a shower before turning in for the night. In the morning. They'd talk in the morning.

Something woke her. She blinked into the darkness, tried to pinpoint what had crept into her sleep. She reached for Rafe, and the space beside her was empty. She sat up, peered into the darkness and made out his figure sitting in the chair by the window. The full moon cast him in a forlorn halo.

"Rafe?" She tossed the covers aside and got out of bed and padded over to where he sat. "You okay?" She caressed his cheek and sat on the arm of the chair.

"Yeah. A little restless. Didn't want to wake you."

"Can I get you anything?"

"I am kind of hungry. Fell asleep before dinner."

"You needed the rest." She stood. "I'll heat up something."

"Nothing too heavy."

"How about a bowl of lobster bisque and a small salad?"

"Lobster bisque! Don't tell me Alice fixed her secret weapon?"

Avery chuckled. "A tall container full."

"You have *got* to have some."

She stood. "Maybe I will. Be back in a minute."

* * *

What he told Avery was only partially true. He was restless, but it wasn't because of pain. It was because he couldn't shake the notion that he'd seen Janae in the crowd. Only an instant, like mist. You know it's there but can't really see it. Maybe it was his imagination and the drugs they'd given him that had him seeing things, but his gut told him differently. What would she be doing here?

He shifted in the chair and slowly lifted his injured leg to rest it on the footstool. Coming to terms about Janae was the most difficult thing he'd ever done. Walking away after seeing her, hearing what happened to her and all that she'd endured, tore him up inside. From the moment he walked out the door he'd questioned—off and on—his resolve to not look back.

"Mind if I turn on the lights?"

He pulled away from the turn of his thoughts. "No. Go ahead. Hmm, smells good."

Avery walked over and gingerly set the tray down on the small square table.

"Looking mighty good in that little pink nighty," he teased and ran his fingers along her bare thigh.

"Bet you say that to all the girls." She sat in the opposite chair and reached for the bowl of soup. "Now let's see what makes this legendary."

"I need to tell you something."

Avery stopped the spoon halfway to her mouth. "Okay." She took a spoonful, and her eyes closed in bliss. "Oh. My. Goodness. This…this is…" She took another mouthful. "Heaven."

Rafe grinned. "Yeah, told ya."

She set down her spoon with a soft click against the white porcelain bowl, focused on his distracted expression. "What's wrong? What do you have to tell me?"

Rafe looked right into her eyes. "This will sound crazy, but today when we were leaving the hospital, I swore I saw Janae."

Her nostrils flared. "Janae? That's…why would she be here? You said she was in Florida."

"She is. I don't know." He shook his head. "It was only a couple of seconds and when I looked again she was gone."

That was it. He *had* seen something or thought he had. She didn't know what to think or how to feel. She gripped the arms of the chair. "Tell me honestly, are you really over Janae?" He started to speak but she held up her hand to stop him. "I'm not accusing or…whatever. I just need you to be as painfully honest with me and yourself. What the two of you had and how it ended or didn't changed your life, your heart, and then to find out that she's still alive… well it's not something that you simply 'get over.' I wanted to believe that you could. I needed to believe it. But that's not reality. The fact that you think you saw her in a crowd after your own near-death trauma says volumes."

Rafe hung his head. "You're my psychiatrist now?"

"What!"

"Forget it." He slowly lowered his leg to the floor. "I love you. I *loved* her. I won't deny that. I can't. But she was *then*. You are *now*. The fact that I think I might have seen her in the crowd doesn't mean that I have some sort of distorted fantasy about me and her reuniting. Or that we're bound in some kind of way because of what happened to each of us."

Avery pursed her lips. Why was she still so afraid? He'd proved his love for her time and again. He'd loosened the reins on his business so that he could relocate to DC for her. He'd come back to her even after she'd accused him of thinking she was a gold digger. He didn't run when she was terrified of her own health; instead he simply said

they were in it together. Time and again he'd confirmed
his love for her. So why?

She linked her fingers together. "I've never had a love
like this," she said slowly. "I know I've said it all before,
and I thought that I was finally finding that space in here,"
she pointed to her chest, "to simply accept that I'm capable
of being loved the way you love me."

"Avery, darlin', you're the toughest, most intelligent,
determined woman that I know *when* it comes to your career. You would move mountains for your job. Actually risk
your life for your job. But when it comes to us—me and
you—the slightest thing and you're ready to jump ship."

"Rafe, I—"

"No. I need you to listen. It took me sixteen damned
years to even take a chance on falling for anyone. Anyone. Sure, there've been women in my life. I admit that.
But none of them got beyond the walls I'd built—until
you. When I met you, Avery, I knew I wanted to try again.
But it seems like the harder I try, woman, the harder you
push back. Maybe it's all the fucking years of second- and
triple-guessing people, always on high alert, waiting for
the shoe to fall, to uncover the bad guy that has you in a
place where you can't trust." His eyes roamed over her
face. "Everyone is suspect—even me."

She drew in fluttering breaths. "You're not—please
don't believe that."

He limped to his feet, wobbled for a moment and then
steadied himself. "It's not me that shouldn't believe it, darlin'. It's you." He stood over her. "If we're going to make
this work you're going to have to trust me and trust yourself. Trust that what we have is real and that the boogeyman is not behind door number two."

Avery slowly stood. She cupped his face in her hands
and he slid his arms around her waist. "Please be patient

with me." She kissed him. "You had sixteen years and multiple trial and errors to get where you are now."

He started to respond but decided against it.

"I promise it won't take me sixteen years."

His lips flickered with the beginnings of a smile. "You sure about that?" He pulled her close.

"I'm not sure about anything." Her eyes caressed his face. "But when I'm with you, I believe anything is possible."

"That's all I need," he said, lowering his head.

"Oh really?" she cooed and raised her mouth to meet his. "You sure that's all you need?" She brushed her lips across his.

Rafe palmed her rear and pulled her tight against him. "Far from it. Anything you can do about that?"

"I'm pretty sure I can..."

Chapter 28

"I don't know, Q. Some days I figure it's gonna be all good, and the next I'm not so sure." Rafe absently ran his finger across the small scar over his eye. He picked up his mug of coffee and put the phone on speaker.

"I hear ya, bruh. Look, if anyone knows what you're dealing with, it's me."

Rafe could kick himself for being such an insensitive prick. Quinten not only lost his twin sister, Laci, to gun violence, he lost Nikita, the first true love of his life, in a tragic car accident. No one was sure if he would ever come back from that. He'd given up on everyone and everything and then one day he met Rae. He and Quinten had bonded years ago, but their bond was strengthened by the experiences that they shared. Yeah, Quinten did know.

"Do you still think about her?"

"Nikita?"

"Yeah."

"All the time. Not the same way or with the same pain, but yeah I think about her."

Rafe was quiet. He slowly turned the mug on the counter.

"You're not being disloyal to Avery to think about or even still have feelings for Janae," Quinten said, filling in the space and the unasked question.

"How do you balance the two, make it work?"

"Man, you know I was beyond f'd up after Nikita. But Rae helped me get better. I let myself go with how I felt instead of trying to fight it. Wasn't easy. You, my brother, have a very rare circumstance."

"Yeah, for real."

"Doesn't mean you can't move past it. I'm pretty sure part of what's spooking Avery is Janae literally coming back from the dead. It's one thing to fight off a ghost, but flesh and blood is a whole other story. Look at it from her perspective. And you gotta remember that less than six months ago she was nearly killed, and then your plane crash. I'd be spooked, too."

"When did you get so insightful?" he teased.

"Man, while you was busy running the streets and dating supermodels and whatnot I was being domesticated. Tapped into my 'feminine' side."

Rafe burst out laughing and Quinten joined in.

"But on the real. We lucky, bruh."

"Lucky?"

"Yeah, both of us got a serious second chance."

Rafe sipped his coffee. "Yeah, we did."

"So like she asked you, give her a chance and give yourself one, too."

"Thanks, man."

"Not a problem. My bill is in the mail."

"Along with my check," Rafe said laughing.

"On another note, how you feeling?"

"Day by day. Ribs are still sore. They took the staples out of my thigh yesterday. At least I can get in the shower now."

"I know that's a relief. Hey, I'm working on some new stuff. I'll send it to you. See what you think."

"Cool. I need to get back to my music. Going stir crazy."

Quinten laughed. "Anyway, bruh, like I said, give Avery a chance. And give yourself one, too."

"That's the plan."

"Later, man."

"Later. Give my love to Rae."

"Will do."

Rafe turned the speaker off the phone.

Alice poked her head in the door. "Going to run some errands. Need anything while I'm out?"

"No. Thanks. I'm good."

"Okay. See you in an hour or so."

Now that he had the house to himself, he decided to take a long, hot bath to get some of the kinks out, and then grub on one of Alice's magic containers and head to his studio. Maybe he'd compose something for Avery and surprise her when she got in from work.

Garbed in his favorite pair of grey sweats, with a bowl of homemade chicken soup in his hands, he headed to his studio.

His in-home studio was modeled after the major recording studios. The soundboard was state-of-the-art and the soundproof plexiglass-enclosed recording space came equipped with standing mics, a keyboard, a drum set and a six-foot couch to crash on.

Playing the keyboard was not his strength, but he knew his way around enough to write his melodies. He'd been playing with some lyrics in his head that he needed to get down on paper. He grabbed a notebook and pencil from the shelf, stretched out on the couch and started to write.

He got up, sat at the keyboard and began teasing out a melody.

Suddenly Alice appeared and tapped on the glass. Rafe waved her in.

"Good to see you in here again."

Rafe grinned. "Feels good. Didn't realize how much I missed it."

Alice stood in the doorway, folding and unfolding her hands. Finally, Rafe looked up.

"Something wrong?"

Her expression tightened and loosened. "I don't know how to say this—I swear I just saw Janae."

The pencil slipped out of his hand. He sat up straighter. "What?"

"It's crazy. I know. But when I was coming up the street there was a car on the corner at the red light. As I was passing the car she turned and looked at me. I was so stunned that I couldn't react. The light changed and she drove off." Alice shook her head. "But it couldn't be Janae." She gave a little shiver.

He thought back to the day he was discharged from the hospital. Her face appeared in the crowd and was gone.

"Oh, I'm so sorry. I didn't mean to upset you. I know all that you—"

"Sit down, Alice. Please."

Hesitantly she slowly lowered herself onto the end of the couch.

"Something you need to know. Probably should have told you sooner."

"Told me what?"

"Janae isn't dead."

"Oh, my God." Her hand flew to her chest. "I don't... what are you saying?"

"Aunt Jacquie got a call..."

Rafe unfolded the story for Alice, who sat in opened-mouth silence, an expression of utter disbelief etched on her almond-brown face.

"I don't know what to say or what to feel. All these years," she said, the sound of awe mixed with sadness laced in her voice. "Are you okay?"

"Getting there. I mean it rocked me. I won't lie."

"You said you think you saw her at the hospital and now she's at the house."

"Pretty sure if that was her that you saw, then it was her that rang the bell a few minutes earlier. I ignored it."

"Rafe, I don't like the sound of this. How did she know where you lived? You bought this place after—"

He pushed out a breath. "I don't know. But there isn't much you can't find out on the internet. For all I know she may have followed the car home from the hospital."

"That was weeks ago. She's been here in Virginia all this time?"

"Apparently."

"I don't like this. Did she seem...okay when you saw her in Florida?"

"I guess. I mean I think I was so rocked by seeing her again I didn't focus in on anything that could be wrong." *I still love you, Rafe.* "The last place I expected her to be is here."

"Avery knows?"

He nodded.

"Maybe you should call her, Rafe. If it really is her, then you need to find out what it is that she wants."

Rafe stared off into the distance. "I'll think about it."

Chapter 29

"How's everything going with the new position?" Rafe asked while he washed Avery's back.

She lifted her face up to the shower and then turned toward him. "Getting the feel of things. It's different. A lot more responsibility, learning the culture of the department, new personalities. But it's good."

"Hmm."

She brushed her wet hair away from her face and studied his closed expression. "Something wrong? You've been weird all evening."

He blinked and focused on her. "I'm good. Just thinking about this piece I was working on today."

Her brows shot up. "You were in the studio?"

He bathed in her enthusiasm. "Yeah."

"And?"

"Got started on a piece. Still some more work to do." He reached around her and turned off the faucets.

"Can't wait to hear it." She grabbed a towel from the rack, handed it to him, took one for herself and then another to wrap her hair in.

"Soon as I'm done." He kissed her forehead. "Promise." He tucked the towel around his waist and strode into the bedroom.

"We haven't talked much about your health since you started the new job."

Avery curled closer to Rafe and pulled the sheet up over her shoulder. "Wow, now that I'm actually thinking about it—I haven't had an attack in weeks."

"Really, nothing at all?"

"No." The excitement rose in her voice. She rose up halfway. "Pain free. I haven't had to take any medication. With all that went on with you," she draped her leg across his, "and the new job I hadn't even noticed."

Rafe kissed her forehead. "Aw, darlin'."

"The doctor did say it would take a while."

"Yeah, so that doesn't mean to go buck wild because you're feeling good." He chuckled.

She playfully swatted his chest. "Guess everything happens in its own time. And speaking of things in their own time, we never did get to go to New Orleans."

"Hmm, true. I'm free as a bird." He laughed. "We have to work around your schedule."

"Could we do a weekend?"

"Whatever works."

"And we're going to fly in a regular plane, like regular people."

"Yes, ma'am."

She ran her hand gently along his chest. "Better?"

"Almost good as new. Just a twinge every now and then." He turned toward her and ran his hand along her bare side. "Maybe we should test it out." His mouth pressed against hers and his tongue teased her lips before dipping inside her mouth.

She shifted her body beneath him.

"Love you, cher," he whispered.

She stroked his cheek and parted her thighs for him. "Show me."

He made a noise deep in his throat. "With pleasure."

Alice usually arrived around eleven and Avery was gone by eight. He paced the bedroom, debating while he turned the phone over and over in his hand. He had to know for sure. He tapped in his password, swiped for his contacts until he reached her name.

The phone rang and rang on the other end until the voice mail kicked in.

"Janae, this is Rafe. Look, I know this may sound crazy because you should be in Florida, but I'd swear I saw you at the hospital when I was discharged, and Alice says she saw you near my house yesterday." He paused a beat. "Are you here in Virginia? I don't know what's going on, but I need to know that I'm not crazy. Call me."

He exhaled and put the phone into the back pocket of his jeans just as Alice came through the front door with a shopping bag and headed straight for the kitchen, bypassing Rafe in the living room.

"'Mornin'."

"Hey, good morning." He followed her into the kitchen and watched her unpack the shopping bag. "Alice, we couldn't possibly need more food in here."

Her brows shot up and then drew together. "What would you know? Fast as I fix it, it's gone." She threw her hands helplessly up in the air.

Rafe came over, wrapped her in a bear hug and kissed

her cheek. "That's 'cause you put some of that black-girl magic in every pot."

She swatted him away. "Oh, go on. How's that leg?" She put clear plastic bags of fresh vegetables in the refrigerator bin.

"Good." He instinctively rubbed the area. "Stronger."

"You eat yet? Hungry?"

"I'm good. Don't worry about me."

"Been worryin' about you since forever." She waved her hand in dismissal. "I'll fix something. Then get to the laundry."

"Why do you ask if you're gonna do what you want anyway?" He took a grape from the bowl and popped it in his mouth.

"To make you think you're in charge!" she said.

Rafe chuckled and wagged a finger at her. "Right."

"You make that call?" she asked. She took a tray of eggs and put them on the table.

"Yeah… I did."

Alice stopped puttering and stared at him. "And?"

"No answer. I left a message."

"Humph. That thing worried me all night long." She shook her head and then began cracking eggs in a bowl.

"Anyway, we'll see if she calls back. I'm going to the gym. Haven't been able to work out in more than a month. Making me crazy."

"Maybe you shouldn't fall out of planes, and you wouldn't have that problem."

"Love you, too," he called out as he headed down to the basement.

"Don't overdo it!"

"Yes, ma'am. But I gotta get in shape. Getting married in two months!"

* * *

Avery walked past several of her seated colleagues to the front of the small conference room, opened her laptop and turned on the big screen. After several link connections her computer was paired to the big screen.

"Good morning, everyone."

The hum of "good morning" rounded the rectangular table. There were a dozen agents present from the joint task force that had been hand-selected by Avery, the director of the FBI and Homeland Security. As she took a brief look around the table she was pleased at the diversity—a good mix of not only cultures and gender, but expertise.

"As you all know for several months Homeland Security has been receiving chatter emanating from these areas." She pointed to spots on the map to areas of Turkey. "We have reason to believe that some kind of plan is in the works. Our intel suggests that it will be a cyberattack, much like what happened to the credit-reporting agencies, Wells Fargo and the pharmaceutical companies last year, only bigger, more widespread and potentially crippling. Mike, would you bring everyone up to speed with what we know so far."

Avery took a seat and all eyes turned toward Mike. As she listened to his detailed explanation and precise intel she was once again reassured that she'd made the right decision in bringing him on board. They may have had their problems over the years, but she could never deny that Mike was one helluv an agent and investigator. He'd actually turned down the promotion that would have been hers in order to join this team. To her that spoke volumes about his character and dedication.

"In your folders I've prepared a list of all the possible targets that we anticipate being hit."

Everyone opened the red folders and began to scan the list.

"Wall Street, the stock market?" one of the agents said.

"Any attack on Wall Street would create worldwide panic and instability," Mike responded. "*And* we have elections coming up. We know what happened last time. It's inevitable that another attempt will be made, and we have it on good information that it will be. We have teams fanned out across the country, evaluating the voting machines and registration sites."

"Thanks, Mike," Avery said. "In the coming days you'll begin receiving your assignment and your partner. I need everyone to stay on task. As we know there is no item that is too small or insignificant. Don't ignore anything, no matter the source, even if its 1600. Understood?"

"Yes, ma'am," they chorused.

"Thank you, everyone."

The team dispersed, but Mike hung back.

"I haven't really had a chance to tell you thanks."

Avery glanced up and tucked her laptop and folders under her arm. "For what?" She pressed a button and turned off the big screen.

"For asking me to be part of this team."

"Nothing to thank me for, Mike. You're a damned good agent."

"That I know," he joked and got her to smile. "I also know that I've been a real prick, but whatever I threw at you, you let it go, rose above it. A page right out of Michelle Obama's playbook," he added with admiration.

Avery smiled slightly. "Mike, after it's all said and done, the bottom line is it's about the work, what we're charged to do. It's about protecting the public, keeping us safe and stopping anyone or anything that threatens our way of life. We took an oath. That's what I think about."

Mike nodded with understanding.

They walked together to the door.

"How are the wedding plans coming?"

"Full steam ahead now that Rafe is fully recovered."

"Lucky man."

"That he is," she said with a smile and walked with an extra bounce to her step back to her office.

When she got off work she was thrilled to find Rafe waiting for her in the lobby.

She beamed with delight. "What are you doing here?" She gave him a quick kiss and then looked him up and down. "Suit *and* tie?"

"We haven't been out on a date in much too long. Figured tonight was the night. I made reservations."

"Reservations! Rafe, look at me. Dark blue pantsuit, white blouse. I reek 'government,'" she joked.

Rafe put his arm around her shoulder. "You could wear a sack and still be beautiful to me. Preferably a short one to show off those fabulous legs that I love wrapped around my back," he said into her ear.

A shiver scurried up her spine. She nudged him in the side. "You always know how to charm a girl. So, where are we going?"

He held the glass-and-chrome door open for her. "The Lafayette."

"How in the world did you get reservations? It's usually weeks."

"I wish I could take all the credit. I told my father I wanted to take my girl out—someplace special. He put in a call."

Avery giggled. "Pays to have people in high places."

Chapter 30

The Lafayette was located inside the Hay Adams hotel on 16th Street Northwest, a stone's throw away from the White House. Although renowned for its exquisite cuisine, there were few restaurants that could compare to The Lafayette's décor and superior service.

"At least I have on heels," Avery murmured as they approached the maître d's podium.

"Good evening. Welcome to The Lafayette. Reservations?"

"Yes. Lawson."

"Oh, yes. Of course. Your table is ready. Let us take your coats." He signaled one of the staff.

Rafe helped Avery out of her white trench coat and handed it over.

A waitress appeared. The maître d' murmured something to her.

She turned to Rafe and Avery. "I'll show you to your table. Please follow me."

They were shown to a semi-private dining area with an incredible view of the DC skyline, which was already lighting up for the approaching evening. The iconic outline of the White House stood out against the twilight.

Rafe helped Avery into her seat. "Fan-cy," she murmured and bit back a cheesy grin.

"Only the best for my woman." He kissed her cheek and then took his seat.

They were seated near the pianist, who teased the keys with soft music for a perfect backdrop.

The waitress appeared and poured sparkling water into crystal goblets that seemed to shimmer like diamonds when hit by the soft light from the chandeliers. She placed a menu in front of each of them and recited the specials for the evening. "I would recommend for an appetizer the lobster-and-butternut-squash soup and for your entrees perhaps the pan-seared halibut fillet sautéed with maitake mushrooms, white wine, togarashi spice and a side of wild rice pilaf. Or if you prefer a meat dish I would recommend our Shenandoah Valley rack of lamb. It is lamb croquettes, with ratatouille, lamb jus seasoned with Georgian spice."

"Everything sounds delicious," Rafe said.

"Can I get your drink orders while you decide?"

Rafe deferred to Avery.

"Apple martini."

"Bourbon."

The waitress gave a short nod and hurried off.

Avery folded her hands on the white-linen-topped table and admired the inlaid walls that framed the portraits and landscapes of Renoir, van Gogh, Basquiat and others whom she couldn't name.

"So, tell me, what prompted date-night?"

"Just felt like we were falling into a routine and a change in atmosphere was in order."

The waitress returned with their drinks and they placed their orders for the house specials. Rafe opted for the lamb and Avery took the halibut.

They raised their glasses and toasted to their happiness.

"Did you work on any of your music today? I'm eager to hear it."

"Coming along. Didn't get as much done as I wanted to. Was actually listening to some stuff that Quinten sent over."

She tilted her head to the side in question. "And…"

"Just got me thinking about how much I miss playing on stage."

She reached across the table and covered his hand. "Then you have to play. You're back on your feet. Nothing is stopping you."

"Actually, me and Q have talked about playing together again at the upcoming jazz festivals—the big ones, Monterey, New Orleans, New Port, Montreal, and there's also Tuscan. That one's pretty new but getting a lot of buzz."

The appetizer arrived.

"Oh, God, this smells good," Avery said. She snapped open her napkin. "Then you have to go. Simple as that." She took a spoonful of soup and her eyes closed in rapture.

"Starting to look into it. We'll finalize everything after the wedding." He winked.

Avery pushed out a sigh. "Another month. I have to admit. I know I gave you a hard time about your sisters taking over the wedding, but the truth is I don't know what I would have done without them. I mean Dominique is a one-woman machine," she said and laughed.

"That she is."

"I mean she's handled everything from finding the perfect invitations, color scheme, the flowers, linens, selecting the menu, locating the designer down here to design my gown." She shook her head in amazement.

"No one could be happier than me that it all worked out," he chuckled.

Avery laughed along with him.

The waitress returned with their entrees and between bites of the mouth-watering food they talked about the wedding and their planned trip to Bali for their honeymoon, and Rafe broached the topic of house hunting.

"I'm thinking that your place is fine for the time being. It's close to your office. But I'd really like something that's *ours*."

She put her fork down and leaned in. "Are you sure you're okay with moving down here to DC? I know how much you love New Orleans."

"When I'm with you, cher, anyplace is home. I have everything worked out at the foundation, the housing projects are moving along. I can play music anywhere. It's all good. Besides, I'm a phone call, Skype or a plane ride away."

"My place doesn't have an in-home studio or gym *or* Alice."

"While you're at the office doing spy stuff, I can work out or record at my place. I'm pretty sure Alice would be happy to help out."

She sighed. "Sounds like a plan."

He lifted his head a bit and looked at her from beneath lush dark lashes. "My plans don't end there."

"Meaning?"

"I have a little surprise for you."

Her eyes lit up. "What? Tell me."

"If I told you, it wouldn't be a surprise. After dessert. Promise."

She huffed. "Fine."

After a dessert of strawberry soufflé, Rafe paid the bill

and collected Avery's coat. When they got to the exit, Rafe asked Avery to wait while he went to the car, which she thought was crazy, since they were leaving.

He returned shortly with his trusty go-bag and a black garment bag.

"What is going on?"

"Date night isn't over yet, darlin'."

He guided her past the restaurant through the lobby of the Hay Adams hotel to the check-in desk.

"Rafe…"

He held her hand. "Reservation for Lawson."

"One moment, sir." The clerk checked the computer and glanced up with a smile. "I see you'll be with us for one night, Mr. Lawson, in the penthouse suite."

"Yes." He turned to Avery and winked.

"How many keys will you need?"

"Two."

"Any luggage?"

"No. Just us." He grinned and pulled Avery close.

"The bellman will take you up to your room. Enjoy your stay."

"Thanks."

A red-vested young man appeared as if by magic, took Rafe's bags and took them up to the penthouse floor and opened the door for them.

"There is a full bar and separate seating and dining area." He opened double doors. "Master bedroom with an en suite bath. There is a second bathroom down this short hallway. And there is seating on the balcony, as well." He turned to Rafe. "Anything you need, someone at the front desk will assist you."

"Thank you." He reached in his pocket, took out his wallet and handed the young man a sizeable tip.

"Thank you, Mr. Lawson. Mrs. Lawson. Enjoy your stay."

The instant the door closed behind him, Rafe swept Avery into his arms. "Mrs. Lawson. Love the sound of that."

"Me, too," she said softly. "You had this all planned out. You're pretty good at keeping secrets."

Inwardly he twinged with guilt. Yeah, he was getting good at secret-keeping. "Only when necessary."

"What's in the bag?"

"I took the liberty of selecting your outfit for tomorrow." He laid the garment bag on the bed and unzipped it. "Voilà."

Avery burst into laughter. "Dark suit, white blouse."

Rafe shrugged. "Aw, that's nothing. The real goodies are in my go-bag."

"I can only imagine." She rubbed up against him.

"And I ordered some champagne."

"Of course you did," she said, and kissed him like she'd been wanting to kiss him all evening.

It was clear that Rafe was fully recovered in every respect. There wasn't an inch of her body that he'd left untouched. Her blood still simmered, her skin still tingled. Would it always be like this between them? Would she always need him like the air she breathed? It was a scary thought for the girl who only needed her wits and her gun.

She eased out of bed, careful not to wake him, and tiptoed to the sitting area. In a few hours she'd have to be up and ready for work but for some reason she was restless, unsettled in a way that she couldn't quite get her head around. They'd had an amazing evening. Not one wrong note. They'd talked and laughed and made real plans. There was no reason not to be curled up next to her man, deep in the throes of sleep. Instead she sat in the dark—looking as she always did for the boogeyman.

A buzzing noise coming from the end table drew her attention. The light from the cell phone lit up the darkness. She reached for the phone and her breath caught. The phone continued to vibrate until she crossed the invisible line and answered Rafe's phone.

"Janae…please don't hang up." She heard the quick intake of breath. "This is Avery."

"I shouldn't have called."

"But you did. I need you to tell me why." When she didn't get an answer, she continued. "I know that he came to see you. Rafe told me everything. I can't even imagine what you've been through." She waited a beat. "It was you at the hospital when he was discharged wasn't it?"

"Yes. But you have to believe me, I didn't want to cause any problems. I needed to see for myself that he was okay."

Avery heard the pain in her voice and a part of her heart went out to the woman who'd loved him first.

"I came to his house the other day."

"What?"

"I didn't see him. No one answered the door. I don't know what I was thinking other than I was going back to my life in Florida, and it might be the last time I'd ever see him. I think Alice may have recognized me as I was driving away. I'm not sure."

Her head was spinning.

"I'm…actually returning Rafe's call. After I came by the house he called me wanting to know if it was me at the hospital and his house, and what was I doing in DC. I didn't get his message until I landed in Florida." She paused a moment. "There was a part of me that believed I could never let him go. But when I saw him with you, the way he looked at you, the way you looked at him, I knew it was time. I came by the house to tell him that and see him for the last time. He's happy and in love with you, and all he and I ever wanted for each other was our happiness. He's an incredible man and when he's all in, he's all in. Take care of him. He deserves it more than anyone I've ever known."

"I will."

"Avery, you okay? What are you doing up?" He rubbed sleep from his eyes as he stood in the arch of the doorway, silhouetted by the moonlight.

Avery drew in a breath and slowly stood. She crossed the room and handed him the phone. "Someone needs to speak with you. It's okay." She kissed his cheek and returned to the bedroom. This time she slept through the night.

Epilogue

The first weekend in June arrived in spectacular fashion. The cloudless sky was coupled with a hint of a warm breeze, which was just enough to lift a curl, stir the blooms that lined the walkway leading into the church or ruffle the tulle skirts of the bridesmaids. After months of planning, near losses, breakups and makeups, the day they'd dreamed about had arrived.

The white velvet runner led from the door of the church to be met on either side of the altar with five-foot urns overflowing with Sprengeri ferns, and bridal veil, mixed with Queen Anne's lace and light pink and lilac roses. The pillars and pews sprouted feather-light ferns and baby's breath, giving the entire space a fairy-tale feel. Melanie Harte, long-time family friend, matchmaker extraordinaire and premier party planner, had worked with Dominique to decorate the church and plan out the reception, which was to take place later at the Lawson mansion.

There was no getting away from the press, but Avery no longer cared as she exited the stretch limo—a vision in white, diamonds and pearls—and was hustled into the church by her bridesmaids, to shouts of "turn this way," clicks of reporters' cameras and what would certainly be cell-phone video.

They entered the church vestibule and were directed by an attendant to the ladies-in-waiting room.

"Perfect," Dominique announced the instant they opened the door.

Two overstuffed couches, comfy side chairs, a portable rack for hanging clothing, a food cart with light snacks and bottles of ice water and ceramic white bowls of floating calla lilies waited for them, and a full bathroom finished off the area.

Avery's gown rustled softly as she entered and looked around. Her throat tightened. She turned to Dominique, who was busy fussing with the flowers. She placed her hand on Dominique's shoulder.

Dominique turned, wide-eyed. "Everything okay?" The beaded bodice of her cocktail dress twinkled under the lights.

"Dom," she turned toward her sisters-in-law to be, "Lee Ann, Desi, I really… I can't thank you all enough. I know I was being bitchy and difficult in the beginning, but none of this," she looked around and waved her hand, "would have happened without you." She put her arm around Kerry. "While Kerry was keeping my head screwed on straight and making sure that I didn't run away from the most wonderful man in the world, ya'll were here making all this happen." She took a breath and blinked hard to stem a flow of tears. "Thank you."

"You're family," Dominique said. "And Rafe's our big brother. He loves you and we love you, too."

"And don't even start crying and messing up your makeup," Desiree said, surprisingly fit only two months after having her twins.

"Besides," Lee Ann added, "we were just happy to get that man settled down with someone who could tame that wild side. Now you can deal with him!"

The sisters laughed in agreement.

Avery sniffed and laughed along with them. She was ready and one thing she knew for sure was that her new sisters would have her back.

"Make sure that you eat a little something," Lee Ann advised. "So you don't get light-headed."

"I will. Promise." She turned and was awestruck at her reflection in the full-length mirror.

Kerry came up behind her and placed her hands on Avery's shoulders. "Ready?" She adjusted Avery's tiara.

"Girl, I'm more than ready to marry my man."

"You and me both!"

There was a light knock on the room door.

"Come in," Avery called out. She turned around on the stool. Her father stepped in. "Dad."

"Look at my baby." He smiled in admiration.

"I'll leave you two alone," Kerry whispered and then eased out with Rafe's sisters.

Horace Richards stepped fully into the room. "You look beautiful. Just like your mother."

Avery drew in a deep breath. "I wish she was here."

"She's watching over you, sweetheart." He pulled up a chair and sat. "I know I haven't been the best father—"

"Dad, you don't—"

"No. You need to hear this. I don't think I ever got over losing your mother. We had our troubles, but I loved her. I guess I believed that if I allowed myself to love you like I should have, I'd lose you, too. So I kept my distance, closed off my heart. I was hard on you. But I still only wanted the best for you. I wanted you to be tough, independent so that you could never be hurt." He paused. "And I'm sorry. So very sorry. I love you, sweetheart, and you now have someone to love and care for you. The way it should be."

"Oh, Daddy." She leaned into his arms and pressed her cheek to his. This was what she'd wanted all her life. To hear him say those words, and she finally understood with vivid clarity that they were more alike than different. She'd fought off love and being loved the same way her father did.

Kerry poked her head back in the door. "They're getting ready to play your song."

Avery straightened and beamed at her dad. "You ready to give me away."

Horace stood. "Never. But I know you'll be in good hands."

The bridal party was led in by Lee Ann and Justin, followed by Desiree and Spence, and Dominique and Trevor. Then the maid of honor, Kerry, and best man, Quinten, walked in to Luther Vandross's "Here and Now." Once in their places, the attendants opened the doors to the sanctuary. The congregation rose to their feet as Rafe and Avery's wedding song, "When I'm With You," began to play.

When Rafe set eyes on Avery, walking down the aisle on the arm of her father, it felt like a dream. He'd never seen her look more surreal, more magnificently beautiful as she appeared to float along the white runner that led to the altar.

The fitted gown embossed with hundreds of hand-sewn pearls and splashes of diamonds hugged her body, save for the dangerous right-side split that stopped mid-thigh.

The tiara crown sparkled beneath the lights, but nothing was brighter than the smile she held for her husband to be.

When Avery stood to face Rafe at the altar, she couldn't tear her eyes away from him. This was it, their moment. They'd been through hell and back. They'd survived.

"Dearly beloved..."

Branford and Jacqueline sat in a place of honor as she tried and failed to stem the tears that rolled down her cheeks. Branford turned to his sister, took her hand and held it.

"Who gives this woman to this man?"

Horace stepped forward, gazed lovingly at his daughter. "I do," he said with a catch in his throat. He kissed her cheek and stepped aside.

"Do you, Avery Aleise Richards, take Raford Beaumont Lawson as your husband...?"

"I do."

"Do you, Raford Beaumont Lawson, take Avery Aleise Richards as your lawfully wedded wife...?"

"The rings please."

Avery turned to Kerry and took the ring for Rafe. Quinten handed Rafe the ring.

"I understand you have something to say, Rafe," the minister said.

Rafe took Avery's hand and slid the blinding diamond on her finger. "Avery, I knew the moment I met you that you were meant for me. I just didn't know how much. You've stuck with me. Understood me, made me believe after all that had happened that I could love again. You made me want to live life again. When I'm with you, I know that anything is possible, and I can't wait to start our life together and all the possibilities. I love you, cher."

Avery could barely keep the tears from her eyes. "Rafe." She took his hand and slid on the platinum-and-diamond band. "I was scared, difficult to deal with and unsure. I thought all I needed in life was a career. But you never gave up no matter how hard I pushed you away. You just kept on loving me. I want to spend the rest of my life loving you and basking in your love for me. We can accomplish anything together. Our love is unbreakable. When I'm with you, I know that there is a God because He gave me you."

"Now, by the powers vested in me, I pronounce you husband and wife. Please salute your bride."

Rafe took Avery in his arms and kissed her as if there was no one else in the world except them, and she melted into the embrace of her husband, knowing that today was the first day of the rest of their lives, and together she knew they were in for an adventure.

* * * * *

LET'S TALK
Romance

For exclusive extracts, competitions
and special offers, find us online:

[f] facebook.com/millsandboon

[🐦] @MillsandBoon

[📷] @MillsandBoonUK

Get in touch on 01413 063232